For Steam and Country

Jon Del Arroz

ISBN: 978-1-951837-03-7

Book design by Logotecture

Published in the United States of America

To my wife, Samantha

FOR STEAM AND COUNTRY

JON DEL ARROZ

CHAPTER I

"We received a new assignment for disaster relief in Portsgate, on the southwest coast of Rislandia. The city has flooded to the rooftops and there is no way to reach the residents other than by airship. My crew is long overdue for leave, and I long for my home and family. Plainsroad Village would never have a disaster like this. Who had the bright idea to build a city in a swamp?"

An excerpt from Baron von Monocle's log
Day 35 of the Month of Dukes
15th Year of Malaky XVI's Reign

LEGEND HAS IT that whenever the earth quakes, a giant has fallen in a faraway land. My mother used to tell me the story when I was a little girl. A giant by the name of Golgmarsh wanted to touch the tip of the sky and climbed to the highest peak of the tallest mountain. The ground beneath him couldn't support his weight, so he fell off the mountain and *thudded* to the ground below. The resulting shake and thunderous *boom* cracked the world. Water spewed from beneath the ground, which created the Golgmarsh Ocean that lined the coast of Rislandia.

I figured out at an early age that most tales my mother told had the sole purpose of frightening children into good behavior. My father, on the other hand, had a wicked sense of humor about it.

One night, my mother had told me the story of Golgmarsh for the hundredth time and tucked me into bed. My father tiptoed into my room. He leaned over my pillow and whispered in my ear, "Zaira, giants are real. I've seen them."

I hid under the bed that night eight years ago, and I wished I could do the same now.

The earth rattled, rocking the field behind my farm. Tree branches from the orchard just past the lane leading to my house snapped. The world rumbled. Solid ground shifted and gave way. Mr. Gentry's thresher, billowing steam from its engine, swayed against the backdrop of the summer sun.

I didn't need a children's tale of giants to scare me. My legs wobbled, and I lost my balance. The tomato plant to my side became the first casualty. Even though I considered myself to be quite lean, my entire weight atop the poor plant squished it and ruined its potential crop.

Moisture trickled through my clothes. I glanced at my coveralls. They were sure to stain. On the bright side, I always wanted red clothing, though I always expected it to be in the form of an elegant crimson dress, something I could wear to a ball in Rislandia City. Something flowing and less sticky.

I pushed myself up and wiped my dirty hands on my coveralls. I didn't have time for these frivolous thoughts of clothes and balls. My life on the farm prevented those fantasies from ever becoming a reality.

I needed to make sure my barn and house took no damage. I grimaced at the lack of productive harvesting I'd done today. Living alone allowed me little leeway in time. My neighbors and I went to market in the village once a week with our crops and goods. This week, I wouldn't have much to sell.

Ever since my father disappeared two years ago, I'd done my best to provide for myself. It wasn't that big of a difference from when he was around, except that I had less coin than I ever did before. He'd often disappear for months, but would bring back spoils from his latest adventure. He showered my mother and me in exotic gifts, from the stationary ferromagnetic high-frequency howler, which helped scare off wolves from the farm, to beautiful porcelain dolls. Before he disappeared for good, I'd been blessed with far more than most farm girls could want, at least in a material sense. Selling off his spoils lasted me for a while, but I needed to find a way to increase my crop yield, and fast. Today didn't help matters at all.

Darkness covered my field as a long shadow spread across the land. I shielded my eyes from the sun and peered at the sky. A large shadow in the shape of a ship blocked a portion of the sun. It moved with tremendous speed. Giant brass pipes protruded from its hull, brightly reflecting as it passed.

The sight sent shivers down my spine. The last time I'd seen a ship in the sky, my father had come home to tell me he'd be there for me more often. He'd shut everyone out since my mother had died, and then he had spent a year sorting out his life. That was three years ago. He'd left and hadn't returned since.

This airship didn't set down in the large field by Plainsroad Village's main street as my father had done so many times before. It flew at tremendous speed and shrank into a small dot in the sky before finally disappearing.

As startling as it was to see that airship, I had more immediate problems. My house rumbled again. I scrambled to my feet, momentarily forgetting my own inconveniences, and bolted toward my abode. The quake had knocked me over, and I hoped my poor country home wouldn't suffer a similar fate.

Shutters hung at odd angles. The screws stripped from the hinges several months ago, but I hadn't had the opportunity to fix them. My gutters overflowed with leaves, and the wood shingles of my roof desperately needed replacing. I'd have to find a way to fix those before the rainy season set in.

I rushed toward the house, ignoring the tall weeds growing at the entrance along with its general state of disrepair. With all the farming work I had to do, I had to make hard choices when it came to day-to-day chores. My poor home suffered because of that.

"Toby!" I screamed as I ran through my front door, the worst of scenarios playing out in my mind. I imagined the kitchen in flames and poor Toby whimpering and trapped beneath some beam as he slowly suffocated to death. By Malaky, my thoughts were morbid.

Part of the roof had collapsed over the table in my kitchen, which I could see from the entryway. My home consisted of a large open room that spanned into the kitchen, with my bedroom to one side and my parents' former room to the other. Bright sunlight trickled over the kitchen where the portion of the roof had given way. Dust and debris covered my now-tilted kitchen table, one of its three legs having snapped under the weight of the roof material.

A whimpering *squeak* came from under the table. I rushed over, pushing aside fragments of plates, baskets, and the remains of a flower arrangement. "Oh, Toby!" I said, holding my breath in hopes he hadn't been crushed.

My ferret poked his head up from under a fruit basket, staring at me like I was crazy. He held a half-eaten apple between his front paws, but lost his grip on it when he stumbled on the tile floor in excitement. His apple rolled toward my feet. Toby scampered and clawed up my pant leg, moving with fervor around my body. His paws tickled me with each step. When he reached my shoulder, he nudged me lovingly with his nose.

"I'm so glad you're alive, Toby. Don't know what I'd do without you," I said, leaning my face toward him. His whiskers slid across my cheek. He sprawled over my shoulder to make himself comfortable.

Toby's frantic chittering brought me relief. It scared some of the other children in Plainsroad Village the first time they heard him, but I'd likened his noises to their kittens purring.

I surveyed the damage. Broken dishware covered my counter and floors. My lamp had fallen over and, as I'd seen before, the table and the roof were in a shambles. All in all, I was lucky, considering how violently the earthquake had rocked my old house and the surrounding area. I leaned against one of my cupboards. The roof patching could take me the better part of the day, which would set me further behind for the market. How many coppers did I have left? I didn't relish thinking about how I'd pay for more supplies in the coming days.

More dust and debris fell from the roof, forming a cloud of dirt in my kitchen. I coughed and sneezed. Toby buried his head in my thick, curly hair. His wet nose pressed against the nape of my neck. "Stop that!" I said, pushing his head back. He hissed at me in reply. Both of us jumped when someone knocked at the door.

"Anyone in there?" a muffled but distinctly male voice called.

I turned to see my door wide open. James Gentry stood in the doorway. He wore his farming coveralls, similar to mine, but his clothes hung loosely on his body, giving him an air of confidence and impassiveness. With his chin up and an elbow leaning against my doorframe, he exuded a masculine quality that few of the other boys in town could match. His curling bangs fell into his face as they had so many times before. I kept telling him he should cut his hair, but I think he enjoyed brushing the strands from his face.

James and I were best friends from the moment my parents settled outside of Plainsroad Village. We both had a farming life. We also had the privilege of being only children. So many others had siblings, but we had to grow up on our own. That led to him treating me like a sister over the years. But, for some odd reason, the way he stood in the doorway today made my hands tingle. I shifted uncomfortably, not sure what to make of that sensation.

Toby scurried around to reclaim his place inside my hair. He poked his little nose out from beside my ear and sniffed around, bringing me out of my reverie.

"Hey, James." I moved to open my large pantry door and grab my broom and dustpan.

"Is everything all right? That was one crazy earthquake. I saw your roof caving in from my house," James said, surveying my kitchen. "Looks worse from outside. This shouldn't be too much trouble for you to clean up."

"Not even going to ask me if I want help? How *chivalrous*." Teasing James came all too easy sometimes. I knew very well he dreamed of becoming a Knight of the Crystal Spire in the capital. Ribbing him about chivalry was the best way to get him to help me out.

James lifted the fallen side of the table off the floor. He studied the broken leg. "No, I know you better than to offer help. Last time Da made me ask if you wanted me to mend your broken fence, you nearly ran me out the county. 'Just because I'm a woman doesn't mean I can't do the hard work myself!'" He mimicked my voice.

"That was different. Besides, it's a lesson you needed learning." I wagged my broom at him. It amazed me how many people thought I couldn't handle myself because I only had sixteen years to my existence. How many of them had lived on their own for more than two years and managed a farm?

Toby chirped from his perch atop me. Sometimes it seemed as if he could hear my thoughts.

James and I spent the next couple hours cleaning the rest of the place. As much as my words sounded strong, his being there comforted me.

I spun the round tabletop out of the way of the other debris. James brought in a shovel to clear most of the roofing material. Toby did his best not to get stepped on, though we tripped over him a couple of times over the course of the afternoon. The table leg had split off, but without much damage to it, and I nailed it back together while James held it in place.

When the kitchen was tidy, we wiped our respective brows and looked up through the caved-in roof to the plain blue sky above our heads.

"You know, when the earthquake hit, I thought of this story my mother used to tell me about giants," I said, carrying a bucket of water into the kitchen for mopping.

"The one about the Golgmarsh Ocean?" James asked, hovering over my countertop as if he were looking for a snack.

"That one. You think there's anything to it?"

"Naw, I've heard enough stories about giants and faeries and hobgoblins growing up. We all have. The most interesting things I ever see in the night are owls. They have it out for me, I swear, hooting for hours and making sure I don't sleep."

I laughed. "Yeah, but we're just in Plainsroad Village. There's a whole world out there we haven't seen."

"Your father went and saw that world." James bit his lip. His eyes widened as if he realized he'd said something inappropriate.

We fell silent, standing there in the kitchen. I squeezed the handle of my mop. James cared about me, he really did, but that didn't mean he couldn't get under my skin. "It's okay, James. I don't want to forget my father. It just reminds me I'm alone, is all."

James squeezed my shoulder and brought me into a big hug. "I'm sorry, Zair-bear. I miss your parents too, but you're not alone." His voice had a low, serious tone. "You have me."

"Can you stop calling me by that idiotic pet name?" I said, unsure of how else to respond. The reminder of my parents' untimely demise had struck me to my core. I bit my lip to make sure I wouldn't cry. By Malaky, James made it hard when he was so right. I nodded instead. "Thank you, James."

"And you have my parents too, you know. It's like you're my sister in a lot of ways," James said, pulling back. His voice reverted to his usual cheerful, energetic tone.

Silence descended upon the room again. Why did him calling me *sister* sting so much? What would my father have said in situations like this? He had a way with people that few others could manage.

James cocked his head toward the hole in my roof. "Probably should patch that before nightfall. It won't look pretty finishing up that quick, but at least it'll do what a roof's s'posed to."

"Thank you, James. For all your help. I mean it."

He locked eyes with me and smiled. Then a knock came at the door.

"Might be Da, wondering where I'm at," James said.

"You didn't tell him you were coming here?" I asked. James did little without his father's approval. My eyes widened. "What about your house? Shouldn't you be helping there?"

"Our house is fine. I was inside when the quake hit." James waved off my concern and took hold of the doorknob. He swung the door open, and immediately stumbled backwards. "Who are you?"

At the door stood an older gentleman and a woman who appeared to be in her late twenties. The man stood much taller than either James or me, lanky in his build, with a gaunt face and a small divot in his chin. Despite it being the height of summer, he wore a black suit with a jacket that had its lapels curling outward, and a burgundy vest beneath that with clockwork designs and brass buttons. His pants matched his coat, and his white shirt ruffled at the sleeves, protruding from his pockets where he'd stuck his hands. His musky cologne with a hint of cinnamon filled the air. I held back the urge to plug my nose from the distasteful scent. No rural farmer would dress or smell like that. He had to have been from a real city.

His companion wore a military uniform, laced boots up to her knees, with black pants and a black jacket that had purple stripes across the front. She had a leather holster, which held a sword on one side and a pistol on the other. A metal pin with angel wings and the Crown of Malaky atop it adorned her right breast pocket. Her face was cool, with dark, tanned skin and pale blue eyes. Her similarly dark hair fell just below her ears, covered by a military cap, which also bore a gold pendant with the angel wings and Crown of Malaky.

They both struck me as fancier than I would ever expect of a visitor in my home. I dropped my mop, and the handle clanked on the floor.

"Can I help you?" I asked. A lump grew in my throat. If they had intended on intimidating me, they were certainly succeeding.

"I'm here to speak with..." Before the suited man could finish his sentence, his companion produced a scroll. The lanky man brandished an eye piece, which he squeezed under his right eyebrow, and glanced at it. With a tsk, he shook his head. "I don't need that, I know very well to whom I wish to speak." He turned his attention back to me. "Miss Zaira von Monocle."

"That would be me." I crossed my arms. Toby scampered away to my room. I suspected the cologne disturbed him.

"What would someone like you want with her?" James asked, star struck. He held a wide-eyed stare upon the woman, then blinked. "No offense, Zair-bear."

It took everything in me not to roll my eyes and punch him in the gut for calling me that in front of proper company, but also because of them, I had to act accordingly. "None taken. It's a valid question."

The lanky man inclined his head toward James, letting his eye piece drop. It dangled from a chain on his vest. "I'm afraid it's a private matter, and, according to my documents, she is of proper and legal age and doesn't have a husband."

"Ha! That's darn right I'm not her husband," James said incredulously. He crossed his arms.

First the sister comment, and now this. Before a few moments ago, I'd never thought of James as more than a friend.

Well, *never* might have been a bit strong of a word. Yes, he was handsome and older folk made so many comments about how we would be married one day, but farm work took precedence over any energy I could expend toward those kinds of relationships.

But that didn't excuse his outburst. Was the prospect of marrying me truly that awful? I turned to the side in hopes he wouldn't see the pain on my face.

James noticed my distress and frowned. He stepped toward the door, possessively placing himself in front of me despite his prior words. "Even though we ain't married, I'm not about to leave her with some stranger in a fancy suit and some military officer all by her lonesome. I'll tell you that right now."

The military woman mirrored James and stepped in front of the lanky man. She stared James down.

The lanky man grabbed her by the arm. "Now, Captain von Cravat, stand down. This is a friendly proceeding. Or it should be," he warned.

I'm not sure what it was about the man, but something in my gut told me he was no threat.

"James," I said, touching his arm. "I'll be fine. If you want, you can wait outside while I talk to him. You can keep your eye on me. It won't be but a couple of minutes, right? Why don't you get to know Captain von Cravat?"

Captain von Cravat took a step back to where she'd stood before, holding herself in a much less threatening posture. She motioned to my porch.

James frowned, holding steady, and then dragged his feet as he moved away. He glanced over his shoulder at me when he crossed the threshold. "Holler if you need me, Zair-bear."

Captain von Cravat handed the man her scroll, then ushered James out of earshot.

The lanky man slipped the scroll into his coat pocket. He grimaced, brushed some dust from his suit, and entered my home. He removed his top hat and frowned at the state of the residence. Though we'd done the bulk of the cleaning, there were still piles of debris that needed to be removed and very little in the way of formal furniture.

I noted my own attire. If he thought my house didn't hold to his standards of society, he must think worse of me. My hair was in tangles, and I was covered in sweat and dirt, not to mention dried tomato juice. If only I'd had time to make myself presentable before they arrived.

"I'll take that." I grabbed his hat from his hand. I set it on my kitchen table behind me. The man didn't seem pleased with the choice of hat racks, but it was better than having him standing there frowning at my home.

He raised his chin and paced my front room. His long strides left little space for maneuvering. He appeared lost, as if unused to such a quaint structure as my house.

"I suppose I should introduce myself," he said, extending his hand toward me in a regal, yet almost feminine manner. "My name is Matthias du Gearsmith. The reason for my sojourn out to the country to greet you is that I am, rather was, charged with this duty as your father's attorney."

A blank expression crossed my face. "What does that mean?" My words came out as a mere whisper. I sounded exactly like the fool young girl I tried so hard not to be in front of these fancy folk.

"An attorney is a person given power to... No, no. I can see that's not what you meant by the question." Mr. du Gearsmith dropped his eyes to the floor with a genuine emotion I hadn't expected. I thought nothing could faze a man like him, but looks could be deceiving. "Indeed. Your father has been missing in action in the Wyranth Empire for two years now, which Rislandia Kingdom law defines as formally deceased. I regret that we meet under such circumstances. And though it is far too late, I must give you condolences with regards to your mother as well."

My strength broke. A few tears trickled from my eyes, though I squinted to try to hold them back. I laughed despite myself. Two years since my father disappeared and four since my mother died in the cholera epidemic. I should have moved on by now. Wasn't that how adults acted? "I see."

"I've been charged with executing his will, which brings me first and foremost to your residence. Your father bequeaths you this land, as I'm sure you presumed, but the primary object of your inheritance is several hours away. You must forgive me that it wasn't something I was capable of transporting myself," Mr. du Gearsmith said. "You are to come with me to Loveridge, where I will give you further instructions."

FOR STEAM AND COUNTRY

"Loveridge?" I didn't understand what sort of business I could have there. I'd been to Loveridge once when I was eight years old. The city had five times the number of people as Plainsroad Village and a market so big I couldn't believe my eyes. "That's hours from here, I can't just leave." I glanced to the hole in my roof. "I have repairs to make before sundown."

"Your repairs can wait. Besides, I doubt you'll be coming back this evening to have to deal with the elements. My time, however, is short. I must return to the capital soon," he said. His heels clicked on my floor as he moved to my table. He retrieved his top hat, dusted it off, and motioned toward my front door. "If you would be so kind."

"Wait a moment," I planted my feet and crossed my arms in front of my chest. Toby regained some of his courage and poked his head out from my room. "How do I know you're telling the truth? I don't know you from—"

Matthias held a lone, crooked finger squarely in front of my face, cutting my sentence off before I could finish. He reached back into his coat and produced the scroll Captain von Cravat had held earlier. Unwrapping it carefully, he spun the scroll around so I could see. It read:

> I, Baron Theodore von Monocle, under the laws of the land of Rislandia under the stewardship of King Malaky XVI, grant power of attorney to one Matthias du Gearsmith, that he might execute my will and seek out my daughter Zaira von Monocle at such a time as I am deceased or incapacitated.
>
> Zaira, if you are reading this, it means time and fate have caught up with me. I've been very lucky over the years, but it was only a matter of time in this line of work. I'm sorry I didn't spend more time with you. In retrospect, I should have dedicated myself to being a proper father. King and Country can fill one's mind with a sense of duty and purpose which cloud what's important in life. Try to keep that in mind when you have a family of your own.
>
> I, likewise, have to apologize for saddling you with the

burden that my attorney, Mr. du Gearsmith, will impart. Some will see it as a great treasure, but as with any great gift in life, there comes great consequences. Know that I love you, and I always will, even from beyond the infinite.
Signed,
Baron Theodore von Monocle

I staggered backward. Mr. du Gearsmith had warned me, but seeing the words penned by my father's own hand made the facts so much more real. My throat dried, and I skipped a breath. My father wouldn't be coming home again.

CHAPTER 2

"We've successfully resettled the refugees from Portsgate and are rushing to assist the Grand Rislandian Army with a budding crisis at the Wyranth border. I do try to send letters home even when duty has me toiling past sundown. I hope Liliana and Zaira will forgive me one day, and wish I could bring myself to lie and tell them I'll be home soon, safe and sound."

An excerpt from Baron von Monocle's log
Day 42 of the Month of Dukes
15th Year of Malaky XVI's Reign

"I PRESUME YOU are acquainted enough with your father's signature to account for its validity?" Mr. du Gearsmith asked me.

Narrowing my eyes, I scrutinized the scroll. The writing had my father's flair, a little twist in the beginning of his capital letters. I'd known it was his long before Mr. du Gearsmith posed the question. "It looks like his handwriting."

"Then you will follow me," he gestured to the door again.

I glanced back at the house and shook my head. "No, I still can't leave like this. I don't even know you."

"Please, Miss von Monocle, I'm asking you to trust me. I can show you my credentials as attorney at law, licensed by the Rislandian Lawyers Association. I have my papers back in the horseless carriage."

14

"I believe you. Your credentials aren't a problem. It's just so sudden, and I have so much work to do." Too sudden, though it had been a long time since my father originally departed. Nothing changed with this news, did it?

I considered what to do. With the repairs I'd have to make, I wouldn't be able to keep my farming schedule for the market anyway. If I received an inheritance as Mr. du Gearsmith said, it could provide for needed supplies and perhaps even some hired help to fix my home. Not only with the roof, but with all the other maintenance I'd ignored over the past two years.

"How much coin will I receive from the inheritance? I presume you'll be taking me to additional lands, seeing as my father held the title of Baron?" I asked, trying to keep the firm tone of voice I used at the markets to conduct business.

Mr. du Gearsmith pursed his lips. "There is an adequate trust, yes. However, I did not mean to mislead you to assume that there would be additional lands. There are two distinct types of nobility in Rislandia, I'm not sure if you would be aware, given your upbringing."

His question irritated me. Just because I didn't live in a fancy city didn't mean I couldn't read or understand what he said. My mother made sure I went to school every day and made me read her books every night, until she passed. I wanted to slap him, but that wouldn't have been the adult action to take. I acted as if I followed his every word instead.

"There are legacy nobles, those with families and lineages that have helped foster Rislandia since the kingdom's founding, and then there are nobles who earn their titles in military service. Traditionally, those nobles don't receive grants of lands or power in politics until they have retired from such service. In your father's instance, he had unfortunately not yet retired."

I slumped my shoulders. Perhaps I shouldn't have counted on receiving enough income to fix my home. "So what is this inheritance then?"

"Your father, needless to say, enjoyed dramatic presentations." Mr. du Gearsmith shook his head, a look of amusement on his face. "He specifically requested I show you. In Loveridge."

I snorted at the thought of dramatic presentations. It reminded of the time my father swung from a rope ladder from his Grand Rislandian Army's airship, landing several steps in front of me. Not to mention the exaggerated stories he would tell me of far off lands, faeries, pirates, and secret treasures. His service to Rislandia sounded much better than a farm life. It was no wonder he never came back to spend time with me.

Perhaps it was a foolish decision to leave with Mr. du Gearsmith, but I needed the money, and he *did* have my father's written word. I'd read father's letters dozens of times in all the time I'd spent alone for the last two years. He cared in his own way. This inheritance would be in keeping with the way he showed it. "I'll have to make sure James will watch Toby," I said.

Mr. du Gearsmith nodded in agreement.

When we stepped outside, James and Captain von Cravat stood next to a huge wheeled contraption in the front yard. It had four seats, some large levers, and a steamstack protruding from its middle. Its wheels were connected by a long strip of metal, which was bolted to gears below the vehicle, some of which protruded outward. The steamstack hissed, and steam burst into the air above it.

"By Malaky," I said.

"You've never seen a horseless carriage before?" Mr. du Gearsmith asked with a cocked brow. "They're quite common in the capital. They have been for a couple of years now. Once you've travelled in one, you'll never go back to the old buggy again. It's a much faster means of transport, and it doesn't spook."

Captain von Cravat grabbed James by the back of his coveralls and forced him upright.

"Aw, come on. I was only taking a peek at the engine," he said, glancing toward Mr. du Gearsmith and me. "Zair-bear, you have to see this."

"I see it, and I believe I'll be riding in it," I said, moving toward him.

"You get a ride? Captain von *Boring* here said she wouldn't let me," James said, pouting.

Captain von Cravat held a stoic expression, but I could see in her eyes that it was all she could do not to whack James upside the head. His teasing would get him into more trouble than he realized when it came to strangers. I'd have to have a talk with him about that when I returned.

"It's not a carnival attraction, James. I have to take a trip to Loveridge with these people." Though I tried to sound mature, the prospect of the carriage ride thrilled me nearly as much as it did James. I'd ridden many a horse to a canter, faster than James would dare to go. Speed thrilled me.

"Loveridge?" James asked, confused. "You can't go off with strangers that far! We've still got work to do on the house, and I know you're behind on your pickings."

"I have to, James." I took his hand and squeezed it gently. "Remember what you said about my father earlier? Well, Mr. du Gearsmith presented me his will. I need to take care of his final business, okay?"

James shifted his eyes from Mr. du Gearsmith to Captain von Cravat. "Okay." His voice betrayed his concern.

"Will you watch Toby for me while I'm away?" I asked.

"Sure," James said. He forced a smile at me. "Be safe."

"Thank you." I stood on my tiptoes and planted a kiss on James's cheek. His growing stubble prickled my lips.

Mr. du Gearsmith opened the door to the backseat of his horseless carriage and used his free hand to help lift me the rest of the way. I plopped myself down into the leather seat, which was far more comfortable than the seats in any other carriage I'd ridden in before. Gold trim lined the interior doors, a reminder of how out of place I was in my soiled coveralls.

In Loveridge, I could find a nice gown or dress to wear, if the inheritance afforded me one. That would be a waste of good money though. I had to be practical and think of the farm.

Captain von Cravat took the driver's seat and slipped her hands into gloves. She turned the key and the motor churned.

My door slammed shut. Mr. du Gearsmith circled around to the other side. He carefully seated himself, making sure his coat tails wouldn't wrinkle behind him.

James waved from where he stood. Worry drowned any former excitement his face had held.

"I'll be back in no time, James," I said, waving in return.

Captain von Cravat spun the steering wheel and turned the carriage around. The vehicle had made tracks on their way in which she followed back out again to the main road. James and my farm faded in the distance.

We picked up speed, which thrilled me at first, but when the road bumped, I had to grip my seat to make sure I wouldn't bounce out. Farms, fields, and trees flew by faster than I could have imagined. The wind brushed my face and my hair blew behind me.

After I took time to bask in the thrill of the ride, I leaned toward the front where Mr. du Gearsmith sat. "How long did you know my father?" I asked.

"Since before you were born," Mr. du Gearsmith said.

My curiosity piqued. "Do you know what he was doing the last time he left? He rushed out the door that day, barely had time to say goodbye. I think something frightened him but he didn't say what," I said, leaning toward the steamstack.

"Don't touch that!" Mr. du Gearsmith shouted. He tried to keep his eyes on the road but couldn't help but turn toward me.

Captain von Cravat looked backward to see what I was doing. The horseless carriage swerved and her eyes went wide. She jerked her head to face forward. With a turn to the wheel, she set our path straight.

"That can burn you faster than you can say fire. I should have warned you before, my apologies," Mr. du Gearsmith said, returning his attention to the road. His voice became measured once more, as if he had never been angered. "What was it you were asking? Ah yes, your father's final mission. I'm afraid that is a classified matter."

"But isn't he declared legally dead? How can it still be classified?"

"Because classified matters stay such until King Malaky himself says otherwise," Mr. du Gearsmith said and turned back to face forward.

I didn't have the nerve to ask any more questions after that and relaxed into my seat.

* * *

I awoke to violent bumping and rattling in the horseless carriage. My head smacked against the metal divider between seats. With a groan, I sat up. The carriage had slowed in its pace and its engine no longer made the cranking noises of the gears.

"What's going on?" I asked.

Captain von Cravat and Mr. du Gearsmith held their attentions fixated on the road in front of them. Judging from the reds and purples in the sky, I'd been asleep for well over an hour. The landscape changed from farmland to thick trees all around us, shading the road and the carriage. The air had cooled since our departure.

"Shh!" Captain von Cravat hissed, glaring back at me. "There's Wyranth soldiers ahead."

I lowered my voice. "Wyranth soldiers? But we're still in Rislandia." Our location I knew from my geography lessons in Plainsroad Village. There was no possible way we travelled out of our kingdom in that time. I hadn't attended school in two years, but I could still recall Mrs. Everley's large map in the back of her classroom. I used to make doodles of our continent and dream of traveling the countryside with my father. Rislandia had such a beautiful shape, almost like a bell. If Wyranth soldiers had crossed the border here, it would have made an ugly crack right down the middle.

"That we are," Mr. du Gearsmith whispered. "Something is amiss to have them this far into our kingdom. Should we turn around?" He tilted his head at Captain von Cravat.

She shook her head. "No, too dangerous to turn the engine back on. They'll hear the sound for certain. I'm lucky I have keen eyesight or they'd already be on us."

I couldn't see any soldiers off in the distance. The night sky won out over daylight. Shadows fell upon more shadows beneath sprawling tree branches. I didn't dare doubt Captain von Cravat's word on the soldiers, however. "What should we do?"

"If they see my uniform, they'll detain us for certain, likely kill us," the captain whispered. She tapped her fingers on the steering wheel in consideration. "I'll leave the carriage. Mathias, you take the wheel. I'll disappear into the forest, do a little reconnaissance on the Wyranth soldiers in the area, and meet you in Loveridge, okay?"

"I trust your plan implicitly," Mr. du Gearsmith said. He bowed his head to her in deference and motioned for her to move.

Captain von Cravat hopped out of the driver's seat and turned to face me. "You haven't been trained. If they interrogate you, think about your farming for as long as you can hold out. Don't let them know I'm here. It could be life and death, you understand?"

I tried to speak, but she had instilled enough fear into me that I couldn't do much but chatter my teeth. I nodded hastily.

"Good. Best of luck to you both. See you on the other side," Captain von Cravat said. She ran for a group of trees to our left and faded into the forest.

"She sure makes decisions quickly." I peered into the trees, trying to ascertain where she went. "And she's really good at hiding."

"Talyen is one of the finest officers Rislandia's ever had," Mr. du Gearsmith agreed. "Now, no more mention of her. I'm going to restart the carriage."

Mr. du Gearsmith stood and stepped over the center console to the driver's side, one leg at a time. He settled himself into his seat, bracing his descent with an arm on the steering wheel. With the turn of a key, the horseless carriage engine whirred back on, steam puffing upward into the night air.

The carriage nudged forward, bouncing on the rock-filled road through the forest. Within moments, the Wyranth soldiers appeared ahead, just as Captain von Cravat had warned.

The soldiers' uniforms were far more ornate than their Rislandian counterparts. The base garments were a drab gray, but with a golden belt that wrapped around, forming two snake heads that bit each other at the clasp. Around their necks, metal guards clasped and covered the top buttons of their coats. Their heads stayed protected by hard shells, again with a metal line clasped by snakes, adorned by a golden point.

Their uniforms alone inspired awe, but the fact that they stared, shouted, and drew their guns washed away any interest I held in their attire. My heart thundered. No one had ever drawn a gun on me before. I didn't know how to react and forgot to breathe for several moments.

"I can't believe they're being so brazen this far north of the Wyranth border! Where is our army? Don't worry, Miss von Monocle. Follow my lead and let me do the talking," Mr. du Gearsmith said, remaining focused straight ahead of him.

The carriage slowed and we approached the soldiers. One of them stepped to the side and leaned onto the driver's door. A scraggly beard protruded from his chin. It might have been a trick of the light, but his eyes seemed unnaturally dark, pupils fuller than normal. "What do we have here? This is quite the expensive vehicle. We may have to commandeer it for the service of the Iron Emperor," the bearded soldier said.

One of the other soldiers patted his pistol in his palm as if to lend his companion credence. They wanted to steal the carriage? These soldiers were no better than ruffians! I clenched my fists but remembered what Captain von Cravat said and bit my tongue.

Mr. du Gearsmith remained calm and held his hands above his head to show he was no threat. "Gentlemen, I would certainly wish to assist with your demands, but please, would you hear me out before taking such an action?"

The bearded soldier narrowed his eyes. "Continue."

The third soldier fumbled with a vial, which contained a blue, glowing liquid. He popped the stopper, which fell onto the road in front of us. "Oh no," the soldier said, bending and running his hand across the ground in front of him to try to find it.

Mr. du Gearsmith stayed silent while the other soldiers turned to see what was happening with their companion.

"What did you do, Corporal?" the bearded soldier asked, sounding irritated.

"I lost my ether stopper. It's too dark. I can't see!" He sounded alarmed.

The soldier holding the gun pulled his own vial from a pocket. "Here, you can pour your unused ether into mine."

The corporal searched the ground awhile longer, and then returned to his feet. "Doesn't seem like there's much of a choice." He tilted his head back and dropped a small amount of the liquid from the vial onto his tongue, then handed the vial to his colleague.

The corporal shook. He grinned in as eerie a manner as I'd ever seen. His eyes had an almost glowing quality to them. "Better," he said.

The other soldier carefully poured the remaining ether into his own vial and sealed it with his stopper. He held up the vial to show the corporal, then tucked it into his pocket.

Mr. du Gearsmith gulped. "Is something the matter, sirs?"

The bearded soldier's eyes widened and embarrassment crossed his face. "No, nothing to concern yourself with, Rislandian."

Mechanically, he drew his gun and leveled it at Mr. du Gearsmith's head.

Mr. du Gearsmith didn't flinch, didn't breathe, but kept his eyes trained ahead, hands on the steering wheel.

The bearded soldier paused in a strange manner, as if his entire body shut down and then righted itself. He glanced down the road. "I've decided to be lenient with you, considering you have a girl child. You may continue with your vehicle. Remember the Iron Emperor's mercy."

Mr. du Gearsmith bowed his head and tipped his hat toward the bearded soldier. "I will, thank you very much. My...daughter and I appreciate it. Have a good night, gentlemen."

We continued down the road at a slow pace, to be sure not to alarm the soldiers as to anything out of the ordinary. Once we were certain we were no longer within their field of vision, Mr. du Gearsmith shifted a lever to increase the carriage's speed.

"A gun. That soldier pointed a gun at us!" I said, hand clutching my chest. The small comfort of reacting to the situation provided me with immense relief.

"Your first time then?" Mr. du Gearsmith asked. He didn't appear in the least bit flustered.

"James has accidentally turned his hunting rifle in my direction several times, but that's not the same by any means. I can't say I'd want to have that experience again anytime soon."

"I hope you won't have to."

"What was that blue, glowing liquid?" I asked, turning my head to see behind us. By now, darkness had overtaken the road and forest, but I still feared one of those soldiers jumping from behind us and grabbing me.

"I don't know. I've never seen anything like it before. The person I'd ask about such things in ordinary circumstances would be your father. He's seen many wonders, far and wide," Mr. du Gearsmith said. "We'll have to report this to King Malaky. It could be crucial intelligence."

"But how are we going to get all the way to the capital? Especially with those soldiers guarding the road back?"

"Wait and see, Miss von Monocle. Wait and see."

* * *

Night blanketed Loveridge in deep darkness by the time we arrived. I sat on the edge of my seat, trying to get a good view of the city. Aside from a couple of lamps, I could only see silhouettes of buildings and a few late-night stragglers walking through the street. Hardly the bustling city I had envisioned on the drive.

Mr. du Gearsmith continued driving through the town and back into the forest that surrounded it.

"Aren't we supposed to stop in Loveridge?" I asked, pointing my thumb back the direction we came.

"Our destination lies soon ahead," Mr. du Gearsmith said ominously.

True enough to his word, we parked against a high wall outside the city. The wall stood much too tall for me to see beyond in the dark, though it arced outward over my head. Long boards lined it in horizontal stripes, an odd construction. I noticed long, brass piping protruding from the side of the boards about two stories above me. The piping looked oddly familiar to me.

Several carriage lengths away from us, a ramp descended from the wall. The ramp wasn't quite large enough for our horseless carriage to drive through, but three people could walk on it and be comfortable. Mr. du Gearsmith opened his door and stood, straightening his coat. "We're here," he said and gazed toward the wall as if it were an incredible work of art.

I twisted the handle to my own door, which popped open after a jiggle. I braced myself on the frame of the carriage, unable to keep my balance after the long and bumpy ride. After I regained my bearings, I followed Mr. du Gearsmith toward the ramp. A lone figure stood at the top, a dark silhouette surrounded by the light from the other side.

24

Mr. du Gearsmith waved at the figure. "Marina! I've brought Zaira von Monocle," he said, trudging forward.

I kept pace with him.

Marina descended the ramp. She wore the same black uniform with purple stripes as Captain von Cravat. A small pin of red and gold rested below her angelic wings and Crown of Malaky pendant. She had beautiful, flowing red hair and the lightest of freckles below her hazel eyes. I almost missed the hand she extended before me. "How do you do? Lieutenant Commander Marina Willett, at your service."

I took her hand a little more strongly than she expected. People who didn't know farm girls firsthand tended to underestimate my strength. I couldn't help but smirk when she recoiled. "Pleasure to meet you. I'm Zaira."

Mr. du Gearsmith tapped his foot on the bottom of the ramp. "Is Harkerpal here as well?" he asked Marina.

She shook her head. "He's gone to get parts for his repairs. I think he mentioned something called a Giffard capacitor. You know Harkerpal." Marina shrugged.

That evoked a laugh from Mr. du Gearsmith. "Indeed I do."

"What is this place? Is this what you were going to show me? My father had some big log fort outside Loveridge?" I shook my head with confusion.

Mr. du Gearsmith wrapped one arm around my shoulder, motioning to the entirety of the large wall before me with his other hand. "No, my dear, this isn't a fort at all. This is the *Liliana*. She is your father's claim to fame."

My eyes widened. I recalled where I'd seen that brass piping before—up in the sky. "This is an airship!" I said.

"The Rislandia Kingdom's most infamous airship at that," Mr. du Gearsmith said. "But how do you know what one looks like? Did your father fly her home?"

I couldn't believe this airship belonged to my father. The curvature of the hull took on a new beauty for me, enough that I was unable to focus on Mr. du Gearsmith's words. I reached out and touched it, the old wood rough against my fingertips. The grain prickled my fingers as I ran my hand across it. This was how my father used to travel around the world. This was the reason he'd left my mother and me alone for so long. "Yes, he said it was the Grand Rislandian Army's ship. I thought they were just dropping him off. And I saw one overhead, just today. This...this was his?"

My father hadn't told me much about his career over the years. His dresser drawer contained several medals, which I found when I snooped in his room, having lost hope in the idea that he would return home. All of these supposed adventures only served to make me seem uneducated. I didn't know the first thing about my own family. I supposed he wanted to insulate me, allow me to live a normal life. I'd never had the opportunity to ask. If that had been his plan, it'd been a bad one. With no parents to guide me, little I did in my life could be considered normal.

"Pardon," Marina asked. Her eyes lit up with concern. "You said you saw an airship overhead, today?"

Her words brought me back to ground. I shrugged at her. "That's right. It appeared after the earthquake in my village. Do you think it could have caused such a thing?"

Mr. du Gearsmith grimaced. "Are you certain, Miss von Monocle? What you claim to have seen is an impossibility."

"I know what I saw." I crossed my arms over my chest. I'd had enough of his routine of doubting my word.

Marina scanned us, her face paling as the friction between Mr. du Gearsmith and I escalated. "We can talk about that later. Would you like to know anything about the *Liliana*?"

I stared at Mr. du Gearsmith, not ready to back down. Doubt my word, would he? The urgency in Marina's eyes calmed me, however. She had the right of matters. I glanced back upward and tried to calm myself. "How does this fly? It looks heavy."

Marina pointed above the top of the wooden siding. It took some focus to see it in the night sky, but two towers protruded upward, each with long flaps that curved to the side. "You see those large poles?"

"I thought they were towers."

"Those are turbines. The engine room has giant gears that make them turn. Our engineer, Harkerpal, can tell you more. I'm a cannoneer and commando, so I'm not as familiar with the workings of machines and contraptions."

Mr. du Gearsmith padded up the ramp, followed by Marina. I satisfied myself with the view, and then jogged to catch up with them.

"It's one of only five airships of this caliber ever built, which is why I told you the sight of another is an impossibility," Mr. du Gearsmith said as we walked through the threshold into a vast cargo hold. Brass lamps adorned the walls, providing ample light. The hold was empty save for several metallic barrels. Our voices echoed.

"Where are the other four then?" I asked.

Marina and Mr. du Gearsmith slowed their pace to allow me to lead and explore. I opened the door from the cargo hold to a hallway of a row of crew cabins and a stairwell. I chose the stairwell, hoping to find my way up to the deck.

"Three of them were destroyed in skirmishes with the Iron Emperor's forces several years ago on the border with the Wyranth Empire. The final airship..." Mr. du Gearsmith paused thoughtfully, "disappeared six years ago. It's presumed to be destroyed as well. If what you say is true, this could mean more trouble with the Wyranth than we could imagine." He turned to Marina. "Speaking of the Wyranth. I must speak with you later. Captain von Cravat and I came across Wyranth soldiers on the road here."

Marina jolted to a stop, bracing herself on one of the stairwell's handrails. "This far north?"

"Indeed. It's disconcerting. We need to have the *Liliana* operational as quickly as possible. King Malaky needs to be informed."

"How frightening," Marina said. She tensed visibly.

I stopped on the stairs ahead of them. "Let's not forget the glowing blue ether those soldiers had," I said, trying to further assist the conversation.

Marina's head jerked up. "Blue ether? What kind of blue ether? I—I've never heard of the like. You've had quite the day indeed."

"So many oddities with the Wyranth lately." Mr. du Gearsmith furrowed his brow. "I'm afraid these are matters far beyond a poor old attorney like me."

I snorted. "I doubt you're poor or anything's much beyond you."

"Yet you do agree I'm old."

"Farm girls don't lie," I said.

Mr. du Gearsmith flashed the smallest of smiles. "I appreciate your faith in me, Miss von Monocle."

"Zaira," I corrected. I'd let him go on calling me Miss Von Monocle for too long. The title didn't feel right, like it was something that belonged to my parents and not me. Similar to everything else that had occurred this day.

My head whirled with thoughts of the Wyranth, my father, and how all of this connected. "You told me earlier that my father's mission was classified, but you seem to know about it. If I'm to have this airship and meet the King himself, I need to know as much information as I can."

Marina arched one of her crimson brows.

"I suppose you're right, Zaira. It's my understanding that the ship was boarded in the midst of one of the worst battles the Knights of the Crystal Spire and the Grand Rislandian Army had ever seen."

Mr. du Gearsmith sighed and continued up the stairwell. "Two years ago, thousands of Wyranth soldiers descended upon the Border River. Your father led a valiant surge, along with several of his crew, keeping the ship airborne until they could reach the water. That is where the *Liliana* went down. Such bloodshed occurred that it's been said the river ran red for three full days, heavy casualties on both sides. Nearly half of the *Liliana's* crew of fifty perished that day.

"Your father was last seen swinging off the bow from a rope, charging onto the enemy shore. He'd planned to provide a distraction while Chief Engineer Harkerpal worked on getting the ship airborne again. Harkerpal succeeded, but no one can give an account of what happened to your father. The King and I held out hope he was taken prisoner, until recently. As I told you before, enough time has passed that he has been declared legally dead."

I cast my eyes low as I walked the narrow airship corridors, able to visualize those ugly Wyranth soldiers decapitating my father. The image stuck in my head, too powerful to shake away. "So, he could be a prisoner somewhere?"

"We'd never heard any evidence that the Iron Emperor had your father. With a hostage as famous as Theodore, we surely would have been offered a large ransom for his return, or he would have been publicly displayed somehow. It would have been the largest moral victory Wyranth had seen in a generation."

We reached the top of the stairwell. Marina twisted the crank to spin the gears and open the hatch to the deck.

They allowed me to take the final steps first. My cheeks flushed when struck by the cool night air. I couldn't help but shiver and wrapped my arms around myself.

The deck spanned a distance similar to my corn field. The turbines loomed, massive above me. It would take four of me, with arms extended and fingertips outstretched, to wrap around their bases. At the front of the ship rested three large cannons. The rear had a small structure, which appeared to be where the command staff worked. Where my father had worked.

I spent a long time spinning around, gawking at the enormity of the airship. Despite the beautiful views, I couldn't help but think on Mr. du Gearsmith's story. "My father meant that much to the war effort?"

"The name Baron von Monocle strikes fear into the hearts of many. Even more still owe their lives to him," Marina said. She paced to the ship's rail, staring at the forest and Loveridge below. "You should see this view."

I took my place beside her. Mr. du Gearsmith stood behind us.

Loveridge appeared so serene. Granted, we had arrived very late at night. The only lights shining were street lamps down on the main street. Rows of houses nestled between thin lines of roads, which disappeared into the heavy forest. I could almost make out the shine of the Border River in the far distance, seeing a faint reflection from the moon. "This is incredible."

"It never ceases to amaze me, either," Marina said. She closed her eyes and took in the night air.

Mr. du Gearsmith cleared his throat. "It's very late. I took the liberty of booking us rooms at the Loveridge Inn several days ago via the post. There will be plenty of time for a tour later," he said and turned back for the stairs.

"Wait," I said, glancing back at him. "Is the ship operational?"

"That's why Harkerpal went to get parts. I believe she's almost ready to fly," Marina said.

"So, when can we try it? Flying that is," I said, heart nearly leaping from my chest in anticipation.

"If all goes well, tomorrow," Mr. du Gearsmith said.

CHAPTER 3

"Thank Malaky for my chief engineer. I swear if he didn't have the supplies he needed, he'd morph into the part and perform the function himself."

An excerpt from Baron von Monocle's log
Day 55 of the Month of Dukes
15th Year of Malaky XVI's Reign

I SAT UP in the iron-framed bed of the Loveridge Inn, sinking into the plush mattress. Sunlight danced across the curtains, trickling through to spots on my sheets, signaling dawn. I'd been awake for nearly an hour already, waiting for a time when others might join me. As a farmer, I'd become used to waking predawn to get ready for the day and accomplish all that needed to be done in the fields before it became too hot.

At my door hung a beautiful dress—brown with a golden sunflower pattern all the way down, far more ornate than any article of clothing I owned. It was there when I awoke earlier, but I hadn't gone over to see the contents of the card attached to it.

I picked up the card, opened it, and looked inside.

I thought you could use a fresh change of clothes for our day today.
Regards,
Mathias du Gearsmith, Esq.

Before I could give another thought to the matter, I found myself tying the final strings on the dress. I observed myself in front of a full-length mirror. The dress trimmed my already thin waist and belled down to the floor. The pattern helped to obscure my strong shoulders, which other girls in my schooling had pointed to as one of my less desirable features. I didn't take too much time to admire myself before hastily leaving the room and padding down the inn's stairs.

The common area held few people at this early hour—the innkeeper, a serving girl, and a man who sat at a long table, eating cooked eggs and drinking a glass of juice. The man had darker skin than the tan Captain von Cravat. He wore a bright red, silk shirt that drew my attention in a less than flattering manner.

The innkeeper noticed me standing at the stairs. He called over to me. "Morning, miss. May I help you?"

I turned and the bottom of my dress whirled behind me, tickling my legs. "I'm looking for a Mr. Mathias du Gearsmith. Has he been down from his room yet? He was supposed to take me to the airship outside the city first thing in the morning."

"Haven't seen Mr. du Gearsmith yet. I'm sure he'll be down shortly," the innkeeper said. He held a rag and turned to wipe down a counter behind him.

The man in the red silk shirt dropped his fork, which clanged against his plate. "Airship, you say?"

I bit my lip, knowing I'd said something foolish. With Wyranth soldiers guarding roads, and given the cause of my father's demise, I shouldn't have been so liberal with my tongue. My skin prickled at the eagerness the man displayed. I'd already given too much information that a lie would be unconvincing, but I certainly couldn't let him know my heritage. "Yes, um, I'm an airship inspector."

"Inspector?" the man questioned, sucking on his lower lip. "So, you'll be looking at the calibration of the turbine gears. Could you refresh me as to which way they turn?"

He'd caught my lie. Beneath my skirts, I dragged my toes on the floor. There were only two possible answers, right? I had a fifty-fifty chance at outsmarting him. "Clockwise, of course," I said with faux-confidence.

The man erupted into laughter, setting his napkin on the table. He stood and approached me. I could smell his eggy breath on my face as he peered down at me. "The gears turn in different directions depending on which maneuvers you are conducting in flight. It's true they'd both turn clockwise, but only if you're flying straight up in the air and forward."

I backpedaled to avoid how uncomfortably close he stood to me and tripped over my dress. Before I could fall, the man grabbed me by the arm and kept me upright.

"I'm sorry," I said.

"No need to apologize, Miss von Monocle."

He knew me? By Malaky, I was a walking target with my namesake. "I'm sorry, sir. I think you have the wrong girl. I'll be going now." I shouldn't have come to Loveridge at all, not alone. I wished I had insisted on James coming with me.

The man took two steps backward, realizing he had intimidated me. Pity crossed his face. "I'm sorry I startled you. Don't leave just yet," he said. "I was about to head to the airship myself."

"Who are you?"

"Your father never spoke of me? My name is Harkerpal."

I clapped my hands in excitement. All of my prior fear evaporated. "Harkerpal! The Chief Engineer!"

Harkerpal flashed a proud grin. "That I am. I could tell you were the daughter of Theodore von Monocle when you walked in the door. You exude such confidence in the way you walk, like you're very determined to be where you're headed–and quickly. You also come across much taller than you are in actuality. That and your nose. You have the von Monocle nose for certain." He bobbed his head in several small nods.

I blushed, unused to someone talking about the way I looked. "Thank you, I think. Did you want to come with me? Marina said you may be able to have the ship sky-bound today?"

Harkerpal scratched his chin. "I obtained the parts I needed, though I was hoping to run a few more tests on the equipment. I suppose it couldn't hurt to test by doing." He tilted his head. "Do you know how to fly an airship?"

"Well, no, but I hoped between you and Marina, you could teach me?"

"I spent the better years of my life keeping that ship running. You don't know how much I sacrificed. The chance for a wife, a family..." he trailed off and rocked back and forth on his feet.

I wasn't sure if I should say something or not, so I stayed quiet while I waited for him to collect himself.

"The Wyranth captured me twice when I was off with your father," he continued. "The Iron Emperor's men knew that I was invaluable to the *Liliana*, and we were such a thorn in their side. You don't know what it's like inside one of their prisons..." Harkerpal stopped himself again.

The innkeeper eyed me, mumbling something to himself. I wondered if I should tell Harkerpal that we should continue this conversation elsewhere. The man could talk at length.

Harkerpal clicked his tongue then sighed. "Of all the tortures I endured, your father was always there for me. He never left a crewman behind. He saved my life on more than one occasion. As much as I regret some of my choices, I also owe him my life several times over."

"So..." I prodded, hoping to lead him to a conclusion before he further drifted into conversation with himself.

"So," Harkerpal said, "I am as much obligated to assist you, as you are his heir. I also long for the *Liliana* to fly again." He produced a strange smile. "I made my life decisions years ago. I live and breathe the *Liliana*. It's too bad there aren't more ships like her. Shall we, then?"

* * *

I stood at the entrance of my father's cabin. The place he spent most of his time. The place he abandoned me for. It seemed too harsh to think of it as abandonment, but no other word fit. I kept my hand on the door and noticed it had started shaking. How could I tell whether I was ready to open it and see what lay inside?

Harkerpal had disappeared into the engine room and warned me, at length, that he would be spending the next few hours installing the new Giffard capacitor. By the time he'd finished explaining the details of every engineered system he could conceive of, I was thoroughly overwhelmed by the workings of an airship.

Perhaps the presence of my father's history overwhelmed me. Either way, I had to become acquainted with this ship, *my* ship. I pushed the door ajar and stepped inside.

The room arced like a pie wedge and was much more spacious than I'd envisioned, suitable for a captain, or a baron for that matter. My father's decorative sense carried over from our farm house—not too ornate, with a rustic touch. He had a wooden chair with a couple of tables, a desk, and a bed, but what caught my eye was the large dresser with a single framed photograph on top. The photograph was of my mother and me when I was perhaps five years old. I didn't remember the moment. It had seemed so long ago when we lived together as a real family. I scrutinized the black and white photo carefully. We posed in front of a large stone wall, and there was an odd man in the corner, face obscured by the frame.

I flipped the photograph on its back and popped the frame open, removing the picture. Outside of the frame, I could see the man clearly. He was a dark, handsome man, with clothing so ostentatious it made Mr. du Gearsmith appear a commoner. "I wonder who that could be."

"Found your father's belongings, have you?" Mr. du Gearsmith appeared behind me.

Startled, I jumped and bumped into the dresser behind me, clutching the photograph in my hand. "You scared me half to death!" I said.

"My apologies. I should have knocked before intruding. What's that in your hands?" Mr. du Gearsmith asked.

"It's a photograph of my family, but there's someone else in the picture, off to the side. I don't recognize him."

"Let me see," he said, holding his hand outstretched to take the picture. I gave it to him, and he held it loosely between his fingers. "Ah, yes," he said with nostalgic fondness, "that's a young King Malaky."

"What?" I asked, astonished. While I knew father had met King Malaky in his military service, I had no clue the king was close enough to appear in a family photo. How much more of his life had he hidden from me?

"Your father and King Malaky were great friends, did you not know?" Mr. du Gearsmith flashed a bemused grin. "Why, back before he ascended to the throne, your father and he were nearly inseparable. His majesty held a profound affinity to airships. It was only with my advice that he stopped flying on them and commissioning new ones to be built. A dangerous sport, being shot at by the Wyranth. Certainly not the best hobby for a king. They are far too expensive to construct, considering they make for giant, airborne targets."

"How could he have never told me he knew the king?"

"Your father once told me that he didn't intend his perilous life to endanger you or your mother. He set aside the farm so that the two of you could live in peace while he made sure you'd be well provided for. With Liliana's death, I'm afraid he withdrew inward. I lost contact with him around that time." Mr. du Gearsmith frowned at the thought, his forehead wrinkling and exposing his age.

Did father think I was incapable of dealing with the realities of the world outside of the farm? And if he did, why did he give me this airship? I slid off the bed. "Perhaps I should give this ship back to the king. I don't have any military experience. Everything I've learned is daunting, and it'd be a waste of a valuable resource if the Wyranth are invading."

"Miss von Monocle," Mr. du Gearsmith said, stepping back to me and placing his familiar, reassuring hand on my shoulder. "Your father, despite making it appear to the contrary, never made any decisions in haste. I trust him, and so should you."

I gazed up at him, uncertain. That much I trusted. My father knew best, but this wasn't the world I'd prepared to live in. Kings and airships made for good stories, but they were never things I actually expected to see up close. "I'll try. I am very excited to fly the ship."

"Why don't you take a look at what's in those drawers?" Mr. du Gearsmith suggested, motioning toward the dresser. He stepped aside to allow me the honors.

I popped open the top and largest drawer and saw a pile of clothes. Digging further, I found a large piece of red velvet that wrapped a solid object. I took the object into my hand and removed the cloth, revealing a sword, shiny with a brass hilt. I'd never cast eyes upon a more beautiful object. "This looks expensive."

"Ah, your father's sword. I'm sure that would fetch a pretty penny indeed," Mr. du Gearsmith said. "And it's wrapped in his cape."

"Cape?" I asked, glancing at the velvet cloth I had cast aside. I picked it up and wrapped it around my neck.

"Ah, Baron von Monocle's signature look! He had one other item to his ensemble. Hmm..." Mr. du Gearsmith pursed his lips and surveyed the room. With a single finger held high, he trounced past me to the closet, opening the door with a flamboyant flair. "Here it is," he said, then reached to a high shelf and pulled down a black top hat. He placed it atop my head and patted it down. The hat was slightly too large for me. I had to have looked ridiculous. My father's clothes still held the smell of a musky old man.

Mr. du Gearsmith stepped back to survey me. "There you are. If only your father had the foresight to have a mirror. I'm afraid your mother was the practical one."

I snickered. "My father fought in this?"

"He told me it served to distract his enemies."

"Well, how do I look?" I asked with amusement, giving him my most intimidating grimace.

"Why, you look like Baron von Monocle!" Mr. du Gearsmith laughed. "You have several of your father's features. Albeit you're shorter and more feminine, naturally."

"I should put these away. Harkerpal said we'd be ready to fly soon," I said, setting the sword on my father's bed.

"Talyen hasn't returned yet. I thought it'd be best we not leave Loveridge until she arrived with whatever further information she could find."

In my excitement, I'd nearly forgotten about Captain von Cravat. I turned to the window in hopes of seeing her approaching the ramp to the cargo hold down below. No one came. "What about a quick test flight? We should know whether the ship is airworthy before trying to fly all the way to the capital, right?"

Mr. du Gearsmith frowned in consideration. He tapped his foot several times, and then nodded. "I must say, much like your father, you present a convincing argument for an adventure. If Harkerpal has finished with his repairs, I suppose a test run couldn't hurt."

For the first time in a long while, I smiled in true happiness. I ran over and gave Mr. du Gearsmith a tight hug. "Thank you! Let's go find him."

CHAPTER 4

"I received word by carrier pigeon that Liliana has been terribly sick for several days. Her fever wouldn't break, and she died in agony. How selfish am I that I could not spend her final days by her side? And for what purpose? War? Many speak of giving their hearts and their souls to another. She was my heart and soul. I know not how I can go on."

An excerpt from Baron von Monocle's log
Day 2 of the Month of Queens
15th Year of Malaky XVI's Reign

I TOOK MY place on the bridge of the *Liliana* along with Marina, Harkerpal and Mr. du Gearsmith. I'd never felt this alive in all my sixteen years, but something crept inside of me, giving me the impression I was an imposter.

How could I possibly live up to the man that everyone else on the bridge told stories about and revered as legend? Each time someone mentioned his name, I learned more reasons that I could never be half the person he was. But that didn't matter now. All I needed to do was focus on launching an airship. Nothing a farm girl couldn't handle, right? I let out a deep breath, stood at the controls, and gazed out the front window.

Harkerpal had completed his Giffard capacitor installation, lubricated the engine and the main gears, but warned that the ship might not fly for long, and several of the finer components required a few more days' work. He vouched for the safety of this test flight as long as we kept it short.

Given what I'd learned of Harkerpal, I figured he understated his analysis of the ship's safety. Harkerpal had a perfectionist streak to him. I, on the other hand, wanted to have fun. "Harkerpal, how do I turn the turbines on again?"

The engineer loomed over me, his gaudy red coat nearly blocking my view. As he showed me the controls, he teemed with a similar level of excitement to my own. "Turn this knob, and that will fire up the engines," he said. "These levers are for altitude. Very important to know your position in that regard at all times. The next set of levers will bank the ship left or right, and, finally, the ones at the end will turn the ship."

"Why would it have two separate sets of levers for banking and turning?" I looked out the window, trying to visualize it. Perhaps I had overestimated a farm girl's airship piloting capabilities.

"Start her up, and I'll show you."

Mr. du Gearsmith clasped his hands together and Harkerpal stepped back. Marina smiled at me from across the bridge, standing in front of her own dashboard that had a strange cone protruding from it. The flight console shined with its brass lining and levers. Fine wood held the panel in a robust encasement. Even though I owned the *Liliana*, I couldn't help my gut feeling that I had my hand in the cookie jar when my parents had already told me no. Closing my eyes, I turned the knob and started the engine.

The *Liliana* trembled as she came to life from her deep slumber, protesting as the steam and gears struggled to remember their functions. A loud squeal came from the room down below, but was soon replaced by a repetitive clanking. I turned to Harkerpal to ensure these sounds were proper, but he didn't appear worried. A whirring noise took over all sound. The turbines had engaged.

I pushed the lever for altitude control, and the ship rocked. It whined, being removed from what its resting place for the last two years. Moments later, the *Liliana* lifted off the ground with astounding speed. Through the window, the skyline changed from a view of the trees to a vast blue horizon with little green dots below. "It's working, it's really working! We're flying!"

It's impossible to describe the exhilaration of buzzing through the air. Mr. du Gearsmith's horseless carriage seemed like a hay ride in comparison. I was further off the ground than most birds could fly. We ascended into the clouds and above. I shifted the altitude lever to hold our position and stood on my tiptoes to get a good view of the front of the ship—Marina called it the *fore,* but it was the front to me—through the window. How small everything looked down below! The whole town was but a speck on an emerald green world. The view sent chills through my whole body. I smoothed down my dress.

"Amazing, isn't it?" Mr. du Gearsmith said from behind me. "Your father and his crew had the luxury to experience this every day."

I looked back at Harkerpal. "I can't believe it worked!"

Harkerpal bowed courteously. Marina gave a small inclination of her head toward me.

"Where should we go?" I asked, mostly to myself, skipping back over to the controls.

"Now, now, wait a moment. I never said the ship was in good enough condition to go anywhere." Harkerpal moved toward me, eyes lit up in panic.

I wanted to see more, but knew if I wasn't quick to the draw, the others would take over and force a landing. We'd just taken off. Sure, we might have to keep the trip short, but I hadn't even had the opportunity to really fly. I threw the lever into full forward and banked us hard to the left. Harkerpal stumbled and fell against the cabin wall.

Mr. du Gearsmith grabbed onto the ship internal communications device to steady himself. "Miss von Monocle, what are you doing?" he hollered at me. His eyes betrayed the same furiousness he had shown the other evening.

Marina braced herself on a handrail on the opposite side of the cabin.

"I'm exploring!" I shouted back, pushing the *Liliana* for all the power she could muster. This would be my one chance to see what my inheritance could do. As soon as Captain von Cravat returned, this ship would no longer be mine. I'd own the *Liliana* legally, but we would be on a mission to deliver information to the king. When he saw us, would he really allow a ship like this to be taken by a young girl for her own pleasures? Even with my limited experience, I understood the answer to that.

This was my only chance to drive my ship on my terms.

Land zoomed past us below, so fast that I couldn't make out our location. I couldn't believe my eyes.

As we settled into our flight, the others calmed themselves, realizing that the ship wasn't going to buckle as Harkerpal had warned. I banked the ship to the left again, this time much more gently. I learned the sensitivity of the flight controls with that first hard bank. Next, I played with the other lever, the one that turned the ship, and saw the distinct difference in how the ship reacted. "This is a better control for full turns left or right. The other works better for sharp maneuvers," I said, proud of my self-education. Learning by doing was how we farmers took care of business. My father might have worked the *Liliana* like it was a part of his body, but he had several years of experience on me. I'd pick it up. Flying a ship wasn't as difficult as I had first thought.

Mountains appeared in the distance. We approached a wide river, one much grander than I had seen in my lifetime. "Where are we?"

Mr. du Gearsmith stepped to the window, gazing outward. He spun around and waved his arms frantically. The anger in his face made me cringe. "Zaira, *turn this ship around!*"

Harkerpal stumbled up to the front of the bridge to peer out the window. Marina stood on tiptoes to see over the side of the ship. "We're in Wyranth territory. Past the Border River," she said. "How did we get here so quickly?"

Harkerpal and Mr. du Gearsmith shouted, their words blurring together into meaninglessness. I hyperventilated. The room spun around me. I heard a loud blast and collapsed to the floor. "I...I don't know what's coming over me," I managed to spit out in between gasps of air.

"Move over!" Mr. du Gearsmith pushed me to the side and grabbed the controls for the craft. He banked hard right and pushed us back into full throttle once more. I stumbled to regain my composure and leaned on the console to try to right myself. When I did so, I accidentally pulled the altitude lever.

The ship dropped. We all stumbled. Through the window, I saw some strange looking devices with large gears and what looked like the barrel of a gun. Several of those lined the border river. Those gears turned and *boomed.* Several large cannonballs flew through the air—directly toward us.

A sharp *crack* resounded at the back of the ship. The nose of the ship tilted downward. Before I could lose my footing completely, Mr. du Gearsmith regained control and leveled us. The whole cabin filled with smoke. I coughed.

"You almost killed us all!" Mr. du Gearsmith said. His face remained tight, rage hot in his eyes. The divot in his chin wrinkled further with his frown. "We've been hit with the Wyranth's anti-airship ballistics. How, by Malaky, did we travel so fast?"

"This ship is capable of incredible speeds," Harkerpal said proudly, seeming to forget the looming danger.

"I'm sorry," I said. My face flushed redder than the glowing light on the console. I had no idea where I was or how fast I flew. Being on the airship, it had tempted me a little too much, preying on my desire for speed and excitement.

"You took us much too far with that little charade of yours," Mr. du Gearsmith fumed. "This is a very fast ship, and you weren't paying any attention to your course. I should have never let you take the helm. Not at your age. Not without experience."

Harkerpal and Marina stood staring, but said nothing. I'd disappointed them, that much was clear. My heart sank all the way to my stomach. "Will we be able to make it back to Loveridge?" I asked.

More *booms* came from below, followed by cannon balls shooting past us. This time, none of them hit.

"I don't know, I'm going to try," Mr. du Gearsmith said, focused on the controls. His composure in the face of the anti-airship ballistics from below astounded me. The ship turned smoothly, and settled into a comfortable speed.

"I'm going to head to the engine room to ascertain the damage," Harkerpal said, bobbing his head. He scurried away quickly, reminding me of Toby. I missed my ferret. More, I missed home.

The Wyranth stopped firing at us. We must have flown out of range. The tension in the cabin still held thick.

I'd thought flying my airship would be the best day of my life. How quickly Mr. du Gearsmith reminded me my upbringing was inadequate for adventuring. Airship life took someone with military training, or at least some form of piloting experience. All I knew how to do was to maintain a farm and grow crops. I'd never be able to fill the role my father had in mind for me with this inheritance.

As if sending me a message from the grave, my father's top hat slipped from my head, covering my eyes. Irritated, I pushed the hat off my head. It fell to the deck.

Marina picked it up. "You dropped this," she said, offering it to me.

"It's not something I should be wearing anyway." I crossed my arms.

Marina bit her lip. She kept ahold of the hat, but held it at her waist.

Before either of us could say anything further, the ship stuttered, a different sensation than the ballistics had caused. I gripped onto the console with all my strength. "What was that?"

"Engines are failing," Mr. du Gearsmith said. Irritation filled his voice, and he didn't bother to spare me a glance. He kept his hands on the control levers, adjusting them with precision.

I rubbed my face with my hands, betraying my frustration with myself. I wished I could redo the last few hours, tell Mr. du

Gearsmith he should take the helm. In fact, I should have gone back further and gifted my airship to Rislandia. "For steam and country!" as my father would have said.

We flew in silence for some time. The sputtering continued from the turbines and the forested earth below passed at a far slower pace than before. I didn't have the courage to ask whether Mr. du Gearsmith thought we would be able to make it back to Loveridge.

Harkerpal popped his head through the hatch by the corner of the bridge. "Miss von Monocle," he said, eyes fixed on me. He paused, glancing at Mr. du Gearsmith as if he were uncertain who he should address. "The ship is no longer flight-worthy. We have to land as soon as possible."

Mr. du Gearsmith peered ahead, narrowing his eyes through the bridge's periscope lens. "There's no good clearing ahead of us to land."

"If we don't land soon, there will not be an option for long. Better to take a chance while we have control." Harkerpal took his final steps up the ladder and back onto the bridge.

The hatch slammed shut behind him. The turbines ground to a halt and the engines made the loudest popping noise I'd ever heard. My ears rang. The ship fell once more.

Harkerpal who threw himself at the console this time, turning the ignition over in rapid succession. "No, no, no! Not like this!" he yelled at the ship.

Marina braced herself against the hand railing. I did the same. Mr. du Gearsmith backed away from the console, letting Harkerpal work. The ground grew ever closer.

In one last act of desperation, Harkerpal kicked the control console with all his might. The engines restarted and the turbines began to spin.

The ship couldn't warm up fast enough to halt our descent, but it slowed us down enough that Harkerpal could maneuver. He jammed the banking controls hard, trying to clear us from the

FOR STEAM AND COUNTRY

forest. It wasn't enough. The *Liliana* brushed over the treetops. As we sank further, branches *snapped*, *cracked*, and *boomed*.

We collided with the ground below. I bounced in the air, feet above my head as I held onto the handrail for dear life. My head smacked against the rail, and my body whacked against the ground. By Malaky, I stung everywhere. My vision blurred, and I lost my grip, collapsing to the floor. The *Liliana* bounced and slid across the ground.

The smoke from the engines combined with a thick mixture of dust and debris that flooded the cabin. All of us coughed. Mr. du Gearsmith grabbed onto my wrist and pulled me to my feet. I had trouble standing, so he braced me. "We need to get out of here in case of fire," he said.

The smoke was too thick to see behind him. "Where's Harkerpal and Marina?" I asked in confusion.

"We need to go now. They can look after themselves," he said, his tone of voice heavily implying I could not do the same.

I hurt too badly, and my mind had gone too fuzzy, to argue. I brought my free hand to my temple and rubbed it. My head throbbed.

Mr. du Gearsmith moved before I could collect myself. He grabbed me by the waist and flung me over his shoulder. I didn't expect such a lanky man to be so strong or swift. He found his way to the hatch and descended the stairs.

Even more smoke filled the lower cabin than had the bridge. Sweat trickled down my face. Something burned and generated considerable heat. Nothing slowed Mr. du Gearsmith's determined stride. He navigated the hallways of the airship as if it were his second home.

I coughed more. My lungs burned, and I inhaled, starved for air.

"Don't breathe too deeply! The smoke is a carcinogen. Shallow breaths, and cover your face if you can," Mr. du Gearsmith said, hustling into the main cargo hold. He set me down against a wall.

He grabbed the cargo door crank and churned in a circular motion. The door hatch opened and descended to the ground. Smoke drifted outward. I could barely move or keep my eyes open any longer. The smoke irritated them as much as my lungs. I almost lost consciousness before Mr. du Gearsmith grabbed me once more, jolting me awake.

We sped down the ramp, and out into the forest, where Mr. du Gearsmith set me at the base of a tree. I gasped for air. He bent over in an effort to catch his own breath. Then I fell into another coughing fit.

My stomach did flips inside of me. I couldn't stop coughing, and I forced myself to my knees, bending over in hopes to get the smoke out of my system. The movement further unsettled my stomach. My skin felt clammy, and then in the most embarrassing act yet, I vomited at Mr. du Gearsmith's feet.

Mr. du Gearsmith jumped backward. "By Malaky, girl!" he shouted, unable to withhold his frustration.

I looked up at him apologetically. What else could I have done?

He appeared far gaunter than I had seen him thus far. The smoke had harmed him as well, but he appeared able to compose himself nonetheless.

My head spun again, and the projecting hadn't settled my stomach. I settled back against the tree, resting my head on its trunk. I frowned. "I'm so sorry. I didn't mean to..."

I couldn't finish my words before my world went black.

CHAPTER 5

"I can't bring myself to return home and face my beloved daughter. How could I look her in the eye and tell her I must leave again? By Malaky, I hope she understands."

An excerpt from Baron von Monocle's log
Day 15 of the Month of Queens
16th Year of Malaky XVI's Reign

THE INNKEEPER INFORMED me that my companions had secured a table in the common room. I'd apparently slept well over two days, which had me scrambling to get back to life. I had so much to think about. What had happened with the airship? What would I to do now?

It turned out I didn't have much time to deliberate. The others waited for me, whether out of compassion and concern or wanting to chastise me, I couldn't be sure. They were the last faces I wanted to see, and this inn was the last place I wanted to be. I longed for my quaint country bed where no airships or Barons or Wyranth would ever bother me.

What would I say to Mr. du Gearsmith? No one had ever been so angry with me before, and he had good reason to be furious still. I'd almost killed the man, and then repaid his saving my life by soiling his shoes.

I dragged my feet all the way down to the common room. I kept my chin down, not wanting to look the others in the eyes.

With a brief glance upward, I saw Marina, Harkerpal, and—to my surprise—Captain von Cravat. "Where is Mr. du Gearsmith?"

"He was called away on urgent business," Captain von Cravat said, ice dripping from her voice. She motioned to a chair at the table, which had no food or place settings. This wasn't going to be a friendly meeting. "Sit."

I complied, settling into the chair. A lump grew in my throat, and I tried to swallow it back. "How is the airship?" I asked.

Harkerpal bobbed his head before speaking. "Several gears need to be replaced, and the steam pipe has cracked in at least three locations. The outer hull has been penetrated on the aft starboard side. There is significant damage. It's going to take a number of parts, and that's just for the critical systems. All of the interior cabins need repair from smoke and debris damage."

"That doesn't sound so bad," I said, phrasing my words half as a question. The room had more tension than a plow's harness behind a horse.

Marina and Captain von Cravat glanced at each other.

"If the damage were any worse, I'd recommend rebuilding the *Liliana* from scratch. She is in dire shape, Miss von Monocle," Harkerpal said.

"Your father would be extremely disappointed," Captain von Cravat said.

Those words pierced me. If Captain von Cravat hadn't known how to get to me, she faked it with amazing precision. I withered into my chair. I already felt terrible enough about my mishandling of the ship. Was this necessary? Older adults from big cities sure liked to hammer on younger folk with less experience. When I'd made mistakes back on the farm, Mr. Gentry took the time to teach me. "It's a matter of survival that you learn this. You're not all on your own. We're your neighbors. It's almost like family," he'd told me.

It wasn't just me who'd made mistakes. James once set a bale of hay aflame in the Gentrys' barn, nearly burning the whole place down before Mr. Gentry could find a bucket brigade. Mrs. Gentry

FOR STEAM AND COUNTRY

shook in fear, but she and Mr. Gentry never used the occasion to make James feel inhuman. Unlike the way these three stared at me. I couldn't be smaller to them.

"I'm sorry," I said, keeping my eyes firmly on the table. I didn't want to look at any of my father's crew any longer.

"You should be, but sorry won't fix this," Captain von Cravat said.

"Don't be so hard on the girl, Captain. She only—"

"*Captain*." She made sure Harkerpal understood who held command. "I'll make the decision on how to handle this. By Marina's account, the girl is completely reckless. She took no consideration as to her whereabouts or the condition of the ship. We've never been in a situation where the *Liliana* came that close to becoming refuse."

I glanced over at Marina. She frowned sympathetically and mouthed an apology. All I could do was to cast my eyes aside.

"Do you have anything else to say for yourself?" Captain von Cravat pressed. She leaned into the table to try to force eye contact with me.

"I'm not my father. You can't expect me to know how sensitive airship controls are or where I should avoid going." All I wanted to do was have some fun with an airship—*my* airship. But I couldn't say that to Captain von Cravat, or even Marina for that matter. "He never taught me anything. He wasn't around." My voice cracked.

"No, I suppose he didn't," Captain von Cravat said as if it validated her position. She stood. "I believe we're done here for now. Harkerpal, I expect an estimation as to the costs to repair the ship within the hour, as well as your best guess as to when you can have the repairs completed. Marina, find one of the crew and buy the fastest horse you can find from one of the merchants in the town square. I have a report that needs delivering to King Malaky posthaste. If we can't get the airship running in a timely manner, we need another means of transporting the information."

"Aye, sir," both Marina and Harkerpal said in unison. They scrambled to their feet and saluted her.

Captain von Cravat saluted in return. She turned and marched out the door, each step measured with the military pomp that would be expected of her.

Marina and Harkerpal returned to their seats after she left the inn. Marina tried to give me a reassuring smile. "Talyen can be a little rough. She's taken your father's death to heart, but she's the finest military commander I've ever met. In some ways, better than your father."

"Different. The Baron had a knack for unorthodox strategies. The enemy couldn't predict him because he liked to take risks. There's more of him in you," Harkerpal said, pointing at me, "than you realize."

I shook my head. "No, Captain von Cravat is right. I'm nothing like him. I shouldn't have come out here in the first place. I belong back in Plainsroad Village."

Marina reached into one of her pockets and pulled out a purse, from which she produced a gold coin. She set the coin on the table and slid it across to me. I'd had gold Rislandian marks from what my father had left me, otherwise I couldn't survive as a lone girl on a meager farm. This coin had different markings on it, ones I didn't recognize.

"What's this?" I asked.

"This is a good story of how your father seized the day, just like you tried to do. Sometimes it works, sometimes it doesn't. Right Harkerpal?"

Harkerpal nodded several times. "That's always the gamble. And that's why he had people like the Captain behind him to keep him on a steady course."

"What's this got to do with anything?" I asked, taking the coin between two of my fingers. I flicked it, and the coin spun on the table in front of us.

Harkerpal pinched the coin, stopping its spin. He held it so I could see the markings clearly. "If you look at the imprint on this, you'd see this isn't a Rislandia Kingdom gold mark, but the markings of a strange tree on the tail's side, and the face of a man known as the One-Eyed King on the other."

"What's that got to do with my father?"

"Have you ever been to the ocean, Zaira?"

I shook my head. "There's a big lake about a day's walk from my farm, though."

"Even the biggest of lakes don't compare to the ocean. Its vastness is astounding, and the effect it has on air currents, well, it's challenging to an engineer." Harkerpal slid the coin back over to Marina. "Your father liked to take your mother to see the ocean before you were born. There was one place in particular, the Ebony Sands Coast. I'm sure you can imagine where the name came from."

I shrugged. "Somewhere with ebony sands, I'm guessing?"

"Got it in one," Marina teased with a wink. She dropped the coin back into her purse.

"That's where these coins come from," Harkerpal said. "The One-Eyed King's name was Renawl, and he set up his domain by preying on travelers along that coast. These days it's safe. Rich nobility from Rislandia, Wyranth, and beyond build themselves vacation residences there. A true example of what peace in the world could look like. The black sands are such an attraction, so beautiful and rare. I've never seen another place so breathtaking, and the weather. Oh my, the weather!"

Marina nudged him in the side with her elbow. "Baron von Monocle. Rash adventuring. Focus, Harkerpal."

I wasn't the only one who noticed how Harkerpal loved to hear himself speak. That made me smirk. If I could relate to anyone since I'd left Plainsroad Village, it was Marina. She understood me.

"My apologies, my apologies." Harkerpal said. "What your father found there was someone who established himself along that peninsula who lived a king's life due to his thieving and pillaging, his kind heart couldn't allow the poor peasants to live in that kind of fear. He landed the *Liliana* by the One-Eyed King's domain, feigning to be impressed by the king. He offered to work for Renawl as a mercenary. While he had the One-Eyed King occupied in contract negations, the *Liliana's* commandos secured the rest of the island. The Baron meant to trick him, however. His job was to convince Renawl that he would be leaving his castle to receive his own airship with a full crew and supplies. An incredible negotiator, your father was, even when it was false."

Was there anything my father wasn't incredible at? If this story was supposed to make me feel better about myself, it failed. "I'm sure he had great skill," I said, wrinkling my nose.

"Ah, but the Baron fooled himself with his own prowess, overconfident in his abilities. The One-Eyed King smelled that something was amiss. Baron von Monocle found shackles waiting for him in the One-Eyed King's palace. His plan of going in alone, being both military force and diplomat, was rash. Like a certain young von Monocle who tried to test the limits of her new airship."

I bashfully ran a hand back through my hair.

Marina chimed in, spinning the coin on the table herself this time. "I should mention that the One-Eyed King had two eyes at this point—he hadn't earned his name yet."

With both of their expectant gazes upon me, I could tell I was supposed to bite at that. I took the bait. "How did he lose an eye, then?" This time I stopped the coin, letting it fall on its heads side, which displayed the visage of this One-Eyed King.

"He put a knife to your father's throat, ready to slay the shackled Baron. Oh my, this is the most exciting part." Harkerpal wiggled his fingers over the table. "Even chained, the Baron kicked the knife right out of the king's hand, grabbing it midair, and driving it into Renawl's good eye! The guards were so stunned and distracted, it allowed the Baron to escape from the square and make it back to the airship. Once there, he had his crew to protect him again."

Several people at another table took note of our conversation and whispered amongst themselves. The innkeeper shook his head and disappeared into the kitchen.

I silently reminded myself not to bring Harkerpal with me the next time I wanted to be in a subtle situation. "That's awful violent," I said. "I don't see how it's funny at all. Or how that's supposed to apply to me. His story worked out in the end because he knew what he was doing. I crashed the ship."

"Yes, but he put himself into peril, just like you. He relied on others to get him safely off the island. He couldn't have done it without his crew," Marina said. She crossed the table, crouched down, and patted my arm. "What you need is a balance, someone to guide and teach you. You need a crew of your own to make up for your deficiencies."

"What Marina is trying to say, is that the *Liliana's* yours now," Harkerpal said. "We understand where you come from, and your lack of experience. Like I told you before, I owe your father my life several times over. We would be glad to help. Captain von Cravat will come around eventually."

I sat thinking for a long moment. They were trying to cheer me up after Captain von Cravat verbally ripped me in two. The part they left out of their story, however, trumped any reason I could think of to restore faith in myself.

My father was larger than life. He'd had talents that no one else could replicate. No matter how perilous the situation, he had the wit, experience, and combat capability to find a way out. The list of his skills didn't stop there, either. Every story I heard only made the man sound like the greatest hero that ever lived. That wasn't me. My capabilities only included digging postholes and growing vegetables. I could make a mean vegetable stew, but that didn't help.

"The *Liliana's* more than a job to you, Harkerpal." I said. He was so selfless, and I could tell from his eyes he truly wanted me to assume my father's mantle, even after the mess I'd caused. I took a deep breath. "But me, I'm not sure I actually want to fly the airship again."

Harkerpal tried to stay impassive, but disappointment overcame his face, revealing wrinkles that showed his age. "I see," he said.

His lack of verbosity jolted me in surprise.

Marina stood from beside me. "It's okay, Harkerpal. We did what we could. If she's not ready, she's not ready. This is a big shock to her, you have to remember. The Baron kept his worlds separate. It's probably safer for her without the weight of a whole airship on her shoulders anyway."

"I'm sorry I crashed the ship, Harkerpal," I said. This time I stood, ready to return to my room. "Sorry to you too, Marina. I hope you can figure out what's going on and stop the Wyranth."

"Where are you going?" Marina asked.

"To my room. I need to collect my things. It's time I went home." Back where I belonged.

CHAPTER 6

"Over the years, I've looked many an enemy in the eye before I slew them, yet today marks the first time I've experienced fear. There's something different in this current crop of Wyranth soldiers. Something inhuman."

An excerpt from Baron von Monocle's log
Day 23 of the Month of Queens
16th Year of Malaky XVI's Reign

THE SUN LOOMED high above me, beating down with its relentless heat. I pulled weeds from the field. Sweat dripped down my face. Those three days I'd been gone had decimated my weekly crop yields. Without the help of the Gentrys, I wasn't sure how I'd survive. Since my return, I'd spent far more hours working than the usual sunrise to sunset. Even with the hard labor, I couldn't help but think about the different way of life I'd briefly gleaned in Loveridge.

War with the Wyranth crept over the horizon, and I would have never known about it if I had minded my own business. Outside of crashing the airship, I had fond memories of the beginning of my lone flight. I couldn't escape thoughts of the unparalleled rush when we lifted off, the weight of the air pushing against me when we accelerated, each sensation more thrilling than the last. I daydreamed of leading soldiers into the battle, raining down death from above. My laughter resounded throughout my fields at the ridiculous thought. "That's not me. That's my father. What am I thinking?" I asked no one in particular.

Toby flipped over to his backside, puffing out his chest at me and wiggling in the dirt. He chirped.

"That's right, Toby. It is much better to be here with you," I said.

A round object whizzed past my head.

Panic overcame me, and I dropped to the ground. Thoughts of war loomed in my head. Could the Wyranth be this close? Did they know who I was? I relived the shock of anti-airship ballistics bombarding the *Liliana*. Two more objects flew from behind, narrowly missing me.

I quivered, just as I had that day on my airship. Shouting for help would do no good. It would lead whoever was targeting me that much closer to me before any of my neighbors could respond. As always, I was on my own.

Toby showed no fear. He climbed atop me and hissed at the assailant. My eyes were shut tight. I hoped whoever it was wouldn't hurt my little ferret.

One of the objects smacked against the back of my skull. I tensed, but it didn't hurt like I expected. The sting of the hit was quick. My hair became slimy and moist. Juice dripped down my neck and crept into my blouse. I smelled a familiar odor, faint, yet somewhat acidic.

For the second time in as many weeks, tomatoes made a mess of me. My fear waned and returned as rage. I balled my fists and pushed Toby off me. He fell to the ground, landing on his feet. Within moments, I regained my own footing. I spun around, eyes narrowed. Only one person would be brazen enough to pull such a prank. "You scared me halfway to Wyranth, you numb-witted, imbecilic—"

James doubled over in laughter in front of me, dropping another tomato he held in his hand. "The look on your face! Ha! Oh, I'm going to die, Zair-bear," he said, laughing so hard it interfered with his breathing.

"You have to stop calling me that. I can't think of anything more embarrassing than being called Zair-bear in front of proper strangers from the capital," I said, pushing him with both my arms. James was a complete idiot, and he needed to pay for his shenanigans. Before he could regain his balance, I pummeled him and drove fist after fist into his belly. It felt good to show him who was stronger.

James's eyes went wide. My shoulder knocked him square in the chest. He lost his balance and gripped onto my coveralls to try to steady himself. In a far more embarrassing situation than the moment I had admonished him, James crashed to the ground.

I fell atop him.

Neither of us moved. Our eyes locked. I was but an ear of corn away from his face, and I mean the width, not the length. I could feel his hot breath on my face. It was... pleasant.

Looking in his eyes just then, seeing his depth and genuine concern for me, I seriously considered the possibility of more than friendship with him. He was sweet and handsome, though I wouldn't tell him that. He didn't need the ego boost.

I held still, eyes staying fixated on his. Neither of us moved. Was I supposed to kiss him, or was he supposed to kiss me?

Toby poked his nose between us, chirping, removing the question altogether. He licked my face.

Both of us laughed heartily, and I rolled off to the side. The moment had passed, but I'd not soon forget the brief connection we shared. I had to think on it. Decisions like kissing or courting, especially a friend since my childhood, deserved more than an impulsive response.

"Your ferret sure is a character," James said, dusting his clothes and popping back to his feet. He took my arm to help me up.

I accepted his assistance without protest for once. Though I was still splattered with tomatoes, my clothes had no holes. No worse for the wear. "C'mon knucklehead, least you can do now is help me carry back some of these baskets."

"To my folk's place?" James asked.

I nodded. Everything I harvested on my farm these days, I brought back to the Gentrys. Mr. Gentry took it to market and did the selling for me—said it wasn't a place for a young girl alone. I wasn't particularly interested in selling anyway. All the better to focus on growing and harvesting.

James helped me harvest the remaining tomatoes until the baskets were filled to the brim. We each picked a basket up and started for the Gentry's house.

"What was your big inheritance all about?" he asked.

The question nearly made me drop my basket. I recovered my grip and considered. Was there any harm in telling him what occurred? The story made me look like an idiot, but he'd seen me make plenty of blunders before.

After determining there was no harm, I repositioned my grip on the heavy basket, and told him about my misfired adventure. I spared no detail about Mr. du Gearsmith, Captain von Cravat, Harkerpal, Marina, Loveridge, and the airship. As the Gentrys' home came into view, my arms burned from carrying the basket for so long. I set it down, finding a clean spot on my blouse to wipe sweat off my brow.

"If I hadn't seen the horseless carriage myself I wouldn't believe your tale," James said with the shake of his head. "Put it to song and maybe you can become some sort of traveling minstrel!"

I gritted my teeth. Did he always have to tease me?

"Maybe I should make a tall tale of my own." James furrowed his brow as he thought. "While you were gone, I joined up with the Knights of the Crystal Spire and travelled to Panderica. We ran into some brigands and—"

"I wasn't making up stories about the airship, and you know it, you jerk!" I reached for the tomatoes, but held myself back, knowing that I'd lose that battle.

He saw what I was doing, and smirked at me with a knowing gaze. It was no fair, not being able to beat him at his own game.

"I'm serious," I said.

Uncertainty crossed his face as he picked up his tomato basket. He motioned for me to do the same. I crouched and tried my hardest to lift with my legs, supposing it was enough of a break. The basket felt twice as heavy as it had before, and the burn in my arms became a familiar friend. This was the life I knew. Could I have truly left it for airship adventuring?

We arrived at the Gentrys' barn, setting our baskets inside. The barn had two horses in stalls, a cart, as well as some of their equipment. It was a small barn, enough for the needs of our families, with a chicken coop attached to the side closest to their house. It was quite the relief to be able to set the tomatoes down. My arms felt like noodles.

Toby hurried through the barn, doing a lap and pausing by the horses. He enjoyed the smell of their dung. I was too tired to yell at him.

James paused at the barn door, frowning with a scrunched forehead. He looked cute when he was thinking. "So, Mr. du Gearsmith was truthful? You have your own airship?"

"Yes," I said. Toby bolted from his spot and used me as a ladder until he reached my shoulder. From the smell of his face, he'd grazed horse manure at some point, which he rubbed into my coveralls.

"And you gave it up? Are you crazy? That's the chance of a lifetime!" Horror filled James's face.

"I was no good at it, James. I told you."

"I'm sure it takes practice. Where is it now? Can we go? We could work for the king aboard an airship, enter into the service. This is my ticket to becoming a knight!"

I crossed my arms. "Do I have to repeat everything to you? It doesn't work. I'm not going back. That's not my life."

"Can I have it, then?"

"Ugh!" I didn't dignify him with a real response, storming away from the barn and over to the Gentrys' house. James followed, but I was finished dealing with his immaturity. I resolved to no longer think about airships or war, but important things, like Mr. Gentry selling my tomatoes. I needed to speak with Mr. Gentry about his plans, how much coin he thought he could obtain. Then I could go home and take a bath and forget about James.

"Hey, wait up!" James jogged after me. "What'd I say?"

"You don't ever consider other people's feelings, do you? It's whatever strikes your fancy in the moment. I hate boys." I rapped on the door to the Gentrys' house.

Though James lived there, and could have opened the door, he waited. "That's not fair, Zair-bear. I have feelings too, and I care about you," he said.

Those words plucked me like a fiddle. I stopped and turned toward him. "You do?" I asked softly.

"Yeah, of course. That's why I'm telling you how great of an opportunity you have. How many of us have the chance to become something more than this?" James motioned toward the farm land.

"It's not so bad of a life," I said.

"It's not bad, but it's not interesting, either. It's just work every day until we die. Look what fell in your lap. You have the chance to become a hero, and you're going to drop that over one mistake? You shouldn't let a dream die over that."

James's eyes glittered and forced my attention to them. Which was the real him? The teenage idiot-boy out for laughs, or this serious, thoughtful James? Lost there in his eyes, his advice held weight over me. "Okay, I'll think it over."

"When you do go get your ship, you have to promise to take me with you, though. Okay?"

"Take you with me?" I couldn't help but laugh. There was the idiot-boy again. "I haven't even decided if I'm going to yet."

"You will. Trust me. I know you, Zair-bear, better than anyone." James grinned. "And you'll help me become a Knight of the Crystal Spire for real."

"Oh, James," I said. I patted his shoulder. Toby chirped over at him from mine.

We both laughed again.

"You know, even though you made a huge mess, I'm happiest here, spending time with you on our farms. As much as you tell me I'm turning away from an opportunity, I can see us growing old here instead. Don't you ever think about that?"

James made a face and stuck out his tongue. "All too much. Ma bugs me about..." he shook his head. "I don't want to talk about that. Let's go find Da and ask him what he thinks." James edged past me, opening the door. He glanced over his shoulder and motioned with his head. "C'mon, Captain Zair-bear!"

"Idiot." I rolled my eyes and followed him inside.

CHAPTER 7

"We'll be returning to Rislandia City, the capital, after a brief sojourn home. My daughter looks more like her mother every day, for which I am grateful. This is the first I've seen her since Liliana passed. She is a strong girl. I hope she understands that much of my strength died with her mother."

An excerpt from Baron von Monocle's log
Day 34 of the Month of Queens
16th Year of Malaky XVI's Reign

THE GENTRYS' HOME was small, like my own, though the rooms had more space between them. James and I entered through the back door by the barn, which opened into a quaint room where the family hung their drying laundry.

I followed James into his kitchen, closed in and detached from their main sitting room. Mrs. Gentry stood in front of one of her countertops, chopping vegetables on a wood board. She sang to herself:

"Over the hills and far away
My love comes to sweep me off my feet
Never would I regret the day
The embrace of the wind, I one day would meet."

Mrs. Gentry shook her whole body to the beat of music that only played in the rhythm of her chopping. Her gray hair was tied back into a bun, and she wore an aging apron over her somewhat stocky body. Though she could be a reflection of me aged thirty years, the way she moved to her own music gave her an air of energy that made me smile.

I almost joined her to harmonize the chorus, but James cleared his throat.

Mrs. Gentry jumped. She dropped her knife on the cutting board with a *clang* and turned toward us. "My goodness," she said, placing a hand over her chest. "You scared me, James! How long have you been standing there?"

"Long enough to hear a song that's far too old," James said, smirking.

I nudged James with my elbow. "That's rude, James. Mrs. Gentry, you have a lovely singing voice," I said.

Toby scampered off my shoulder and immediately pawed at vegetable scraps on the floor.

"I'm sorry, I should have left Toby outside," I said.

"Toby's always welcome here," Mrs. Gentry said. She returned to her chopping, but spared a glance over her shoulder. She slid a couple of carrot pieces off her board, which dropped to the floor.

Toby gratefully scampered over and gnawed on the scraps of food.

"Zair-bear's got another load of tomatoes for the market tomorrow," James said. He picked a couple of diced carrots off his mother's cutting board and popped them in his mouth. They crunched when he chewed.

"Did you load them in the barn?" Mr. Gentry asked.

"Yes, Ma," James said.

"Good. Zaira, would you join us for dinner?" Mrs. Gentry turned to smile at me. "We'd love to hear what you've been up to these past few days. My son says you went off with some city fellow and a military woman?"

"It really wasn't all that exciting," I said, casting my eyes down to where Toby gnawed on his scraps.

"That's not true. Zaira got to fly an airship!" James said.

"Really?" Mrs. Gentry raised a brow. She moved to light a fire in her stove.

I bit my lip and moved to the vegetables to assist her. I'd made this particular stew on my own several times over the course of the last two years. All of my recipes came from Mrs. Gentry. She taught me how to cook, how to mend clothes—basically everything I knew came from her.

Annoyed by my silence, James spoke up and told my story, embellished with his own personal flair, but I didn't contradict him. His version made me sound much more important than I truly was. He blamed the crash on the Wyranth and not my own failures. My cheeks became hot when he mentioned it.

Dinner cooked in the pot while we talked about my misadventure, all of which I found embarrassing when relayed to an adult. "Is this true, Zaira? I've never done anything so exciting in my life," Mrs. Gentry said.

I glanced at the window. By that time, the sun was almost set, casting a pale crimson light across the horizon. Mr. Gentry unlaced his boots on their porch.

"It's true," I said. The way James told the story, I didn't sound so bad as I'd felt about the adventure.

The main door swung open and Mr. Gentry stepped inside.

"Hi, Mr. Gentry!" I said with an eager wave. He provided a good subject change.

He nodded in return and reached over to his cabinet to pick up his tobacco pipe.

"Just in time for dinner, dear," Mrs. Gentry said. She grabbed her pot holders and removed her stew from the fire. With a lift of the lid, the aroma of fresh vegetables and rabbit meat filled the kitchen.

"Glad I could make it," Mr. Gentry said. He lit his pipe and gave Mrs. Gentry a kiss on the cheek before moving to the table. "Hello, Zaira."

"Hello, Mr. Gentry," I said.

We all sat down to eat, talking about the harvest and market. Sitting around the table with them made me remember all the times I'd sat down for dinner with the Gentrys. They made me so welcome, never hesitating to look out for me. As much as I worked hard, I wasn't sure I could manage my own farm without the support they provided.

It was almost enough to forget about my father and his airship.

Until Mr. Gentry spoke. "What happened with that attorney a few days back?"

"Zair-bear got to fly an airship," James said.

I was about to stuff a chunk of meat into my mouth, but the reminder made my stomach churn. I set my fork down and stared at the plate. "Yes. I crashed it on the first go around, I'm afraid."

"Only because the Wyranth shot you down," James said with a mouth full of food.

Mr. Gentry considered both of us, cutting a piece of meat. "There's no shame in that, Zaira. I'm sure James is right that circumstances were extenuating. You know, your father took me aboard the ship when he first took her out. Amazing piece of machinery. Theodore nearly killed me that day, as I recall. I've never travelled at such speeds. Don't intend on it again, either."

"You never told us that, dear," Mrs. Gentry said.

James chomped on a carrot. "You flew on the airship and never told me? That's incredible. Are you secretly a knight?"

Mr. Gentry laughed. "I'm afraid not, m'boy. Theodore was the only one who did the adventuring. Amazing man, he was. I'm truly sorry for your loss, Zaira," he said.

I prodded my stew. "He'll probably be the last one of us to do adventuring, too."

"Hey, you promised to take me on the airship!" James protested.

"James!" Mrs. Gentry said in a scolding tone.

"It's all right, Mrs. Gentry. I did promise. *If* I go back to it," I said.

A noise like one of the clockwork rotors at the mill down the road *clacked* in the distance. The mill wasn't loud enough to make noise at this distance. The *Liliana* had made a similar sound when its turbines engaged. Did Harkerpal work his magic with the ship? Perhaps they were coming to get me after all. I glanced to the window, but curtains blocked the view.

"What's that noise?" James asked.

Clack. Clack. Clack.

Mr. Gentry stood. The noise grew louder and louder. He rushed to the window, pushing the curtain back. It was just before dusk, difficult to see outside. "I've heard that sound before," he choked out the words. This marked the first time I'd heard fear in Mr. Gentry's voice.

We all stood, following him to the window, the sound growing still louder.

Clackety-clackety-clackety. CLACKETY-CLACKETY.

"That's no airship," Mr. Gentry said. He protectively pushed James and me from the window. "You kids need to get away from the front of the house. We're under attack!"

CHAPTER 8

"Our new assignment is a suicide mission over the Border River. But there is no other way. We must press on for the sake of Rislandia."

An excerpt from Baron von Monocle's log
Day 42 of the Month of Queens
16th Year of Malaky XVI's Reign

"DEAR? WHAT'S WRONG?" Mrs. Gentry asked, wide-eyed.

I peeked around Mr. Gentry to get a glimpse out of the corner of the window, clutching at the back of his shirt.

An army marched from the east, toward my farm. Toward the Gentrys' farm.

They had to be about a half a mile in the distance, only silhouettes in the darkening sky, but it was unmistakably a wall of men moving in our direction. There were hundreds of them. They carried torches and lanterns and had shiny silver helmets with long points, the same as I had seen on the road to Loveridge.

"Wyranth infantry," Mr. Gentry said. He didn't move but continued to stare out the window. "I never thought I'd see a sight like this again."

"Wait, again?" James asked from off to the side. He clambered for a place at the window to see. "I knew you weren't telling the truth about not adventuring! You've fought in the Grand

68

Rislandian Army, Da. Haven't you?" He sounded more in awe than annoyed.

"It isn't something I like to relive."

"That still doesn't explain the sounds," Mrs. Gentry said.

CLACKETY-CLACKETY-CLACKETY.

The sounds stopped.

Outside, some of the soldiers parted. A giant metallic device I hadn't seen before rolled into our view. Steam spewed from its top. Gears as large as the ones I'd seen in the *Liliana's* engine room protruded from its side, and a giant open barrel cranked out of its front. The barrel pointed straight at the window.

"Down!" Mr. Gentry shouted. He lunged and tackled me. I hit the floor with a *thud*. My lungs burned. James and his mother fell prone to the floor with me.

I gasped for air.

Thunder shook the house and the window before us shattered. A round metal ball crashed through the room, tearing apart everything in its path until it punched into the back wall. Shouting men barked orders outside.

"What was that?"

"Mobile artillery. Cannons become a lot more effective when you can maneuver them quickly. By Malaky, during the war..." Mr. Gentry trailed off.

"Should I grab your musket?" James asked, sounding eager to fight. His mother wrapped her arms around him protectively.

"No," Mr. Gentry said. He rose to his knees and pulled me up. "Zaira, you know why they're here."

I hadn't had time to think about it, but when I saw that look in his eyes, I understood. The Wyranth came for me. I'd alerted them to my presence once I'd launched that airship. Someone back in Loveridge must have overheard my conversations and found my name. Could it have been the innkeeper listening in on my conversations? We should have talked in private.

"What do I do?" I asked. My bottom lip quivered.

Another blast hit. This time off to the side of their kitchen, hitting one of the posts. The house creaked in response, but one of the load-bearing walls sagged. One more barrage and it would collapse for sure.

I thought about the earthquake, the beginning of this rush of madness that I called my life in recent days. It had caused part of my roof to cave, but nothing like this.

Mrs. Gentry screamed. "The oven!"

Had she left the oven burning? I glanced over. No, it wasn't that. It was far worse. Wood beams from the ceiling fell right onto the oven. Fire blazed. It would have died out, but now it had fuel.

The wood pillar caught fire, and before I could move, that flame trickled up to the wall. Within moments, the Gentrys' kitchen became a smoldering inferno.

Mr. Gentry shook me. "You need to get out of here, fast." He snapped a finger at James. "James, you protect her. Take Lightning and ride west. Don't stop until morning. Your mother and I will stall the soldiers."

The soldiers. In the flurry of the flames, I'd nearly forgotten them. I glanced back out the window. They moved ever closer. Would we have time to escape with them marching so quickly?

I scrambled to my feet, not arguing, not stopping to think. I'd been used to doing what Mr. Gentry told me, and that was a blessing. James grabbed me by the arm and hauled me toward the back door.

I looked back. Mr. Gentry grabbed his musket, getting ready to shoot from his window. Mrs. Gentry grabbed a rake, holding it like a weapon, standing loyally at his side. They were going to lose everything for James and me. I wanted to protest, I wanted to stop them.

"Go!" they both hollered at once.

James and I rushed to the barn behind his house. Lightning was their cart horse. She had a milky-gray color to her and a sweet temperament—anything but what her name implied.

"Are we going to make it?" I asked, a slight warble to my voice.

James saddled Lightning with expert speed. He thrust his foot into the stirrup, and swung his other around. I could envision him as a real Knight of the Crystal Spire, as a hero. My chest lightened at the sight of him. He held out his hand to me. "Take my hand. Hurry."

I complied. His grip was firm as he pulled me up. I swung behind him and wrapped my arms around his stomach. My nails dug tightly into his shirt.

"You all set?" James asked.

"Yes," I said.

James turned Lightning and kicked her hard before we left the stable. The horse lunged into a full gallop.

Lightning had never been speedy like Mr. du Gearsmith's carriage. Tonight, though, she seemed as spooked as we were by the artillery and shouting soldiers. The wind blew against my face, and my hair flew everywhere in the cool night air.

I glanced back at the Gentrys' house. Flames engulfed the kitchen area and spread across the roof. Hopefully Mr. and Mrs. Gentry made it outside. Even if they did, they had to face those soldiers. And from the way they had attacked us, I doubted they were in the mood for talking.

The *crack* of musket fire echoed over the farmland. A man's voice howled in pain.

James tensed but said nothing. He focused on maintaining control of Lightning. We sped down the open road toward town. Poor James. His parents wouldn't survive the next several minutes. What could I say to console him?

We rode past several more farms in silence. More neighbors, lesser friends who I might never see again. Would they be in danger, too? Or, once I was gone, would they be left alone? Given the stories I'd heard of the Wyranth Empire's advances in my school, I doubted they'd leave the poor farming village alone.

We arrived in town before I could collect my thoughts. The markets were closed, boarded up and locked until morning. The only light came from the Plainsroad Inn, which would still be serving some of its patrons.

We passed the constable's office, attached to a small jail, which typically held unruly drunks from the inn more than any other serious criminals. I couldn't remember hearing of a crime worse than that. I'd never participated much in town life, content to stay on my farm, do my work, and have Mr. Gentry go to market for me. This could be the last time I'd see the place. Oh no. I'd done something terrible. I panicked, gripping James's shirt hard.

"What is it?" James asked.

"Toby, I forgot him. We have to go back." I tugged at James's shirt.

Lightning pressed on. "Zair-bear, there's no way. The soldiers are there. We'd be killed."

My eyes became heavy and damp, tears streaking away from my face in the wind. I'd made so many mistakes these last few days. Of all of them, this hurt the worst. "I'm sorry, Toby," I whispered to myself.

"Which way should we head?" James asked. We approached the main road at the end of town. One direction led toward Loveridge, the other to Rislandia City, the capital. Mr. Gentry hadn't given us advice on which way to go when we arrived in town, but we couldn't stop for the night. Not with that many soldiers trying to find us.

"Well, the *Liliana* is closer to Loveridge. Maybe I can find Harkerpal there and we can get to the safety of the skies," I said.

James pulled Lightning to a halt. The safety of the skies. Funny that I'd think that, so soon after the skies had proven anything but a place free from Wyranth attacks.

"But if the army's after the airship, won't they have scoured that area first?" James asked, glancing back over his shoulder toward me.

"Oh, yeah," I said. That should have been obvious. "But if we know that, won't they know we know and realize we took the road to the capital?"

"Or they might know we know they know we know..." James said.

"Do you think they're that clever?"

"I'm messing with you, Zair-bear." He laughed, but it came out hollow. "Rislandia City is the safest bet." He kicked Lightning and steered the mare west toward the capital. The city itself was at least a three-day ride, if we pushed ourselves. I already started to feel the effects of weariness, having worked hard in the sun all day.

We rode on for hours. Every sound along the road made me glance behind us in fear, expecting to see a troop of Wyranth soldiers. After a while, the pounding of my heart subsided back into normalcy. James slowed Lightning's pace to a trot so she wouldn't wear out before we arrived somewhere we could rest. I was so tired, I could hardly think straight. Lightning protested even her slower pace, bucking her head and snorting.

James suggested we pull off the main road, travel a few more minutes and find a nice place to camp by some trees or foliage. Even though sleeping on the ground sounded unappealing, any sort of sleep would have been fine by me.

James found a good clearing soon thereafter and tied Lightning to a nearby tree. She grazed, and I sat down on some long grass. "If only we could have packed a pillow or some blankets," I said. Then I laughed at myself. "Look at me, we're running for our lives and I'm thinking about the comfort of blankets."

I had hoped James would laugh along with me, but instead, he frowned and gazed off toward home. Reality set in for him, his somberness overcoming me. James lost everything he knew. His home. His parents. I'd been through that before and understood his pain completely. Though I could scarcely find any words for him.

I forced myself to stand, legs wobbling from resting so long atop a horse. I walked over to James and wrapped my arms around him from behind, pressing my head against his shoulder blades.

James held his body tense, solid as a rock. I would have thought him impenetrable, but he sniffled and wept softly. Once he started, his soft cries escalated into a full bawl. He shrugged at my touch and I let him go. He collapsed to his knees. Then he started tugging some of the tall grass until the leaves snapped off their roots, as if killing them would ease his pain. He kept at it for several moments, sniffling in between heavy breaths.

"I'm sorry, James," I said, reaching down to squeeze his shoulder. I didn't know what else to say. This was my fault. His life was ruined, and it was all my responsibility because I had drawn the Wyranth's attention. What more could I do wrong?

"It's not your fault," James said, wiping some of his tears on his sleeve. He stood. "My dad made a decision. He wanted to protect us, give us lead time to get out of there. I...I just hate those Wyranth scum! Why do they keep attacking our kingdom?"

I swallowed. As much as he said it wasn't my fault, I knew that wasn't true. I let him have his space. He probably didn't want me touching him. "Your father was noble. You heard him, he was a soldier. I bet he did incredible things. Saved many people's lives," I said, hoping my words would comfort him.

James turned to face me. He looked like a wreck. I never wanted to see him in that much pain again. I wouldn't allow it for as long as I lived, I swore to myself. He started to say something, but his words were stifled by a loud *click* behind us.

Something prodded me in the back. "Don't even think about moving, or I'll blast you," said a voice with a harsh, guttural accent.

Wyranth. We'd been discovered.

Three soldiers circled, surrounding us. The rifle dug deeper into my back. What could we do? I didn't have a weapon, and neither did James. Even if we did, we were outnumbered, and we faced trained soldiers.

James put his hands up in surrender. I followed suit.

The soldier behind me lifted his gun and frisked me. Another patted James down. They were not tender with us. The soldier behind me groped my buttocks. By Malaky, I wanted to vomit. I was completely helpless. What if he didn't stop there?

"Enough of that," said one of the onlooking soldiers. He appeared to be an older man, gray in his trimmed beard. The look on his face was anything but amused. "I know you have a daughter, Private. Do you want Rislandian soldiers giving her a feel if she's captured?"

The soldier behind me released me, using his rifle to push me. "No, Major Anton, sir," he said.

The rifle hit hurt. I was already tired, and I wasn't built for pain. I stumbled forward. Were they going to kill me? If they were, what did the leader care how I was treated?

I side-glanced at James. His eyes caught mine, worry overcoming his face. We had no hope for escape, at least not now. All we could do was wait.

Major Anton moved in front of me. He gripped my face by the chin and forced me to look him in the eyes. "Zaira von Monocle, in the flesh. Oh, if we would have taken you when you were younger. I bet we could have saved so many Wyranth lives. Your infamous father would have turned himself in with you as ransom." He grinned at me. All semblance of compassion disappeared from him.

These men were responsible for destroying my friends' farm. They likely killed Toby and the Gentrys. Without thinking, I spat in his face. How dare he invoke my dead father?

Major Anton jerked back and raised his hand as if to strike me.

I cringed, raising my shoulder to protect my face from him. Perhaps I deserved his slap for my foolish move, but I was in no place to accept that kind of pain.

Oddly enough, Major Anton's eyes softened when he saw how I reacted. He wiped the spit from his face. "You're lucky I'm ordered to capture you and that I have a soft spot for young girls." He pointed to the other soldiers. "Men, bind their hands and let's get going, the captain will want to see them. And he won't be so lenient if you're not cooperative, Miss von Monocle."

CHAPTER 9

"I hardly believe it myself, but we survived our recent assault. A third of the crew was killed or captured, but it would have been all of us if I didn't have my quick-witted second in command."

An excerpt from Baron von Monocle's log
Day 45 of the Month of Queens
16th Year of Malaky XVI's Reign

THE SOLDIERS LED us back toward the main road. One of them took Lightning, commandeering the horse for the Wyranth army. We had ridden so far only to be captured. Mr. Gentry's sacrifice meant nothing now.

The soldiers ahead of us spoke with Major Anton, though I had some trouble understanding their words through their thick accents. From what I could make out, it sounded as if little remained at Plainsroad Village. Their artillery leveled nearly the whole town. I snuck a glance at James, but he had his head down, staring at the dirt in front of his shoes. His eyes had a glassy quality to them.

One good bit of news was that no airship had been found, even though a large number of Wyranth soldiers scoured the countryside. Harkerpal must have been able to get the *Liliana* airborne.

Where were we in relation to where I had crashed? My memory became fuzzy when it came to thinking about specifics of that day. If only I had been more cautious, we might not be in this mess.

The soldiers seemed to content to take me as a hostage and hadn't asked many questions. Their conversations revolved around the *Liliana* and further searches for the airship.

The more I considered our walk, the more I realized it would only be a matter of time before they questioned me on the ship's whereabouts. They would probably torture me, and then James, if my answers didn't satisfy them.

That pressed upon me a need to stall before we arrived at their main camp. The more I could delay them hurting James or me, the better. If I were my father, I'd think of some ingenious plan. It'd make for yet another of dozens of stories where he grabbed one of the soldiers' knives from their belts and whirled around his guards before they had time to react.

But I wasn't my father. So, what could I do? I could only think of one possible way to delay them. I pretended to trip over my shoes.

This act had to be convincing, so I didn't brace myself when I came tumbling toward the ground. I yelped in surprise. My face hit the dirt road, scratching my cheek.

The soldier who groped me earlier forced me to my feet, rough with his grip. I winced.

Major Anton stopped in his tracks and turned back. The other soldiers followed suit. "What's the matter? You're not getting fresh again are you, Private?"

The private released his grip of me. "She tripped, sir. I helped right her."

I played up my weariness, stumbling and fluttering my eyes like I could barely keep them open. "I'm so tired. We've been riding all night, then this. I... I don't think I can stand anymore."

Major Anton frowned, glanced further down the road, then back at us. "A break, then. But we will be walking again in short order," he said.

"But sir, the Captain—"

"The Captain doesn't know when we found the girl, or even that we have yet. We have time before we can get back to the airship search. Now take a break. If she can't walk, you'll be the one to carry her. I'm going to scout down the road." Major Anton gave a firm nod and started away from us.

The other three soldiers set down their packs and their guns and seated themselves, motioning for us to do the same. I did as was told and sat next to James. With Major Anton gone, our odds were better if we tried something.

"You're that tired?" James whispered to me, sounding concerned.

I winked at him in return. He nodded, understanding.

Moments later, a noise rattled in the distance. It was much like we'd heard at the Gentrys' home before.

Whap-whap-whap-whap.

The noise grew in intensity as each moment passed. The guards rushed to their feet in response, scrambling for their guns. "Where's Major Anton?" the private asked to the other soldiers.

A younger, slightly unkempt soldier shrugged. "He went off to scout the road ahead."

"I know that, but he needs to be back here. Find him!" the private shouted, taking matters into his own hands by rushing in the direction Major Anton had gone. The soldier he spoke to followed, leaving one final soldier who held his wits about him, staying to guard James and me.

The noise intensified.

WHAP-WHAPPEDY-WHAP.

"The mobile artillery group is still running their machines? Are they trying to alert the whole countryside to their arrival? Maybe all the farmers could have time to band together," James said, eyes lighting up with his cute idealism. He shook his head. "They'd be overrun, wouldn't they? Just like Mom and Da."

We hadn't had a moment to pause to continue the grieving process since the soldiers had captured us. Poor James. I wished I could give him some comforting words. Instead, I listened to the sound. It didn't have the same timbre as it did back at the farm. It was somehow softer, a little higher pitched.

Something about it was familiar.

The sounds swirled around us in a tornado of noise. Hearing anything else became impossible. Wind picked up, blowing leaves, sending my hair into a frazzled jumble.

I pushed my hair out of my face. James shouted something, but I couldn't understand it. The lone Wyranth guard pointed his rifle up toward the sky and fired.

The shot rang out, but the soldier appeared displeased with the result. I looked up. What I saw was the most beautiful sight I could have imagined. The *Liliana*. Those sounds came from the turbines!

Six people in dark clothes descended from the side of the ship's hull, rappelling down long ropes. They hollered like maniacs, brandishing guns and swords.

Our guard stumbled backward, mouth agape. He shook where he stood, staring at me. His Wyranth uniform had several holes in it. Before he could do or say anything else, he fell to the ground.

Blood pooled around his body. I dragged my feet and backed away. Bile rose in my throat faster than I could suppress. I'd never seen a dead man before, let alone one killed so brutally.

The six commandos from the airship dropped to the ground. They spread out, five of them circling around me and James. One I recognized as Marina, but the sixth member of the party surprised me—Captain von Cravat. She glowered at me, but her attention shifted when more shots rang out.

One of the *Liliana's* commandos collapsed. The three Wyranth soldiers who had left stood with their guns trained on us, using a nearby tree as cover. My rescuers returned fire, several shots hitting one of the Wyranth soldiers in the shoulder. He fell.

The other two Wyranth soldiers wasted no time. Major Anton moved the quickest, charging the circle of my rescuers. His companion fired his gun behind him to cover him, keeping Major

Anton from getting shot. Before I could think to yelp, Major Anton had a knife to my throat.

"Weapons down, or I'll kill her!" Major Anton shouted from behind me.

The five remaining rescuers looked at me. Captain von Cravat's eyes flickered as if she were assessing the situation for action. Her dark hair was tied back behind her head, remaining still as her head moved. She took a step toward me.

"I'm serious," Major Anton said. His hand shook despite his threats. The knife grazed my throat. "Weapons down and hands up. I'll spare the girl if you comply."

"Wyranth soldiers. You all think you're so smart, so brave. Really, your tactics are anything but. Taking a mere girl hostage? Is this what your empire has come to?" Captain von Cravat asked, scorn in her voice. "Pathetic."

Captain von Cravat leveled her gun right at my eye level. It pointed right at me! Could she be so cold as to shoot me to alleviate the situation? It couldn't be possible. Her finger pressed on the trigger.

I shut my eyes tight, tensing every muscle in my body. The shot rang out, a deafening noise even with the whirring of the airship above.

CHAPTER 10

"We retrieved a whole supply wagon that was captured by Wyranth soldiers. They escorted it down the banks of the Border River. I love the looks in their eyes when my team and I descend from above. The others on the ship prefer guns, but I prefer the sword. It's a more elegant weapon."

An excerpt from Baron von Monocle's log
Day 46 of the Month of Queens
16th Year of Malaky XVI's Reign

MAJOR ANTON'S KNIFE went slack against my neck, scraping downward. The blade nicked me in a couple of places as he fell to the ground. The wound he'd created stung. My eyes fluttered open. I couldn't believe I still lived. "You... you didn't shoot me," I said to Captain von Cravat.

"Of course I didn't. Now get behind me. I have more of your mess to clean up," Captain von Cravat said. She motioned to a couple of her commandos to flank around the tree the final Wyranth soldier used as cover.

Everyone moved so fast. I gingerly touched my neck, still in disbelief at the fact I lived. James rushed to my side and steadied me.

The lone Wyranth soldier became desperate. He stayed behind his tree, but blindly fired two more shots from his rifle.

"Duck!" Captain von Cravat shouted.

James wrapped his arm around my waist and pulled me to the ground. I braced myself with a hand, crashing to the dirt. When I looked up, Captain von Cravat's commandos had flanked the Wyranth soldier. Captain von Cravat closed her hand into a fist in a pronounced motion, and her crew fired simultaneously. The Wyranth stumbled out from behind the tree, falling to the ground soon after.

I felt a hand on my shoulder, shaking me. "Zaira, snap out of it," Captain von Cravat said.

I looked up, blinking. "What's happening?"

"Later. There's a lot more soldiers out there, and we need to get you back up on the airship before someone notices the commotion we made here," she said.

Marina produced a small lantern that had a handle and some gears attached, spinning slowly as the light pulsed inside. She pointed it up toward the airship and flipped a switch. The lantern blinked on and off four times.

Four more blinks returned from the airship and several rope ladders dropped from the sky. The ladders swayed in the wind, the airship hovering at least five stories off the ground.

I stared up at the *Liliana*. Did Captain von Cravat expect me to climb that? "There's no way I can get up there," I said.

"You'd better, or you'll be found when the next patrol gets here. Get a move on. I didn't risk our necks so you could be afraid of heights." She took the end of one of the rope ladders and shoved it into my hands.

"Zair-bear," James said, "You'll be fine. I'll be right behind you." He smiled at me, warm, reassuring.

I cocked my head upward again, daunted by the prospect of the long trek up to the ship. There was no other choice. I could do this. I had to do this. I started on one of the rungs. Captain von Cravat helped to lift me up. Her men hoisted themselves onto other rope ladders, swinging easily from the ropes and making good time up to the sky above.

I stopped on the rope ladder, wooden rung slipping beneath my shoe until it caught on the rough grain. My hands sweated, and I tightened my grip on the rung above me. "What about Lightning?" I asked.

Captain von Cravat climbed the first rungs behind me, stopping when I did. "We can't descend to load a horse right now. We have to keep moving. She'll be fine. Someone will find her and will give her a nice home. Now keep moving!"

I climbed, gut wrenching with each step. The higher I ascended, the more likely a fall would kill me. I moved far too slowly for Captain von Cravat's tastes. I could see impatience in her eyes when she waited for me in between steps. But what was I to do? I had never tried acrobatics like these before. It was hard enough hold on. The rope wobbled, and the wind pelted us.

About halfway up the rope, I looked down at the ground and froze. At that point, I noticed that the airship didn't hover. It moved forward. Dizziness overcame me. "By Malaky, tell them to stop!"

"We can't stay in one place or we'll be a target for the rest of the Wyranth army. You don't want to get shot off this ladder, do you? Keep. Moving," Captain von Cravat said, her voice even more stern than before.

My palms could barely grip each rung, the sweat dripped from me like I was a leaking sieve. I scanned for James, who had already climbed to the bottom of the airship hull. If he could do it...

I moved up the rungs with determination, hand over foot. Before long, all the others were up on the *Liliana's* deck with only Captain von Cravat and me lagging behind.

When I reached the top rung, a couple of the crew hoisted me onto the deck, pulling me up by the shoulders. My legs hovered in the air in a fearful moment.

Captain von Cravat crouched onto the deck before lifting herself, smoothing down her Grand Rislandian Army uniform. "I find it harder and harder to believe you're *his* daughter," she said under her breath.

Those words stung worse than the knife wounds on my neck.

James rushed to my side from where his rope ladder attached to the ship, linking his arm with mine. After the strain of the climb, his muscles were taut as the rope ladders themselves. He held me steady through the heavy wind blowing on the deck. "You know, you could be kinder," James said to Captain von Cravat. "She's never done anything like this before, and besides, this is *her* airship. She might very well order you off it, and it's a long drop down!"

I flushed. James defended me so much lately. While nice, after Captain von Cravat had saved our lives, it wasn't the most appropriate of jabs. Anything I could have said would only make Captain von Cravat angrier, so I kept my mouth shut.

Captain von Cravat did what I couldn't expect—she laughed. "That is a good one! I'll have to tell the rest of the crew about that." She straightened herself, grinned, and ruffled James's hair. "You're a feisty one, I like that. Spunk goes a long way toward being a good member of the team."

James did not look amused. Neither did I. What was wrong with her? I glanced at the other crew, who all watched us with curiosity. Were they all this crazy?

Pity filled Captain von Cravat's eyes. "Okay, it's high time we talk. Woman to woman. Come to the mess cabin. Let's get you something warm to drink, and I'll fill you in."

I followed her inside, recalling the direction to the mess cabin from my previous jaunt. The rest of the crew that had gathered to look at us had scattered, attending to their jobs. I didn't see Marina. She had a dual function with the ship, though, I'd learned before. I imagined she'd returned to her cannoneer station.

Other crewmen pulled up the dangling rope ladders. Some descended stairs to the lower decks. Each stopped to salute me as I passed in spite of the scene they just saw. Eyes trailed me as if they expected something. What did they want?

The mess cabin held four long tables and a serving area that had the food strapped in and covered. The ship's chef carried a tray and moved to secure it. I was in awe at how many people assembled on the ship so quickly.

Captain von Cravat called the chef over, ordering him to fix us hot tea. The chef nodded and complied without hesitation. Everyone appeared to be firmly under her command. No wonder she found James's threats to be amusing. We'd be thrown off the ship before Captain von Cravat ever would.

James and I seated ourselves on a long wooden bench across from Captain von Cravat. The benches were hard, uncomfortable and immobile, bolted to the floor. Inside the mess cabin, the whirring of the ship's turbines became a muffled, constant hum.

Captain von Cravat tugged on her uniform's tunic as she sat. "At least we'll be able to talk without too many people bothering us." She cocked her head at James, concern on her face. "Are you well, Mr. Gentry?"

I glanced over at James, seeing that he had turned bug-eyed like he wanted to bounce off the walls. This had been one insane evening that neither of us would have believed if the other had told the story. His own emotions must have been as confusing and overwhelming as my own.

"Yes... I..." James frowned. "I can't believe I'm on a real airship. I can't believe any of this."

"Of course, this is real," Captain von Cravat said. She paused whatever thought was going to follow that as she inclined her head. "Miss von Monocle, raise your neck some. I'd like to see your wounds in the light."

I did so. The stretching motion exacerbated the dull pain that lingered from Major Anton's knife scraping against me.

"Not too much blood. Are you well enough, or do you want medical attention?"

"I'll be okay," I said.

The chef returned with a tray containing a pot of steaming liquid and three metal cups—one for James and me, and another for Captain von Cravat. He set them before us and poured the three cups.

Captain von Cravat hooked two fingers through a handle and brought the cup just below her face, inhaling. "A floral flavor. Theo used to like more of a bitter, black tea, himself."

"I never really drink tea, unless I'm sick," I said, but took the cup into my hands all the same. She was right, it reminded me of the flowers that bloomed in the spring along the dirt road from my farm to the village.

"Now, where was I?" Captain von Cravat asked to herself before taking a dainty sip of the steaming liquid. "Ah, Mr. Gentry, would you care for a tour? There's no need for you to be involved in this conversation. It's... personal."

James frowned, but then looked over at me as if wanting my decision on the matter.

"Don't get into trouble," I teased, hoping it would lift his spirits.

James gave me a tight hug, then stood. "Where do I go?"

Captain von Cravat waved over another of the crew who appeared to be sitting at a bench enjoying a meal. The crewman didn't protest when he was ordered to take James around the ship. He waved and motioned to James. They departed out the mess cabin, leaving Captain von Cravat and me alone.

I gazed into my tea, steam warm on my face. What could I say to her? One moment I'd crashed the airship, the next she saved my life. I owed Captain von Cravat, and she was right to scold me. I couldn't be of any use to her.

"I suppose you're wondering how I assembled the crew so quickly," Captain von Cravat said.

"More wondering what I'm going to do. My farm...it's gone. I'm so lost."

"We'll get to that in a moment," she said, reaching out to pat my arm reassuringly. "I know I was hard on you. I'm used to a military crew, you have to understand. I issue orders, they obey. I may have been unfair to you because of that and because of—"

"Because of what?"

She took a longer sip of her tea before replying. "Because you're not him. You look like him, in a feminine way, of course. Your mannerisms, they're very similar as well. I expect certain things when I hear the words von Monocle, you understand?"

"I've heard enough stories to know he was more of a giant than the creatures in the bedtime stories my mother used to tell me," I said.

Captain von Cravat nodded. "Some are exaggerations, but he was also the kind of man who would do whatever it took when there was necessity. And don't tell him something's impossible! I swear if I said, 'You can't move a mountain,' he'd find a way to do it."

I didn't know what to say, so I sipped the tea. I found this floral blend much better than the tea my parents used to have.

"When you left, I impressed upon Harkerpal how imperative it was that we get the ship airborne again. I know the Wyranth. If they understood the ship went down, they'd stop at nothing to obtain it. Harkerpal said he needed supplies and men, and so I borrowed Mr. du Gearsmith's horseless carriage to make some quick arrangements. She's not in the best shape, but she'll get us back to the capital."

"So you're returning the ship to King Malaky?" I asked.

Captain von Cravat focused on me. "That depends on you. King Malaky is very protective when it comes to his subjects' private property. I would honor his wishes as a loyal subject. This ship belonged to your father, and by all rights belongs to you. Though without an airship, Rislandia would lose quite an advantage against the Wyranth. I would hope you'd consider that."

"Mm," I said. I couldn't commit without knowing more. My body felt hot, and I wasn't sure whether that was because of the tea or the conversation. Everything moved so quickly. The day before, I'd harvested crops, played around with James in the fields. I'd almost died out there on the road! And now I was headed all the way to the capital?

I longed for home, my room, my bed. It occurred to me then I hadn't slept since the day before. My eyes must have been puffed up like a pastry. They felt heavy all of a sudden. I missed my old life. I missed...

"Toby," I said to myself, heart fluttering.

"You're not making any sense," Captain von Cravat said. "What's wrong?" she asked, standing. "Do I need to get you a doctor?"

"It's...my pet ferret. We left him back at the house. I took off in such a hurry from the Gentrys' that I forgot him." Was it childish to worry about a pet like this? I'd lost much more than that, James lost his parents. But in some ways, Toby was my child. I abandoned him without a thought. But what could I have done differently? If I had stopped, returned to my house to get him, the soldiers would have captured us far earlier. Captain von Cravat and her crew wouldn't have rescued us.

Her strong hand squeezed mine. "I'm sure he's all right. When we have everything cleared, I'll make sure someone's sent to look for him."

"You'd do that for me?" I asked, confused.

"You're Theo's daughter. That makes you family."

Before I could say anything else, Marina bounded in from the deck. She looked so proper in her uniform, similar to Captain von Cravat, and greeted us with a salute. "Captain, Miss von Monocle."

"At ease, Commander Willett. Have you made some progress with..." Captain von Cravat shifted her eyes in my direction, appearing to make a determination. "...the prisoner?"

Marina gave me a once over as if unsure she should talk about it in front of me, but accepted Captain von Cravat's judgment with a nod. "We have. Apparently, all of the soldiers are given the serum you mentioned to us before. This soldier is either not aware of its purpose or he's holding out on that fact. Whatever it is, it's clearly addictive. Without it, our prisoner's gone into violent fits."

I wanted to ask about the prisoner, where he came from, but I knew better than to interrupt. Having a Wyranth prisoner was probably how they knew which direction I'd gone to in the first place. The *Liliana* was a tight operation, that much was certain. These people were as much heroes as my father.

"Disconcerting," Captain von Cravat said. She set down her tea. "We'll have to report this, as well. Good work, Commander."

"Captain, there's one other thing," Marina said. She shifted uncomfortably. Whatever information she had, it was big. The air seemed to electrify.

"What's that?" Captain von Cravat asked.

"It's Baron von Monocle, sir. According to our prisoner, he's still alive."

CHAPTER II

"It's been nearly a year since I've written in this log. We'd been relegated to transportation duty for the most part. A most recent return to the capital brought us new orders, and we've set our sights for an offensive within the Wyranth Empire. Mr. du Gearsmith, my attorney, recommended that I formulate a will, just in case. I followed his advice, but poor Zaira has been missing a father for far too long already. What difference would it make should I actually meet my demise?"

An excerpt from Baron von Monocle's log
Day 13 of the Month of Kings
16th Year of Malaky XVI's Reign

AFTER I'D HEARD the news, Captain von Cravat told me I needed to rest. I had to get some sleep while she conferred with some of the others to determine our plan. The information that my father could still be alive impacted far more than just me. Some of the crew in the mess cabin voiced that they should be heading for Wyranth territory immediately. The thought was that no one ought to be left in the hands of the Iron Emperor for that long. Others, Captain von Cravat included, said that the crew's duty was to Rislandia, and that King Malaky needed to be informed of both this and our other recent reports of the Wyranth soldiers.

Captain von Cravat hurried me along before I could get into the discussion. "Go and rest now, before I make you. Trust me, that won't be pleasant and will result in a lump on your head as big as this airship."

I went to my father's cabin and lay down. My eyes wouldn't close, however. How could I stop my head from spinning?

My father might actually be alive. Alive! I'd become so used to him being gone, the possibility stopped occurring to me. What would I say to him? How would I react? He'd been gone for so long, even before his official disappearance, I barely knew him.

I wanted him home, to work on the farm and help me become an adult. But wasn't I an adult already? I had worked hard and provided for myself since he'd disappeared more than two years ago. That had to count for something.

I frowned, sitting on the large bed that rested in his cabin. If my father lived and I found him somehow, I had no idea what I would say to him.

Even if I wanted him back home, my world had crumbled in these last several hours. There wouldn't be a farm to return to. I wouldn't have Toby. I still couldn't believe I'd left him back there.

A knock came at the door of my cabin—*my father's* cabin.

"Zaira, are you awake?" Marina peeked her head around the door.

I waved to her. "Yeah, come in."

She stepped fully inside, glancing around in awe at the room, a perfectly preserved treasure trove of this airship's past. "I've never been in his quarters. No reason to have me here," Marina said.

"Well, here it is. The great Baron von Monocle's personal sleeping space," I said in a mock-ominous voice.

Marina moved over and sat on the edge of the bed next to me. "I'm sorry. It must be hard for you with everyone singing the praises of your father. He meant a lot to a lot of people though, so try to take it as a compliment."

I stared straight down at the sheets. "I know, I can't help but feeling—"

"Inadequate?" Marina asked.

"Yeah." I blushed.

91

"Trust me, anyone new to this ship goes through that. I still don't feel like I completely fit in. If you look at people like Captain von Cravat or Chief Engineer Harkerpal, they know their respective crafts so well it's daunting. I just follow orders," Marina said. She caught my eye with a small grin and shrugged.

"I'm glad I'm not the only one, but it still doesn't help me. It doesn't feel right for me to be here." I glanced to the small window at the end of the cabin. The *Liliana* moved through the clouds like they were waves in the ocean. The clouds themselves looked like mist.

Marina stood and paced the room, stopping at the large dresser of my father's belongings. The pictures above the dresser caught her attention, and she took one into her hand. "This one's of the Baron, you, and Liliana. I don't mean the ship either," she said.

"Must have been a long time ago," I said.

She further inspected the photo. "He doesn't wear a monocle."

"Of course not, it's just a name. You don't expect Captain von Cravat to wear one all the time, do you?" My words came out defensive, but I wasn't sure why. All nobility in Rislandia had similar names. Tradition dictated it be so.

Marina chuckled. "No, I suppose not." She pointed to my mother in the photo. "You know, he named the airship after her. Did he ever tell you the story of how they met?" Marina tilted her head at me curiously.

I shook my head. For all I knew, my mother was a country girl from Plainsroad Village. The more I thought about my parents, the more I came to understand I was disconnected from them. It wasn't my mother's fault—she died when I was twelve, before I understood the importance of these questions. But my father left me. He'd had a choice.

"It was one of the first outings of this ship, far before I came aboard, but it's a hard one to forget once you've heard it. Harkerpal told it me originally," Marina said.

I laughed. "Of course, he did."

"King Malaky commanded that each of his airship captains name their own vessels so they would be tied to it by a stronger bond than just their oaths to the king. Silly, really, since the Grand Rislandian Army oath is one of the strongest I've ever heard. But that's neither here nor there. The naming, combined with granting each captain ownership over their own ship, had the intended effects."

"Why would the king do that?"

"It is odd thinking. But kings and emperors do as they will, not much us little people can do otherwise but to follow as we're commanded." She shrugged. "Baron took the ship on its first mission, off to the Tyndree Kingdom, northeast of the Wyranth Empire."

I'd never heard of the Tyndree Kingdom before. I tried to picture the school maps but didn't recall seeing that name. "Wait, there is no kingdom northeast of the Wyranth Empire."

"Not now, there's not. The Wyranth control it. Back during that war, your father's mission was to resupply the duchess of High Mesa Castle, give her some relief in the fight, as her lands were nearest the border. When the Baron arrived, he found the castle overwhelmed by the Wyranth forces. He fought his way into the castle and rescued the duchess. The crew says that he was so captivated by her, even in the midst of a battle, that he had to profess his love somehow. And so, he did, by naming his airship right then and there," Marina said. She reverently touched the glass on the picture frame and set the picture back down.

I blinked. My mother? A duchess? My heart sank again. She was a wonderful woman, a great cook, but she was simple, just like me. She had never told me anything to the contrary. If this story held any truth, I couldn't relate to anyone in my family. "That can't be right," I said.

"It's the truth, as far as I know it."

That meant *I* had royal blood. James would shoot steam out of his ears when he heard. My lineage was anything but comforting to me. "I miss my mother. And my father," I said softly. I didn't know what to think anymore. I wouldn't be surprised if someone told me Toby invented the airships to begin with.

"Well, hopefully we'll be able to get him back," Marina said.

"We're going to rescue him?"

"We discussed a lot without you, Zaira. I apologize. The Wyranth soldier told us the Baron is being held in a prison in the Wyranth capital, in the Iron Emperor's castle dungeon. Captain von Cravat is already working on a rescue plan, granting that King Malaky signs off on it."

"Iron Emperor's castle dungeon? That doesn't sound safe at all," I said. My hopes and happiness dwindled. From earlier, I'd thought my father had been found somewhere I could reach him. Deep in the heart of the Wyranth Empire, though? Our airship couldn't even cross the Border River without being shot at.

"No, he's most definitely not," Marina said. She moved back over to my bed. "But it's better than dead, right?" She offered a hand. "Come, now. I came to get you so you can be on deck for the landing. The others will be wondering what took us so long."

I took her hand and she pulled me to my feet with ease. There were so many questions I had about my mother, father, this ship, and so many other things. I followed Marina out into the hallways and back up through to the mess cabin.

It struck me that I'd be meeting King Malaky soon. That excitement dwindled some as I my feet dragged. My body had such intense weariness I wasn't sure I'd be able to keep my eyes open. Yes, Captain von Cravat had made it clear I was supposed to have been napping. With having almost been killed, flying again on the airship, all this talk about my father, I'd hardly been able to sleep. I'd been awake for far too long. I wanted to cry, to take a moment and forget the whirlwind I'd been spun into, and maybe sleep for a couple of days. I kept my chin up though, forcing myself to feign some energy. At least I'd been able to lie down for a while.

When we reached the mess cabin, the chef lingered behind the buffet, cleaning the remains of lunch. James sat alone at one of the long benches. He looked up at us, hair a disaster, face gaunt, his eyes cracked and bloodshot, cheeks flush. Tears had definitely drained down his face while we were gone. A lot of them.

I tried to smile at him. "Hi, James. Did you sleep, too?"

He shook his head. "Can't. My parents..." His voice cracked, soft as it was.

I walked over and wrapped my arms around him. "Marina says we'll be in the capital soon. We're going to meet King Malaky," I said, as if that could be any consolation for what he'd been through. When his dog had died when he was little, I stirred James from his melancholy by promising to play as if he were one of the Knights of the Crystal Spire.

His eyes twinkled at the mention of the king, but it didn't seem to lift his spirits completely. "I know," he said.

"Do you want to stay back in the airship?" Marina asked. "That can be arranged."

"No." James scrambled to his feet. "I'm fine. I'll just need a moment to get myself together, okay?"

"Of course, I think we have a little bit yet, right, Marina?"

"Correct. We have to land, be taken to the castle, and then the king will have to be roused. I suspect he won't be in tip-top shape himself," she said.

"Isn't Rislandia City pretty large? Where will we land?" James asked.

"The Crystal Spire has a landing pad beside it for airships. It was cleared when the ships were originally built."

"The Crystal Spire?" James's eyes returned to life from their stupor. That did it. He was nearly his old self, remembering his dreams. "Can we see it?"

"We should be coming up on it soon—would you like to go look? We can head out to the main deck."

"That's a lovely idea," I encouraged.

James rubbed his face on his sleeve. "Let's go."

Captain von Cravat met us and led the way, one of her men opening the door from the mess cabin out onto the deck. The door swung ajar, the wind slamming it back against the cabin. Turbines whirred so loudly we would have to shout to speak. I wrapped my coat more tightly around myself, but even so, the wind and cold pierced right through me.

But before we could step outside, a silhouette buzzed in from the deck. I suspected who it was by the peppy step, even before the cabin's lamps illuminated his face. Only one person could be that excited to be working at this hour, someone who loved his craft more than anything else.

"Harkerpal!" I said. I ran to him and gave him a hug.

"Zaira! I heard we picked you up. I would have come and seen you earlier but I had to man the engine room, make sure the *Liliana* was working properly. After the crash a couple of the turbine gears... Well, I won't bore you with that. It's a long story," Harkerpal said. He returned my hug with a squeeze.

"Friend of yours?" James asked.

I pulled back from the embrace. "Yes, this is the chief engineer, one of my father's most trusted men. Harkerpal, meet James. He's my neighbor, and my most trusted friend."

"A friend of Zaira's is a friend of mine. Well met," Harkerpal said, bobbing his head.

Those words struck me. I'd done nothing to inspire the loyalty of Harkerpal—quite the opposite. I crashed the ship and abandoned him. He had told me he owed his life to my family. Heaviness gripped me like I was skirting some obligation.

Still, his loyalty was sweet. I would have to make it up to him somehow, if I could find a way.

"We were just heading to the deck," Captain von Cravat said. "I realize you're going the opposite direction, but would you care to join us?" "

"The lower gear assembly needs a thorough greasing," Harkerpal said, then glanced back toward the deck. "But I suppose that can wait." He held the door for us.

We stepped out onto the deck. Outside the cabin, the wind was strong enough that it was difficult to stand. I had to hold my hair back so it wouldn't repeatedly slap my face. I longed for what I had thought was the cold before. This was torture.

A few of the crew manned the deck, keeping watch, not seeming to notice the breeze or the chill at all.

James rushed ahead of us, to the railing on the port side of the ship. The Crystal Spire shone like a beacon, lights bursting out into the night in all directions. Long cables wrapped around the outside. Guards kept posts at various balconies. The building stood tall, not quite to the clouds itself, but much higher than any James or I had ever seen.

"Magnificent," James said.

The rest of Rislandia City looked dull in comparison, especially in the evening. A blanket of lights covered the city, very different from Plainsroad Village, which shut down at night. The ship banked, giving us a view of a smaller, though more elegant, bulbous building that sparkled silver in the late night. That had to be King Malaky's Palace.

James remained fixated on the spire. "It really does tower over everything."

"And inside are some of the greatest military minds in the world. Without the knights, and this crew, Rislandia might have fallen like so many others," Captain von Cravat said. She leaned on the rail alongside James.

I thought both of them were crazy. No way was I getting so close to the edge. If a wind picked up, or the ship banked wrong, it would be so easy to fall over. I shivered, both from the cold and the memory of looking down from the rope ladder.

The *Liliana* banked again, but slowly, not enough to cause a stir in any of us standing on the deck.

"We're about to land," Harkerpal said. "It must be so exciting to see this city for the first time, and meet the king. Oh, how I envy the young."

His words made me think of all James and I had lost in the last few days. We didn't deserve envy. Quite the opposite. I had no farm anymore, no Toby. This airship was more of a curse than a blessing. Ever since Mr. du Gearsmith showed up in my life, delivering the letter of my father's will, one thing after another had gone sour.

We hovered in place, and then began a slow descent. Whoever was at the controls of the ship worked with a precision garnered from years of experience. Reminded of how I had blundered when I took the controls, I blushed. Harkerpal placed his hand on my shoulder, as if he fully understood what I was thinking.

It served as another reminder that I didn't belong here. What good was I to this crew? I had no place aboard this ship, no place left anywhere. It wasn't as if I had some dream of becoming a Knight of the Crystal Spire. My attention shifted to James and Captain von Cravat, who were talking about that very subject.

"Now that I'm at the capital, I'm going to work extra hard on my swordsmanship. Maybe I can garner one of the knights' attention," James said. In a lot of ways, this city was just what he needed. He could put his parents out of his mind.

"I'm sure you will," Captain von Cravat said. She nodded at him approvingly.

One of the deck watchers approached. "We'll need everyone except for the landing crew back inside and braced for our final descent," she said to Captain von Cravat.

Captain von Cravat took the lead and ushered us inside as the ship touched down.

CHAPTER 12

"We're almost at the border. King Malaky gave me medals of his crest to pin on the entire crew's lapels in our honor. Though such a commendation is quite prestigious and carries many benefits in normal times, I don't expect many of us will live to reap the benefits of it."

An excerpt from Baron von Monocle's log
Day 14 of the Month of Kings
16th Year of Malaky XVI's Reign

WHEN WE ARRIVED, a guard in ornamental silver armor over a Grand Rislandian Army uniform ushered us into the royal apartments by the palace. The sun began to rise over the horizon, glinting a reddish reflection off of the tall Crystal Spire. The apartments were as gaudy as I expected, with expensive art, vases, statues, and furniture adorning every corner. If it weren't for guards guiding our every step, I'd have become lost in the immense space. Ceilings towered higher than anything in Plainsroad Village, where we had nothing of the lavish decorations covering every wall and every table.

Our guide escorted us to the *ambassadorial quarters* as they were called, where servants took us into their stead, offering a light snack and some water, promising a big breakfast later. After we accepted the refreshments, the servants took our measurements, sizing us for appropriate clothing to meet with the king.

I complied with each of their requests, so tired I could barely stand, let alone cause a fuss. One of the servants touched my hair, sniffed at me, and offered a bath. I jumped at the opportunity. James and I were separated then, sent into separate rooms. A servant started to undress me, but I batted her hands away and told her I could handle that much on my own. Perhaps that's not how people took baths in the city, but in farm country we retained some modesty.

I stripped inside a changing room and tiptoed over marble flooring toward a steaming tub the size of my former kitchen back home. In the time it took for me to undress, the servants had left the room, giving me the privacy I wanted. I sank into the bath proper, the warm liquid soothing my legs and body as I descended. I couldn't remember a bath with a more perfect temperature. This was certainly the difference between what I could do on my own and what a king's servants could prepare.

A bar of soap rested on a ledge by the bath, set for me along with a towel just beyond that. I scrubbed myself, wetting my hair, which was dry, oily, and tangled after the day's work and evening's escapades. The warmth of the bath made my eyes heavy. My body relaxed, and I slid down until I was nearly on my back. It wouldn't hurt to close my eyes for a moment...

I awoke to servants rushing to help me out of the tub. My privacy apparently evaporated sure as the steam from the bath. "You were in here for such a long time, and feel your hands! They've become prunes!" said one of the servants.

The second servant wrapped the towel around me and grabbed a brush. She rapidly stroked my hair, forcing the tangles undone and pulling out several strands in the process. Her companion powdered my face and helped me into my smallclothes. I tried to bat her away again, but she persisted, and before I could fully regain my consciousness, I found myself dressed in a bizarre outfit.

I looked in the mirror. "Is this some sort of joke?" I asked.

"This is proper royal meeting attire," the servant said flatly.

The ensemble was one a giant poof. A poof around the neck, a poof around the shoulders, and even a poof at the waist, which did not flatter my skinny, but muscular, figure. Every aspect of the dress had ruffles, nothing about the attire functional in the least. I'd barely be able to walk straight. Who, by Malaky, came up with this as proper? I opened my mouth to protest, turning to the lead servant who had gone to answer a knock at the door.

It opened to reveal James standing in the doorway.

If I had been thrown into a forest of various poofs, then the servants had erected a poof mountain atop poor James. The garment layered up from an elongated base into a peak on top of his bulbous head, and if I didn't know his head was attached, I would have thought it would roll off like a big boulder. His neck had all but disappeared in ruffled, white fabric. The rest of the outfit was an equally unflattering hunter green color.

"What's so funny?" he asked, his face red hot.

"Nothing," I said, stifling a snicker. If James had to wear that atrocious thing, I supposed my dress looked okay after all. I turned to the servant. "What now? Do we see the king?"

"Not yet," a voice came from the corridor, shoes tapping one after another and echoing across the expansive floor.

That deep voice had familiarity. I turned. "Mr. du Gearsmith!" I said. "I didn't expect to see you again." Though we hadn't parted on the best of terms, I ran over and hugged him.

Mr. du Gearsmith hugged me in return, still wearing one of his dark suits. He held a firm and tall posture, as one would expect from a lawyer of his stature. "Zaira, my dear, I'm happy to see you're well." He glanced over at James. "And you've brought company."

"Mr. du Gearsmith, you remember James Gentry, my neighbor?"

"Mm," Mr. du Gearsmith said, face stoic.

"I'm afraid the Wyranth overran his farm." I bit my lip, hoping that wouldn't throw James into another emotional spiral. The memory and wounds were still fresh. I could still feel the house shake as it was pounded by those mobile artillery machines and could only imagine what ran through his head.

"James, well met," Mr. du Gearsmith said. "My condolences regarding your parents. The Wyranth are not known for their civility."

"Don't be sorry," James said, offering a small smile. "I've reason to believe they made it out."

"What?" My jaw dropped. No one had told me anything of the sort. Was James in denial?

"Why do we have to wear this ridiculous clothing if you can wear your suit?" James asked, flicking one of the larger ruffles that circled his wrist.

"It's tradition for non-nobility greeting the king," Mr. du Gearsmith said.

"But I'm technically nobility," I said.

Before Mr. du Gearsmith could reply, Captain von Cravat entered the room, circling around and finding an unobtrusive place to stand. She remained in her Grand Rislandian Army uniform. I would have killed to wear one of those right now, instead of this nightmare of a dress.

"Yeah," James said. "Since, you know, your father's still alive, and we didn't see anything happen to my parents, it's just as likely that they escaped, or are captured somewhere. If we find where your father's being held, they might even be in the same place."

"Oh, James," I said softly. Denial. He sounded as if he wanted to convince himself as much as us. Arguing wouldn't help him, however. I had to let this drop, for now.

"Ah yes, your father," Mr. du Gearsmith said as if it were a perfect segue. "Zaira, I'm sure you know that the king has invited you here to discuss your father, and I have been invited as well. The news of your father still being among the living is fresh for me as well. Much remains uncertain in these matters, but know I am still in your family's employ, and it is my duty to advise should you need any assistance or have any questions as to the legal ramifications of your father's reemergence."

"Wouldn't the king's word be all that matters?" I asked. If Mr. du Gearsmith hinted regarding the airship, I didn't expect to be keeping possession of it. What good would it do me?

"The Malaky line upholds the rule of law, which is what makes them great, and has preserved their line through all these generations. It is what makes the name worthy of recognition in our daily speech through moments that bring us to awe," Mr. du Gearsmith said, as if reciting a poem. I'd heard that mantra before in school.

"Then, *by Malaky*, I'll plead with the king to rescue him. Even if there's just a small chance of him being alive, we should do something!" I said.

"We'll see." Mr. du Gearsmith turned his attention to Captain von Cravat and bowed toward her. "Talyen. A pleasure to see you again. I trust all is well?" His tone sounded as if he were asking after my behavior.

I clenched my teeth. Captain von Cravat was not my mother and had no say over me. I remained quiet, however.

Captain von Cravat shifted her eyes to me and back to Mr. du Gearsmith, bowing in return. If she took the cue from him, she didn't show it. "The pleasure is mine, Mathias. And yes, all has been well as can be, considering that the Wyranth have pushed across the borders into Rislandian territory. Though I'm certain that takes precedence in terms of King Malaky's considerations, I have to agree with Miss von Monocle that rescuing her father would be my priority as well."

Mr. du Gearsmith paused, studying Captain von Cravat. "I see," he said and turned to me. "Zaira, are you familiar with the customs on how to present yourself to the king?"

I'd never even considered meeting King Malaky before this evening, but I wanted to redeem myself with Mr. du Gearsmith and Captain von Cravat present. "Yes, majesty, no majesty. Speak only when spoken to, I'm sure," I said. Those had to be safe ways to act around the king.

"Yes, but slightly more than that, Zaira dear. Attitude is paramount. Kneel when you come before him or he arrives. Defer to him. He is still a king, though a fair one, as I have described."

"Okay, I'll do my best," I said.

"Well, then, let's go," Captain von Cravat said, motioning for one of the servants to lead the way.

The servant started down the hallway, and we walked behind. "Where'd Harkerpal go?" I asked.

"Back to the ship. It was a long voyage considering his new repairs," Captain von Cravat said. "He needs to make sure his work held. We may be back out on assignment by the time we're done here. At least, I hope so."

"We?" I asked, but there was no time for a reply as we approached the royal chamber.

Two guards turned and pulled open large double doors, embroidered in gold and with the crimson crest of Malaky carved into the wood. We entered a large throne room, several chairs adorning each side and a carpet leading up a few steps to the throne. The throne itself was simpler than I would have imagined, an ordinary chair save for the Malaky crest carved into the backrest, and a matching cushion. To the throne's right was another chair, one step lower. A long curtain hung behind the throne. Several other chairs adorned the sides of the room, below the dais, providing places to sit for courtiers or royal guests.

A tall servant came in from the back door and pulled back the curtain. She wore similar poofy attire as the rest of us, with golden ruffles up to her throat. The servant turned to us. "Presenting his royal majesty, King Malaky the Sixteenth," she said.

Everyone knelt, leaving me gawking. Captain von Cravat tugged my sleeve, jolting me enough to drop me to my knees. "Ow!" I whispered.

"Quiet, eyes on the floor," Captain von Cravat said.

I cast my eyes downward. Footsteps traversed the back of the throne room, the *click* on the floor edging closer. I saw those boots in front of me, and behind them, a heavy burgundy cape with a white ruffled fringe. A hand fell upon my shoulder. "You must be Zaira," a kind and gentle voice said. "Please, arise. That goes for all of you."

I stood, and met King Malaky's eyes, deep brown pools that held years of wisdom. His face was pale, age showing in several wrinkles on his forehead.

"You look just like your father, it's incredible," King Malaky said. "Though I'm certain he would be wearing one of these." He motioned to his cape.

I glanced to Captain von Cravat, not wanting to risk speaking out of turn. She nodded to give me leave. I met King Malaky's eyes once more. "My father's belongings are aboard the *Liliana*, Sire. I was told this was the proper attire for an audience with you," I said.

King Malaky laughed heartily. "My servants dressed you, did they? I keep telling them that people don't have to dress in those antiquated costumes. They were originally meant to humiliate audiences so they would remember their place before the king. I don't view my subjects in such a negative light to think they require it. You've certainly grown since I last saw you."

"We've met before?" I asked, wide eyed.

"The king was present at your name day, Zaira, though of course, you wouldn't remember the ceremony," Mr. du Gearsmith said, nodding to the king with familiarity.

"Indeed. It's good to see you, and you as well, Talyen." King Malaky walked past each of them as he said his greetings. Then he stopped before James. "And who might you be?"

"James Gentry, humbly at your service, Your Majesty," James said.

King Malaky took his hand and clasped it in greeting before pacing back toward his throne. "You've all had quite the evening, so my advisors tell me. Would you care for any refreshments while we speak? Food? Wine?"

"Your servants have cared for us well, Your Majesty," Captain von Cravat said. "We are ready to attend to whatever matters you choose to discuss."

King Malaky sighed and seated himself upon the throne. A servant flocked to each side to ensure his cape didn't bunch. "You never were one for friendly conversation," he said to Captain von Cravat. That was an understatement. "The *Liliana* has returned to the air. I wasn't sure I'd live to see the day. And Zaira is in command?" he asked.

"Not exactly," I blurted, though unsure why. My cheeks flushed a hot red.

"It's her airship by right. Though Miss von Monocle hasn't the...training necessary for true command as of yet," Captain von Cravat said.

As of yet? What was that supposed to mean? I couldn't help but stare at Captain von Cravat, her face still holding the stoic coldness that she had the first time I met her. What was she thinking behind those calculating eyes? I'd thought she would want to wash her hands of me and send me packing.

"I've received some formal reports, but Zaira, I would be interested in hearing your version of recent events," King Malaky said. A servant poured wine into his goblet, which he took into his right hand. "Please, don't remain standing on my account." He motioned to the chairs.

Servants scurried to reposition the chairs so they would face the king from the center of the room. One moved a chair to the back of my knees. I fell into the seat. This was all so nerve racking. "Our farms were attacked by Wyranth soldiers," I began, shifting in the chair and crossing my legs.

"Mr. du Gearsmith told me they'd pressed into Loveridge, but they've truly advanced so far north?" The king asked, concern flashing over his face. "I find it hard to believe they'd be able to make it to Plainsroad Village. The general and I were just discussing mobilizing the army to patrol the southern roads. Talyen, can you confirm this report?"

Captain von Cravat nodded gravely. "The Wyranth inflicted a great deal of damage to the village. The farmers will require aid. We lucked upon Zaira and James when they were captured on the open road."

It hadn't occurred to me to consider how Captain von Cravat and her crew found us. It all happened so quickly and she appeared so coordinated. Was it truly simple luck that led her to us?

"How many Wyranth were there?"

"A legion for certain," Captain von Cravat said.

"I'd say at least a thousand, Your Majesty," James said. "My father held them off. They brought mobile artillery as well and barraged our home with it."

"Please, continue." King Malaky motioned to me. "It's strange they should attack such an insubstantial target."

"They were after me. I believe they think I could be a valuable ransom, given that I've inherited the airship," I said.

"I see," King Malaky said. He tilted his goblet back to take a small sip of his wine. "I'm going to have to speak with General Carwell and form a plan. This is dire news indeed." Worry crossed the king's eyes.

"I trust we will defend our homeland and prevail, Your Majesty. As we always have before," Captain von Cravat said. Strength dripped from her words as if she were delivering King Malaky a personal oath.

"Hmm," King Malaky said.

I watched the exchange. The king did not appear nearly as confident as Captain von Cravat as to Rislandia's ability to defend itself. My heart sank, but I remembered my father. If anyone could help save the kingdom, it'd be him. "There is good news, however."

King Malaky raised a brow. "Do tell."

Captain von Cravat inclined her head. "As I sent in my report with Mr. du Gearsmith, we captured a Wyranth soldier, one of who was carrying a vial of the blue liquid. In interrogations, he revealed that Baron von Monocle is still alive, being held in the Wyranth Castle dungeon."

"Yes. I was briefed on that," King Malaky said. "While it is good to hear my old friend might not have drawn his last breath, the source is suspect, to say the least."

"I did not get the impression this soldier lied," Captain von Cravat said.

"Still, it's a product of interrogation. We have no corroborating evidence, and even if we did, the Wyranth Castle isn't a place we could extract him from. It's too dangerous, in the heart of the Iron Empire. The throne room itself sits above the dungeon. I've been there when we still had diplomatic talks. Before the Iron Emperor changed so suddenly." King Malaky stared into his goblet.

"A team of trained commandos could—" Captain von Cravat began, but was cut off by King Malaky raising his hand to her.

"Could get killed. We're not going to risk our best soldiers on a fool's errand when we have troops who have penetrated our borders. We need our best to be fighting and ensuring the safety of our people," King Malaky said.

"What about the *Liliana*?" I asked.

"Even more valuable than a team of commandos. Your airship, Zaira, instills fear into the hearts of the enemy. That she flies the skies again is a rallying cry for Rislandia. No, we couldn't risk the *Liliana* or her crew on hearsay."

I gripped some of the ruffles of my skirt in to my fist, my nails piercing through the fabric. It wasn't fair. My father might be alive, probably *was* alive. I couldn't lose him again, not like this! Not because the king was afraid. "Baron von Monocle would never hide from a mission like this," I said.

"Zaira!" Mr. du Gearsmith chided, his eyes wide.

James looked as if he were about to burst out laughing but clamped his lips tightly.

"My apologies, Your Majesty," Captain von Cravat said, covering for me. She had an expression on her face the same as that day I'd come into the inn in Loveridge to talk about the crashed ship.

The blood drained from my face. Did I make such a terrible error?

King Malaky eyed me for a long moment, then returned his gaze into his goblet. "Don't chide the poor child for speaking the truth. She is right," he said.

Emboldened, I pressed. "Well, what are we going to do about it?"

The room fell silent save for a small gasp from a servant. King Malaky waved toward the servant as if he didn't have a concern. "It's a good question. It's something that will require some deliberation, but for now, I'm afraid the answer has to be nothing."

"Nothing?" Captain von Cravat and I asked in unison.

"I would risk my life for Baron von Monocle," King Malaky said, sadness in his eyes. Sincerity dripped from him as his eyes met mine. "But I can't risk this kingdom. Sending a team into the heart of the Wyranth Empire could be the fuel the Iron Emperor needs to legitimize his invasion, which would be the last thing we would need."

Captain von Cravat's gaze cooled so quickly it could have frozen my crops over in the middle of summer. "He doesn't seem concerned about legitimacy now."

King Malaky met her stare, eyes narrowing in focus.

Mr. du Gearsmith's eyes went wide. "It has been an exhausting couple of days, Your Majesty. If you would permit, I believe it may be best to sleep on the matter. Your faithful servants are weary and a rest might assist in their understanding of difficult strategic decisions.

"Indeed," King Malaky said. Anger still radiated from him. "Perhaps some in the ranks have been on their own for too—"

"Father, what's going on?" a feminine voice asked as the door opened.

I glanced up, as did everyone else in the room. King Malaky turned around. By the door stood a girl about my age who embodied every essence of objective beauty from the fairy tales my mother read me when I was little. She had long blonde hair with a slight curl, big blue eyes, lengthy legs, and a perfectly proportioned body. She stood in her night clothes, soft pink silken layers that dangled down to the floor. No poofs or ruffles in her ensemble. I couldn't help but wrinkle my nose, in jealousy I hate to admit. For some reason, I hadn't been gifted with a body that might be considered perfectly feminine. Back in Plainsroad Village, most of us girls had to do hard farm work along with the boys.

I glanced over at James. His mouth hung open like an ape. I wanted to sock him one good, but I had to maintain my manners in front of King Malaky.

"Reina, Sweetie," King Malaky said softly to the girl. He beamed with pride.

Mr. du Gearsmith bowed before Reina. "Might I introduce Princess Reina, heir to the throne of the Rislandian Kingdom." He pointed to each of us. "Zaira von Monocle, Captain Talyen von Cravat, and James Gentry," Mr. du Gearsmith said.

Princess Reina curtsied in her night clothes. "A pleasure."

Each of us followed Mr. du Gearsmith's lead and bowed to her.

"We were just discussing some matters of state. No need to trouble you at this hour," King Malaky said to his daughter.

"I hope to train with the Knights of the Crystal Spire and be in your service one day, Princess," James said. No one else likely noticed, but he stood on the tips of his toes to look a little taller. I'd seen that attempt to impress a girl before.

He'd done it to me. I'd thought it was cute. This time, I couldn't help but be stricken with sickness and a pain in my chest. I tried to keep my expression flat, but Captain von Cravat locked eyes with me, concern in her own. She was well attuned to more than just the airship.

Princess Reina gave a cordial and political smile that appeared to be directed at us all and at none of us specifically at the same time. "To train with the knights is a noble goal, Mr. Gentry." She turned back to King Malaky, taking a step toward him. "I was only worried because I heard a commotion, Father. I shall return to my bedchambers and sleep. I hope we can take breakfast together in the morning?" Princess Reina then planted a soft kiss on King Malaky's cheek.

King Malaky grinned. "Of course, my lovely daughter. See you in the morning," he said.

With another curtsy toward the group, Princess Reina spun on her heels and returned to the door in which she came.

James's attention lingered on the Princess's backside for much too long. My face went hot with fury, more than for my own feelings. If King Malaky noticed his leering, who knew what he'd be liable to do?

The king remained fixated on his daughter, his chest swelling. "She'll grow up to be a great ruler someday, mark my word. Now, where were we?"

"Theodore von Monocle," Captain von Cravat said, "and his rescue."

"Ah yes," King Malaky said. He turned his attention to one of his servants. "It's been a long evening with a lack of sleep for all of us. We should rest before discussing strategic matters further."

My heart sank. If there was any hope my father still lived, I needed to pursue it. Captain von Cravat appeared equally distraught. At least we had something in common. Did father really inspire that much loyalty in his crew?

"Of course, Your Majesty," Mr. du Gearsmith said after none of the rest of us replied. He gripped me by the arm. "I'll take Miss von Monocle to her sleeping quarters. Thank you very much for the audience."

"Of course. It's good to hear from old friends, even if much of the news is dire," King Malaky said. He gave a nod and turned for the back entrance of his chambers.

Captain von Cravat and James said nothing. A king's dismissal was final. They each bowed before the king and servants guided all of us away, back down the winding hallways of the palace.

When we came close to our quarters, Captain von Cravat stopped me. She nodded to Mr. du Gearsmith who continued past us to where he was staying. "Zaira, I know you're tired, but would you mind stepping outside and getting some air with me before you sleep?"

I blinked. Captain von Cravat wanted to talk with me? The only times she'd wanted anything to do with me was when she had no other choice. "Sure," I said.

"See you tomorrow—or, later today, I suppose—Zair-bear," James said, stifling a yawn.

I waved back at him.

Captain von Cravat motioned, leading me the opposite direction to the others. I followed toward big double doors that a servant opened for us. It led out to a giant balcony.

The balcony was as ornate and beautiful as I could have imagined, a perfect viewing pad that looked out toward the Crystal Spire on one side and down upon the rest of Rislandia City on the other. The balcony itself could have held at least fifty people, and I imagined it was used for various proclamations and formal functions more than a simple place to talk. It reminded me of how big of a world I'd stumbled into. I missed Plainsroad Village.

The servant closed the balcony's door, leaving us alone. Captain von Cravat leaned over the outer railing, staring down toward the town below.

I walked up to her, unsure what to say. The morning light made me squint. In the stillness and quiet of the outside, weariness came over me once more. I'd kept pushing myself too hard far before I'd met with the King, if falling asleep in the bath had been any sign of that. My body felt like a great weight, but Captain von Cravat needed me. If I could get on her good side somehow, I had to try. "Is everything okay?" I asked.

"No, Zaira. It's not okay," she said, her voice stern. She turned back to me and sighed. "I'm sorry. It's not your fault. I'm angry at the king, I suppose."

"Because he won't let you go rescue my father?"

Captain von Cravat nodded. "Our source was not lying to us. I've been in enough interrogation situations to know the difference. Theodore is alive and I... I have my hands tied. If he were here, he wouldn't take no for an answer."

If my father were here, I had doubts that King Malaky would tell him no for any mission he proposed, but I couldn't voice that and hurt Captain von Cravat further. "Well, what can we do about it?"

"I don't know, Zaira. Perhaps the king is right. We should rest. It's been a trying few days. But how can I rest knowing that Theodore is in that tyrant's hands? Who knows what kind of tortures each day brings to him."

I frowned, not having considered how my father must have been treated. He was the Wyranth Empire's greatest enemy, and they had him imprisoned. Whatever he endured might well be worse than death. But if Captain von Cravat didn't have a plan, what could I do? I didn't have anything.

Then I remembered how Mr. du Gearsmith made clear that the *Liliana* was my airship. King Malaky gave these ships to its commanders more than symbolically. This ship was a reward for my father's service. "What if..." I started, then shook my head. "No, I'm being foolish again."

"What?" Captain von Cravat asked.

"The *Liliana* is mine by inheritance, right? Technically, I can do what I please with the ship."

"The king as much as ordered us not to do anything."

"But like Mr. du Gearsmith says, I own the airship. It's my choice to make. If my father's not in the prison, or if we fail, I'd have far more to worry about than King Malaky's anger. We'd be in the middle of Wyranth territory. And if we bring him back, how mad could he be?"

Captain von Cravat frowned. "Zaira, what you're suggesting could be considered treason."

"It's my father. How could I not try? You said it yourself."

The older woman looked me in the eye for a long moment as she considered. "I know I've been distraught by the king's orders, but I don't want you to rush into this. I don't want to have manipulated you into it, either. We should try one more time to reason with King Malaky first, sleep on it, as he suggested. But if you're sincere about this..." she said, pausing for me to reply.

"I am."

"Then I'll start formulating a backup plan. You have to follow my every order, each step of the way, if we go through with this. You understand?"

I nodded. Pride swelled in me, that she'd even consider me as someone who could assist her. Captain von Cravat was perfectly capable of taking the ship and mounting a mission on her own. But I knew as we talked that she had far too much honor to steal what wasn't hers, even if it meant rescuing my father. I saw why the crew had so much respect for her, and hoped one day people could see me in that same light.

Then, in a final shocking move, Captain van Cravat hugged me. "Thank you, Zaira. I may have been wrong about you. Let's meet here after we've had time to talk to the king again."

Captain von Cravat turned for the doors, where a servant waited and opened them again. I followed her inside and went to my quarters.

CHAPTER 13

"Every time I'm about to go into a skirmish, I wonder, will this be my last? The Wyranth attacks have been so ferocious lately, half of my own crew have turned over due to deaths. Some sense of duty keeps me persisting in my foolish errands. The ideals of the Rislandian Kingdom must endure. They are more important than me or any individual."

An excerpt from Baron von Monocle's log
Day 17 of the Month of Kings
16th Year of Malaky XVI's Reign

DESPITE BEING SO tired that my eyes felt heavier than a basket of corn, I still found I couldn't sleep. Captain von Cravat said she might have been wrong about me. It might not have been the highest of compliments, but compared to how she'd reacted when I crashed the airship, I'd made huge strides. But what had I done differently? Planning to steal an airship and go into Wyranth territory to rescue my father was just as rash as my decision to test the airship's speed capabilities days ago.

My world had changed so much since that day. In my mind's eye, I could still see the ship descending, smoke rising. But I didn't have Captain von Cravat behind me then. With her leading, we wouldn't fail.

A servant knocked on the door and peeked her head inside. "Mistress von Monocle?" she asked.

I opened my eyes to see light trickling through the window curtains. I must have fallen asleep at some point if the day was already that bright. I sat up, rubbing my eyes. "Come in," I said.

"King Malaky has requested you at breakfast. I've brought suitable attire for you to wear. Do you require assistance?"

"No, I can dress myself," I said, sliding out of the plush bed in the guest quarters.

The servant set a fresh poof-dress at the foot of the bed, nodding to me as she departed. I held the dress up, noting its similarity to the one I wore the night before, this time a deep crimson hue with white lace frills.

I slipped into the dress and fastened the buttons on the back before heading out into the hall. The servant waited for me and motioned for me to follow. We stopped next at James's guest quarters.

His door was open and we looked in upon him standing in front of a mirror, practicing thrusting an imaginary sword at his reflection.

"That's an interesting dance. You aiming to try that out at the harvest festival talent contest this year?" I teased.

James spun, his face flushing bright red. "Zair-bear! By Malaky, you scared me half to death!"

"You should close the door if you're going to make moves like that. Less embarrassing that way."

"Don't act all high and mighty just because you're Miss von Monocle with her own airship. I happened to have a royal visitor this morning," James said, crossing his arms and lifting his head proudly.

"I have no idea what you're talking about, James, but if you're going to start some game with me, I'm much too tired for that. And there's a breakfast with the king I need to get to," I said. It was my fault, heckling him to put him on the defensive. Worse that I'd told him not to joke with me. It'd been a rough few days, and we were both on edge.

116

"Since you asked," James said, ignoring my response and straightening his collar in the mirror, "I had little discussion with Princess Reina. Alone. In my quarters this morning." James glanced at his fingernails as if they were freshly manicured.

All of the tiredness disappeared from me, his words shaking me toward being alert. My stomach tied into a tight knot. Princess Reina? She came to him alone? It couldn't be real. "That's a load of ground gears, James. She went back to bed, we all saw it."

"Swear it on my life," James said. The excitement in his eyes emphasized his sincerity.

"So, you talked to the Princess." The bitterness in my voice couldn't help but seep through. Was this jealousy? Or crankiness because I was so weary?

"I did. She told me she liked my plans to become a knight and would ensure my name was spoken to the high knight himself! She's going to recommend me for training, Zaira!" James said. Then he hugged me.

His touch surprised me. Much like that moment when he fell atop me in the tomato field, my body tingled. He felt so warm pressed against me. I wrapped my arms around him. The sickness I'd felt when he'd first mentioned the princess dissipated. "You talked about the knights," I said, relieved.

"Yeah, though I think she likes me. Why else would she come to my quarters?"

I pushed James back from the embrace. "You're such an idiot."

"What?" James asked, frowning with no clue as to what he'd done.

"Never mind. I have breakfast with the king. We'll talk later." Without waiting for him to respond, I spun around and stomped out the door. The servant led my way without a word, cautious of my foul mood.

She led me around to the king's study, a large room, bigger than Plainsroad Village's grange hall. It had books stacked from the floor to ceiling in ornate wooden cabinetry. I had to calm myself, and quickly. So, I took a deep breath and thought of more peaceful times. A few days ago, I would have never said memories of shucking corn would be something I'd use to give me solace, but nothing was the same anymore.

King Malaky had a table set for a meal away from some larger leather chairs. With him was a man I didn't recognize—older and bald, with a wire mesh patch over his left eye. A single plate of food lay on the other end of the table, where I was presumably to sit. The man with the patch laughed at something the king had said before I entered.

Both men looked up from the map. King Malaky's eyes lit up as he saw me, and he flashed a grin. "Zaira! Come, come. We were just going over the strategy to run the Wyranth out of our Northern provinces. I've had my servants provide me food. Forgive me that I don't join you, I've already eaten with my daughter. Come discuss our plans for your airship."

"My airship?" I said, forgetting for the moment that the *Liliana* was mine. Moving over to the table, I glanced down at the map. It had details of every town, village, mountain, hill, and river between Rislandia City and the Wyranth Empire. Whatever mapmaker had made this took extreme care. I saw where the king held his finger close to Loveridge.

"Yes, your airship. Though the kingdom is in dire need, I do try my best to respect my subjects' property," King Malaky said, eyes intent on me.

I would do whatever little I could to help with the war effort, but I'd been intent on rescuing my father. I never imagined that King Malaky would need my airship this quickly. But, of course he would. It was a tactical advantage like nothing else, or so I'd been told.

"With the use of the *Liliana*," the bald man beside King Malaky said, "we could run the Wyranth off in a matter of days. It would be much more difficult with mere infantry."

King Malaky took a glass cup filled with juice into his hand and drank before wiping his mouth with a napkin. "Forgive my manners. I've been so involved in the battle plans I forgot to introduce you. Zaira von Monocle, meet General Carwell of the Grand Rislandian Army."

General Carwell held out a hand to me. I took it and shook. "A pleasure to meet you," I said.

"The pleasure is mine, daughter of Baron von Monocle. I do hope you grant us use of your fine ship."

"I... couldn't say without Captain von Cravat's input," I said, holding back from cringing in fear. Mr. du Gearsmith would have chastised me for not agreeing to King Malaky's requests. The king seemed like a nice man, though. Surely, he wasn't so quick to anger?

"Of course," King Malaky said, inclining his head to the servant who still stood at the doorway. "Fetch her at once."

The servant dashed away, and I was left with the two men and their map. They spoke of my father, yet more stories about the battles he'd won and how he'd outsmarted his enemies. This time, I didn't listen. I focused on the map, seeing where General Carwell had placed markers representing the Wyranth's defenses and where I'd crashed the *Liliana*. If we were to mount a rescue of my father, Captain von Cravat would have to guide the ship around the anti-airship artillery set across the border river.

Captain von Cravat arrived. She remained in her Grand Rislandian Army uniform, with goggles set above her head, appearing ready to take off in the *Liliana* on a moment's notice. "King Malaky, General Carwell, Zaira" she said, bowing.

"Thank you for coming so quickly," King Malaky said, motioning her over. She moved to stand next to me. Her presence gave me comfort in a protective sense.

"How might I help you, Your Majesty?" Captain von Cravat asked.

"We're planning an assault on the occupying Wyranth forces in our northern provinces based on the intelligence provided by your crew," General Carwell said, his single eye locking on Captain von Cravat with incredible intensity.

Captain von Cravat's face went flat as she looked down at the map. "You'll use the ship to drop explosives and cause the enemy to retreat?" she asked, sounding as if this plan had been used before.

"Which will soften them for the infantry's later assault, yes," King Malaky said.

My stomach rumbled, breaking the silence in the room. King Malaky smiled at me and motioned to the plate of food in front of me. "Zaira, eat. I promised breakfast. Captain von Cravat, I apologize that I did not anticipate you joining us."

I moved to a chair and picked up a fork. "Thank you," I said and glanced at Captain von Cravat.

She still stood, staring at the map. "I'm not hungry," she said. "Very well, I'll lead the mission."

Mid-bite of a scrambled egg, I nearly choked. "What?" If the airship went on this mission, we wouldn't be using it to rescue my father. I stared up at Captain von Cravat, who didn't bother to glance in my direction.

"Very good," General Carwell said. He grabbed a pointer from beside his chair and extended it, placing the tip on the map. "As you can see, the airship is currently here, in Rislandia City. We will provide a strike force to assist with the crew of the *Liliana* to depart in three days' time. In the meantime, our first infantry division will deploy to the south of Plainsroad Village. The airship will fly a route over our infantry units, and they'll wait two days before engaging with the enemy."

"Is that satisfactory, Zaira?" King Malaky asked.

I'd hoped that Captain von Cravat would argue, fight for the rescue of my father. That sounded like what she intended to do the night before. Bringing her to the table did no good. She was a military woman, having to follow orders. My expectations were the trouble. "Yes. If Captain von Cravat is comfortable, then I can have her use my airship."

"I would like to request, Your Majesty, that Zaira accompany me on this mission," Captain von Cravat said.

"I'm not certain that's the best idea, Captain," General Carwell said. "She's only a child."

"So were many of us when we joined the Baron's crew," Captain von Cravat said. "This ship is hers, she needs to learn the ropes, and there's no better time than the present. If something were to happen to me, someone needs to be able to take command of the ship."

"And she'd be the one to command?" General Carwell raised the brow over his mesh patch.

"If it's truly her vessel," Captain von Cravat said.

"Are you certain she won't be a distraction for you and your crew?" King Malaky asked.

"I'll manage," Captain von Cravat said. "I can always lock her in her quarters if there's an issue."

I wanted to protest, but they talked about me as if I weren't present. It was nice that Captain von Cravat was willing to teach me after all I'd done to disappoint her, but it made me feel so small to be talked about as if I were a nuisance. This also flew in the face of everything we'd discussed the prior evening. What of that?

"Very well," King Malaky said. "She can join your crew."

I bit my tongue, unsure of what to say, watching Captain von Cravat the whole time. King Malaky and General Carwell proceeded to go over the plan with her in detail, with troop movement, supplies, and timing. General Carwell moved pieces across the map, representing the different divisions of the Grand Rislandian Army, while I watched, studying.

There was much more to war than I'd heard of the stories with my father. How many meetings like this had he attended before he became comfortable with the idea? I looked at Captain von Cravat, who intently studied the map, making suggestions to General Carwell and King Malaky. I had a lot to learn if I were to follow in my father's footsteps. If we never found a way to rescue him.

CHAPTER 14

How do I keep morale high when there's such a death toll? The old crew are beaten down. The new crew is scared. Harkerpal is telling stories of our past exploits, but it hardly seems enough.

An excerpt from Baron von Monocle's log
Day 19 of the Month of Kings
16th Year of Malaky XVI's Reign

I JOGGED TO catch up with Captain von Cravat in the hall. "What was that about?" I asked, voice echoing down the long chamber.

She maintained a brisk pace. "Not now, Zaira," she said.

"Well when's a good time? Like you said in there, I have to learn from you if I want to take over my father's role, and I want to know when you gave up on finding him!"

She paused her step then, forcing me to turn as I passed her. Then Captain von Cravat looked me straight in the eye with an ice-cold stare. "I will never give up on finding Theodore. Do not ever suggest that again."

Her words and her expression silenced me, my mouth hanging agape before I could manage a small nod. "I'm sorry."

"I need to go prepare. Wait until I send for you, understand?" Captain von Cravat said, her eyes sternly holding mine.

I nodded, unable to find anything worth saying. Captain von Cravat continued past me down the hall as if I had never been there.

Unsure what to do, I wandered around the castle. Long hallways connected to each other. Several formal reception rooms lined one hallway, one after another, each with a different style and décor. I passed through the servant quarters. Many of the servants scurried about, and a couple gave me confused looks and asked me if I were lost. I politely let them know otherwise and continued through the winding corridors.

Eventually, I found my way to a courtyard where I saw James standing in a metal protective mesh with a taller person in front of him in the same. Both had swords in their hands, and the taller man explained how to hold it properly. James took the sword and assumed a wide stance. "Like this?" he asked.

The two went through a series of motions, mostly involving footwork. James protested about wanting to swing the sword, but the instructor told him there would be plenty of time for advanced lessons earlier. "Footwork is the most important," the instructor said.

"I already know how to stand," James said.

Instead of arguing further, the instructor jolted forward, pushing James with a flat hand to his chest. James stumbled and nearly fell over.

"Now if it had been a real battle, you'd be dead. Footwork and balance are the most important part of swordsmanship. Now let's try your basic stance again." He spread his own feet apart in a wide manner to demonstrate.

James followed without talking back this time, and they proceeded to go through several different motions. Over the course of several minutes, the instructor gave James tips on how to hold the sword to not be run through. James caught on fairly quickly. It was amusing to watch.

"Very good," his instructor said. "That should be enough for today. Let's pick this up again tomorrow."

James wiped the sweat from his brow and nodded. He bowed to his instructor, and the instructor bowed back. The taller man moved toward me and passed without seeming to notice I was present.

"Impressive," I said to James.

James looked up to me and smiled. "Zair-bear. That was a real Knight of the Crystal Spire! His name is Cid, and he's been assigned to train me. He says I have good raw strength. Probably from tilling fields. What've you been up to?"

"A strategy meeting with the king," I said.

James set his practice sword back in a cabinet against a wall, closing the trunk, and placing a lock on it. "You don't sound excited about that. How insane is that to be in on the king's strategy meetings? Just a week ago we were going to be stuck farming forever."

At least all of this work had distracted him well enough from the thought of his parents. Did he still hold on to the delusion that they made it out alive? I kept a warm smile and wouldn't mention anything that could possibly hurt him. "I don't know. There's so much to think about. I don't even know if I'm cut out for all this."

"You are. It's in your blood." James walked over to me.

I nodded to his reassuring comment. "Thanks, James. We'll see. Right now, I'm just confused. Captain von Cravat is acting strange, and the king is too busy planning a war." I shook my head. "I think I just want to be home."

James stopped in front of me. His eyes met mine once more, and a long silence fell between us. His facade of happiness broke, and he frowned. "Home isn't there anymore, Zair-bear."

Watching him like that, the pained look in his eyes, everything that he was holding back—it made me want to cry. I wouldn't, I couldn't. I had to be strong, for him as much as me. "No, I guess it's not." That home had gone, and so, in some ways, had the comfort of being around him. Things were different now—I couldn't explain it. It might have been because of that princess, but I didn't have the capability to think about that on top of everything else.

Not yet. "I should see if I can take a nap. I couldn't sleep again this morning."

James reached and scratched the back of his head. Then he yawned. "Yeah, me too, now that I think about it. Sword training is hard work."

"See you later?" I asked, and before we could meet with another awkward moment, I turned and headed back for my quarters.

* * *

I spent the next three days waiting for news of our mission. At least I had the time to get well rested, well fed, and back to normal. As normal as I could be in Rislandia City, that is. After the first day I'd noticed that when no adults could monitor me, servants found ways to confine me to the castle walls and courtyard. It wasn't a stated imprisonment, but whenever I ventured into the city without the company of someone older, they would be close at hand to distract me and ensure I went somewhere else or obtained a *real adult* to come with me.

Because this was the king's domain, I didn't fight it. That said, if I were capable of owning the kingdom's sole surviving airship and allowed to go on a mission to the Wyranth Empire, why couldn't I come and go as I pleased? The more I thought about it, the servants probably operated for my own safety. Wyranth spies could certainly be lurking outside the castle, waiting for me to misstep again. That thought frightened me.

James practiced in the courtyard every day from sunrise to sunset. I watched several of his practices, and it both amazed me how much natural talent he had with a sword, and that the Knights of the Crystal Spire provided someone for him to train with for each of those days. He must not have exaggerated about his conversation with Princess Reina.

Harkerpal spent most of his time making calculations and repairs. He requested various supplies from King Malaky's servants, and they provided everything he needed. Airship life was the good life if all it took was a few words to have everything you wanted handed over. He seemed content to tinker with the engines and spend his time doing little else. At least it kept him away from barraging me with stories at every opportunity.

General Carwell oversaw munitions and arms deployments to the ship. Originally, the *Liliana* never had much in terms of an artillery component, instead relying on personnel drops and the fear of the ship itself to batter the enemy. Marina and a couple others had been cannoneers, true, but the raw firepower of their older weapons left much to be desired. General Carwell, therefore, proposed a few upgrades with gear-based rotating cannons and a steam-powered crank turret at the ship's fore, a word I'd gotten used to using when speaking with the *Liliana's* crew.

I saw the designs for that with its various copper gears on the side both allowing a pitch and swivel. It looked like a lot of fun to fire, though I doubt I'd be allowed to touch it. The ship would be stocked and ready for battle, though it should be a quick in-and-out mission.

The only person I didn't see much of during those three days was Captain von Cravat, much to my chagrin. Did she avoid me because she'd given up on the plans to rescue my father so quickly? I had in many ways wished for her approval since we'd met, and now that I'd had some semblance of it, she hid from me. Or at least that's how it seemed.

I spent hours of the first day of waiting looking around the castle for Captain von Cravat, but she eluded me. A couple of the servants shared rumors that she disappeared. I asked one of the munitions stockers for the airship if he'd seen her, and he shrugged saying, "The cap'ns always off somewhere. She's got important things to do, that woman. I don't question her, just follow orders."

Other crew responses were close to the same. After a couple more attempts, I gave up on trying to find her. It could be that her avoiding me was all in my head. Surely, she had to train with her commandos if we had the Wyranth to engage. With their acrobatics and hauling down rope ladders, they had to stay in shape somehow.

If I couldn't keep up, would she follow through with what she'd said to the king? I could see it coming, her locking me up in my father's quarters while her team descended onto Wyranth troops without me. Though I couldn't call myself a soldier, I vowed not to let that happen. I would make myself useful somehow.

On the third day, a couple hours before we were supposed to have our final meeting with King Malaky and depart, a servant knocked on my door. "Miss von Monocle?"

"It's just Zaira," I said. "Come in."

The door opened. I sat on the bed, reading a book on the history of the Rislandia Kingdom and Wyranth Empire's past wars. I couldn't find much else to do, so I'd resigned myself to at least becoming knowledgeable of history. I looked up at the servant.

Before he could speak, the ground trembled, just as it had outside my farm a little over a week ago. But this one quake lasted longer, the ripples across the ground having far more strength. The castle shook and creaked, walls rumbled, and the servant nearly lost his footing, bracing himself in the doorway.

I gripped the sheets of the bed as the world vibrated, watching my book slide off the bed and hit the floor. I heard a *crash*, which certainly didn't come from the book. I glanced to the side. A vase had hit the floor, shattering glass into bits and pieces. Water pooled and dead flowers sprawled across the tile.

A scream sounded down the hall. Then, the rumbling stopped.

"That was unnatural," the servant said, still standing in the doorway. His eyes had gone as wide as a bug's. He released his grip on the door frame, moving cautiously away from it as if not trusting his feet to hold upright. "I've felt quakes before, but nothing in all my years was like that."

Someone ran through the halls. "I saw a building collapse from the balcony! The streets are filled with panic."

"I have to go," the servant said. "If there's trouble in the streets the king will assign us to help soon." He turned, then held a finger up. "Oh, the woman, Captain von Cravat. I came here because she is looking for you. She should be out in the courtyard, though, after this," he motioned all around him, "I'd be surprised if anyone was in the same place."

"Thanks," I said.

The servant took off running.

I slid off the bed and onto my feet. The stone floor felt good, solid. Much better than the rattling bed I'd been on. I frowned, thinking about the collapsed building. People had to have been hurt, maybe worse. I was lucky to be in such a sturdy building. What of the Crystal Spire? That structure was so tall, so thin compared to the castle. Could it have survived the ground shaking for so long?

It must have, or I would have heard far more than the small amounts of crashing I did. I headed toward the door.

Out in the hall, I saw more people running, some carrying water, others swords. I tried my best to keep out of their way and not interfere with their duties. If Captain von Cravat were looking for me, perhaps it was best we left without any fanfare anyway. King Malaky certainly would have his hands full now.

I wandered through the halls until I found the larger entry room that led to the courtyard. It still amazed me how big the palace was. Over the past few days, I tried to figure out how many people it housed and counted at least two dozen individual servants.

"Zaira!" Captain von Cravat called as I entered the courtyard. She jogged in my direction. "I've been looking for you. Are you okay?"

"I heard, and yes," I said. Having been mostly alone for the last three days, I considered giving her a hug, but I stopped myself. "What did you need?"

"I had good news and wanted to surprise you. I suppose it'll be a small consolation now," she said.

Glancing around the courtyard, I saw that many people had gathered. Most of the castle's population must have assembled here, in an open-air area where rogue items wouldn't fall on them. Many of the servants huddled together, but several Grand Rislandian Army uniforms of the *Liliana's* crew stood out among them. James waited in his sword practice clothes along with the man who trained him. Several others lingered in their formal poof gowns. Everyone seemed agitated, none paying attention to the luscious gardens and statues that adorned the courtyard.

I turned back to Captain von Cravat. "That was quite an ordeal. I think the whole city's stirred."

"I'd be surprised if the whole *kingdom's* not frightened."

"You think it carried that far? There was a bad one before you came to greet us in Plainsroad Village. Did you feel it?"

Captain von Cravat shook her head. "It must have been when we were on the road. The horseless carriage bumps enough that I wouldn't feel much."

"The last quake brought me to my knees out on my farm," I said.

"I do recall seeing your home in disarray. Still, it's hard to say how far these quakes carry," she said dismissively. "Anyway, the surprise..." Captain von Cravat brought fingers to her mouth and whistled a high-pitched call. Several of the courtyard's population turned their attention toward us, but a *Liliana* crewman buzzed over. As he turned, I saw a small crate under his arm.

"What's that?" I asked, cocking my head in curiosity.

The crewman stopped in front of us, setting down the crate to salute Captain von Cravat. She returned the gesture. The crewman opened the crate. At first, I couldn't see anything in the dark interior, but then came a snout and two beady little eyes. A ferret.

"Toby!" I yelped with excitement. Tears streaked down my face. Toby heard my call and leapt from the box to my shoulders, nuzzling against my hair and neck. I returned his attention with such a tight hug and squeeze that he yelped. "I can't believe it," I said, sniffling with joy. "I thought I'd lost him forever."

Captain von Cravat smoothed down her leather jacket and adjusted her goggles on her forehead. "General Carwell ordered a scouting party to the area to make sure our estimates of the Wyranth by Plainsroad Village were accurate. I remembered you mentioned a pet ferret and told the crew to look out, even though the odds were very low. Sometimes miracles happen when von Monocles are involved. I've learned that lesson long ago."

"Thank you, thank you!" I smiled, rubbing Toby's head. "You're the best."

"I know." Captain von Cravat winked at me. "Anyway, there was another reason to track down those troops, and we were successful. I'll show you once we board the airship."

"Are we leaving soon? Will we still be meeting King Malaky first?"

"I just sent a messenger to address that very question. I'd think likely not. The king has far more important things to deal with now, and we know what to do," Talyen said.

James had stopped talking to his knight trainer—Cid, I thought he'd said—during our conversation and come over. I'd just noticed him. "Hey, you found Toby, that's great," he said. His eyes darkened and he looked to Captain von Cravat. "Did you find anything of my parents?"

Captain von Cravat shook her head. "Nothing. The house has been completely demolished, and my people didn't linger around long enough to go through the rubble. They looked out, but didn't report anything back."

"So, they could still be alive," he said. Hope still radiated from him.

I wasn't about to crush his spirits. Not now, not when the ground below was giving cause for fear and hesitation. "We'll have to search for them when we return."

Captain von Cravat grimaced but nodded. "Yes, we could do that."

"You're leaving now?" James asked me.

I nodded. "Yeah. Are you sure we can't get you to come with us?" *I could use a friend*, I thought but didn't say so to him. I only wanted to show strength around Captain von Cravat, else I would never prove my value to her.

James glanced back to Cid. "My place is with the knights. I'm making good progress," he said. His eyes sparkled when he returned his attention to me. Yes, this was his place. I hoped I could find mine.

A messenger rushed to Captain von Cravat, and they moved a couple of paces from us. The messenger whispered and Captain von Cravat nodded. She returned to us a moment later. "It's like I thought, King Malaky is far too busy with the crisis to send us off personally. He recommends we depart."

I nodded, then looked at James. He was my last vestige of home, and our fates tore us apart already. When would I see him again, if ever? This time, I kept my tears at bay. *Be strong.* I bit my lip. "Follow your dreams, James."

"You too, Zair-bear," he said, eyes locking with mine.

We stayed gazing at each other. Was I supposed to kiss him? That's how the stories ended that my mother told me as a child.

I didn't make any gesture, however. It had to be James who took the lead. He made a move toward me, but only for a hug. It was a good hug, but one between friends. No more. I wished I could tell him how I felt, but this was not the time. People counted on me. I had to act however an airship owner should act. Whatever that meant, it didn't involve gushing out strange feelings.

I pried my attention from him to turn to Captain von Cravat. "Okay, let's head to the airship."

She motioned and moved through the courtyard. Her fingers pressed to her lips once more for another loud whistle. This time, everyone in leather in the courtyard turned. "*Liliana* crew, time to move out!"

The rest of the crew hustled into pairs behind her. They lined up in perfect formation, trained and tried. Everything I wasn't.

I walked with Captain von Cravat, Toby nuzzling his wet nose against my neck.

As we left the courtyard, I looked back, fantasizing that James would come after me, shouting that I should wait. That would be the true fairy tale ending. But he didn't follow. A quick glance revealed him deep in conversation with Cid, not sparing his own longing gaze for me. He'd already forgotten me.

Captain von Cravat caught my wistful glance. "Is there something between you two?" she asked. A look of amusement crossed her face.

As teasing as it may have been to her, the question gave me a lot to think about. Mrs. Gentry often had referenced our inevitable future marriage, but she likely perished when the Wyranth attacked our village. In some ways, I couldn't be anything but a reminder of pain for James. The knights, his dream, didn't have room for that pain. For him, it was better this way. If I loved him, I had to acknowledge the fact and let him go. "No," I said. "We're just friends."

Captain von Cravat shrugged as she continued on and didn't press me. I silently thanked her for that.

The airship landing pad was a five-minute walk from the castle. We had to venture into the city and outside the protection of the castle walls. Smoke rose from a distant section of the city. Several buildings had collapsed, at least in some of their supports. An inn had a huge crack down its walls but still remained upright. Several of the city's residents hurried down the streets. Tension filled the air with everyone around.

I glanced up at the Crystal Spire. It remained standing tall, not impacted in the least. It comforted me to think the building made a statement that it was stronger than anything the ground could throw at it. If only the Wyranth soldiers could see that strength in our kingdom. Perhaps they would back down.

Soon enough, we arrived at the pad. A couple of horseless carriages unloaded crewmen and supplies. Several of the king's guard attended to the ship. A fuel line pumped whatever strange aether made the turbines turn, and Harkerpal directed that process. More crew hurried supplies up into the hold.

Captain von Cravat made a motion to the crew behind us, and they broke their formation, heading for the ship. She stopped to look at the *Liliana,* and so did I. Toby climbed around me and perched on my shoulder.

"It feels strange to be on a mission again," Captain von Cravat said.

"Without my father?" I asked.

That caused her to frown. She let out a deep sigh. "Zaira, there's something I need to tell you."

I froze, panicked. Did this mean she meant to leave me here in Rislandia City? Had she been stewing over a moment to rid of me? I tried to stay strong. "Yes?"

"This mission—we're not going to follow the king's orders."

My heart pounded. "We're not?" My voice couldn't help but betray my nervousness.

"No. I'm taking the ship, and we're going to go look for your father. There's no way I'm going to leave him if he truly is alive. He would never leave one of his crew in enemy hands like that, and so I owe it to him to return the favor." Her dark eyes pierced into me. "Are you okay with that?"

This whole time I'd thought she had betrayed my father by agreeing with the king. I'd been torn about it, wondering why she wouldn't talk to me. Now it dawned on me. "You didn't say anything so I wouldn't be held accountable if someone sniffed it out."

She nodded.

A voice behind me stopped me. "Zaira."

I turned. Mr. du Gearsmith stood there. Toby sniffed at him.

"Matthias, come to see us off?" Captain von Cravat said.

He nodded. "I thought someone should be here since King Malaky is indisposed."

"Well, thank you." I looked to Captain von Cravat curiously. Something about Mr. du Gearsmith felt solemn, as it always did.

But this was different than when we first had met. I wasn't sure why.

"He knows, Zaira. I told him so he would be able to inform the king and General Carwell. We don't want to leave the ground troops stranded, expecting support. I wouldn't do that to those innocent people."

"Oh," I said. That made sense. It made me feel a little better about what we were about to do. Though in a lot of ways, I couldn't help but think our next moves would be stealing this airship. Why should I think that when the *Liliana* was rightfully mine?

"Zaira, what you're doing, it's important. I'm sure you know that," Mr. du Gearsmith said, eyeing me seriously.

I nodded. "Of course."

"This isn't like our jaunt on the *Liliana* from before. The Wyranth will be targeting this ship. As soon as it's seen over the border, there will be no quarter. You especially—you're a symbol, whether you know it or not. I won't try to change your decision to go with the crew, but you should stay hidden as much as you can. You can still learn much from them, but don't take undue risks. Let them do their jobs. These people are..."

Adults, I thought.

"...professionals, and they know exactly what they're doing. Don't get in their way, and they will bring your father home safely. The kingdom needs that more than you know."

Though his words stung, he spoke in my best interest. He was my attorney, he'd said so a dozen times. He wanted me to survive this, as much as it sounded like a chastising of my capabilities.

I held my head up. "Mr. du Gearsmith, I appreciate all you've done for me. This is my ship, and this is my father we're rescuing. I will do what is necessary."

Captain von Cravat didn't interject, but let me have my piece.

His expression held sour, but no different than I'd seen him at any other time. He studied me for a long moment, then nodded. "I hope you're right," he said. "Godspeed. Zaira, Talyen," he said with the tip of his hat. He turned, walking with that professional and aristocratic bounce he'd maintained since I'd met him.

Captain von Cravat patted my free shoulder, and then turned for the *Liliana*. A lot fewer people remained on the landing pad, and so I hustled over to the ramp, Toby digging his paws into my shoulder as I moved.

Harkerpal looked up as he detached the fuel tube. "Just about ready, Baron!" he said with a few bobs to his head.

Even if no one else believed in me, Harkerpal brought a smile to my face. "I'm glad you're part of the crew, Harkerpal."

He beamed back at me at that before returning to his work.

I followed Captain von Cravat up the ramp up into the hold of the airship. A few moments later, Harkerpal jogged the length of the ramp. He wound the crank to retract it, and soon we soared into the skies once more.

While we flew, I explored the ship again. It had been a while since my first tour. Last time, I focused on my father's quarters, the main cargo hold, and the engine room. Now that I'd had some experience with the ship, I wanted to see how the crew lived. After all, dozens of people had spent their lives gallivanting about with my father. It was only right I should try to understand them while I still owned the airship.

There were twenty crew-quarters rooms, most of which had double bunks, but a few of which were given to individuals. Captain von Cravat's room was at the end of the hall, and she had her door open. She was at her desk penning some sort of letter when I passed. I decided not to bother her, continuing on to explore the ship.

Then I found my way into the cannoneers' hall. Five cannons lined up on each side of the ship, poking out of holes with a view port for the cannoneers to find their aim. These were the new, more robust cannons that General Carwell had his men install. Each cannon rested on a rotating platform controlled by a gear-based crank for aim. Marina sat on a chair by one of the stations reading a book. She looked up and waved at me. That looked like a fun job, but if all went well on this trip, this crew wouldn't have much to do. Probably why Marina had a dual role on the ship. Still, they manned their stations, giving me respectful nods as I passed.

All that was left was the storage rooms, the fore and aft lavatories, and the kitchen. Having spent some time in the mess hall, the kitchen made me curious. One chef served the entire crew, and he was busy at work, skinning potatoes for the next meal. To cook for that many people on a regular basis had to have been taxing. I'd only cooked for one for many years. Toby perked, sniffing the mouth-watering odors. He was hungry, but I doubted the chef wanted to give my ferret anything but scraps.

I decided not to bother him, and so I made my way up to the main deck. The wind blew hard as ever, but in the daytime the chill didn't bite quite as hard. Rislandia City disappeared far below and behind us as we sailed through the clouds. I looked back to see the Crystal Spire, now smaller than my pinky finger on the horizon. The view took my breath away, and I doubted I'd ever get used to it.

We headed northwest, to fly out over the ocean as planned so we could avoid detection by the Wyranth soldiers along the border. It would also avoid any confusion for the Rislandian troops on the ground. We'd continue out over the ocean and bank hard east into the foothills behind the Wyranth capital. In theory, we should arrive just after nightfall, giving the ten of us time to descend from the ship.

At that point, the *Liliana* would go back to hide over the vast ocean as we made our way down the coast. The route was circular, true, but it would help to avoid any potential tracking by spies. The ship had more than two weeks' worth of fuel and food, which gave us adequate time to be careful in rescuing my father.

We wouldn't cross into Wyranth territory for several more hours, but time felt like it crept up on me. A nervous shiver went down my spine as I paced the deck. The rest of the crew ignored me, going about their tasks, making sure the ship continued to fly.

Two hours into the journey, I stepped outside to see the coastline and glanced back to the bridge. A man I didn't recognize sat at the helm, with Captain von Cravat at his side, monitoring his maneuvers.

Suddenly, a *boom* resounded to our port side. Everyone on the deck rushed over to the rail see what happened. I followed the crew, and Toby ducked into my coat, clinging to my shoulder. "What was that?" I asked. Loud noises had been ill portents thus far on my journey.

"Don't know. Maybe someone spotted us," one of the crew said.

"But we're out over the ocean. No one should be here."

Another *boom* came. This time, the pilot banked the ship hard to starboard. Several of us lost our footing and slid down the deck.

"Brace yourselves!" Captain von Cravat shouted from the bridge.

I looked up at her and, for the first time I could remember, Captain von Cravat had fear on her face. This wasn't good at all. Whatever made that noise had to be much worse than I could have imagined.

I gripped onto the port side rail, narrowing my eyes to peer off toward land. No artillery could hit us from that distance, or even come close enough to make those exploding sounds. I couldn't see anything but ocean from my vantage.

I lifted my head. A tiny speck grew in the sky, not a cloud or a bird. It was something else, and it flew right toward us.

CHAPTER 15

This will be my final reckoning. I face the full might of the Wyranth Empire today.

An excerpt from Baron von Monocle's log
Day 21 of the Month of Kings
17th Year of Malaky XVI's Reign

"WHAT'S THAT?" I asked one of the crewmen on the deck, pointing at the bulb in the sky that had been a speck a moment before.

The crewman stared at it for a long time. His eyes widened. "It can't be. But we're the only..."

"Enemy airship!" someone else on the deck shouted.

The crew scrambled, rushing for guns and swords. The cannoneers hustled to their posts below deck. Captain von Cravat burst from the bridge and slid down the ladder to the deck in one fluid motion. She turned and raised her sword. "Battle stations, everyone! For steam and country!"

"For steam and country!" the crew on the deck shouted back.

The gunners took their positions, kneeling and taking aim toward the growing shape. The swordsmen braced themselves, huddling by rope swings. The speed at which everyone had moved to their station told of how well Captain von Cravat had the crew trained.

I, on the other hand, with no duty and nowhere to be, stood there gaping like an idiot.

Captain von Cravat grabbed me by the collar, barely missing crushing a concealed Toby inside my jacket. She shoved me toward the cabin door. "Get into your father's quarters and lock the doors. I have no idea how the Wyranth got this airship, but I'm not going to lose another von Monocle on this mission."

"But I want to help," I pleaded. Despite my words, her orders were right. I wouldn't do anything but get in the way.

"Now's not the time, Zaira. Now go, I have too much on my plate to—"

Another boom rocked the ship. This time I saw the cannon ball whiz right past us, finding the wooden rail on the starboard side of the ship. The rail split with a *crack*. Both the cannon ball and rail pieces fell to the ocean below.

The airship swayed, and I struggled to maintain my balance. That would have taken off my head if I were another few feet to the right! Captain von Cravat had moved back to barking commands at some of her soldiers.

The other ship moved ever closer. I backed inside the main mess cabin, watching as it came into full view as a mirror image of the *Liliana*. The pilot turned the *Liliana* to face the other ship. The crewman at the front of the ship wound the turret crank as fast as he could. The turret made *rat-a-tat-a-tat-a* piercing noises as it fired. I plugged my ears.

Two more crewmen rushed passed me, guns drawn. I took the opportunity to duck into the cabin. The door closed behind me, and the blasting sounds from outside were muffled, but reverberated through the ship all the same. Was I any safer in here than I would be outside?

It struck me that this crew had never faced another aerial foe before. Only the Grand Rislandian Army had used airships in combat prior to today. I recalled that one airship had gone missing from the original fleet, one that could have been repaired and brought to life in recent times. Could this be the one that had passed over my house the day Mr. du Gearsmith had come to give me my inheritance? Images flashed through my mind of Wyranth soldiers torturing my father, extracting information about the airship technology. I shivered at the thought.

No matter what I pieced together about missing airships, or what might have happened with my father, it wouldn't help them now. I moved through the ship corridors to my father's quarters.

Soon I arrived, another *boom* echoed through the hall. The ship rocked hard this time. As the enemy airship came closer, it would be easier to hit us. I could only imagine what went on outside of the cabin.

I rushed inside my father's quarters and closed the door behind me. Toby peeked out from my jacket and let out a frightened chirp. "Me too, Toby. Me too," I said to him, squeezing him close to my chest.

I glanced around the room. Everything had stayed much the same place as I had left it. What if a cannon ball came flying through the room? I'd be just as dead as I would be outside. I paced the small area by the bed, finding myself too antsy to sit still. After a few minutes, the sound of cannon fire had stopped, both from our ship and from theirs. The ship swayed hard to one side like it never had before. I stumbled, gripping onto my father's bedpost to hold me upright.

I went to one of the portals on the port side and pressed my face against the glass to get a look.

The enemy vessel had butted right up against ours. The rocking must have been from when the two ships collided. I could see the soles of shoes from people jumping across both ships. Others swung on ropes from one ship to the other. My vantage was below them, but I still caught small glimpses of gunfire and sword fighting going on outside.

"Hmm," I said to Toby, who jumped out of my jacket and onto my father's bed. "If someone makes it in here, I'm going to need a way to fight them off."

I reached into my father's drawer and grabbed the sword that I had left the first time I'd visited the cabinet. It rested firmly in its scabbard, keeping me safe from any cuts my clumsiness might have caused. Then, I moved over to the closet, opening it up. The hat and cape that signified my father's garb had been placed there. I wondered who had brought these items back after my first airship mishap. Regardless of who had returned my father's attire, seeing those items got me thinking. King Malaky had said that even rumors of his presence were enough to throw the enemy off at times. I picked up the hat and placed it on my head. It still didn't fit right, so I set that aside. Then I took the cape and wrapped it around me.

I glanced in the mirror. When I had tried on my father's accessories before, Mr. du Gearsmith seemed pleased, but I still was surprised to see the cape fit me well. It flowed around my shoulders, the bottom hovering inches from the ground. It complimented my white blouse, and my hair looked better without the hat. It still needed something, though. Perhaps a nice pair of goggles? I made an angry face at the mirror as if trying to intimidate my own reflection.

The door *creaked* open behind me, and I spun around. Out of the surprise of hearing someone come in, I dropped the sword. Before me stood a Wyranth soldier, just as I had feared. His eyes widened when he saw my garb. "Baron von Monocle himself? But he was captured!"

In that moment, he froze, giving me time to reach for the sword on the floor and draw it. I had no experience with the weapon, and its weight made my arm shake.

The Wyranth soldier didn't stay stunned for long. He drew his pistol, though fear still lingered in his eyes. My father had the reputation everyone kept boasting to me about. That would be my saving grace if I survived this encounter.

I yelled a visceral holler and charged, pointing my father's sword in the direction of the soldier. The unexpected move made the man step backward and lose his footing. He fired his gun. I closed my eyes and dove for him, driving the sword with all my might. At the very least, I would slow him down so he couldn't hurt anyone else on the ship.

I heard a loud *crash*.

When I opened my eyes again, I found myself on the ground in front of the soldier, who lay crumpled on the floor. His shot must have missed, as I felt no pain. I would know if I was hit, wouldn't I? Glancing behind me, I saw that his bullet had hit the mirror, shattering it and leaving a hole in the wall. The confusion of my attack made him misfire. I'd survived!

For the first part of a first battle, at least. Overcoming the Wyranth soldier filled me with pride. I scrambled to my feet, tugging hard on the hilt of my father's sword, now stuck in this man's belly. The moment of elation from my small victory evaporated. The sight of blood, coupled with the feel of the flesh squishing against the sword, made my stomach knot.

Toby scampered over to the body, sniffing it. He looked at it curiously.

I turned, closing my eyes tight. I killed someone. Me. Little Zaira the farmer girl. I needed to get out of here. I needed to—

Another *boom* came from outside, followed by an ominous *crack*. The ship stuttered in the air. Everything toward the back of the room shifted and for a moment I felt like I was floating. We were falling. The picture frames flew off the cabinet. Intense vertigo replaced my sickness, and I doubled over onto the bed, dropping my father's sword on the ground. Toby slid across the floor, smashing into the wall.

It was all I could do to concentrate on breathing. In and out. In and out.

The *Liliana* regained its stability. Whatever had hit us had only felled our vessel temporarily. But it made me think how easy it might be to shoot us out of the sky. That would amount to a much better and more permanent strategy than swashbuckling between ships. Why weren't the Wyranth focusing on that?

Because no airship had ever done battle against another. This was the first time in history. I'd learned that back at the castle, when I had read those books at the about the wars between the

Kingdoms. The Wyranth were unskilled at aerial battles. Even the *Liliana's* crew was used to fighting against a ground force.

Had I thought of a strategy that no one else had? No one else could? It seemed far too simple to knock the enemy ship out of the sky while the hand-to-hand fighting waged on. At the same time, when people were caught up in the heat of battle, thinking tended to evaporate. I'd been victim of that myself. At the moment, I would be the only one on the ship out of danger and not engaged in fighting. That gave me time to consider that we should still be firing those cannon balls! I had to find Captain von Cravat again. She needed to know.

Or did she? It was simple, just like I'd thought, and I'd only conceived of a generality that could be a waste of her time. To be of any use, I needed to bring her more than simply *fire the cannons*. How could one knock the enemy ship out of the sky in a quick shot?

Harkerpal would know.

I righted myself, using the bed for balance. Toby gave me a curious chirp. He jumped onto the bed and hid between two decorative pillows, snout sticking out and sniffing toward me. "It's all right, Toby. I stopped the bad man, but I need to stop the rest of them, so wait here, okay?'

Toby retreated into the pillows. He'd be safe.

I turned around, avoiding looking at the dead Wyranth soldier in the doorway by cocking my head to the side, keeping focused on my father's dresser. I fumbled for the sword beneath me, carefully making sure I grabbed the hilt. Once it was back in my hand, I leapt over my dead adversary. My cape flowed behind me as I entered the hall.

The corridor outside remained empty. It held an eerie quality, but I told myself silently that it's better empty than filled with Wyranth soldiers. I counted myself lucky as I bolted down the hall, then descended the steps toward engineering.

When I arrived from the stairwell, I heard the *clicking* of a gun to my side. Steam filled the floor of the room, obscuring some of my view of the engine room. "Drop the sword!" someone shouted.

I complied. The sword clanked to the ground. I put my hands up over my head slowly. Sudden movements could be bad. I wanted to be careful and not cause a stir.

Harkerpal came around from one of the steam furnaces, covered in grease and with tools in hand. The cores of the turbines turned and creaked along with their gears around us. "Don't shoot!" Harkerpal shouted. He dropped his tools as fast as I had dropped my sword. "That's Baron von Monocle!"

"What? That's who we're rescuing...oh!" The gunman said, lowering his rifle from my head. "The girl!"

I turned around to see that the person who had me hostage a moment prior wore the Grand Rislandian Army colors. Though my heart still raced faster than I could ever remember, I relaxed. "Yes, that's me." I knelt to pick up my sword.

A couple of other crewmen moved behind Harkerpal, carrying metal piping. They seemed to be in a hurry. Harkerpal ignored his task for the time being and approached me. "Sorry, Miss von Monocle. We stationed one of our gunmen here in case the Wyranth tried to break in here and do damage. Take the engine room, take the ship, hmm? We learned that lesson once when we were on an exploratory mission by the Island of Fae—"

"No problem, Harkerpal," I said, cutting off the beginnings of his story. I glanced at the gunman, who returned a sheepish smile. We didn't have time for Harkerpal's babbling. "You're right about the ship being most important, though." At that point I noticed a large metallic crate with handles on all sides, several feet in length and tall enough to reach my chest. It hadn't been in engineering the first time I'd been on. It looked out of place in engineering. I pointed to it. "What's that?" I asked.

Harkerpal looked back. "Ah, some kind of weapon, I think. They didn't tell us, just asked us to store it down here in case of future use."

I shook my head at that. Another thing I could find time for later.

"How's it going up there?" The gunman asked.

"They sent me away, but it appears to be a full-fledged fight on the deck. One Wyranth soldier broke through to my father's— *my*— quarters. I, uh, got to him before he could shoot me." I motioned to my sword, noticing the blood on the blade for the first time.

"Zaira! How horrible. Should we should set soldiers to guard you? You're as important of a resource as the ship herself," Harkerpal said.

The gunman sized me up after my explanation and nodded. Was that approval from him? "Baron's daughter all right. Taking out the first Wyranth soldier she sees."

I opened my mouth to protest that it was more luck than anything else, but thought better of it, shaking my head to refocus on my purpose. "Harkerpal," I said, "the reason I'm down here is that I think we're making a mistake with the hand-to-hand fighting. We have an airship at our disposal, and the enemy has neatly lined up next to us to give us a clear shot."

"They have?" Harkerpal asked.

The gunman understood my line of reasoning. "We'll sink them." He chuckled. "First time we've *fought* another airship before. We're so used to thinking about air-to-surface tactics that it slipped by us. Always helps to have fresh eyes."

"That's right, and what I'm looking to be. Harkerpal, you know the ship better than anyone. Do you know where we could aim our cannons for one quick volley that would do a single burst of damage and end this?"

"The engine room, of course."

"And where is it within the ship?" With all the corridors that wound within the hull, in somewhat of haphazard of a design, I wouldn't be able to place a finger on an exterior schematic of the ship and show our location. Our plan assumed the design would be the same between the two ships. But what were the odds the

Wyranth, having captured my father and another vessel, had gutted the original ship and created a new design?

"The center, about midway down on the hull if you're looking at it from the outside," Harkerpal said without missing a beat.

"Great," I said and spun back toward the stairwell. My cape spun behind me, not-so-graciously hitting the gunman.

"Hey!" he said, batting the fabric down.

"Sorry," I said, glancing over my shoulder.

"Where are you going now?" Harkerpal asked?

"To Captain von Cravat so I can let her know about the strategy," I said. I didn't like lying, but with how fast the fighting had descended into the lower decks, we needed to move more quickly than proper channels would allow. Even though they respected my name, it would make them more comfortable to think this plan would have the approval of real authority.

"By Malaky, I hope it works," the gunman said with a nod. The look in his eyes told me I had impressed him again. If only it were that easy for everyone aboard the ship.

Harkerpal had already departed the conversation, bent over to get his tools. He rushed off in the direction his helpers had gone. They held piping for him to repair.

I rushed up the stairs. When I reached the top level, I ducked into the corridor that led to the cannoneers' stations and moved through that door. For the second time, a gun to the head greeted me. This time there would be no Harkerpal to vouch for me.

I shut my eyes tight, hoping this one was equally patient with the trigger as the gunman in the engine room. "Zaira von Monocle, don't shoot!" Hopefully my saying it would have similar impact to those words coming from Harkerpal.

Mutters of, "The girl," came from the cannoneers. Someone patted my arm.

"You can open your eyes," the person said.

My eyes fluttered open.

Marina smiled at me, lowering her gun. Her uniform looked so crisp, not a wrinkle, despite all the fighting. She belonged with this crew. "I like your Baron outfit," she said. The cannoneers had prepared to have their space invaded. Each of them held guns and had them trained at the door, where I stood. When Marina motioned to them, they lowered their weapons as well.

My luck had to be impeccable not to have any of them fire on sight. More mutters of agreement came regarding my fashion choices. The cape and had a gravitas among the crew, enough that it improved morale.

"I have orders from Captain von Cravat," I lied again. These crewmen were just as wont to require real orders as Harkerpal and his team. "We need to point all the cannons we have toward the direct center of the hull of the other ship and fire one after another. We're going to ram through their engine room and sink them."

"But some of our fighters are up on the other ship!" one of the cannoneers said.

I hadn't thought about that. Even I, who had no experience with this crew, didn't like the prospect of sacrificing some of our own to sink these Wyranth. Though if we couldn't do something, and the Wyranth already came below decks, there wouldn't be much left of the crew to consider. But would my father have given the order and let some of his crew die? No, probably not.

"You could return and get Captain von Cravat to whistle them back. They know to respond to her calls," Marina said.

Hopefully that would give enough time for the crew to get back aboard. "Okay, anyone have a pocket watch? We can time the shots so that I can have time to reach Captain von Cravat."

"I do," came a voice from the back of the room.

"Give me five minutes. I'll get the crew back over, and then you fire. On the dot, okay? We can't risk any Wyranth soldiers making their way to our engine room."

"Aye, Baron!" a chorus of cannoneers said.

That sent shivers down my spine. Was that all it took to be a leader? Decisiveness. It came easy to me. Once I thought of this idea, I made a plan and stuck to it, even if it meant fudging a few facts to do so. We'd be better off for it later.

The clock ticked, no time to think about that now. I could consider the finer points of leadership and strategy later. The cannoneers were all still looking at me. I raised my sword.

They raised their guns as well, but stared at me expectantly.

What was I supposed to do? I supposed this was the time for a rousing speech or...that's right, the battle cry! "For steam and country!" I shouted, echoing Captain von Cravat's call earlier.

"For steam and country!" the cannoneers shouted. They cheered afterward with hoots and whistles. I didn't consider myself all that inspiring, but I wouldn't look a gift horse in the face. I spun and headed back out the door again.

I had to get to the deck for the last part of this plan. Though the whole concept was simple, and anyone could have thought about it, it felt good to contribute something to the crew. I hoped Captain von Cravat would see it that way as well. For that matter, who knew if she still lived? A Wyranth soldier had made his way to the lower quarters, after all. What if the entire outer deck had been captured?

I took a deep breath, and then lunged to push the door open and pounce outside. The deck had dozens of people, fighting and crowding the entire surface of the ship. Where did all these people come from? As I had feared, most of those fighting wore Wyranth military uniforms, complete with ugly pointy helmets. Several of our crew and Wyranth soldiers alike lay dead on the deck. Most of our crew had their hands up.

Luck remained with me. Perhaps there was some strange von Monocle magic that guided my family to survive this situation. Instead of spotting me, the Wyranth faced toward the fore of the ship, away from the cabin. I caught Captain von Cravat's attention, who looked as if she wanted to scream at me. My being there had directly violated her orders.

I slipped away from the cabin door and ducked behind the main turbine, hoping it would be enough to conceal me from view. From there, I glanced at the deck of the enemy airship. No more fighting went on. We didn't have crew over there after all. All my planning didn't matter now.

"Who is the commander here?" one of the Wyranth demanded, waving a gun around as he paced in front of the line of the *Liliana's* surviving crew. "You will tell your people below to stand down, or I will execute a member of the crew one by one."

No one said anything. I watched Captain von Cravat's eyes. They flickered to the side when he asked the question. If the Wyranth leader was observant, it would have given her away.

"So that's it then? You'd rather all die than give away your commander? Very well then, you'll have your wish. The rest of you might see what happens when you pay no heed to the servants of the Iron Emperor." The leader motioned with his sword to one of the crewmen. "Bring him forth."

Two of the Wyranth guards grabbed each arm of that member of the crew. The crewman struggled, but to no avail. The guards threw him to the deck, prostrated before the man who spoke.

The Wyranth leader brought his sword to the crewman's throat and held it there. "I'll give you one more chance for survival. Let it never be said that I am not merciful. Tell me, who is the commander of this vessel?"

The crewman, though his body shook, stayed silent with eyes facing forward.

"You, like all Rislandians, are a piece of human garbage," the Wyranth leader said. He raised his sword.

The deck rattled. *Boom. Boom. BOOM!* The sounds came from below deck. The cannoneers had done their job. My ears rang.

Six shots fired in total. I turned to see the other ship, lifting my head to look over the side rail to get the best view I could from behind the turbine.

The Wyranth leader stumbled, then turned toward his ship. He didn't behead the helpless crewman, the blasts serving to distract him. All of the Wyranth turned that direction in shock, as had the captured crew of the *Liliana*. Moments passed with no one moving.

Several of the Wyranth soldiers rushed toward the rail. Only two stayed behind.

Captain von Cravat made the first move, pummeling one of the soldiers. She drove an elbow into his wrist, forcing him to drop the pistol that held them hostage.

Another crewman followed Captain von Cravat's lead but couldn't manage to remove the Wyranth soldier's weapon. They struggled, locked in each other's grips, which forced the pistol to point up in the air. It fired.

The sound of gunfire caused the Wyranth leader to return his attention to his hostages. "Firing cannon shots at the ship to distract us? Where is your honor? Your blood will be all the sweeter," he said.

He raised his sword once more. The prostrated crewman rolled left.

The Wyranth leader brought his sword down, clanking against the deck below as he missed. He cursed.

I could have charged myself, but I didn't have nearly the same training with swords that the crew of the *Liliana* did. Instead, I caught the attention of the crewman on the deck, and slid my own sword across to him. He deftly caught it by the hilt, swinging it around with amazing speed to meet the Wyranth leader's next blow. Steel met steel, sparking as the blades collided. I couldn't help but let out a small yelp to cheer. With the sound of the turbines, the cannon fire and swords clashing, no one noticed.

The Wyranth's airship groaned, its turbines protesting as gears ground into one another. The steam exhaust turned into a thick black smoke. The turbines had all but stopped rotating, but I knew the ship's engineers did their best to keep the ship in the air. Their best didn't matter. The nose dropped, and the rest of it followed. The ship slowly descended at first, its deck sinking just below the *Liliana*'s. The enemy vessel dropped like a rock, shrieking a high-pitched noise on its way down.

A couple of the Wyranth soldiers panicked and jumped off the edge of our deck in a desperate attempt to return to their ship. I had heard that the heat of battle could make people do stupid things, but what could they be thinking? I couldn't help but imagine them plummeting thousands of feet to their eventual demises.

At that moment, I realized I stood exposed. Two Wyranth soldiers at the rails noticed me, and one pointed in my direction. "That's the von Monocle girl. Get her!"

While the cape had served me to surprise the soldier below decks, it made me a target in the midst of so many enemies. I lunged the away from the soldiers, and tried to get to Captain von Cravat. These Wyranth soldiers moved with inhuman speed, however. When they came close, I saw the same large pupils that had so frightened me back on the road to Loveridge. They overtook me easily. One dove for my ankles and tripped me. I hit the deck hard, too fast to break my fall with anything but my face. My jaw cracked, and pain filled my face.

My movements drew the attention of the Wyranth leader, who still parried with the man who held my sword. The brief distraction of my fall accomplished one positive thing. The Wyranth leader turned back to his engagement to find a sword protruding from his chest. He flailed, then hit the deck in front of me.

Captain von Cravat dove across the deck for the pistol that had been freed a moment earlier. Her Wyranth assailant moved after her, though he failed to grab hold of her. Watching her in battle could be described as nothing short of amazing. Her fluid movements surpassed the lightning=quick Wyranth that had knocked me down. Before I could blink, she had the pistol in hand. She spun around to fire.

Her single shot pierced her target between the eyes.

Without pausing to admire her work, she spun her arms to shoot the Wyranth who had the crew member in a tug of war for a second pistol. Only the two Wyranth soldiers attacking me remained. I squirmed, but the soldier slammed me hard back into the deck.

The other soldier pressed the barrel of his pistol against the side of my head.

"Drop your weapons, now," the soldier said.

"Want to bet that I can shoot you before you shoot her?" Captain von Cravat asked. She sounded so sure of herself, but with my life on the line, I couldn't say I wanted him to take her up on it.

"I doubt you'd risk the girl's wellbeing," the Wyranth soldier said.

"Oh? You think she's worth anything? She's just a girl, too young to be of any use. Go ahead, we'll save some food rations for the rest of the journey. And I'll shoot you dead all the same."

Her words stung. She'd let me die? No remorse? I couldn't have been that bad. I'd saved the ship! Then I recalled how Captain von Cravat had acted with the king. This was a ploy to get him to drop his weapon. At least, I hoped that turn out to be the case.

"Last chance," the Wyranth soldier said. His gun shook against my head. He had to know that even if he managed to kill me, he wouldn't make it off this ship alive.

I did everything I could not to move, not to breathe, lest his finger slip on the trigger and end me. Being held down by his companion made that fairly easy a task. Was this what my father's life was like? Since leaving the farm, I'd been at gunpoint twice. At this rate, even if I survived the day, it would only be a matter of time before one of those soldiers pulled the trigger instead of using me as a hostage.

A gunshot rang out. I winced.

My life flashed before my eyes. I saw myself as a little girl, back in the schoolhouse. My mother picked me up and dropped me off. Another girl in class had soiled herself that day, and everyone laughed about it. I didn't laugh. I thought about what would happen to me if I'd been in that situation. She was so scared. It wasn't funny. I'd forgotten that incident. Funny that I should think of it as my last moment.

In the panic of the situation, I realized I had my eyes shut tight. Would I be opening my eyes to Heaven? To a new life? I saw the deck in front of me. My jaw throbbed in pain. Then, the Wyranth soldier collapsed next to me. Captain von Cravat hadn't been bluffing. Her sheer speed, just as when she slid across the deck before, had been too much for her enemy.

The soldier who held me down to the deck scurried away from me. "I surrender!" he said.

Several crewmen hurried over to seize him and drag him away. Captain von Cravat herself grabbed me by the arm and pulled me to my feet. She looked as if she were about to lecture me until she saw my face. I must have had a horrible bruise for her to look at me like that.

"We should get you to a medic," Captain von Cravat said. "I'm not sure what we can do other than give you something for the pain and let it heal on its own, but it'll at least be something."

"Thanks," I slurred, only half of my jaw opening to speak. Even that one word proved excruciating.

The door to the cabin swung open from behind me, revealing the cannoneers. They hooted and hollered, raising their swords and guns in celebration. "We did it! We sank the first enemy airship!" one of the cannoneers shouted.

Marina was quiet, watching the others, subdued. If she were like me, the thought of killing probably bothered her.

"There'll be songs about this!" another cannoneer added.

Captain von Cravat lifted her head toward the cannoneers and smiled. "Well done, my crew. I think we might have lost the ship without your timely distraction. More than a distraction," Captain von Cravat said, glancing over toward the rail where the Wyranth ship had been a moment ago. A large section of it had fallen into the sea, and more had splintered and broken. "You won the battle for us."

Marina stepped toward me and Captain von Cravat. She inspected my wound with a frown. "We wouldn't have done it without Miss von Monocle. She's the one who brought us the order to fire the cannons into their engine room," she said. "Looks like she paid a bit of a price for it, as well."

Captain von Cravat raised a brow. "Is that so? I thought I told you to stay in your father's quarters, Zaira. You've been all over the ship?" Now the scolding tone came.

I couldn't defend myself. The pain in my face overwhelmed me. I wanted to ask how was it that the cannoneers received praised when I was told I should have stayed in my quarters? Instead of saying anything, I pointed to my jaw. Tears forming in my eyes would hopefully prove the urgency.

"Right, the medic. We can talk about this later. Again, good work. We'll open a few kegs of ale to celebrate in the mess!" Captain von Cravat said. "A well-deserved victory."

The crew cheered.

CHAPTER 16

Theo kept a log of all this ship's adventures. I know he would want me to continue here. He's been gone for more than a week, leaving me as acting captain of this vessel. I pray that he comes back to us. I won't give up the search.

An excerpt from Captain von Cravat's log
Day 30 of the Month of Kings
17th Year of Malaky XVI's Reign

SEVERAL HOURS LATER, I awoke once more in my father's quarters, lying in the bed next to Toby. The medic had given me some sort of elixir, and that put me to sleep within minutes. I vaguely remembered being carried back to the bed. My jaw still hurt, but the swelling had come down since I'd hit the deck. "Toby, you awake?" I asked, testing my voice, if anything. I could talk, though I had to be careful with my mouth's movements.

Toby slept on one of the decorative pillows, curled up into a little ball. He didn't respond to my voice. When he crashed, he went down hard. A knock on the door came a moment later, though the person didn't wait for my response. The door opened.

Captain von Cravat stood before me. She carefully shut the door behind her. "Good, you're awake. I wanted to see how you were doing."

"Much better," I said. "I can talk again, though I feel a little woozy. What was in that concoction I drank?"

"I don't ask, and I'm sure you don't really want to know," Captain von Cravat said with a smirk. "The medic does as the medic does. One of the unwritten rules of the *Liliana*."

"Probably a good rule, as long as you can trust the medic."

She nodded. "I talked to the crew about what you'd done. That was very brave of you, Zaira. And you even scored one dead Wyranth solider, reports say."

Scored one? They kept tally of their kills like it was a sport? I wrinkled my nose, finding that distasteful. I supposed one would have to find some way to get used to the violence of war if one were to make a career in it. "That's right," I said.

She considered and then sat herself on the corner of my bed. "Frankly, I'm surprised. I didn't think you had much of a fighting spirit in you. This wouldn't make for the first time I'd underestimated you. You have a little of Theodore in you after all. Perhaps more than that..." Captain von Cravat stopped herself and stared out the portal.

"More than that?" I asked.

Captain von Cravat sighed. "There's a lot I wasn't going to tell you, for your own sake. I didn't think you'd want to hear it, but you've earned the right to know. The crew is coming to respect you, and this is your ship. When we get Theo back, I bet you'll be joining the crew."

I had a feeling something like this could come. Not the talk necessarily, but something about Captain von Cravat that lingered under the surface of her hardened soldier exterior. Something about being around me made her uncomfortable. I'd seen enough of her that I could read her in that regard, but I stayed quiet. She would tell me what she thought I needed to know.

"I joined the crew a long time ago. It's been at least a decade, maybe more. Funny enough, I was about your age when I made it. And no, I wasn't the first officer when I joined then," Captain von Cravat said.

"What were you?"

"I was the chef's assistant. I spent most of my time peeling potatoes." She smirked and leaned back against the bed post.

"You? That's hard to imagine." I tried not to laugh. She had nobility to her, her name stated as much. I couldn't believe that she had been in such a low position.

"It's true. Even in that, I trained with a number of the crew. They were exclusively men so it was difficult on a few levels. Theo looked after me, kept the crew respectful. I won't say there weren't instances...but I digress."

"There weren't women in the crew?" From what I'd seen so far, the crew had very few women, but not none.

"It's dangerous for women to be on the front lines of battle, especially with the Wyranth as an enemy. I still am not comfortable with the idea of putting women in harm's way, even in my position." She shook her head. "I was the first, and only because of my ability to prep cook. That's the term for the position where the chef makes you do all the work he doesn't want to."

I nodded. It sounded like a fancy city title for the way I'd helped my mother or Mrs. Gentry cook back on the farm.

"After my hard work, everything changed. Your father first took notice of my skill with a pistol about a year into my tenure here. I was practicing marksmanship with the commandos one day, using moving targets on the turbines. He came out to scold me. If I caused damage to the turbines, they were worth more than my life. He didn't want some assistant chef destroying the ship. Though, after he saw how well I'd shot, he decided against chastising me. I didn't miss a single time."

"I don't think I've ever seen anyone shoot like you," I said.

Captain von Cravat ignored the compliment. "One mission, your father found the crew shorthanded. The Wyranth had taken a toll on us more than once. He asked me if I'd want to go with an away party, and I accepted. Long story short, I became his closest confidant over time. I took command when he disappeared." Captain von Cravat dropped her eyes to the floor. She fidgeted with the frill at the end of the blanket. "But I digress. You don't need two Harkerpals telling you stories."

"But he's so sweet." I said. I meant to sound playful, but with an inability to move my face, I couldn't be anything but deadpan.

"He is, he is. You know what I mean, though." Captain von Cravat smirked.

I wanted to laugh again. Ow, but it hurt!

"Well, after your mother passed, Theo became much more solitary. Some would say he lost the will to fight. His heart certainly wasn't in commanding an airship. And the fact that this ship bore the name *Liliana* made it even harder on him. Imagine hearing the name of your beloved day after day. We should have rechristened the ship." Captain von Cravat shook her head.

"That's when he stopped coming home as often," I said, in some understanding as to my father's motives. I'd been bitter, thinking he'd abandoned me, but his pain must have been far worse than what I endured now.

Captain von Cravat, in almost a motherly fashion, placed her hand on mine. "Zaira, I'm sorry. I know how it is to lose a parent and be alone. This is where it gets hard for me. I've been struggling with how to tell you this."

"What?" I asked. I could almost feel her pain in the way she spoke.

"As I said, Theo came to depend on me. Not just the day-to-day operations of the ship. I handled most of those already. But his personal things. We became...close." Captain von Cravat blushed and turned her head. She kept her hand on mine, but her palm became sweaty. Did I make her that nervous?

As much as she was nervous, it didn't bother me that she had a relationship with my father. A lot of the way she treated me suddenly made sense. My being here had to be a painful reminder for her, as painful as my father having a ship named *Liliana* to command after my mother had passed. When the news came that my father might live, I stopped being a symbol of pain to her, and that's why she started being kinder to me.

"That's why you act so strange when my father's mentioned?" I asked.

The room quieted save for the soft whir of the turbines outside.

"Oh, uh..." She wanted something from me. I couldn't tell what. I tried my best. "Well, my father has good taste in women, that's for sure."

The tension broke. Captain von Cravat burst out laughing. "Thanks, Zaira. You have an innocence to you that's precious. Don't lose that."

"Innocence? I killed a man earlier today," I said. Hearing those words from my own lips sobered me.

The moment of levity disappeared, and Captain von Cravat's face returned to dead seriousness. "Zaira, I'm sorry about that. If I could have done anything to avoid that happening, I would have. And if you ever need to talk about it, I'm here. Okay? We have to get on with the mission. I know you care about it as much as I do. Just be strong for now. It'll be okay."

I pulled back my hand. "Does it ever get easier? Do you ever not think about it?"

Captain von Cravat slipped off the bed and moved toward the door. She'd said what she needed to, and she didn't ever linger when there was work to be done. She looked at me over her shoulder. "It never gets easier, but you learn to trick your mind into not thinking about it. I need to go check on the rest of the crew and figure out our estimated time of arrival outside the Wyranth capital."

"Thanks, Captain," I said.

"You're not military, you're nobility. Call me Talyen."

I could hear in her tone how much those words meant to her, allowing me to call her by her given name. It was a permission that signaled that I was at least a friend, perhaps even family. "Talyen," I said to myself as she departed.

After Captain von—Talyen— left, the elixir the medic gave me swirled through my head again. I wanted to be able to think clearly, but at least I couldn't feel anything from my jaw. I tried to stay awake and think about the conversation I had with Talyen, but my eyes became so heavy. I closed them for what felt like just a couple of minutes. Eyes need rest. In no time, I'd be going over plans of attack and...

Another banging on the door. This time, I nearly jumped out of my bed. I'd drifted off to sleep. Toby scampered onto my chest, sniffing and rubbing his wet nose against my face. "Toby," I said, pushing him off me. I would have been nicer to my ferret with all he'd been through, but he knew better than to pester me when I'd just woken. How long had I been asleep?

The person at the door knocked again.

"Yes, yes, come in," I said. It couldn't be Talyen, because she would have let herself in.

The door opened, and Marina slipped her head through the door. "The others were getting worried about you, wanted to send someone to check on you," she said, her tone apologetic. She gave me a soft smile.

"It's not a problem," I said, still orienting myself. I looked out the portal. It was bright outside. "I must have slept a long time?"

"Most of the evening and through dawn today. I thought you might want to get to the mess before the chef stops serving breakfast," Marina said.

"The whole night?" I scrambled out of bed. By Malaky, how did that happen? We would be almost to the Wyranth capital by now! I rubbed my jaw. It was sore, but not crippling as it had been the day before.

Marina smirked. "Medic's got some nasty potions, don't she?"

"I guess so," I said. I stood in a nightgown, though I didn't remember dressing in one. My appearance may have been improper for guests, but I was fine with it. I was safe aboard this airship. My Baron von Monocle ensemble hung from a hook across from the bed. I glanced at it. Those clothes caused a lot of trouble when the Wyranth attacked. Should I wear something that made me blend with the crew more? No, the crew would want to see me in it, as a mascot if anything. It would bring them joy and hope. They were dying to see my father. And they very well could literally die for that privilege.

I slipped out of the night gown and put the clothes on. They were a little more wrinkled than the day before, despite my best efforts to smooth them out. Oddly, the costume held its impact on me. I felt more confident than before.

Marina looked on with approval. "You're just like him, you know."

"People keep saying that," I said, stepping over to the door. "But don't I look a bit ridiculous?" She was one of the first people to listen to me, to support me. The more I got to know her, the more I liked her.

"Maybe. But are you so sure he didn't look ridiculous, too?" She gave me a good-natured smile. "Come on, Miss von Monocle."

"You can call me Zaira," I said, hoping that would convey the same friendship that Talyen had granted me.

She giggled, and motioned toward the hallway. "Thanks, but I don't think I'll ever think of you as simply Zaira. Come on, let's get you some food."

When I arrived at the mess, a large number of the crew adorned the wooden benches, finishing their meals. Marina went over to the counter to pick up food for both of us, and I sat at the corner of a table alone. All eyes moved to me while I waited. I felt so small. Did I choose wrong? Did they not want me to sully the image of my father, their hero? I felt like an imposter.

"Baron von Monocle lives!" one of the crew shouted. Shouts of agreement came from each of the mess tables, followed by whistles and cheers. It resulted in everyone clapping.

I must've turned as red as a ripe tomato at harvest time. My face might have gotten lost in the crimson cape I was wearing. I froze worse than any of the times I'd dealt with the Wyranth. That answered my prior question, but I didn't deserve this kind of praise.

Harkerpal rescued me, plopping his own tray down across from me. "They love you, Zaira," he said with his overly eager Harkerpal smile.

"But why?" I whispered.

"You saved the ship with your plan," Harkerpal said.

"It wasn't that big of a deal. Anyone could have figured that out given time. I just happened to be looking out a portal. It wasn't anything special."

He wagged a finger at me and made a *tsk* sound. "That's exactly what's special about you, and about your father, too. You both give credit to the crew, don't take it upon yourselves. It keeps your head from getting big, and people like that. But don't forget, as simple as the plan may be, you were the one to solve the problem, to take that initiative. You gambled when you were told specifically to do something else, and you won. That's what makes Baron von Monocle special."

"You can say that again," Marina said. She returned with our food trays.

"I will," Harkerpal said, his head bobbing with excitement like that first time I'd met him. He stabbed at his food and raised it to his mouth, barely taking time to chew in between talking. "It reminds me of the time your father took us on a mission to the Twin Tops Mountains. There was a small village there, and it was the dead of winter, right after a blizzard. The people there were starved, all skin and bones. Do you know what your father did? Well he—"

"Zaira should focus on eating now, Harkerpal. The medic gave her a potion that took her out for a good amount of hours," Marina said.

Harkerpal stopped, gave a thumbs up, and returned to his food.

I would have to thank Marina later. If anything, she made for an invaluable ally to stop Harkerpal in the tracks of his never-ending stories.

I wolfed down my food. It was like I'd never seen eggs or bread before. And they even gave me a cup of juice. The meal was heavenly, and my stomach let me know it with a satisfied grumble.

"You want seconds?" Marina asked. She may have been the most observant person I'd ever met.

"I would, but I should find Talyen, I mean, Captain von Cravat. I don't know where we're at, and I want to discuss what our plans will be for the descent," I said.

"Captain von Cravat should be in her quarters. She's usually writing around this time of day," Marina said.

I stood, smiling to both Marina and Harkerpal. "Thank you, both."

"For what?" Harkerpal asked.

"For being here for me," I said and left to go find Talyen.

Since Talyen hadn't bothered to wait until I responded to allow her to come in my room, I figured I should give her the same treatment. Her door hung cracked open. All it required was a little push.

There she was, diligently pressing pen to paper beneath a brass lamp with an outstretched arm to shine the light directly down on her desk. Talyen looked up, unsurprised to see me. "Zaira, good to see you're up and about."

"Thanks," I said. "What are you writing?" I stepped into Talyen's quarters, which were a good deal smaller than my own. It didn't have its own walk-in closet. It felt odd that I'd be given such grand accommodations compared to her, when she did all the work for this ship.

Talyen set her pen down on her desk, giving a quick glance toward her paper before she turned. "I write an account of everything that happens on this ship. All of the great battles, our deeds we do when not in combat. Someone needs to keep an accurate record for posterity."

"And you have time to do that?"

"I did before, when Theo was in charge." Talyen said. It was clear from her tone that she missed those days.

"Well, I'll hopefully take some responsibility off your plate as I learn more," I said. "That's what I wanted to come talk to you about. I wanted to go over our plan of attack once we land." I didn't mention our earlier discussion, as that had been more personal in nature. Separating personal and ship business was something I'd have to learn to do if I were to help Talyen like I'd just offered.

"My plan of attack," Talyen corrected.

"I'm here to rescue my father as much as you are," I said. I crossed my arms. "Don't leave me out of this."

"Zaira, I'm going to be honest with you." Talyen placed a hand on my shoulder. "You're not ready for this. Even with having experienced combat a couple of times, we're going to the heart of the Wyranth Empire. It's too dangerous. Before you say anything, I know you did well out there, and I was wrong to try to lock you in your room. But this is different."

"How?" I couldn't suppress the anger in my voice. I dropped my shoulder to remove her hand from it.

Talyen let her hand fall. "What you did was not a direct confrontation. It was a good plan, but the planning's done. This requires skilled espionage."

"I can do it. Just give me a chance."

"It's more than that, Zaira. Because of your name, of who you are, you're too valuable a target. This ship needs a leader in case I don't return. If you look at the Grand Rislandian Army, nobility are never allowed on field missions like this. There's a reason for that, because that person's authority is needed to run the ship. It's irreplaceable."

"You're nobility too."

"It's different. My title comes from my work here on the airship. It was given to me as a commendation. You have a real lineage with the kingdom. Hold on a moment." Talyen moved over to her drawer and opened it, pulling out a brass pin. She came back over and fastened it to my vest.

"What's this?" I asked, inspecting the pin. It was a sword thrust through a gear.

Talyen stepped back, nodding approvingly. "Looks good on you. But then, it always did on that ensemble. This was your father's crest, his symbol. The sword for his ability to fight, the gear for his ability to process. Without the sword and the gear like this, the *Liliana* would be but another mode of transportation. Worth little compared to the fame she's achieved. Do you understand?"

"I understand, but what you're talking about is my father, not me." I touched the pin, feeling the cold metal, the ridges of the gear. It was my father's symbol, but I left it on my chest all the same. "I don't have the same value he has. If anyone does, you do."

"But as I said, with the name von Monocle, you would be the one to make a valuable hostage if we are to be caught. Which, I might add, is a near certainty if you leave the ship," Talyen said.

"You can't stop me from going." I narrowed my eyes.

"Want to bet on that?" Talyen met my gaze with challenging eyes.

We held there for long seconds, and both of us erupted into laughter. "Zaira, you are so stubborn. You're just like him, more than you realize. I also think you'll be more valuable to the ship than you know, given time."

"And I can be valuable in a rescue party too," I said, holding firm. I wouldn't let her back me down with compliments, sure as I wouldn't let her order me about. I owed it to my father to find him. This was for him. Nothing else mattered.

Talyen considered me, bit her lip, and then nodded. "I see there's no way of convincing you otherwise. Very well. I'll include you so you don't run off the ship and do something foolish as soon as I'm out of earshot. But please, you be careful and follow my orders to the letter. You understand me?"

She was a great commander. She listened, yet held authority all the same. I was lucky she allowed this, and lucky she had been so patient and willing to train me. Even with my name, if she ordered the crew to lock me in my father's quarters as she had suggested to the king days ago, they would have followed her words, despite this being technically my airship. I nodded. I would do my best to do right by her.

"Okay then. I've been waiting to talk to someone about this idea. Perhaps you could give me some of your own thoughts before we call in the commandos. Here's the plan..."

CHAPTER 17

It's been another three days, still no sign of Theo. We will have to return to Rislandia City soon and report our losses. Though I've been with the crew a long time, I'm not sure I'm fit for leadership. There's so much despair. How did Theo keep morale so high?

An excerpt from Captain von Cravat's log
Day 33 of the Month of Kings
17th Year of Malaky XVI's Reign

THE SUN BEAT down upon the *Liliana*'s deck as we lingered over the ocean. Talyen's plan had us landing at nightfall in hopes that we could have a better chance at avoiding detection. Hours passed, giving me time to relax and get better acquainted with some of the crew. While we waited, one of the commandos gave me lessons on how to fire a pistol straight.

When evening came, I watched the sun make its slow descent over the water, the sky sucking the light down across the horizon like it was desperately trying drown it in the ocean. A chill hit me as the *Liliana* stopped its hovering in place and sped toward land. Soon we would arrive at the Wyranth capital. I would have wrapped my father's cape around me, but this evening I wore something far more ridiculous than his ensemble.

Thanks to the airship attack, we had procured a dozen Wyranth soldier uniforms. Talyen had them collected and handed these out to the rescue team. "Their attacking us was a gift. This way we can sneak into the capital without drawing suspicion," she said.

My problem was that my physique was a good deal smaller than the average Wyranth soldier. The uniform hung loosely on my lithe frame. The crew folded in and pinned the pants and cuffs of my sleeves so they wouldn't drag. The helmet slipped down over my eyes, but, since it was made of metal, there was really nothing to be done to keep it in place.

I pushed the helmet back for the umpteenth time as Talyen came out onto the deck to rally the rescue team. "Pilot says we'll be reaching the foothills outside of the Wyranth capital in less than an hour. We need to be ready. Everyone in uniform?"

"Aye, sir!" we all shouted.

"You all have your Wyranth weapons?"

"Aye, sir!" we repeated.

"For steam and country!" she bellowed.

"For steam and country!" we all returned the call.

"Good. Keep vigilant. We'll need to be careful and quiet once we land. The turbine noise itself might cause a stir, so she's going to do a full land, stop, and we'll wait to ensure there's no scouts down below. You have the next hour to yourselves. Make sure you're ready," Talyen said. She turned and headed back into the cabin.

The other members of the team talked amongst themselves, leaving me standing alone by the starboard railing. Though I'd proven myself to them in our last battle, I still didn't fit in as part of the crew. There hadn't been time to ensure I'd fully integrated. Even if I did, with my name being von Monocle, many of them looked at me with some kind of awe rather than as a peer.

Someone approached me. I couldn't quite make out the person's features in the dark. The airship ran without any lights, another precaution to avoid detection. The person stopped by me and leaned against the rail. "Miss von Monocle." The voice was Marina's.

"I told you to call me Zaira," I said, shifting to give her a little more space.

"And I told you, I should be calling you Baron or Baroness if anything. The *Liliana's* yours. At least until we get your father back. Then... is there a word for a Baron's heir? Baronheir?"

"Baronette?" I smirked.

"Baronette. I like that. Once we have your father back, that's what I'll get the crew to call you," Marina said with a twinkle in her eye.

I laughed at her teasing. "I'd still rather be called Zaira," I said."

The moon shone upon her and reflected upon the helmet she had secured under her arm. She wore a Wyranth uniform along with the rest of us. I hadn't seen her in the rescue crew before. It made sense that Marina was one of the commandos, but Talyen hadn't called her name on the rolls for this mission either. "You're coming with us?

"I volunteered for this mission, late addition," Marina said.

"It'll be good to have some friendly company," I said, turning back to the rail of the ship to stare out over the side. The ship flew over a rocky area, which became flowing hills that steadily increased in size. The Wyranth capital lay at the base of a mountain, I remembered from my school maps. With the coast behind us, we had to be getting close.

"That it will, Baronette. I look forward to seeing you in action," Marina said, and then turned to talk to some of the other crewmen.

I paced back and forth across the deck during the rest of the hour it took to get into the foothills near the Wyranth capital. My palms became sweaty, and I had to wipe them on my pants several times. The wait grated on my nerves. Despite trying to think about anything else, I couldn't get my fears out of my head. What if Talyen was right? What if the mission failed because I couldn't handle the task? I had never embarked upon something as important as this. I imagined my father shackled in some dank cell somewhere. What if someone asked for my credentials when we entered the city? I couldn't freeze. I had to be convincing as one of the Wyranth. Could I act with the authority and swagger Talyen had?

There was only one way to find out. I took a deep breath as we reached our destination, peering off toward the lights of the Wyranth capital. We kept quite a distance from the city itself. Talyen wouldn't set down too close and risk being discovered. I grabbed my soldier's pack and slung it over my back.

The *Liliana* descended, jolting as she landed on the ground below. The rescue team, about a dozen of us, lined up, and we made our way into the cabin, down the stairs to the cargo hatch, which was open for us when we arrived. The rest of the crew watched, wishing us luck in whispers as we left the ship.

Harkerpal stopped me to give me a hug. "Bring him back safely," he said. "I know you can. I know you will."

"Thanks, Harkerpal," I said, hugging him in return. I fell back into line as Talyen ushered us down the ramp and out of the airship.

Though I'd only been back on the *Liliana* a couple of days, it felt strange to leave her. The airship had an air of home to it that it didn't have the first time I'd been aboard. When our team had made it several paces from the vessel, I glanced back at the big wooden planks, remembering how I first felt, believing that a giant wall stood before me. How little I knew then. How little I still knew. But I learned. That was the important thing.

Even though I might not have had the training, this crew had prepared me as much for this mission as possible during the time we had. I had to get experience by doing, head first into the deep waters. How else was I going to live up to the famous Baron von Monocle name? Or Baronette, as it may be.

We all gathered at a point several yards from the ship. The ramp was raised, leaving the *Liliana* behind us. We couldn't turn back now.

Something shuffled in my pack, causing me to jump. My heart raced. What was it?

I slipped the pack off my shoulder to take a look, leaning to one side. I saw a little snout. Oh, no. It couldn't be.

The snout squeaked at me. Toby had stowed away inside.

Talyen buzzed over to me almost immediately, anger on her face. "You thought it'd be a good idea to bring that rodent along with us? What are you, crazy?"

"Talyen, I—"

She didn't let me get a word in edgewise. Her tone was scathing, and rightfully so. "You let it out of the pack right now. It can go live in the foothills here. We are not bringing that into the city, and it's too late to put it back on the ship if you wanted that thing to be your pet."

"He won't get in the way, I promise. I'm not abandoning him," I said. I couldn't lose Toby again. Even if he had stupidly come into my pack, she couldn't make me do it. I bit my lip, not wanting to fight with her in front of the rest of the crew.

Talyen eyed me, appraising. I could feel the wheels turning in her head, coming to a decision. "Don't you remember our discussion, Zaira?"

I did. She told me I would have to follow her every order, and I agreed. "I do, but this I have to stand my ground on."

The others remained quiet, watching us. Not a word was said, and that silence loomed over us both. Talyen needed to show her leadership on one hand, and she had real concerns about the ferret. I could keep him quiet though. He wouldn't be a nuisance. Toby was in tune with me in ways that she didn't understand, couldn't understand. I likewise would die before I would abandon Toby again. I already had made that mistake once.

"Fine, come on then," Talyen said, acting as if it were only a trifle to her, spinning as she trudged up the hill in front of us. Though it was dark, I could see a little bit of the terrain. It was grassy, with a few bushes and rocks here and there, and sparse trees. It offered nowhere to hide. Descending during nightfall had been imperative.

The Wyranth capital seemed brighter from where we stood than when we had looked down on it from the airship. It illuminated the night sky like a halo, though I couldn't actually see the city from my vantage point. At least a couple of hills jutted upward, in the way. This walk would be long and hard.

Our march went mostly in silence, with a couple of the scouts listening for any sign of trouble nearby. Talyen took the lead. Marina fell in beside me, smiling when I caught her eye.

Toby stayed quiet as I expected, as if he understood the gravity of the situation. He stopped moving around in my pack, as well. Perhaps he'd gone to sleep. The lazy mongrel. He was *my* lazy mongrel, though. I loved him. That thought brought warmth to me through the chilled evening.

It felt like hours, trudging through the foothills. My feet fast became sore in the ill-fitting Wyranth boots. The weight of my pack took a toll on my back. What I carried doubled the others because I was carrying the sleeping Toby. Fortunately, I'd been used to carrying heavy things from my farm work.

Talyen looped around and linked arms with me, forcing me to quicken my pace. "Come on Zaira, you're lagging behind," she said in a whisper. "You wanted this. You've got to fight for it like you did your pesky pet."

Like a lot of what Talyen said to me, I could have taken it as an insult. But her intent was to push me, to make me stronger. I wouldn't let her down again. I wouldn't let my father down, either.

We'd reached the most difficult place Talyen could have chosen to pull me along. Our path steepened as we traversed the tallest hill we'd crossed yet. The ground was rough, rocks slipping beneath my boots with only a few grassy spots to regain traction. I had to focus on my feet and slipped more than once on the terrain.

Talyen moved like clockwork gears. Her every step fit perfectly into the grooves of the hill. She never stumbled. Every time I did, she lifted me back to my feet. The others moved along without a problem, used to this kind of operation.

With Talyen's help, I reached the top of the hill before the others. It dawned on me another reason Talyen had grabbed me. Less because I was lagging behind too far, but more because I needed to show leadership. Even with her bitter comments, she helped me more than I realized the whole time I'd been with her. Everything she did had a purpose.

When we reached the peak, I could finally see the Wyranth city down below. Lights splattered across the basin, but the city itself had no grand beacon like our Crystal Spire. A river ran through the center of the city, and the city stretched back to the bottom of a mountain behind it, the culmination of these foothills. A tall wall jutted upward into spiked points. It would be incredibly difficult for an army to invade here.

The main entrance to the city was to the east, a road protruding in that direction. It might have been my imagination, but even with the grandeur of the city, nearly twice the size as Rislandia City, it seemed darker. Even Loveridge at night had more of an illuminated feel. That had to be my imagination though. I could see the glows from the city even back from the airship.

"Everyone, come in close," Talyen commanded, keeping her voice low.

All of us formed a semi-circle around her, awaiting her words. I counted everyone who'd been on the march with us. Only nine, plus Talyen and me. There should have been one more. I scanned the faces to see who was missing, but I couldn't figure out who it was before Talyen forced my attention to her.

Talyen pointed toward the city. "There's another entrance this side of the foothills, less heavily guarded. Our scouts found it years ago. It's used for patrols. The main gate will be inaccessible at this time of night. We should be able to slip through the side entrance as Wyranth soldiers unnoticed. I have stolen papers validating orders. These patrols often go out for two or three days at a time and return at odd hours. It should work fine."

She had done a lot more preparation than I had anticipated. No wonder she'd retired to her quarters so often during the final leg of our journey. I would have asked where she obtained all that information, but with her rank and status, she likely had access to several informants and spies I had no idea existed.

Talyen continued. "Once inside, we'll need to find an alley, change into civilian clothing, and split into smaller groups. We don't want to stand out once we're in the city. Keep the uniforms. You may want them as a fall back, or if we can get into the prison. It'll come in handy. Any questions?"

When she stopped, I resumed my count of everyone present. I scanned the rest of the group and realized who had fallen behind. "I do," I said. "Where's Marina?"

Everyone on the rescue team whispered amongst themselves in concern. No one seemed to recall when Marina had disappeared. When I last had seen her, she was with me, at the back of the pack. That was when Talyen grabbed me and thrust me to the front.

"I think she fell behind," I said. "She brought up the rear with me early on."

Talyen considered and nodded. "I'll go look for her, wait for me to return," she said, moving her way through the semi-circle of her team. She trudged back to descend the steep hill, then stopped in her tracks. I heard rocks grinding against the sole of her shoes. She slipped. I'd never seen Talyen lose her footing on the whole journey. Something was wrong.

I rushed over to her. My heart sank into my belly when I arrived. "No!" I slid to a stop.

We'd found Marina on the hill. She stood at the head of a whole company of Wyranth soldiers. She grinned, her eyes dilated in the way I'd seen several of the Wyranth soldiers. "Ah, the captain and the Baronette together. Perfect. Please deposit your weapons at your feet."

The Wyranth held so many guns trained on us that the mere act of moving would be dangerous. I glanced at Talyen, and she nodded. I saw defeat in her eyes, another thing I would have thought was an impossibility an hour ago. Marina had too many soldiers for us to handle, and they'd cut off our return route to the airship. I still hoped Talyen would think of something. We'd already been in circumstances with impossible odds, and come out the other side with a few scrapes and bruises. Did she truly have no plan here?

"Make sure your little strike force behind you does the same, if you would," Marina said to Talyen.

"Everyone, drop your weapons," Talyen said loudly. "I mean it. We can't win this one."

Some of our team turned back to see what the commotion was, having the same reaction as I did. Everything had been going so smoothly before. How could this have happened? And Marina? The single person on the *Liliana* who befriend me, who respected and listened to me? "Marina, why?" I couldn't help but ask.

"Because I am loyal to my country and my emperor, of course. Someone had to be on board that blasted airship to make sure the infamous Captain von Cravat and her new sidekick Baronette von Monocle didn't muck up this war," she said. "If you hadn't noticed, we're about to win it."

"But you were so..." Something had changed inside her. This wasn't natural, not the way she spoke at all.

"I am a spy, Baronette. This is what I excel at. You're a lovely girl, you really are, but that's not what's important here. Enough of this talk. Men, seize them!" Marina motioned with her pistol and two soldiers came to grab each of us by the arms. They didn't take any chances to allow us leeway.

I exchanged several glances with Talyen in hopes that she would give direction, but she made no move. She didn't have a plan. This couldn't be happening. We were so close!

In a flash, our mission to save my father had been snuffed out. My gut wrenched. What would they do with us? Were they going to kill us? Use us as hostages to take the airship? "If you were spying, why wouldn't you help your people before, when we were in the air?" I asked. Keeping Marina talking couldn't be a bad thing.

"Baronette, you have much to learn. I assess tactical situations and present information to the Iron Emperor. There was nothing to gain from saving a couple of low soldiers' lives. They were not going to succeed on equal ground in capturing the illustrious *Liliana* with her whole crew in their finest element. Home advantage is what was needed and, as you see, my instincts were correct. It'd be a valuable lesson for you, but I doubt you'll live to use it. Anyway, onward! To the capital dungeon!" she shouted her last words. No sympathy, nothing of the old Marina. She had been a Wyranth soldier through and through. Merciless.

The Wyranth soldiers forced us to walk toward the capital, the destination we would have been headed in anyway. We'd been stripped of our weapons, helpless. One of the commandos struggled, punching his captor in the jaw.

The commotion gave me hope as I watched, seeing if the distraction would spur others to action. It didn't. There were too many Wyranth soldiers. They surrounded the man who'd resisted, and one of them knocked him in the head with the butt of a rifle. He fell to the ground.

I turned away, horrified as they fired several shots into his head.

We passed through the gate, all according to our original plan, except for that one little hitch where we were supposed to break up into smaller teams. The Wyranth capital streets were made of cobblestone, rough on the feet after so long a journey. Even in the middle of the night, a horse and cart passed us by, followed by another contingent of soldiers. No civilians could be seen.

The soldiers led us to spiral steps and down to a large, iron-barred door that marked a dungeon. Inside, torches flickered through the underground passageway. Something dripped, and the place felt damp and dark despite the torchlight. It was a relic from the past, before clockwork and steam technology changed the world with gas-powered lanterns. The smell of mold wafted in the stale air as we continued down the corridor. One of the soldiers closed the gate behind us and locked it. I couldn't help but be overwhelmed with a profound sense of dread and hopelessness.

After the hallway, we came to an open room with a guard behind a desk and a second locked door that led to the cell block. The soldiers stripped us of our Wyranth uniforms, down to our undergarments. I tried my best to turn away from the soldiers' view, embarrassed, though truth be told Talyen had a far ampler bosom to conceal than I did. I shivered from the cold and wrapped my arms tightly around myself. The soldiers tossed our packs off to the side, including the one that had Toby inside. He didn't squeak at the jostling, the poor brave soul. I kept my mouth shut for fear they would kill him.

The soldier at the desk processed us, giving us prisoner numbers and writing down our descriptions. Another Wyranth opened the door to the cell block and escorted us down the next hall. At each open cell, the Wyranth deposited three of us, pushing the group into their prison before locking the door. After the fourth cell, where they sent Talyen and one other, I moved as well, but the guard stopped me. I stood there alone.

Marina sauntered down the hall and joined the guards. She motioned for them to follow, and they took me deeper into a complex dungeon with multiple pathways containing cells, to an area where very little light penetrated, and the stench overwhelmed every other sense. Marina grabbed me by the wrist, causing me to lose my balance, then pushed me into a solitary cell. That dark corridor stretched on both left and right for what seemed forever. An empty cell lay across from me, barren, as if they wanted to keep me from seeing the others. The barred door slammed shut.

"Why?" I whispered, mouth dry.

"A Baronette deserves her fiefdom," Marina said. With no further fanfare, she left me behind those iron bars and took steps back down the hall. The soft thuds of her feet echoed the whole way.

My cell contained a cot, a small pot of water, and a second pot, that one empty. It was obvious what it was for. Would they really expect me to use it in the open like this? These conditions could be considered barbaric. They'd stripped us of our decency and humanity. Worse, in this cell, I had no one to share my torture. I almost envied the others' lack of privacy.

I heard the crew down the hall chattering between their cells. Then more footsteps sounded. A guard slammed a baton against several bars. "Quiet in here. Next person to talk gets a beating," he said.

The prison fell silent immediately. I heard drips of moisture echoing, but I couldn't tell where they originated. It was going to be impossible to sleep with that constant drip combined with the cold. All I had was a thin blanket, nothing further to protect me from the elements.

I lay down on the cot all the same, curling up into a ball. Everything moved so fast, and I'd had so little time to think about it. But now I had nothing but my thoughts. Had my von Monocle luck run out? It'd done so well for me before in situations where I might not have had the most experience. After the airship battle, I'd thought we were unstoppable, unbeatable. How could we have been so blind to a traitor in our midst?

We trusted each other. Everyone on that ship relied on one another, and Marina took advantage of that. How long had she waited with the crew before this day? Years? The patience she displayed astounded me. The mark of a true soldier dedicated to her empire. Come to think of it, she might have been responsible for my father's capture. I imagined her informing the Wyranth of the *Liliana's* movements.

I'm sorry, father. I failed you. I thought that bleak mantra over and over as the constant drip droned on through the night. Of course, I did. I was a farm girl pretending at being a pirate, a soldier. Mr. du Gearsmith and Captain von Cravat had been right to warn me off. I could have been...

Where? Home? My home had been destroyed by these very Wyranth soldiers. I could have been cozy in the capital, fretting over news of this mission. I would have been kicking myself for not helping Talyen and the others, especially if I'd found out the rescue attempt failed. No, despite anything else, I tried my best. Even if the attempt was a failure, at least I had that.

Those thoughts brought me no comfort and no closer to sleep in the cold dungeon cell that night.

CHAPTER 18

King Malaky wept at the news. I almost couldn't believe my eyes. He wants us to strike hard again at the Wyranth, to send them a message at the border river. I'm happy to oblige, and so is the remaining crew.

An excerpt from Captain von Cravat's log
Day 1 of the Month of Princes
17th Year of Malaky XVI's Reign

I WOKE TO a guard prodding me with a baton. "Up with you, girl," he said.

I grumbled, stirring. I tried to push away the baton, but with little luck. When my eyes focused, I remembered where I was. This prison hadn't been some horrible dream. I had a new reality, and it meant a Wyranth dungeon until they executed me, or worse. Crewmen on the *Liliana* had told horror stories about what was done to prisoners here, all of which were rumor, but the vivid detail of the torture was enough to give me chills.

"I said up with you. Quickly. You don't want to keep him waiting," he said, a warning tone in his voice.

I pushed myself to a seated position, stretched my arms from their cramped position, and then slid off the cot to my feet. The cobblestone floors brought a chill to my bare skin. I would have given anything for shoes or even socks. "Who am I meeting?"

"No questions from prisoners." The guard scowled at me. He motioned with the baton toward the opened gate of the cell. I could see nothing else other than iron bars and the cold, dark stone of the hallway.

I moved from the cell. The guard locked it behind me. He led me down the hall, through the first gate we entered when we were captured yesterday. My guard nodded to the one seated at the desk, then he took me through another door that led to a second stairway.

Though the winding corridors made it more difficult to get a sense of direction, even compared to the innards of the *Liliana*, I saw that this hadn't been the door we came in through the prior evening. The door was smaller, and the stairway had been outside of the dungeon before, not within. Was this the way to the torture chamber I'd heard about? I imagined being chained, hung from the ceiling, and beaten to within an inch of my life as I screamed for mercy. It would be fitting with the tales I'd heard. This guard, at least, wouldn't be my torturer. Though he wore the Wyranth soldier uniform, he struck me as a man simply doing his duty. He didn't have that cold, dilated-eyed look that some of the more vicious Wyranth had. That, and he hadn't used much force with me in the cell.

We passed through another locked door, and I noticed a change in the architecture. The stones were still there, but now it had some ornamentation. Carved molding adorned the ceilings and windows. Glorious windows. Light burst in through them. With the utter darkness of the dungeon, I had my first semblance of any time since the prior evening. Though I'd only been in the cell through one sleep, I thought I'd never see natural light again. My eyes took a moment to adjust, but the sight gave me hope.

As we passed through this corridor, I saw rugs, decorative tables, goblets, and beautiful purple curtains. It reminded me of King Malaky's palace. Wherever I was, the person who owned this was wealthy. Servants moved down the hall, and I did my best to cover myself, remembering I wore only my smallclothes. There was nothing I could do about my bare legs, exposed for all to see. My face went hot, flushing.

My guard didn't seem to notice or care how I was dressed as he ushered me through a pair of carved double doors. He opened the door and stopped there. "Inside," he said.

The room had a couch made of lush velvet and a wall of books. Those books were old, I could tell by the smell. I found that mustiness strangely comfortable. Though at the same time, this furthered my confusion. Why would someone bring me, a prisoner, to somewhere so elegant?

I passed through the door, and it slammed shut behind me, giving me a start. I wasn't sure what to do, so I crossed to the couch and sat. The velvet seat molded against my body, soft and comfortable. I could have fallen asleep right there and caught up on the rest that I'd missed from tossing and turning through the night.

Someone else came through the double doors. A wiry man, similar in build to Mr. du Gearsmith but younger, dressed in all black save for a ruffled white shirt beneath and a yellow kerchief protruding from his coat pocket. He held a pipe in one hand, which he puffed intermittently. What struck me most about him was his youth. He couldn't have been much older than me.

The man strode over to the couch where I sat, not seeming to notice me for a long while. He puffed his pipe, as if in deep thought. When he helped himself to a seat on the couch, near to me, it brought to light his clean-shaven face and penetrating blue eyes. The most beautiful eyes I'd ever seen. I could stare at them for an eternity. I stifled a gasp.

Those eyes stared at me, almost expectantly. But what did he want from me?

For a long moment, the man held silent. He only sat, watching me, and soon, his eyes closed. He took another deep puff of that pipe, blowing smoke coolly out from one corner of his mouth.

Before I could say anything, the ground and walls trembled around me. I gripped the armrest of the couch, hanging on for dear life.

Though the third such quake I'd experienced in recent times, the violence of this one gripped me with fear. It was more an abrupt pounding than the others, which had been more of a shake. Books fell from the cabinet. The jolt had to have been as rough as the landing when I crashed the *Liliana.*

"Wonderful, isn't it?" the man finally spoke. His eyes fluttered open and glued on me. The fallen books around him didn't seem to bother him in the least.

"Terrible," I said, my knuckles turning white from gripping the armrest. As much as I was curious at first, this frightened me. *He* frightened me. Something about him screamed that he caused the quake. Could a man have such power? I'd heard strange tales about my father, but nothing like that.

"Such an overreaction, but what else should I expect from a von Monocle? It's not terrible, no. It's a mere reminder. Of power. That there's some force greater than all of us out there, and we're not in control." He reached over the side of the couch to a table and tapped his pipe on an ashtray. "What is interesting, is that power can be harnessed. Do you understand?" the man asked. He took a deep puff of his pipe this time, blowing the smoke in my direction.

I coughed and waved the smoke away as best I could. "What do you want from me?" I asked. It might not have been the best tack to take with this odd man, but I had never been one for subtlety. You learn that in King Malaky's court, not growing up on a farm. My neighbors didn't have time for anything but direct as they worked sun up to sundown, sure as I did. This man couldn't know anything of such an experience.

His lip curled upward on the right side of his mouth, and then he stood again and paced over to the bookshelf behind him. He bent down and picked up one of the books that had fallen to ground. Smoke trickled into the air from his pipe as he thumbed through the pages. "Interesting, this book that fell. Fated, really. *Strategies of War*, by Jasyn Wahrpeg, one of the greatest tactical minds that ever lived." The man licked his thumb to turn the page, then glanced up at me. "I don't suppose you've heard of him?"

I shook my head. As much as this man's beautiful blue eyes enraptured me, he gave me chills when those eyes turned away. I had no idea why he would bring up a book on war, or why he rambled like a madman. What would my father do? He would find some way out of this, something to use as a weapon, perhaps? Picking up books on the floor and chucking them at this man didn't seem to be a viable option.

His eyes returned to me. That piercing gaze made me feel more naked than I already was. I wrapped my arms around as much of my body as I could.

"A pity. I can tell by the way you look at me that there are gears turning in your head beyond most others' abilities. Baron von Monocle was foolish to hide you on a farm, ignoring your raw talents for so many years. A girl with such a simple life doesn't read books on the art of war, if you read books at all. And you should. In your blood is the legacy of a great man, and it's a shame to waste such a mind."

He cleared his throat. "Anyway, one of the main philosophies of Warpehg's strategies is that it's not enough simply to subjugate your enemy. You must either woo the populace to think of you as their leader, or push them to believe a fight would be so hopeless they resign their hearts and minds to your rule. Anything else creates rebellion, endless fires to put out. A perpetual disaster. Either way, full subjugation can take several generations."

I still didn't see what this had to do with me, but I'd lost my nerve to say anything else. I bit my lip.

The man came over to me and ran his fingers through my hair. I froze. Had I been given to some strange Wyranth as some sort of toy or plaything for him? Could this be the torture they devised for their prisoners? Horror filled me.

"Don't touch me," I said defiantly, fighting back the bile in my throat from the thoughts of what he might do.

He pulled his hand back, quirking a brow at me. Our eyes locked, those beautiful blue eyes on his awkward frame. Then he dropped his head back and laughed. He laughed harder than I had ever heard anyone laugh before. "Oh, that is grand. Just grand. Is that why you think I've brought you here? Do you think I'm some kind of *monster*?"

"I...I don't know."

"I'm not. That I promise you." The man paced again. "I'm here to give you an opportunity, not take anything from you. You are quite a lovely girl, I assure you. A little skinny for my tastes, but lovely nonetheless. Very much like your mother."

Those words jolted me as much as anything else he'd said so far. And not just because he seemed intimately familiar with my family. I'd spent weeks being compared to my father over and over again. So much like the great Baron von Monocle! So stubborn, so rash, yet honorable! I could be him one day, as I'd been told many a time. But this was the first someone compared me to my mother. "How do you know her?"

"Liliana von Monocle..." he trailed off, voice longing for something I couldn't put my finger on. He thumbed through his book once more before setting it down on a lamp stand. "That's not important right now. We're here to talk about you."

"Me?" His responses to my questions jumped from topic to topic without any form of cogency. I was convinced more than ever that this man was mad as a goat.

"Yes, you. There's a great opportunity, here and now. You have something I want, and I have the ability to make your life very comfortable...or quite the opposite."

I frowned, annoyed. Why couldn't he say what he wanted from me? Did nobility always have this aloof air to them? I thought back and recalled that King Malaky hadn't rambled in tangents. Perhaps it had something to do with the strange dilation in the Wyranths' eyes I'd seen so far. "What's the opportunity?"

"Joining the Wyranth Empire, of course."

It was my turn to laugh, and hard. How absurd! I could barely contain myself and found myself gasping for air soon after. "You have to be kidding me."

The man frowned. "I assure you, Zaira von Monocle, this is no joking matter."

"Why?"

He paused and stared at me again, as if studying me longer would give him a glimpse into my soul. He must have seen something as he clicked his tongue before continuing. "You don't need to be eased into concepts. I see I must be forthright with you. I mentioned war, and ending wars. The von Monocle airship is a symbol of war, more than anything. It's become the representation of all that is the Rislandia Kingdom. If that allegiance evaporated, if that word was circulated... Do you see how many deaths it could prevent?"

His thoughts hadn't been as jumbled as I thought. Everything he said was completely true, but he must have known that I'd think his proposition crazy. How, by Malaky, did this man expect that I could possibly join the Wyranth? After all the pain and heartache their empire had caused my family and friends, I could not be considered an ally. That didn't even count the times Wyranth soldiers had tried to kill me proper.

That said, if he spoke truth, I could hasten the end of the war. It would sink the Rislandia Kingdom. They would lose their most effective weapon in my father's airship, and that would embolden the Wyranth to snuff out our modest kingdom. It was my kingdom as much as anyone else's who enjoyed a life in Rislandia. I happened to like it. "I'm flattered," I said cautiously.

"Ah, that's a better reaction than I thought you might have. It's a lot to think on, but you have an intelligence that few others could muster." He brought a finger to his skull as if to exemplify it. "It's the blood of the von Monocle, as I said before. This could prevent the deaths of thousands, Zaira. Is loyalty such a high price to pay for such a boon?" The man brought his pipe to his mouth once more, puffing.

He spoke of loyalty, though he asked me to betray my kingdom. Thousands of lives meant a lot to me, and if I could keep those alive, I would. But on the other hand, if the Wyranth had control of the airship, and rolled over Rislandia, would it actually save lives? I couldn't trust him to keep his promises.

Moreover, my fight was personal. He had my father in prison, and I was a prisoner in enemy territory, with no one to back me up. "What would this loyalty entail?" I asked, trying to keep my voice neutral.

The man set down his pipe across the ashtray on the end table. In an odd maneuver, he dropped to one knee in front of me and took my hand. His hands were cold, his skin soft. This man had never done a day's field work in his life. "Marriage, my dear," he said.

I nearly choked on my own breath. "What?" I recoiled my hand.

He didn't pursue the touch, but stood again. "Don't you see? A union of Wyranth and Rislandia. It would unify our countries, bring peace to the world."

He was as loony as I thought. How could I even consider marrying some strange man in an enemy empire where I had been taken prisoner? This was no torture chamber, excepting for the tricks being played on my mind. He didn't offer peace but, instead, lulled me into some strange thought process where I would do his and the Wyranth's bidding. He'd picked the wrong farm girl for that.

I smiled my sweetest fake smile at him. "I would rather have my throat cut from ear to ear," I said and made a gesture with my hand across my neck.

The man breathed in deeply through his nose, clearly angered. "A von Monocle through and through," he said as if it were a curse. "Very well then." He turned to the door. "Guard!"

The Wyranth soldier burst in and stared at me as if he were primed to follow through on the idea I'd just given the strange man. Once he saw I posed no threat to his master, he bowed. The pointy tip of his helmet reflected our warped images.

"Take her to her cell," the man said. He turned away to face the book cabinet. "And send for a servant to clean up these books. Do tell them to take care with them. Some of them are very old and worth a considerable amount."

The guard rushed to the couch, grabbed me by the arm, and forced me to stand. My arm ached where he gripped me. I grunted at the jolt.

"Let's go," the guard said and pushed me toward the door.

I stumbled, then walked of my own volition.

"Oh, and Zaira," the strange man said.

The guard gripped my shoulder and spun me back around. I shook off his hand, annoyed with the rough treatment.

Those deep blue eyes fixated on me again, the anger gone as soon as it had arrived. It was as if two men lived inside this one body, one ferocious and bursting out, the other keeping his darker side at bay. "Do think about it. This isn't the last offer. You will have two more chances. Let it never be said I'm not a patient man. But after the third...well, I'm afraid I can't vouch for the safety of your father. Do you understand?"

I paled. My father. This was the first real confirmation I had that he had survived after all, but that sweet news soured with the coupled threat. I could barely breathe. "I understand," I said.

"Good," the man said.

The guard pushed me again through the doorway, and I stumbled once more, bracing myself on the wall at the opposite side of the hallway. The guard shut the door behind me, then pulled his baton from a strap on his belt. "Move it," he said.

I complied, but glanced back over my shoulder toward those ornate double doors where I had the strangest encounter of my life. "Who was that?" I asked the guard.

"You don't know?" Shock filled the guard's voice. "That was the Iron Emperor himself!"

CHAPTER 19

Sometimes this ship feels like a cell. I used to be excited when we travelled on missions. Now I only feel loss.

An excerpt from Captain von Cravat's log
Day 7 of the Month of Princes
17th Year of Malaky XVI's Reign

THE NEXT TIME I awoke in the cell, I felt moisture on my face. My first thought was that the dripping found its way to the stone over my cot and formed a crack specifically to torture me. I winced and turned on my side, not ready to wake just yet. In the dungeon, no light shone through save for the small lamps in the hall, so I had no ability to tell whether I'd slept long enough. My grogginess told me I could afford to fall back asleep for a while longer. It wasn't as if I had pressing matters to attend to.

Even in my new position, the cool moisture touched my face once more. Someone had to be playing a prank on me—the prison guard? This time, it didn't feel like a drop of water at all. The moisture I felt had a solid component to it. I flipped from my side to my back and raised my head a little. Then I opened my eyes. In the dim light of the lamps that lined the hall, I saw a silhouette on the bed. A ferret.

"Toby!" I said. His name echoed down the hall. I brought my voice to a whisper. "Toby," I whispered, wrapping my arms around him and squeezing him. "How did you get here?"

My ferret nuzzled against me as if attempting to dig into me. He loved me, and I loved him.

I noticed something he had brought with him, dropped on my cot next to me like a present. It glimmered in the dark room. Toby must have picked it up because it was shiny. I grabbed the item— Talyen's pen.

I remembered seeing that very pen in her quarters before we departed the *Liliana*. Talyen wanted to chronicle every detail of our adventures so, of course, she would have kept it in her pack when out on our mission. Toby had rummaged through the same store room since he had stowed away in my pack. He must have found it while digging around. The rascal. Always getting into things he shouldn't.

The pen brought me more hope than I could have imagined, lying there in that bleak cell without any possibility of escape. I looked around for something to write on. The guards hadn't given us any amenities like paper. Chronicling my days wouldn't do me much good even if they had. I crinkled my nose as I thought of how I could utilize this gift. My cot's sheet! It was white like paper. That gave me an idea of what to do. I could write a message. But then what?

Toby nuzzled more.

"Do you think this will work, Toby? This was your idea."

Toby stopped, as if considering. He sniffed the air, then jumped off my cot. Next, he skittered around the dungeon floor in circles like a crazed animal.

I couldn't help but laugh at the sight, but that gave me the second part of the idea that could make this writing thing work. Toby could get through the bars. He could run around this entire dungeon without being noticed. That meant I could get messages back and forth with some of the crew, as long as he cooperated. "Great idea, Toby," I whispered.

While he continued his energetic run around, I tapped the pen to the corner of the sheet. Toby crawled onto my lap a moment later. What should I write? Something simple, no doubt. In big letters, I scrawled:

Hello. I'm stuck in a cell, and it would be nice to hear from someone.

Nothing profound, but it would establish a dialogue with someone else in the dungeon. I longed to hear from anyone on the airship. It had only been a couple of days of being alone, save for the chat with the Iron Emperor, which I didn't count as company. I'd been used to solitude before on the farm, but never so confined like this. I'd always had the option of running over to the Gentrys' or other neighbors if I needed anything, even a chat

I told myself to stop thinking about it, lest I go crazy. I had this hope of correspondence now, and that's what I'd focus on. I took the sheet between my teeth, unable to tear it another way. The sheet ripped as I chewed through it. The chewing didn't create the cleanest cut, but it would do. I wrapped the scrap of sheet around the pen, and tucked it into Toby's collar.

Booted footsteps pounded down the hall. I couldn't let them see Toby or find my attempts to communicate with the others. "Shh," I said to Toby and buried him under the sheet to hide him. The guard appeared a few moments later, baton in hand.

I spun to face him, hands on my knees as I sat on the cot. I scooted in front of where Toby hid so as to obscure the strange bulge under the sheet. The darkness helped matters, but I didn't want to take any chances.

"Come on," the guard said. He unlocked the cell and opened the door.

I slid off the cot. The stone floor under my feet was freezing, but I did not protest. He must mean to take me to the Iron Emperor's company, the same as yesterday. Without the fear of the unknown, it didn't seem so bad.

"What are you smiling about, prisoner?"

"Nothing, nothing at all," I said, holding my head proudly as I exited the cell. Seeing Toby gave me an odd sense of bravery. I would survive this. *We* would survive this.

Fear didn't grip me at all during the walk to the palace. I felt a renewed urge to fight. If this was the worst they would throw at me, nothing could stop me. My will was stronger than iron. Stronger than the Iron Emperor. Was this what it meant to have the blood of a von Monocle coursing through me?

When the guard opened the doors to the palace study, I saw the Iron Emperor had already seated himself, smoking his pipe and reading a book. He read a different book today, and I couldn't see the title from the angle he held it.

I stepped in. The door closed behind me. I carefully moved to the couch. Only when I seated myself did the emperor glance up from his book. "Zaira, you should have some courtesy and bow before your betters."

"I do bow before my betters," I said with defiance. Perhaps my newfound confidence was too much, but it felt good to not follow his commands.

The Iron Emperor slammed the book shut. His face became grave, much more serious than I'd seen before. He stood and leaned over me, face close to mine. His hot breath lingered on my face. "Girl, I think you may have misunderstood me yesterday. I have patience. I'm willing to wait to get what I want, but I will not suffer indignation."

Then he raised his hand and backhanded me across the face.

The hit stung, but not as badly as I would have expected. It still left my mouth agape. The move left me more shocked than anything. The confidence I had just gained drained from me. Yesterday he had acted like such a gentleman, though eccentric to say the least. But to use brute force?

Fear came back to me as I recalled the stories of torture I had been warned about. I recoiled on the couch, trying to distance myself from him, but the Iron Emperor still loomed over me.

"Well, girl? Bow. To. Me." His voice pierced like ice. He leaned back to give me space to compile with his demand.

I met his eyes. Those beautiful eyes had a different quality to them today. Dilated hard, like his soldiers I had come across. This was not a man in control of himself. I didn't want to bow to him, to show him that subservience. I couldn't do it. It would have made me a traitor to Rislandia, to my father. "Get away from me, you monster!" I blurted out of fear.

The Iron Emperor brought his hand up as if he were going to strike me again. He stared, then lowered his hand and blew a puff of smoke. "Disappointing, it really is. Here I thought we could make progress, person to person. There are very few who understand positions of power, Zaira, how they operate, how they feed off one another. I thought you did. I see I was wrong."

All I could do was sit there frozen. Did his moods change so drastically? How could he go back to his philosophizing? I sat on the couch before a madman. That was the only explanation. He had two sides to him: the harsh, Iron Emperor part, and then this man, the eccentric thinker. What could analyzing him accomplish, though? Now more than ever, I needed to figure a way to escape before he did more damage than a cheek that smarted. A von Monocle would find a way out. I hoped some of my father's luck still dwelt within me.

I scrambled to my feet, ready to bolt on first notice.

The Iron Emperor shook his head, making a *tsk* noise. "Zaira, even if you were to make it out of here and past the guard in the hall, this is my domicile. Where do you expect to go?"

He was right. After a hard glance around, I confirmed there was no means of escape. The double doors behind me were the only way in or out of the room unless he had some hidden passage in the bookshelf. That was a silly thought since I had no idea where a passage would be if there was one. Even if I found one, I wouldn't be able to overpower the man in front of me. "Why are you doing this?" I asked.

"I am protecting my empire, Zaira. Mark my words, it gives me no joy to bring you pain. Quite the opposite. My end goal is to have you join me, I've told you as much," he said, stepping to me again. This time, he softly placed his hand on the cheek he had just struck, caressing as if I was a porcelain doll. I tried not to recoil, but I couldn't help but flinch at his cold touch. "I don't wish to hurt you, Zaira. You know that. Have you given thought to our discussions yesterday?"

"About subjugating empires?" I asked, trying not to sound too biting.

"Of marriage. The concept is more important than you realize. It's not just the joining of our peoples in a way that would end the war. The Wyranth Empire has no lady empress, nor does it have an heir." His finger traced down my neck and my arm, all the way to my hand, which he took into his. "I find that solution would be enjoyable as I find, for some strange reason, that I like you."

I stayed quiet. Did he expect that I should thank him for that?

He considered me, reading me as he had done the day before. "I don't know if you are aware of our laws, but the empress would be second only to me. You would be able to control policy, control the entire empire. You understand what a gift I am offering you?"

If I thought he was mad before, it was nothing compared to now. Did he think I longed for that sort of power? Despite his beautiful eyes, I found him repulsive. Though in some ways, his idea did give me pause. Wouldn't accepting and bringing peace be a worthy thing to do? Could I sacrifice myself for the good of everyone like that? Would it even be for everyone's good?

No. As much as he tried to tempt me, he would still be in charge. I would be second. The offer sounded slick, but he would be able to countermand everything I attempted to do. It would be as useless as my attempting to escape this room. It would serve the same purpose as my defecting, to demoralize Rislandia's army, make the invasion easier. He had said he wanted as much yesterday, and he'd use whatever means it took to achieve that. This man viewed everything as a battle.

I pulled my hand back from him, but slowly, not jerking away. "My marriage is not on the table for discussion," I said, trying to sound as strong as I could.

His blue eyes pierced me again. Could he see that I had considered his offer? If he did, he gave no indication. "Zaira, I'm so disappointed in you. You're so shortsighted. But of course you are, it's the nature of youth. Not all of us can be raised to be emperors from birth. You haven't had the life experience I have. You may think you're invincible, that there are no broader considerations to your actions."

"I am fully aware of the *broader considerations*. Rislandia is my home. And I am loyal," I said.

"True loyalty would save lives. And at what cost? A life of comfort? Do you not know how this empire would shower you with praise?" He jerked his head to the side, frowning. "No, this will not do. I told you that you had three days to consider joining me. I shall give you one more chance to reconsider. You will agree tomorrow, I will see to that. Your father will be brought here. And he will receive a lash each time you resist, until his death if need be. Now out!" He shouted the last words.

The guard opened the door upon the shout, trudging over to me.

I went limp, letting the guard take me by the arm. My father. He was all I could think about. My heart thundered. On one hand, I would see him again, which was what I'd been longing for since I'd first left my little farm village.

The guard dragged me all the way back to my cell. I wasn't in the mood to cooperate today. He roughly tossed me back inside. I fell, bracing myself with my hands as he locked the door behind me.

I immediately moved to my cot and felt around for Toby. He was gone. Wandering, or with purpose? I might never find out.

I dug my face into the pillow, and bawled into it. Did I really break this easily? The thought of my father getting lashes had been the final straw. The only alternative would be to marry that terrible, terrible man. And I might have to do it. I must have lain there sobbing for almost an hour, I still couldn't keep good track of time. My soul hurt. I had no way to win, no way out. My delusions about rescuing my father and gallivanting about on an airship to save the kingdom had been just that—delusions. Talyen had bought into them, and look where it got us.

I had no business being here, no business running around as if I were some hero. It was like the first time I flew the airship—I'd led us into danger and crashed. Every time I took action, that was the end result.

Just when I thought there was no hope left, Toby returned and snuggled up against me. I pulled myself up from my pillow and sat, inspecting Toby's collar. In all likelihood he'd wandered around, not found someone. Toby was loyal to me, but was a little chicken when it came to other people.

I pulled the note from his collar and unfolded it. My original scrawling was there, asking if anyone was there. When I flipped the scrap of cloth over, I saw writing that didn't come from my hand.

Zaira? Could that be you?

Toby had found someone for me to correspond with! And this person knew me. Someone from the ship had responded. Or, it could be my father. The crew always called me Miss von Monocle, after all. This hand was more familiar. It had to be him or Talyen. My spirits lifted, and I sniffled. I wished there were more of a note there, but this was at least something. I could communicate, assuming I could get Toby to go again.

I tore off another scrap of cloth from my sheet, this one larger. What would I say? *Yes! This is Zaira. I tried to lead a rescue mission but failed.* That presumed too much that my new correspondent was my father for certain. I snorted, and that sound echoed down the hallway. No, nothing like that. Instead, I wrote:

Yes, this is Zaira. It's good to talk to someone. The guards are so cruel, and so is this country. Who are you?

I tucked the cloth and the pen into Toby's collar again. It wasn't much of a conversation starter, but I was sure anyone in here would agree that the Wyranth were an oppressive people. All of them I'd met had this anger to them that could flare out of control at any minute.

This time, I walked to the front of the cell, where the bars were, and set Toby down. "Go find our mystery writer again," I told Toby.

Toby squeaked and scampered down the hall.

I still stood there when the guard came by to see why he had heard noises. I remembered from the first day how he didn't tolerate chatter. "What's going on down here?" he asked.

"Nothing. I miss people, is all," I said.

"The Iron Emperor is being gracious to you," the guard said. "You should be grateful in return."

"He's giving me an ultimatum. That's not grateful, it's terrible."

"You haven't seen terrible, girl." The guard shook his head. "Most prisoners are executed. Slowly. I shouldn't even be talking to you," the guard said. He turned to go back to his station.

I don't know why it was then I thought about this, but it was the first time I'd had to question it. "What's the Iron Emperor's name? That's a cold title to be called." Cold like the iron bars at my hands.

The guard stopped and looked back. "It's blasphemy to utter his name. You should stop thinking such things. Heed my advice." This time he walked away before I could get any more information from him.

In truth, I'd enjoyed the conversation. Beyond the one line of my note, this was the first I'd had outside the strange emperor with the blue eyes. I built a little rapport, even if the guard had taken to simply warning me. I had to remember that these guards weren't necessarily evil themselves, but held down by oppression. All soldiers did what they thought was right, for loyalty, for country.

Thinking of my people made me miss my friends all the more. Talyen and Harkerpal, James, Mr. and Mrs. Gentry, and even Mr. du Gearsmith. One way or another, all of those people took care of me. As I considered it, there had been a profound difference between those I knew and loved and these Wyranth. It was compassion. The Wyranth seemed to have none. The world to them was but forwarding some grand plan of the Iron Emperor.

What that plan was, I had no idea. I wished they would just stop. Rislandia was no threat to them. If they left us alone, we'd leave them alone right back.

I hung my head as I moved back over to my cot. Then I plopped down. How could a simple note get my hopes up so high? That's how far I'd fallen. I had such freedom before, whether on the farm or on the airship. Now I had anything but freedom. If I didn't give into the Iron Emperor. I certainly would be tortured or killed.

I sat and waited. For a while I tried to count the drops I heard in the hallway or try make out some of the whispers from further down the hall. After a time, sitting became tiring, and I needed to get up to stretch. I looked out of my bars, trying to see down the hall, but it was too dark, too huge to see anything other than the empty cell across from me. Just how many prisoners did they keep down here?

I had no one to answer my questions. I wished I'd been thrown in a cell with some of the others, even if it would be cramped and with no privacy. Instead, my cell had been down the hall. I didn't even have someone I could whisper across to. The Iron Emperor might be my only human contact for the rest of my life. My shoulders slumped, and I pressed my head against the bars.

I'd been rambling to myself in my own head. This was worse than despair. It was boredom.

More time passed, and finally I heard the scampering of little ferret feet. I perked. "Tobytobytoby," I called to him in a whisper. I made a clicking sound with my tongue.

Toby came right back to my cell. I crouched, and he hopped into my arms.

"There's momma's little boy." I kissed him. He kissed me back with a little slobbery tongue.

I set him down and pulled out the cloth. That couldn't have been time enough to find someone to reply, could it? I opened the cloth, seeing my bigger note this time. I flipped it around. I was nervous, wanting so desperately for real conversation with one of my people. This note had many more words to it, I could see as

I unfolded it. I held my breath as I held it up toward the meager light. Then I read the note.

Zaira! There's so much I need to tell you. How it both brings me joy and pains me to know you're here, my daughter. I love you. – Father

CHAPTER 20

We struck them hard, but they have a new form of anti-airship artillery. The mission didn't go as planned. Harkerpal made us set down at Loveridge in hopes that the heavily forested area would conceal the Liliana while we figure out repairs.

An excerpt from Captain von Cravat's log
Day 9 of the Month of Princes
17th Year of Malaky XVI's Reign

MY FATHER WROTE that line. I couldn't believe it. He was close. I squealed in excitement, and that echoed through the dungeon.

"Quiet back there!" came the angry voice of the guard. I ignored it. What did it matter? I had a note from my father. For the first time in years, I'd actually talked to him. He penned these words! I traced the letters with my fingers. By Malaky, how I missed him.

Tears streamed down my cheeks again. It embarrassed me to think about how much I'd cried these last few weeks, but I'd had some of the biggest emotional ups and downs. My tears had been justified in every occasion, but these were different. Words from my father brought me tears of joy. I kept being told he was alive, first by Talyen, and most recently by the Iron Emperor, but this was my first tangible evidence that he truly lived. All I wanted was to hug him, to hold him.

I rushed over to the bed to scrawl another note on my sheet. Toby ran and hid under the cot. I wrote:

I'm so happy to hear from you. I love—

In my excitement, I hadn't seen that the guard followed up on his call for quiet by padding down the corridor. He watched me from outside the cell and banged his baton on the iron bars. "What are you doing, girl?"

I jumped, dropping the pen and the piece of fabric. "Nothing, just..." I couldn't think of a plausible excuse. I'd been caught writing notes. But what did that mean? No one had told me I couldn't.

By the way the guard glared at me, I could tell he couldn't care less about that technicality. He slammed the door to the cell open, pushed me aside, then swiped the pen and fabric off the floor. He stared at the message. "You're passing letters between cells?" he asked, more to himself than me.

He turned his head and yelled. "Tyree! We need to have someone permanently stationed back here. Our prisoners are getting rowdy!"

The guard who must have been Tyree stalked toward the cell. "Everythin' okay?" he asked in a low voice.

"They've been passing letters between the cells. This is supposed to be solitary," the first guard said.

Tyree nodded. "Fine, I'll stay stationed here and let the next shift know."

The first guard nodded. "Very well." He turned back to me, and then jabbed his baton into my stomach.

I hadn't been expecting him to attack me. I doubled over from the pain. His blow both knocked the wind out of me and made me want to retch. He'd hit hard enough that it would bruise for certain. I held my hand to my stomach, keeping pressure on it through the pain. I found myself unable to keep upright and collapsed to the stone floor.

The guard kicked me on my side. He snarled. "Do not test the limits of this dungeon, girl. Remember that."

I couldn't respond. My mouth hung open, gasping for air. I rolled on the ground in pain.

The guard turned and left the cell, locking it on his way out. "I have no idea why the Iron Emperor doesn't just dispose of this one," he said to Tyree. "She's worthless."

I groaned on the ground and, fortunately, Toby didn't come out from under my cot until both guards moved somewhere out of sight. Toby couldn't understand my pain, but looked worried all the same.

I caught my breath as I lay there on the cold stone floor. My stomach still hurt both to the touch and whenever I tried to move, sit up, twist, or turn. It'd be a few days before that went away.

The physical pain meant little to me compared to the sinking feeling in my chest. I'd been on the cusp of a real conversation with my father only to have it taken away. I should have been quieter, more cautious. I banged my fist on the cot. Another failure in a long line of the Zaira von Monocle comedy of errors.

I sat and leaned my head back against the cot. Toby crawled into my lap and purred at me. At least I had Toby. He'd love me no matter what, even if we had to spend the rest of our lives in a dank prison.

It felt like we were going to spend the rest of our lives in this cell. As the shock of the pain wore off, I grew weary. I fell asleep on the cot. Tyree brought a pile of mush that they called our rations, some of which I fed to Toby. The two guards now took shifts walking in front of the cell. I had no alone time save for a few minutes in between the two. I couldn't believe how well Toby kept hidden, like he had a second sense about when they came. My last vestige of hope had been taken away. It had to be close to evening time, which left me but a few hours before I would be back in the presence of the Iron Emperor. This time, he would threaten to hurt my father if I didn't comply with his demands for marriage. Did I have any other choice? It would be the only way I could get out, the only way I might be able to save my other friends down here.

That short timetable filled me with dread. I hoped the next day would never come, that in some bizarre fashion time could stop in this cell. I'd gladly stay in a prison like this for the rest of my life if it meant my father would be safe. Though he probably felt the same way about me. I missed him more than I had realized.

This was all my fault. If I hadn't come on the mission, the Iron Emperor couldn't have used me as a pawn, wouldn't be threatening my father. Even though this prison provided a terrible existence, at least he still lived.

I buried my face in my hands. What a disaster.

Down the hall of the dungeon, I heard a *crack* that sounded a lot like the baton smashing against the steel of a cell. Someone else must have been misbehaving. *Crack! Crack!* I heard more. That couldn't be good. Were the guards beating someone? The sound could have been bones snapping. Despite the fact that I hadn't endured tortures, my gut told me that other prisoners in this dungeon didn't have it so easy.

I lifted my head to peer into the dimly lit corridor. Of course, I could hardly see anything in the soft flickering light, and with the turn of the corridor a few cells down, that cut off any potential view.

A man cried out in horrifying pain. Much worse than I had just endured, though thinking about it caused my stomach to ache in sympathy.

Then I heard what sounded like a gurgling noise. I covered my mouth in horror. Was one of my crew dead?

There had to be something I could do. I glanced around the cell, looking for something, anything that could at least cause a distraction. There were the pots, one of which was filled with urine as I'd had to go before my nap. I shuffled over to the pot and picked it up.

Footsteps fell from down the hall. I had to distract the guard to the point where he'd not be able to think of any other prisoner. I saw a shadow on the stone floor below, and I did my best to hold for the timing. I'd get him before he could see me there.

With a swift heave, I dumped the contents of the pot through the iron bars.

The guard must have jumped back, because I didn't see him in front of my cell. "By Malaky, what the—Is that piss?"

By Malaky? Wyranth soldiers didn't use those words. I'd missed hearing them myself. Thoughts of the king brought me comfort, reminded me of home. I moved up to the bars, clutching at some off to the side that weren't doused in urine. I pressed my head to the bars to see more clearly.

The person there stood in a Wyranth uniform, but I couldn't make him out in the shadows. The uniform didn't fit, however, similar to the way that the clothes had hung on me when I wore them, like they were meant for someone bigger.

The person in Wyranth garb stepped toward my cell.

I edged backward. Dumping a pot of urine was a badly thought out plan. It wouldn't do anything other than make the guards angrier. At least that anger would be directed at me and not someone else. I clutched my stomach, remembering the pain and bracing for what would come next.

The Wyranth soldier tilted his head at me, and I could almost make out his face. "Zair-bear?" he asked.

My eyes widened. James! He looked so ridiculous in the Wyranth guard uniform. Understanding who stood before me gave new meaning to all the sounds before he had arrived. It must have been James taking the guards down, which he did quickly before they sounded the alarm. I rubbed my eyes to make sure I didn't hallucinate.

"I come to your rescue and you try to dump piss on me?" James asked, glancing back at the puddle on the stone floor.

"I didn't know it was you! I thought you were one of the guards. It doesn't matter. James! I'm so happy to see you, and you couldn't have come a moment too soon!" I wanted to hug him, but the iron bars still loomed between us. "I don't suppose you have a key to the cell?"

"Hmm?" James blinked. "Oh," he said, fumbling through his Wyranth uniform. He reached into a coat pocket and pulled out a key ring with several keys on it. "I'm not sure which one is yours."

"Well, try them, dummy," I said.

"Piss and insults. I swear, I'm going to head right back to the Crystal Spire and forget I ever came to this ugly city," James said, trying out a couple of the keys. On the third try, the lock *clicked*, and he pushed the door open.

Even though I was grateful, and this had to be the direst situation of my life, I couldn't help but tease more. "Come on, this is far more fun. This is the type of adventure you've been dreaming about since we were kids." I smiled. Though it had been only a few weeks prior, living on our farms seemed so distant now. We had been so innocent, so naive, and what now? Before he could respond, I rushed out of the cell and engulfed him in the biggest hug I could muster.

"Oof," James said, patting me softly on the back. Then he squeezed me in earnest. "I missed you too, Zair-bear. Now let's find Captain von Cravat and get out of here before the commotion I caused gets noticed."

"It's just you?" I asked, breaking the embrace. I pulled back, and then I realized that I was dressed in only my smallclothes, as I had been since I'd been moved down here. I wrapped my arms around myself to cover my chest, trying not to blush.

"I have two other full knights with me. They're back at the entrance now, guarding in case more soldiers make their way in here."

"They let you come?" I asked, pulling back to look at him.

"I fought for it, Zair-bear. They tried to tell me that as an apprentice, this was too dangerous, but I bested Cid in combat to prove myself." His eyes twinkled in the flickering torchlight.

I beamed back at him with pride. Oh, James! "It looks like you took out the guards?" I looked down the hallway, and saw the body of the original guard crumpled against the iron bars of another cell. I felt no sympathy for him after how he'd treated me.

"Guards? As in more than one?" James blinked.

"You mean you only saw one?" I recoiled.

Tyree charged from deeper into the dungeon, his sword already drawn. It shined in the reflection of one of the lamps. He gauged who posed the greatest threat in the situation and swung for James.

I spun out of the way, pressing against the bars behind me as if they were a safety net.

In a flash, James drew his sword from his scabbard. I recalled the times back in the field when he'd used stick swords. Back then, he playfully attacked me with incredible speed. I could never keep up. Watching him move with a real sword made me tense.

Steel met steel in the dungeon hall. The loud *clang* echoed down the corridor. James kept one hand back, using only his main hand to deflect the first blows that the aggressive Tyree delivered. He kept an open stance, pivoting off his back foot.

Tyree pounded mercilessly. He was stronger than James, with a bigger, more muscular build. James was forced to retreat.

James hopped backward over the puddle of my urine, beckoning for Tyree to come at him. If he'd have acted that cocky with me, I'd have whacked him upside the head. Tyree, however, held a grin on his face, as if he knew he was the better fighter of the two and it were only a matter of time before he would defeat James.

There was little I could do. I thought about kicking Tyree from behind or trying to distract him, but I had no weapon of my own. If I did manage to garner his attention, I would have no means to defend myself.

Luck was on our side, though. Tyree pressed forward, and stepped right into the urine puddle. Surprised by the sudden slippery surface, Tyree lost his footing and had to draw back his sword to stabilize himself. His eyes went wide as James landed a deep cut to his shoulder. When James pulled his sword back, Tyree fell backward. His head landed on the stone floor with a resounding *crack*.

James winced in front of me. "Terrible way to die, head splitting to piss on the floor," he said, sheathing his sword. He looked more disturbed than the way he made light of it.

"Is everything okay?" I asked, placing a hand on his arm.

Toby scampered out of the cell, climbing and circling my body until he perched on my shoulder. He squawked in James's face, making James pull away from the hug.

"Yeah." James hopped the puddle once more and started back down the hall toward the exit. "I've never killed anyone before today. It's weird, Zair-bear. I feel a rush, power in some ways, but I also feel sick."

I jogged after him to catch up, then kept pace at his side. "I know how you feel. I killed a soldier myself a few days back. Something I thought I'd never do."

James glanced to the side to look at me. "You? You'll have to tell me about it when we get out of here." He grimaced. "It leaves this sinking pit in your stomach, you know? Ending someone's life like that. I keep telling myself the Wyranth are evil, and I had no choice, but I see the look in their eyes as life fades from them. It's like the sun setting, only…"

"Permanent," I said, finishing for him. I flung my arms around him again for another hug. We both needed it. "Oh my. In the commotion I'd almost forgotten about my father. He's in here somewhere. And what about the others? We should free them, too."

James pulled back. "I let a few members of the crew out on my way in here. Do you think there are more of them further down some of these rows of cells? How many did you bring down here? I don't think we have much time before we're noticed."

"We can't leave anyone here!"

"The orders were to get you and Captain von Cravat and go. We need to grab her and get out. I figure we send up a flare to signal the airship and wait out in the foothills. Shouldn't be too hard to hide two of us." James started down the hall again.

"James, seriously! This is crew loyal to King Malaky, not to mention it's my father you're talking about. We get everyone out."

The knights had orders to leave other behind? It didn't sound very chivalrous. I still hadn't seen the other two knights that James had come with, which meant they could be helping the others despite James's words. But I wouldn't leave anyone trapped here, especially my father.

James considered, frowning. "Part of our strategy to get in and out is to have as few people as possible. Easier to evade detection that way. This isn't exactly an easy task, breaking into the Wyranth capital. We're all likely to be killed."

"I don't care. My father's here, James." An idea struck me. "What if we took the opposite tack: let everyone out of their cells, our people or not, and cause some sort of mass confusion? We could escape in the process."

"Except you're the most prominent prisoners. Everyone would recognize you."

"Still worth a shot. Besides, who knows what kind of people are held here? We could be doing the world a service."

"You're the boss," James said and reached for his keys.

We moved from cell to cell, heading further into the dungeon and down a couple of branches of yet more cells. Soon enough, we had a few of the commandos opening doors along with us. One of the others thought to grab Tyree's keys from his body, and so we had two sets to open doors as quickly as we could manage.

After the fifth cell, we found Talyen. She sat, eyes closed, with her legs crossed. Her arms rested on her thighs, palms up. I wasn't sure why she sat like that, but I tapped on the bars with my key.

Talyen's eyes fluttered open. It took her a moment to remember her surroundings, but her eyes widened when she saw me. Still, she didn't flinch, strong even in her moment of surprise. "Zaira? You're the last person I expected to see."

"I'm here. And we're getting the others out of here as well."

"We?"

"James and the knights are working on releasing all the prisoners," I said. I turned the key in the lock and held the cell door for her. "And my father's in here. Somewhere. We have to get him as well."

"Theo..." Talyen pushed herself to her feet and followed me out of the cell. "How long has it been? It's difficult to judge time in here, being dark. I think the guards bring food at random times to throw us off."

"A little more than two days," I said. "Maybe closer to three. They've been bringing me out once a day to talk to me."

"Talk? You mean interrogate?"

"Something like that," I said with a shrug. "I'll fill you in when we get out of here. We still haven't found my father yet. I communicated with him, so he's somewhere in here."

Talyen's eyes lit up like I'd never seen. "We have to find him!"

I nodded. "Believe me, I want to find him more than anything."

James opened another cell down the corridor. "I think we're really tempting fate if we don't get out of here soon."

Talyen frowned. "From what I've seen, this dungeon is like a giant underground catacomb. It has all sorts of passages. We could go deeper in and possibly find a different way out."

"One of the guards brought me up through a different route into some fancy building. There's definitely more than one door," I said.

James spun one of the keys around his finger. "If we get stuck though, and there is only one way out, we could be dealing with the whole Wyranth army if we wait too long."

Talyen patted me on the shoulder. "If there's one thing I learned from your father, Zaira, it's to take chances. The *Liliana's* crew doesn't leave people behind, no matter the odds."

That stirred my heart. Much better than the way the knights had been ready to get a couple of people out and leave the rest stranded. I glanced down the hall.

James had gone from opening cells to winding his arm around like a clock hand, imploring everyone to make for the exit. "Rislandians, let's move!" He met my eyes, his look saying he was sorry.

I wouldn't leave my father, there was no way. If it were that dangerous to get in here, that meant another attempt would be impossible, or never be attempted at all. This would be my only chance to free him.

The rest of the *Liliana's* crew and the others flooded toward James, who pointed toward the main exit. Only one person stayed put. Talyen stood by my side. "Let's find him."

"But the others?" I asked.

"Your friend is doing a good job getting them to safety. We're Theo's only hope."

I took a deep breath to muster up my confidence, then I turned and made my way deeper into the dungeon, Talyen at my back.

CHAPTER 21

My life these days is traveling back and forth to the capital. Our crew trains, and I with them, but Harkerpal hasn't been able to fix the engines. There's some gadget or component he needs to fabricate. This might be the end of what's become our home.

An excerpt from Captain von Cravat's log
Day 40 of the Month of the Fool
17th Year of Malaky XVI's Reign

AS WE MOVED in the opposite direction of the sea of people, some of the crew broke off from the pack to follow their captain. Talyen barked orders back at them to follow James instead. It amazed me how many prisoners that dungeon held, and how fast two sets of keys could free people. It felt like I'd actually done some good, modifying James's plan, even though I'd needed rescuing myself.

"Where to? You've been further through this place than I have," Talyen said, maneuvering around one of the other prisoners in the tight corridor.

"Toby was the one who's seen him, but I think he was further down from where they kept me." I moved back toward my old cell.

"What happened anyway? We thought for sure that they would have tortured and killed you once they separated you from us." Talyen asked.

I told her about Toby and the pen, and how I'd used scraps of the cloth on my cot to pen letters, and then how I'd learned it was my father writing back to me. For some reason, I couldn't bring myself to talk about the creepy conversations with the Iron Emperor and his demands to marry me.

"That's incredible," Talyen said. "The ingenuity on your part—"

"Reminds you of my father, I know," I said, making a circular motion with my finger to let her know I'd heard that line before. I kept walking down the hall.

Talyen laughed and followed me. "That's not a bad thing, you know. What I'm more shocked about is that your little rodent actually came in useful. I suppose I was wrong in telling you not to bring him."

"I didn't bring him on purpose," I admitted. "He snuck into my pack."

"Hmm, then, the luck of the von Monocle blood is with us."

We turned a corner. The dungeon seemed to darken and the smell of mold and moisture in the air was more profound the further we went. As we delved deeper into the dungeon, more prisoners came to their respective doors, jiggling the bars, howling at us to get our attention. We'd tried to let everyone out, but there were just too many to stop. I felt terrible, but James was right, we didn't have time to come down here and get to every prisoner. There were just too many. It pained my heart to think of that fact, so I kept my eyes forward as best I could, trying not to make direct contact. Most of the prisoners here looked withered, old, as if they'd been down here for years. Some of the men had beards down to their stomachs. The place had a distinct stench to it, unhygienic. It was as if none of these people were allowed baths the whole time they were in here. Didn't the guards get sick of it?

I scanned back and forth, torn apart at the seams that I couldn't take the time to rescue these others. These prisoners, each were held solitary in a cell as I had been. They had it worse than anyone and probably deserved the most help. But we did what we could.

We'd gotten a good number of people out of cells who weren't from our crew.

Talyen kept her eyes peeled, stepping closer to a few cells when she thought she saw someone that resembled my father. "You know, it's been a couple of years. Who knows how different he might look now?" she asked.

"I bet he's thinner, with a longer beard," I said. Hopefully nothing worse had been done to him in that time.

The hall continued and, again, split into twin corridors that went on forever. We faced a choice. Clanging sounds resounded back from whence we came. That could mean only one thing—the Wyranth had already arrived. We had to pick the right hallway, and now.

"Which way?" I asked.

Talyen frowned, glancing back and forth. "Odd or even," she said.

"Hmm?"

"Pick," she said.

"Odd," I said.

"Left then. I chose odd for left, even for right." Talyen took the left path without hesitation.

"How are you sure that's correct?" I asked, following her. I couldn't have made a decision like that so randomly.

"I'm relying on your von Monocle luck."

"Wait!" I stopped, an idea popping into my head. "If Toby led the way to my father before, he would be the best one to decide which way to go."

Talyen turned to face me. "If you think that would be better. I seem to remember a propensity for him getting lost more than a keen sense of direction."

I ignored the insult, and hoped Toby did, too. "But he has gone back and forth between our cells a few times. He knows my scent, as well as my father's. It's the best chance we've got," I said. I grabbed Toby from my shoulder, though he'd dug his claws into my shirt, and set him down on the ground. "Come on, Toby. This is do or die. We need you. Find him for me."

Toby sniffed around my feet, not appearing to want to move anywhere. He went in circles, and then became distracted by his tail.

"Zaira, it was a cute idea but we have to get going!"

"Just a minute more! Please, Toby." I crossed my fingers.

Toby suddenly looked up and sniffed the air. Then he bolted back the direction we came from.

"Let's go!" I said, and ran after Toby.

I could tell Talyen wanted to protest my choice of direction, or rather Toby's, but there was no time. She had to either follow or separate from us. She chose to follow.

We all ran back down the hall to the original split point when Toby took a hard turn through a little hole in the wall that we'd missed on the way through here. We looped around and found him again. This dungeon was like Talyen said—catacombs. Secret passages, holes in the walls, they could be everywhere. One could get lost in this maze easily. We would have never known without Toby, never been able to find my father.

Toby kept us going at a breakneck pace, running down that new corridor. This hallway had no other prisoners, no longing faces begging for us to rescue them. The Wyranth had enough cells to hold the entire Rislandian Kingdom in here. My lungs burned from the frantic pace.

Toby came to a halt. I had to leap over him not to step on him. Talyen had fallen behind us, moderating her pace. She jogged to us to catch up. I doubled over, out of breath. Talyen didn't have an issue.

She looked around and frowned. "So now what? This looks like everywhere else we've been in these cells."

I raised a finger to Talyen. I needed another moment to catch my breath but could only see more corridors of cells, and none pointed toward my father. Had Toby led us on a goose chase? He could have seen the running and chasing as a game. It was something we'd done in the tomato fields back home on a regular basis.

Toby squawked and ran into one of the cells.

A silhouette appeared from the back of the cell, standing. It was a man, tall and skinny, malnourished as most of the other prisoners, with a long beard, spotted salt and pepper. His face was wrinkled, and his eyes looked like they'd seen the ends of the world itself.

It was also the face of my father, distinct and recognizable with the same chin and nose that I had. I gasped, already short on breath. "Father!" I said and rushed over to the bars. Tears came again, but this time I didn't care. I had the right to cry for my father. This was the best moment of my life.

He came to the iron bars, smiling at me with pride. I was so overcome with joy that I gripped his shirt through the bars to give him a hug, forgetting in that moment that I had the keys to open the cell.

"Might be easier without the bars in the way," Talyen said softly. She had a small smile on her face as well.

"Oh, Zaira. How I've missed you!" father said. "How, by Malaky, did you get here? Oh..." He froze when he saw Talyen. Adoration crossed his eyes, there was no doubt about it. The very way he used to look at my mother. "I see," he said.

"That's all?" Talyen quipped. She maintained her smile.

I broke the semi-embrace with my father, reaching for the cell keys. My hands shook. I could hardly control myself. With a quick twist of the key, I managed to get the cell door open.

Father rushed out of the cell and hugged me again. I'd thought he'd go for Talyen, but he made his priorities clear. He kissed my hair, my forehead, my cheeks. Then he lifted me off the ground as if I were a small child again. When I was above him, looking down on his face, I saw that he cried as well. "I never thought I'd see you again. I never thought I'd get out of here."

"I hate to break up the family reunion," Talyen said. I turned to see her staring back down the hallway where we came. "But I hear footsteps. Sounds like at least two people."

Two Wyranth soldiers appeared in the corridor, both with pistols in their hands. They must have gotten past the knights, or taken another route into the dungeon. "Rislandian scum. This little rebellion is over," one of them said, waving his gun between the three of us.

I hoped the others had been able to get out before the soldiers arrived. Though I feared for the worst.

Father put his hands up, and I followed his lead, watching him from the corner of my eye. "Please, don't shoot. We'll do as you say," he said. His voice quivered. I'd never heard him sound so helpless. Had the Wyranth tortured the fighting spirit out of him? He didn't sound like the Baron von Monocle everyone gushed about.

Before either of the Wyranth could respond, Talyen moved like the wind. It happened in a flash. Her hand went to her back. I blinked, and in that instant, she'd drawn a knife and thrown it. "Down!" she screamed.

The knife flew straight into the Wyranth's left eye. He stumbled, convulsed, then collapsed to the ground.

I knew better than even to hesitate. Talyen had told me under no uncertain terms to follow her orders to the letter. I'd been bad about that so far, but I wouldn't mess around in combat. I dove and hit the stone beneath me, bracing myself with my palms. My skin scraped on the floor. Toby scampered away with the sudden movement. I looked to the side to see my father on the ground next to me.

He didn't have fear in his eyes, at all. They twinkled with pride.

The other Wyranth soldier fired a shot toward Talyen. If we hadn't followed Talyen's lead, one of us might have been dead. The bullet ricocheted off the stone wall.

Talyen charged at the Wyranth soldier, diving to tackle him. The Wyranth was caught by surprise, and Talyen succeeded in knocking him over.

They scrambled along the floor, wrestling. I froze, scared out of my wits. All I could do was watch as they tumbled, each trying to get atop each other, retain control. Talyen grabbed hold of the pistol for a brief moment and smacked the Wyranth soldier in the face with it. He recoiled but took control of the grapple, positioning himself atop Talyen.

Father rushed to his feet, but years of sitting in that dungeon slowed his reflexes. He barely managed to right himself while Talyen and the Wyranth battled.

Talyen tried to pry the pistol from the soldier, digging with her fingernails into his hand. She succeeded, but she lost grip of the pistol itself. Both she and the soldier paused as it flew from his hands and bounced on the floor, sliding across the stone toward my father and me.

It settled just past where my father now stood, right in front of my face.

The soldier drew his arm back to punch Talyen in the face. She fell backward and into his clutches.

I grabbed the pistol and scrambled to my feet, pointing it at the two of them. I'd had a little bit of training with the weapon from the commandos back on the *Liliana*, but Talyen's body stood between me and a clean target. I held it as the commandos taught me, two hands, arms straight forward.

The soldier used Talyen as a shield, wrapping an arm around her neck. "Drop it or I break her in two!"

Talyen stared at me, struggling to get air with the choke hold the soldier had on her. "Shoot," she mouthed to me.

I glanced to my father, who stood facing them, eyes narrowed in calculation. If he moved for them, he wouldn't be able to get to Talyen fast enough. Refocusing on the soldier and Talyen, I saw it would be tough to get a clean shot. What if I hit her? I would never be able to live with myself.

The soldier squeezed her neck tighter.

I fired, the gun recoiling in my hand.

My shot truck true, the bullet hitting the Wyranth soldier in the face. He went limp, arms falling from Talyen. Then he fell to the floor.

I realized I'd been holding my breath in the whole time. I exhaled, relieved beyond belief that I hadn't killed my friend.

Talyen stepped away from the Wyranth soldier's body, gasping for air.

My father stood and walked over to her, placing a hand on her shoulder and looking down at the Wyranth soldier who had a pool of blood forming around his head. When Talyen had caught her breath, she pulled him into an embrace.

My father turned his head to the side to look at me as he wrapped his arms around Talyen in return. "Good shot, Zaira. Better than I could have done. Looks like Talyen here has trained you well."

Before I could respond, Talyen pulled my father into a kiss. I turned away as quickly as I could. Disgusting!

I heard the sounds of their lips smacking together. Those sounds echoed and made me want to retch.

When I looked over, they had concluded their all-too-public display. They walked toward me. Talyen's face had turned a hotter red than I could have ever imagined, visible even in the almost-nonexistent light.

My father had a twinkle in his eye. "Sorry, Zaira," he said. "It's been so long since I've seen Miss von Cravat here, and I couldn't well leave her in a situation where one of us might die without, ah, catching up."

Yuck. "Next time do it in private."

"Okay," Talyen said, her professionalism and tone of command returning as if that display had never occurred. "We're still in a Wyranth dungeon and need to find a way out of here before more soldiers find us." She crouched to search the first soldier's body and found a second gun. The knife she'd used was still stuck in his face. She pulled it out of him while using her foot to keep the body down.

She walked back over to us, handing my father the pistol she'd grabbed. I offered her mine in return but she waved me off.

"Can't you use this much more effectively than me?" I asked, holding it gingerly.

"Yes, but I'm just as effective with this." Talyen flipped the knife into the air with ease, and then swiped it out of the air by the hilt. "A gun's easier to use, might come in handy in a pinch for all of us to be armed."

"Anything is a deadly weapon in your hands, my dear," my father said with a toothy smile to Talyen.

Yuck again. I glanced down at the gun in my hand, and then gripped it properly, keeping the barrel down at my side. "Okay, let's go then. But where to?"

"Before I was captured, my operatives mapped this place. We had a planned rescue of several of our people here, but never got around to it. There was always some other, more pressing mission," my father said. "Fortunately, I have a perfect memory." He pointed the direction we hadn't gone yet. "If we keep following this, there should be a hidden door that leads to other tunnels. Those will lead us to the mountain behind the city. It would make for the best way to avoid the soldiers in the city, who are no doubt swarming around looking for us at this juncture."

"Theo, we had others with us. A few good members of the crew and some Knights of the Crystal Spire who came to rescue us when our own rescue attempt failed. They had already gone up into the city. What do we do about them?"

My father stared back in the direction we had come, brow furrowing in contemplation. "I think it's too late to do anything about it now. If I know our crew, they'll find a way out of this awful place. We have to trust they made it."

"I thought we don't leave people behind?" I asked.

"Not locked in a cell, but your father's right. At this point, our people are either dead or they made it out. Going back to check would be reckless and just get us into trouble. If they didn't make it, we'll find out soon enough."

I nodded, knowing in my heart that was the best strategic decision. All the same, James had been back there, and there was nothing I could do about it. My heart sank in worry. That reminded me of Toby. I clicked my tongue, and he ran over to me from his hiding place, crawling up my leg and back onto my shoulder.

"Come on," my father said, and led the way further down the dungeon's catacombs.

CHAPTER 22

King Malaky has ordered that the ship remain grounded for now. In some ways, I am relieved. It's not the same without Theo. Our crew will still train as a unit. We will operate as special forces, of a sort, for some of the king's more difficult operations.

An excerpt from Captain von Cravat's log
Day 23 of the Month of Duchesses
18th Year of Malaky XVI's Reign

A COUPLE OF turns later, we stopped in front of a solid wall. My father stood staring at it for a good, long moment. "Hmm," he said.

"It's a wall," I said.

"He knows that, Zaira," Talyen said, moving to his side. "He mentioned hidden doors before."

My father turned around, motioning me closer as if he wanted to teach me something. I wished I could share my whole life with him, even though it wasn't the time. He'd been down here for two years, and I'd missed out on that. I wanted to find out what they did to him, to tell him how much I'd learned.

He took my hand and ran it over the surface of the wall in front of us. Toby sniffed his hair from my shoulder.

"Feel that?" my father asked.

"It feels like a wall," I couldn't help but say, amused with myself, even if the older folk weren't.

"What about here?" He pushed my hand further down the wall. There was a distinctive bump where it didn't quite line up. It would have been difficult to find for anyone who didn't know it was there.

"It feels different," I said. For some reason my father's presence made me feel like a little girl again, but in a good way. I liked that he wanted to teach me his ways. It felt good, like I had family back. Even learning from Talyen felt that way to some extent.

"That's right, a slight differentiation between the levels of the wall. This is where the hidden door is." He nodded, sure of his own assertion.

"So, do we give it a push?" Talyen asked.

"That's right," my father said, giving my hand a nudge forward.

At his prompting, I pushed harder on the wall. The hidden door creaked open slowly. The screeching sound of dry gears sounded as wheels turned and opened a passage into whatever existed beyond.

"Ladies?" My father motioned for us to step through to the darkness beyond.

"Wait!" a voice echoed down the hallway behind us.

All three of us spun in one quick motion, though my movement nearly knocked Toby from off my shoulder.

Father had his pistol drawn, pointed over my shoulder in the direction of the voice. "Hold it, and drop your weapons now!" he said. His voice changed, sounding protective, like a leader. It gave me shivers.

At seeing my father's weapon, I fumbled with my own pistol, pointing it the same direction. Two guns had to be more intimidating than one.

Talyen kept her hands at her side, narrowing her eyes. Now that I'd seen them both, I noted a difference in leadership styles. While my father seemed to be more of a shoot first and ask questions later type, Talyen liked to calculate scenarios. That fact made them a good team. Balance.

A figure came out of the shadows, with two others following. It was James. He had his hands up, sword and gun holstered in his belt. "Don't shoot! It's me, James Gentry. Sorry, I should have said that first. Uh..." he motioned behind him. "These are my fellow Knights of the Crystal Spire, Cid and Frances. We're here to help."

Father kept his pistol steady and then returned it to his side. He beamed a smile. "Good, we can use all the help we can get. No telling what we'll run into down that dark path."

Talyen inclined her head as if she knew it would be them all along. "What of the rest of the *Liliana's* crew?" she asked.

"They made it out through the main city gate. On our way in, we set a timer on a device we call a tinsomatic screecher." He waved his hands. "Don't ask. The knights rely on all sorts of strange things to get the advantage. Anyway, it created a lot of chaos back there. Cid said we should leave the city with them, but I didn't see you, and I wouldn't leave. I think we may be trapped down here now though. Unless you have a new path out?" James asked, glancing to the opening where the false wall had been.

"This way will be much safer," my father said. He stepped over the threshold and took the lead. "In theory, at least. I don't suppose we have a way out of this country, do we?"

"Yes, we came in the *Liliana*," I said.

"My ship?" My father's eyes lit up before he turned to lead us. Though he'd motioned for ladies to go first before, that changed now that the knights had arrived.

Talyen followed, and I moved after that, with the knights bringing up the rear.

"You hadn't told me the story of how you arrived here, James," I said, making conversation to ease some of the tension that loomed over us. As this passageway had dirt walls, compacted, like it was a side project that had never been completed, the room was claustrophobic, seeming to close in on us from every angle. If one of those earthquakes happened like the many recent ones we'd experienced, it would be liable to cave in on us.

"Mr. du Gearsmith went to King Malaky immediately after you left. He sounded worried about what you were doing and told the king your plan to come to the Wyranth capital and rescue your father. At first, the king was pretty mad that you didn't follow his orders, but then he said he should have expected it from a von Monocle, whatever that means," James said.

"True," Father said, laughing.

"He dispatched us immediately to back you up, and we took a more direct route over land with a horseless carriage." James snapped a finger. "Hey, I finally got to ride in one. Not as much fun as an airship. The ride's much bumpier. Anyway, the Grand Rislandian Army paved the way forward, allowing us smooth travels. Since there were only three of us, it wasn't difficult to slip over the border and traverse here. We found the *Liliana* in the foothills and flagged down some of the crew still on the ship. They said you were later than anticipated, which led us to believe you'd been caught. That brought us here." He glanced back to his fellow knights.

Cid nodded approvingly as we moved along. "He's my apprentice. A quick study," he said.

"Anyway, then it was about waiting for the right time to mount a rescue of the rescuers. We needed the Wyranth to get comfortable thinking they had succeeded and that there weren't any reinforcements coming. I hope they didn't hurt you while we were assessing the situation?" James asked to me in particular.

"Other than a bizarre marriage request..." I said with a shrug.

"What?" James, Talyen and my father all asked at the same time.

"I'll tell you about it later." I remembered again that I was walking around in my smallclothes, in front of James and two other knights, no less. That with my offhanded remark made the situation far more embarrassing than I thought it would be. I blushed, glad no one could see the colors of my face change.

Talyen nudged my father in front of us. "We're chatting too much. Let's pick up the pace."

"Yes, dear."

We followed my father down the path, which was far darker than the poorly lit cells. It made it difficult to move quickly. The walls closed in around us as we moved, forcing us into a narrow, single file line.

Just as I feared, the cave trembled, growing in intensity as an earthquake hit.

I lost my footing and braced myself between the narrow walls. Pebbles fell from the ceiling, and dust kicked up from the floors, leaving us coughing.

"Another one," I said. "They're happening so frequently now."

"More here in the Wyranth capital than elsewhere, but yes. There's something going on. I aim to get to the bottom of it," my father said. He planted his feet and started walking again.

As we continued, the pathway became narrow enough that we had to squeeze through sideways.

"What do you mean?" Talyen asked.

"You don't think it's natural?"

"Not in the least," my father said. "A lot of soldiers and scientists passed through the dungeon over the years, people you wouldn't have expected to see. I watched, and tried to analyze their movements, but I didn't have any clue what was going on. This secret tunnel may yield answers."

"Is that why you took us this direction?" I asked. He might not have been taking us to the ship after all. The great Baron von Monocle had another agenda beyond getting his people to safety. It didn't surprise me, based on the stories the crew had told me.

"That's right," my father said, his tone of voice making it sound like nothing out of the ordinary.

Even though this certainly sounded similar to the stories the crew had told me about his past actions, I couldn't help but be angry. I'd risked my life. By Malaky, scores of others had risked their lives in a foolish attempt to liberate him from this evil empire. I couldn't let him risk that. "Father, we need to leave. The whole Wyranth army is after us!"

"I agree with Zaira," James said from behind. The other two knights kept quiet. They must have thought this to be an entertaining family argument.

"The both of you are perfectly welcome to walk back to the ship. I'm going to determine the cause of these earthquakes and what's been odd about the Wyranth soldiers these last years. And then I'm going to put a stop to it."

"I'm going with him," Talyen said, her tone resolved.

"If there's some sort of contraption controlling the ground like this, causing these shakes, it's going to be heavily guarded. The two of you alone won't be enough," I said.

"There you go, Zaira. Thinking like a von Monocle," my father said, continuing on his way without even a glance back in my direction. A man on a mission.

Oh, he was infuriating! "Father, don't make me drag you out of here."

He laughed. "I'd like to see you try."

"That's it," I said, pushing past Talyen so that I could reach him. I'd thought my father was dead, never dreaming of a reunion, and this was how it was going to go? Because of his stubbornness? I didn't think so.

One of the knights chuckled behind us.

That stopped my father in his tracks, he turned. "In the back, you think this is funny?"

"No, sir," Frances said, then shut his mouth.

I took my father by the wrist. "We're all obviously on edge. We're in some dark hallway that's far smaller than it should be. We have the ground giving way beneath us, and have been imprisoned. On top of that we've had a few physical battles. We're tired, we're weak. It's why we're arguing. Father, why can't we just go to the airship, get rested, and then come back and figure out what's going on here?"

"Because these quakes are getting more frequent. Something's going on, and it's in the now. Plus, we have a unique opportunity, being in this passage already. You think we'd be able to sneak up on the Wyranth capital again?" he asked me, placing a hand on my shoulder.

"We couldn't sneak up on them the first time," Talyen said.

"Exactly."

"But we still need to keep going," Talyen warned.

It was frustrating, but there was no way I could win against both my father and Talyen. And it wasn't like I could go back the way we came, anyway. I took a deep breath to calm myself. My father needed someone to help him if he was going to pull off whatever he was thinking. If I couldn't change his mind, I might as well help keep him safe.

"Fine, we go find the cause of these quakes, or whatever you're looking for."

"Trust my intuition, Zaira." My father gave my shoulder a little shake, turned around, and started moving again.

"You should, you know," Talyen said to me, stepping around me once more so she could be next behind my father. "He's a great man."

"There's an opening up ahead!" My father said. He sounded excited. "I can't quite make it out, but I think there's some sort of chamber." He quickened his pace, and we all followed suit.

The narrow hallway opened into somewhat of a larger room. It looked like an entry or waiting place, and a sealed metal door loomed at the end of it. A gas lamp was positioned to its side, lighting the area better than the lamps of the deep dungeon.

My father moved to the door, which had no handle from this side. He tugged on it, but it didn't give way. Then he tried the lamp at the other end of the hall, jiggling it when it held still. When he pulled harder, the lamp broke off the wall. He jumped back, losing his grip on the casing. It crashed to the ground, shattering on the floor in front of us.

That left us in complete darkness.

"Everyone okay?" he asked.

"I can't see," I said.

"There were a couple of lights along the way, should we go and get them and try to get this one working?" one of the knights asked.

"No, no," my father said. "Hmm, well I wasn't expecting a dead end here. I suppose there's only one thing to do."

"Turn back?" I asked.

"Of course not. That's not the von Monocle way," he said. I heard three distinct knocks on the door. Was my father insane?

"There can't be anyone but Wyranth on the other side!" I said, panicked.

"And they don't know we're not one of them," he said.

I couldn't see anything, so I couldn't see how anyone positioned themselves. At least I could feel Toby resting on my shoulder. I didn't want him scampering off in front of us. I imagined my father with pistol drawn, ready to pounce and shoot. That's how the stories posed him, at least.

Talyen remained silent, along with the other knights. They all had good military training that kept them following orders and reserved in these situations. Part of me hated that. If there were something foolish going on, someone needed to speak up.

James moved to my side and brushed against my arm. The feel of his light touch made my insides tingle. Even though it'd been only a few days, it felt like an eternity since I'd seen him. I still wasn't sure what I felt about him. He was always there for me, in some ways more of my family than anyone I knew, including my father.

The door opened, swinging outward toward whatever was on the other side. Light filled the other side, slowly bringing our room out of darkness and giving me my first glimpse of my companions since we entered the room. My eyes adjusted. The other side was much brighter than I thought it would be.

A Wyranth soldier stood there, as I'd thought. He appeared utterly confused. "Who—?"

"My good sir!" my father said, taking the lead and moving to the Wyranth soldier. He took the soldier's hand for a shake. "I thank you so much for greeting us at the door. The Iron Emperor himself sent me, you understand, to... inspect what you have inside. Make sure the operation's going smoothly."

"The operation," The Wyranth soldier repeated.

"That's the one," my father said, grinning and putting and extra amount of charm into it. It sounded ludicrous to me, especially as he stood there in smallclothes, like me, but the others looked like they enjoyed his grandstanding, by the adoring looks in their eyes.

"Why are you wearing small clothes?"

"Just woke up, good sir. You know how the Iron Emperor can get. Wants the job done now, now, now!"

"He didn't let you get dressed first?"

"No, my good sir," my father said. Now he placed an arm around the soldier's shoulder. He walked him through the door.

Talyen followed behind, then we all moved after them. James pushed in front of me as if that small act would protect me from harm.

When we stepped into the next room, I saw that it was some sort of staging area. It was well lit, but still enclosed in rock like the last tunnel had been. The ceiling extended out at least twenty feet, and there were large stacks of crates piled nearly to the top of it.

"What are the crates for?" my father asked.

"For the project's sustenance. Shouldn't you know that if you're sent to inspect?" The Wyranth soldier blinked, taking a long look over Talyen, then me.

"I was checking your knowledge, good sir," My father said, removing his arm from the man and tapping his head. "Passed with flying colors. What did you say your name was again?"

"Sergeant Wilheim," he said.

"Excellent, Sergeant Wilheim. Good job standing guard. We'll head on through and leave a good mark on the report when we return. Keep your post, good sir!"

Sergeant Wilheim started to nod, but then blinked at the knights with us. "How come they're armored, if you're in small clothes?" He slid from my father, heading back toward the next hallway behind him. "I'm going to go inform—"

"Oh, no you're not," my father said. He pistol-whipped Sergeant Wilheim in the back of the head. In a fluid motion, he caught the solider before he hit the ground. With his head, he motioned for James and the knights to help him. "Let's stuff him into one of the crates here, make it a little difficult for him to come out and follow us."

"Why don't we just kill him?" James asked.

"He seemed like a nice man. Don't kill unless we have to, m'boy," my father said. "Hmm... Strip him first. I think he's about my size."

The knights took Sergeant Wilheim and did as my father asked. They found a crate and pried open the top. When it opened, a putrid stench filled the room. James went over to look inside, and then choked in horror, covering his mouth. "By Malaky," he said.

"What is it?" I asked.

James turned away, bracing himself against the wall. He shook his head. He looked like he was moments from vomiting.

Talyen moved over to the crate next, and her eyes widened in a shock I hadn't expected to see from her typically stoic face. "Body parts. Bloody ones," Talyen whispered.

"Oh my," my father said, grimacing. "Well, we can't give them a proper burial. Perhaps we should kill this guard if that's what he meant by sustenance. No, he's just following orders, this isn't his doing. This speaks of something far eviler." He rambled to himself, but this was how he worked on the solutions to problems. Whatever he pieced together in his mind, I had no idea.

"Do you know what's going on?" I asked my father.

"No, I've never seen anything like it," my father said. He at least sounded calm. He shook himself into the Wyranth soldier's clothes all the same, and like he thought, they did fit him pretty well. At least we would look like four Wyranth soldiers, with two women in small clothes in tow. That, at least, could generate some sort of rational cover story, though one that gave me shivers to think about.

"Bodies in boxes, bizarre," he said as he plopped the helmet on his head.

"Very," Talyen said. "What could they be feeding?"

"Vampires?" James asked.

"Silly. Vampires don't exist," I said. Then I blinked. "Do they?" I glanced over at my father. I'd heard so many stories as a child, but what was real and what wasn't, well, my knowledge was still limited.

"That's a funny question, Zaira, remind me to tell you a story about—"

"Now's not the time for a Harkerpal," Talyen said.

I couldn't help but laugh at that—same with James. It diffused the tension of the moment and took our minds off the bloody mess in the crates. The knights searched the boxes until they found one that was empty, and stuffed Sergeant Wilheim inside. They placed the top over the crate, then Cid nodded to my father.

"Well then, only one way to find out what we're in for," he said, motioning with his pistol toward the next hallway. He trudged ahead and led us through.

We only had to go a small distance this time. The room opened into an enormous area, larger than I'd ever seen. It could have fit the *Liliana* inside twice. We must have been in the center of the mountain, which meant the Wyranth cored it out somehow. How much work had gone into the construction? This project must have been extremely important.

I moved Toby to under my arm. He probably wouldn't have moved from my shoulder, but I didn't want to risk him running out to where he could be seen.

The center of the room had a large rail that blocked the way to a pit in the middle. The pit itself produced a hazy blue light that pulsed throughout the entire room. It was almost overwhelming to the eyes. Still, I was glad to be in an open room with plenty of light, strange color as it might be. As it pulsed, I could see more crates piled around the room in various places. Several wooden barrels were stacked throughout the giant room, as well.

Wyranth soldiers stood all around, a good dozen or more in the space. One manned some sort of machine that had vast tubes protruding into that pit. A large crane with several brass gears on its side hung over the pit. Those gears turned, lifting a crate attached to a long rope. All the non-soldier Wyranth worked hard, whether holding the crane's robust steam exhaust port pointed toward a small aperture on the other side or turning levers on the first machine.

The machine whirred, and a couple of Wyranth soldiers moved over to it, carrying large buckets. An ooze pumped through the tubes, having the same glowing blue property as the light that came from the pit. The ooze looked just like the blue vial we'd found on the Wyranth soldier when I'd first left Plainsroad Village. The substance must have been produced here.

My father watched the whole scene and frowned.

Talyen moved to his side. "Theo, what are we looking at?" she asked.

"I have a theory, but I need to see for certain," he said and made his way toward the center of the big room. He leaned over the rail and looked down at whatever produced the light below.

From that position, he would surely attract the attention of the Wyranth soldiers. I moved forward, but James stopped me with a hand to the shoulder. "He's got the right uniform, Zaira, you don't. Stay back here," he whispered.

"Oh my..." my father said, hopping back from the pit. His eyes were wide with wonder. "I can't believe it."

Before I or anyone of us could ask what he meant, one of the Wyranth soldiers whistled at my father. "Hey, you, over here. We need some help with this."

My father turned toward the other soldier, who held one of those large buckets being filled with ooze. Without hesitation, my father sauntered toward that soldier.

The rest of us crept back into the hallway, trying not to be noticed. I peeked around the corner to see what my father was doing.

He assisted the soldier to tilt a barrel sideways toward the machine, which had a large valve that another Wyranth soldier had within his grip. As the barrel filled, the soldier controlling the valve closed it. The way that soldier slowly moved, it must have required tremendous strength. My father set the barrel down, wiping sweat from his brow. "Why'd we have to tilt it?" he asked.

"Extremely volatile fluid," the soldier said. He cocked a brow at my father. "You don't know that? I thought everyone down here had been trained."

"I forgot." My father shrugged.

I was so caught up in my father's conversation, that I didn't notice a soldier standing by the wall on our side. He turned to go down our hallway and nearly ran into me. "What are you doing here?" he asked, staring directly at me.

The knights stepped forward. "We're escorting the sergeant's concubines to greet him on his break," Cid said.

The guard didn't buy it in the least. "No one gets in here without the Iron Emperor's direct order." He turned. "Corporal! We have intruders!"

I fumbled backward, raising my pistol toward the soldier. I fired a shot, and it hit him square in the chest. He collapsed to the ground. With how well I'd been shooting thus far, I found myself liking the weapon. Much better than a sword or a knife. My father and Talyen were crazy.

Talyen stepped forward and over the downed soldier's body, waving the others to follow her lead. "Cover wasn't going to last forever anyway. Let's keep to this hallway, it's the most defensible position so far. If they come forward, we'll fall back to the room behind us. The crates will give us cover," She reached out with an arm and swept me behind her.

I didn't have a great view of the larger room. The tunnel was turned just enough to give us that cover Talyen mentioned. I glanced around her and saw several soldiers moving our direction. My father was still out there, which scared me. How long could he maintain the ruse that he was one of them?

James pulled me back from my attempt to peek. Bullets whipped past my head, hitting the rock wall across from me.

"Careful," James said.

One of the soldiers charged into the hall. He was caught by surprise as Talyen jabbed him in the stomach with her knife, drawing the blade all the way up to his chest. She left the knife in him, lifting the pistol right from his hand. Then she pushed his body forward past the aperture.

The other Wyranth soldiers opened fire into their own man, putting several holes through him. Talyen flung her arm around and fired a couple of shots over the dead Wyranth's shoulder before he completely collapsed.

I stood with my mouth agape, shocked at Talyen's ruthlessness. I couldn't see if her shots hit, but I did hear sounds of pain from the room outside. Toby squirmed from my arms and bolted back toward the last room.

"Two more down," Talyen said, turning to the side and pressing her back against the rock. "I think I spotted six more."

"Eight," I corrected her from my own observations.

"You sure about that?" Talyen asked.

"I am. I got a good look when I was watching my father," I said, happy to contribute something of use.

Talyen nodded, pride in her eyes. "Okay. All of you in tight, here's the plan," she said, crouching and turning to face us.

Before she was able to get another word in, several of the Wyranth soldiers rounded the corner and rushed us.

CHAPTER 23

I killed my first Wyranth in months today. It felt good.
Killing shouldn't come this easily, but I find it numbs the
pain of missing Theo.

An excerpt from Captain von Cravat's log
Day 40 of the Month of Duchesses
18th Year of Malaky XVI's Reign

"LOOK OUT!" I shouted, reaching my free hand forward, as if that would be of any help. Hopefully my father would hear my yell. He would be blended in with the other soldiers, at least. I hoped he wouldn't be too far away to help.

Talyen stood faced toward us, helpless against the charging enemy. She tried to spin around, but blasts rang out from the Wyranth soldiers' guns. She jerked and hit the ground, much harder than when I'd seen her duck in the past. Blood trickled from her limp body.

I stumbled backward in shock. Talyen couldn't go down. Not like this. I'd thought of her as invincible, unkillable. Amidst all of the danger before, she'd moved with such speed and precision that I'd thought the whole Wyranth army couldn't be a match for her.

Our knights reacted quickly. Both Cid and Frances fired return shots from behind me. Four of the Wyranth soldiers collapsed.

James tugged at me, dragging me back through the tunnel to the staging room we first entered. "Fall back!" he yelled.

Still in shock from seeing Talyen so helpless in her own blood, I screamed. The sound came out loud and high-pitched, and it echoed through the chamber. It might have been my imagination, but it appeared as if the pit pulsed more brightly in that moment, overwhelming even our hallway. Where was my father? Before I could think on that more, I heard a voice in my head.

ZAIRA. FIRE YOUR GUN.

The words rang in my ears, coming from everywhere and nowhere at once. I looked between the knights, but they remained focused on the charging Wyranth. Was this some sort of ghost of Talyen guiding me? The voice had too much of a male quality for that. No matter where they came from, the words reminded me that I wasn't helpless to sit and watch as soldiers gunned down my friend. Even with James pulling me back around the corner, I leveled my gun and fired three shots, which emptied my pistol's chambers.

A Wyranth soldier grunted in pain. Though I could no longer see the action, I had hit at least one of them.

The two knights who had fallen back to cover us made a push forward, hollering to distract the attention of the Wyranth soldiers. James and I retreated to the entry room, Toby was already there and moved to stay near me. James circled around one of the stacks of crates and led me there. "Stay down," he said.

"I am not sitting this fight out, especially after they shot Talyen!" I protested. "Share some of your bullets with me. I'm out."

"No! I'm here to protect you, Zaira. That's what knights do!"

I narrowed my eyes, expectantly holding out my hand, palm up. I focused my eyes on him, daring him to keep questioning me.

James handed me the bullets. One of the smartest things he's ever done.

I fumbled with the gun, trying to find where to load the bullets. I'd never done that before, even with the training the commandos gave me. It was an embarrassing time to realize that. "James, I need you to help me load them," I said.

He grimaced, then handed me his gun. "Swap you," he said, taking the bullets and my original gun. He loaded the bullets in a swift motion, clicking them into place. Then he crouched and leaned against the crate that concealed us.

The two other knights backed into the room. Frances made an error in exposing himself and several bullets pelted him in the chest. He collapsed. Cid pressed against the wall around the corner, firing his gun at the Wyranth to help draw them away from the rest of us.

James stood from his crouch as Frances went down. "No!"

"Get down, James. We'll have time to grieve later," Cid said.

A bullet whizzed by James's head. He hurriedly ducked behind the crate, joining me again. His face had turned pale as a ghost.

MOVE. KILL THEM.

The voice resonated in my head. My body wanted to comply, but that order made no sense. James and I held in too sure a spot to get up and fire weapons. Despite my rational thoughts, my legs started to move. Then I heard footsteps approaching.

The Wyranth soldiers came to the edge of the hall in front of us, guns pointing outward. I couldn't get a good line of sight on them from behind the crate.

"You should surrender now. We are right outside the capital, and even if we go down, there will be others to take our places. You're outnumbered, thousands to a few," one of the soldiers said.

"You'll kill us anyway if we surrender!" James shouted back at them.

"This is your last warning."

Three shots rang out, one after the other in succession. At first, I'd thought that had been the soldiers firing warning shots at us. What could we do? The soldier was right, we couldn't hope to escape with such odds.

James stood. My own legs wanted to move already so I joined him, dropping my gun to the floor as I assumed he meant to surrender.

He didn't surrender, but stood in awe of what he saw. Each of the Wyranth soldiers fell flat, face first into the room in front of us. I peeked behind the crate to see that they'd each been shot with perfect shots to their heads.

"By Malaky, I hate all this messy fighting," my father said, not bothering to avoid the bodies as he strode forward. He looked like the hero in the stories, gruff, strong, full of purpose. He had Talyen draped over his shoulder. "My apologies for the delay, but I was able to get a closer look at the thing below. Horrific looking stuff. It took those soldiers long enough to not be in a place where I had my back to one of them, as well. Everyone out here okay?"

James and I stood, and his knight mentor moved to my father's side to assist with Talyen. "What of Captain von Cravat?"

My father moved her carefully from his shoulder, helping Cid to place her on the ground below. The wound was clear. Despite all the shots fired before, only a single bullet had pierced her shoulder. That had been enough to soak her small clothes with blood.

The knight tore the fabric away from her shoulder, maintaining her dignity by not exposing her chest. He glanced toward the hallway, and my eyes followed. A trail of blood led back to where she had taken the wound. He frowned. "She's lost a good amount of blood, which is why she's fainted. We'll need to put some pressure on it and stop the bleeding."

"Need my knife to dig the bullet out?" James asked.

Cid shook his head. "I wouldn't take the bullet out unless I knew it caused problems where it rested. Too much risk of causing other damage through the surgery. Further, if we start digging around with your knife, which is not sterilized, there's too much risk of infection. I'd leave that to an actual medic." He pointed to one of the downed Wyranth soldiers. "Quickly, rip off a good portion of his tunic, say this wide." He made a motion with his hands as he spoke.

LEAVE HER. SHE WILL SLOW YOU DOWN.

I jabbed my fingers into my ears, twisting to see if something was stuck in there. I could hear the voice so clearly, but it wasn't coming from the room. All I wanted was for it to go away and leave me alone. It gave the worst commands. By the looks of the others around the room, still focused on Talyen's health, no one else heard it.

James gave me a perplexed look as he saw me picking my ear. He moved to one of the Wyranth and cut off some of the dead man's uniform with his knife. He held a piece of fabric up. "This work?"

"Perfect," the knight said, taking the fabric. He folded it and stretched it tightly around Talyen's shoulder and pulled to ensure it stayed. Then he tied it into a knot. With one more tug to make sure it was secure, he nodded. "This should stabilize her if she hasn't lost too much blood already."

My father paced back toward the big room we'd just left.

"What was that in there?" I asked him.

"Come with me, Zaira. You two stay here and watch over Talyen," my father said. He disappeared through the hallway.

I sped to catch up with him and reached him as he peered over the railing toward the center pit. This time, I came close enough for a good look as well.

My heart palpitated with what I saw, and I gasped. Deep down in the gorge sat a giant blob with bubbles forming across its skin. Each pulsed like a chest taking a breath, and then descended back into the main mass. The bubbles didn't have any noticeable pattern about them. The whole thing was blue and bright, just like the light that it projected. It had large veins that stretched across it, thicker than a person. They pulsed, as well.

"I don't understand," I said.

"A giant," my father said.

HE LIES.

The voice pierced through me, guiding my thoughts this time. "Those are kids' stories, Father."

"No," he said, shaking his head. "They're not. I thought they were just legends as well, but this is proof of their existence."

"Aren't giants supposed to look like a person, but, you know, giant?" I couldn't help but stare down at it.

"Long ago, when I was on... I think it was my third journey across the ocean to open trade negotiations with the Tribes of Zenwey, I came across a book. No doubt you've seen the library in my quarters?"

I nodded. His quarters smelled of old books, and he had enough stacked in his room at the house that anyone understood he read a lot. How he had time for that, I had no idea. I worked so hard from sun up to sun down with my fields that I never had any time to read. I could only imagine how it was with his responsibilities.

"The book I'm thinking of was given to me by a shaman, one attached to one of the Zenwey chiefs. She told me that those of us over on the Areth continent didn't have a grasp of true history. When the first settlers came here over a thousand years ago, they started anew and had forgotten much. This book detailed life before that, so she says. I've never heard any record of events prior to the last thousand years beyond legends and tales, so I was naturally intrigued."

"And it had these creatures, these giants in it?" I asked.

"It was said that there were men who once roamed the land, thirty feet tall, taller sometimes. That their very footsteps caused the earth to shake beneath them. They had machinery that makes our clockwork and steam engines look like children's toys. One day, one of their infernal devices caused a massive explosion, pouring vile chemicals across their land. The giants weren't destroyed, but they transformed.

"They became bulbous creatures, and their skin looked like jelly. Their brains still held intact, but they morphed from normal function as well. They could project thoughts and feelings to those around them. It was rumored that, barring some sort of accident, they could never die, that they would keep growing for eternity."

"Wouldn't they starve if they couldn't move?"

"With their projections, they could convince people to bring them their sustenance. Many tribes delivered human sacrifices to them as if they were gods. Oh my." My father glanced back over to the crates in realization. "Sustenance. It looks like this one here has been feeding off people for some time."

A shiver ran through me. Being around this giant thing gave me the creeps. And the talk of projections, could that be the strange voice I kept hearing? I would have given up anything to be out of this room. "Do they have to eat people? What happens if they don't eat?"

My father shrugged. "The book said they go dormant, lose their glow. They're able to come out of that hibernation over time. But the book also said that feeding on people was just their basic level. As we need food and water, they craved something more than simple flesh."

"What's that?"

"Emotions."

I bit my lip, thinking about the last several hours and even days that I'd been in proximity of this... thing. I'd thought I had a change in me, that I'd become more confident, taking on the roles that I'd inherited from my father. Now that I looked back on it, if my father was correct, there was a force amplifying and manipulating my will to fight. And that voice I'd heard...

"Father," I said. "I think it's been reaching into my mind."

"It has?"

"I heard a voice as we were fighting in there. It was loud. It told me to shoot, to kill." I looked at him with horror. "Can it really dictate what I'm thinking like that?"

"I don't know enough about it, Zaira," my father said, leaning over the rail again to once more glimpse the glowing bulb below. "I sensed similar. Whatever this is, it's dangerous to be here alone. You were right about that. We should leave immediately," he said.

He moved to the hall and called to the next room. "Are you able to move Talyen? I think there's an exit here from where the machines exhaust their steam. It'll be tight, but it's better to head that direction than back through the Wyranth capital."

"It'd be best not to," Cid said, "but I don't see a choice. We have to get her to a medic quickly."

"We have to get to the airship. They have a great medic. It was incredible how fast he healed Zaira before," James said, making his way into the hallway. With the help of the other knight, James lifted Talyen, moving with careful steps.

"Hopefully they haven't left without us," I said.

James reached into his vest and pulled out a small pistol-looking contraption, patting it as he grinned at me. "It won't be a problem. I told them to wait for me to give them a signal. After the rest of the crew returns to them, they'll be just off the coast in flight, looking for us and waiting to swoop down for the rescue."

"What's that?" I asked.

"It's called a flare gun. It shoots fireworks into the air. The knights have all sorts of cool gadgets that I wish I'd known about."

"Wonderful," my father said, peeling himself from me. "I'm glad to hear that the knights are as resourceful as ever." He made his way over to the exhaust shaft, stepping over some of the piping lines from the machinery. He paused, glancing at the goo being extracted from the creature. "Anyone got a canteen or a small jar?"

"I do," Cid said. He motioned his head to me. "It's attached to my belt."

I removed the canteen from its clip and brought it over to my father.

When my father took it, he tilted the canteen back over his mouth, downing the last of the water inside. He shook out the last drops, and dunked the canteen into one of the containers carrying the glowing azure goo. He jutted his head forward, sniffing the substance, and then made a face of disgust. "Whatever they're extracting from this thing smells worse than wombat droppings.

I'm sure some of our researchers would be interested in figuring out what this is."

He twisted the cap back onto the canteen, tossed it to me to hold, and pressed forward into the exhaust shaft.

I caught the canteen and placed it under my arm.

Toby scurried out from the other room and scampered up to his perch on my shoulder as I followed my father into the shaft.

We moved through, one by one, with Cid last, carefully maneuvering Talyen through the aperture created by the exhaust shaft. It was dark inside the shaft, though I could see light out the other side. It gave me a little thrill. The sun! I'd never thought I'd bask in its rays again.

The shaft proved a steep climb. James and Cid struggled to keep Talyen steady through the ordeal. Fortunately for our footing's sake, the Wyranth hadn't spent much time smoothing out the surface. It left plenty of natural ledges and rocks to give us footholds and grips.

My father and I were out first, allowing us to help James and Cid bring Talyen out safely. We'd made it back to the outside world. The area around the exhaust vent was dead. Dirt, rocks, old dried out foliage that couldn't have survived the hot steam they poured through here and whatever chemicals came along with it. Beyond the patch of death was a small clearing with tall grasses and trees that expanded into a dense forest. There were no signs of villages or of people on this side of the mountain—strange, given it was so close to the Wyranth capital.

"They call this Devil's Mountain, you know," my father said. He was like an encyclopedia of knowledge thus far. He'd told me about empires and lands I'd never heard of before, so his intimate knowledge of Wyranth Empire landmarks came to no surprise. "Perhaps that title had a very real meaning to it that was lost in time. If it's true that creature inside has been influencing people for generations, it's no wonder the Wyranth have been so aggressive."

"Huh," I said. "That explains a lot."

"What?" James asked, shielding his eyes as he glanced around.

"The war. What if this aggression is all because of the thing inside? Think about it. The Wyranth attack us relentlessly, almost mindlessly. They don't give up and don't care if it's in the name of slaughter and for little other cause." My eyes widened. "If we destroy that thing, we might be able to have real peace with the Wyranth."

NO. PEACE IS DANGEROUS. MUST DESTROY.

"Whatever's projecting into my head doesn't like my thought process," I said, rubbing my temples. I wanted nothing more than to get that voice out of my head.

My father placed his hands on his hips. It was a thinking pose—I'd seen it before. It was when he got creative ideas. "Zaira, that's a very good conclusion. Hmm, it couldn't hurt to try."

"Try what?" I asked.

"To blow it up," my father said with a grin.

I sighed. By Malaky, my father was exhausting. We'd already been through so much. We needed some time to recharge, heal up before mounting such a dangerous plan. Was this the life the *Liliana* crew had signed on for? They must have had endless stamina.

"Well, we have to get to the airship first," James said, holding the flare gun into the air while propping Talyen up on his opposite shoulder.

"No!" Cid said, nearly dropping his end of Talyen's limp body in the process. "We only have one shot, James. We have to wait until nightfall or they'll never see us."

"We can't wait here, then," I said. "We're too exposed."

"Zaira's right," my father said and pointed away from the mountain. "Some of the trees are pretty thick over there. We'll set Talyen down and rest, take turns keeping watch."

We set off toward the trees at my father's command. Even though we were at the foot of the mountain, the walk still had a slope that made for a descent into the forest. It brought me some comfort to know we had a whole Devil's Mountain between us and the Wyranth capital. However, I wished we could be further away from that blasted place. Once they realized what had happened in their strange laboratory, they would pull out all the stops to search for us.

We waited several hours, sitting, talking, and catching up on the last couple of years. The conversation naturally split between my father and myself, and James with Cid. I couldn't have been happier to have a conversation with my father after all that time. Though he'd spent most of the last couple years in a solitary cell, he told me of how he devised games with himself by scratching lines into the stone. He came up with a strategy game involving armies and their commands, using different numbers to represent different types of units.

"I'll have to develop that into pieces when I return to Rislandia," he said. His voice gushed with pure happiness as if being alive itself held reason for joy. It brought me warmth inside, and that warmth removed a lot of the tension that kept me awake.

I fell asleep under a large stumped tree with thick leaves and branches.

CHAPTER 24

Of all the crew, I believe Marina impresses me the most. I wouldn't tell her that, of course, but she reminds me of myself rising through the ranks. I was happy to give her a promotion today to Lieutenant Commander.

An excerpt from Captain von Cravat's log
Day 4 of the Month of Dukes
18th Year of Malaky XVI's Reign

I JOLTED AWAKE to a fizzing sound, followed by a *boom* and *crack*. "Wyranth!" I shouted, reaching for my gun. I used my free hand to push myself up to my feet faster than I should have, dizzying me in my post-sleep haze. Toby used a nearby tree to conceal himself.

The sky lit up with brilliant white light, much stronger than the moon and stars. It brightened our camp considerably, revealing the faces of my party in the concealment of the shady forest. It was just the flare gun.

I looked at James, seeing his features, his neck stretching upward to the sky and eyes lit up. Seeing him like that made me realize that if our ship could spot the flare, so could the Wyranth soldiers. "Doesn't the flare leave us exposed?" I asked.

James didn't seem to hear my question. "Wow," he mouthed. "I'll have to get my own when we get back."

Cid watched the sky along with James, and then acknowledged me. "We discussed that while you slept. It's a risk, but it's the only

247

way we can be sure the *Liliana* finds us in short order. Traversing through this territory on foot would be far riskier." The fire paled in comparison to what we'd just seen. The night air behind Devil's Mountain held a cool breeze that bent the flame eastward.

My father sat at Talyen's side, his hand clutching hers. She'd been lain down, close to the fire lengthwise, with her head resting atop a Wyranth uniform jacket. Another jacket covered her torso, the best comfort that could be mustered in our current position.

From her side, my father looked up at me, the first to notice that I still held my gun drawn. "Easy there, Zaira," he said. He sounded amused.

I set the pistol down against a protruding tree root I'd used as a pillow for the last several hours. Toby sniffed it. "Sorry. I didn't expect to wake up to such a strange noise."

"You should have seen the look on your face," my father said, then laughed. "I'm so glad that I can see your face again, and that you can make me laugh. You've always made me laugh, Zaira." He sounded nostalgic, then looked away, down at Talyen.

It was then I noticed her eyes were partially open. She groaned.

"She's awake!" I said, moving over. I dropped to my knees beside her, on the side opposite my father.

"Hi," Talyen said. Her voice was weak, and she tried to smile, but winced in pain.

"I thought you... I thought you'd..." I couldn't say it. As much as Talyen and I had had our tiffs, I respected her, and she'd become one of my closest friends. Now that we'd shared a terrible experience, imprisoned by the Wyranth and not knowing if we'd ever be able to get out alive, I daresay she became family. I didn't want to lose her or even consider the prospect of it.

"Now that we have Theo back, there's no way I'm going anywhere," Talyen said.

My father squeezed her hand. "No, I expect you won't." He looked up at me again. "Zaira, I told her about what you thought of the evolved giant back there, and how it might be the thing that's driving this endless war. At the very least, whatever's in that goo is being used to supply something in the Wyranth army. We're all in agreement that it should be destroyed."

"Yes, good analysis," Talyen said. "We talked some logistics."

"You say that as if there's something we can do about it," I said. I knew we'd have to go back to King Malaky and face him after defying his plans. In all of this, I hadn't had time to even think of the consequences back home. I'd been too focused on rescuing my father. From the sounds of things, we weren't going to be heading to Rislandia soon. "Are we going to break back into the Wyranth capital?" I asked, unsure of what Talyen had implied.

My father laughed again. "No, that's not what we're intending at all."

Talyen cleared her throat and shifted. She looked as if the pain were about to overwhelm her.

"Perhaps we should leave you alone, dear. I can fill Zaira in," my father said.

"No, no," Talyen waived him off as best she could. "You may recall that General Carwell made some modifications to the ship before we left, upgrading our combat capabilities. While you saw most of them, there's one that he and I kept a secret for worst case scenarios." She paused, collecting her breath. "There's an explosive device packed into the cargo hold. It has a big enough payload that I'm told it could level the Wyranth castle. We had it in case someone tried to capture the airship. A self-destruct option in case it fell into enemy hands."

The whole castle? I couldn't imagine an explosion that large, and I'd only seen parts of the castle from the inside. My eyes widened. "That's..."

"A last resort. It was prudent. They didn't intend on using it unless they absolutely had to," my father said.

Such destructive force didn't sit well with me, even if Talyen and my father approved of it. If something went wrong, if Marina had discovered it, such a power could be put to terrible use.

I glanced over to James, who hadn't listened at all. He'd returned to his own conversation with Cid seated across the fire from us. He looked so happy, finally getting to achieve his dreams. Perhaps when we left this awful empire I'd feel the same. "How big is it? Are we going to be able to get it into the chamber?"

"I think we'll be okay. Takes about six people to carry," Talyen said. Her eyes drifted off to the side.

"And I think that's quite enough, Talyen dear," my father said, giving her hand a squeeze. He carefully extracted his other arm from behind her, ensuring she was comfortable. Then he stood, stretching. "I'll be happy when we can blow this thing to bits and get out of here."

"It'll be a long time before then," said a feminine voice that came from the dark of the forest.

I scrambled to my feet and spun, hearing James and Cid doing the same behind me. A Wyranth soldier moved incredibly fast, hurtling over the tree root where Toby was hidden. Even though we all stood as fast as we could, the Wyranth had his gun trained directly on me. I couldn't do anything while he approached.

"No sudden movements," he said, his accent thick. None of us dared defy him, as it would have meant my certain demise. He whistled and other Wyranth soldiers approached as well, including someone I hadn't expected—Marina.

She grinned and sauntered toward us before putting her gun directly up against my head. "Well, Baronette, you've caused quite a stir in the capital. I've never heard the populace so panicked. You're infamous on your own right now."

I wanted to shout at her that she was a traitor, that she'd never get away with this, but I didn't want to press my luck.

My father didn't move, but watched Marina, appraising. I couldn't see what James and the knight did, as they were out of my view. Part of me expected Talyen to fire a well-timed shot right into Marina's skull, but Talyen remained still, faded from consciousness.

"Let us go, Marina. It's over. You don't need us anymore," I pleaded. Maybe our friendship could get us through this?

Marina laughed. "Oh, that's rich. It's not over in the least." Her gun didn't waiver. "You see, I intend on taking that ship as soon as it arrives."

I scanned the forest behind her as best I could to look for Toby, but I couldn't spot him in the darkness. "That'll never happen, Marina," I said. "Come on, back on the *Liliana* you were a different person entirely, can't you see that? You're being influenced here. It's not natural. Even if you were convinced into spying, there's someone else within you. There's good. I've seen it."

I tried to communicate my good intentions to her as if by my will alone, hoping that would be strong enough to have some effect, and hoping I was right about her. Whatever that voice had been, the one in my head pushing me to violence, it had influenced her completely.

I heard a distinct *whirring* coming from above and to the west. The *Liliana* had arrived in an untimely fashion.

The airship's arrival served as a small distraction to Marina, who turned her head to take a look. Was this the time to jump her? From all I'd seen of Talyen and the others, that's what the *Liliana's* crew would do. I thought that's what my father would do as well, but he didn't move. Was he waiting for me? I readied myself for action, then hesitated.

The moment I could have overtaken her disappeared as soon as it had come, and Marina had returned her focus to me. She frowned. "I hate doing this to you, Baronette. I really do. You were so kind to me on that ship, and still, you show this faith in me..." She faltered. I saw it in her eyes. She shook her head as if fighting off something. "No, we need to be careful. I've seen how these people operate. One slip up and they'll turn the tables."

Was she talking to the voice inside her? I shifted my eyes to my father, who acknowledged me with the smallest inclinations of his head. How could I reach her? *What would you do, father?* Honesty was my only hope. "Marina, something has control over you. I don't know how, I don't know why. But think. Fight it!

You can come with us, return to Rislandia. I promise you'll have sanctuary there."

The other Wyranth soldiers started to rumble. "Orders?" one of them asked Marina as if trying to get her back on track.

Marina's eyes met mine and locked there. She studied me, curious at first. Her eyes narrowed.

I tried to project acceptance, friendship. I'm not sure if I could pull off puppy-dog eyes but, by Malaky, I tried. *Please, Marina!*

She lifted her gun into the air. The turbines from the airship caused the wind to pick up around us. My hair blew into my face. A couple of the Wyranth soldiers covered their own faces with their arms. Trees and branches shook. Leaves blew everywhere.

My father pivoted toward Marina, but I held up a hand for him to stop. I don't know why I did. He had experience in these matters. My gut, however, told me reasoning with Marina would be our best chance to get out of here. It felt right. We'd already had the oddest of days with a strange blob creature being pumped for strange goo. The normal course of action didn't seem to be the right procedure in any of this.

In keeping with that oddness, my father followed my lead and stopped.

"Soldiers, I have this covered. The girl is a defector and will assist me in securing these others," Marina said. "The ship will have sent landing parties west of here, though. I overheard them before we took them. Go and find them."

The soldiers muttered. Her story smelled fishy. None of them moved, despite her orders. Perhaps Marina didn't have the rank she appeared to when she arrived? Or they could have come to the realization that she had been the one defecting.

"Now!" Marina shouted at them, with a deep, guttural command that mirrored some of what I'd heard of Talyen projecting over the turbines on the *Liliana*.

With that, the soldiers spun and followed her orders. They retreated into the forest.

Before I could blink, James and Cid had flanked my sides, edging in their shoulders in front of me so to shield me from any potential weapons fire from the Wyranths' direction. My father was on Marina a moment later, twisting her wrist and knocking the gun out of her hand.

It fell, but my father grabbed it right out of the air. He twisted it around to press against Marina's side. "Well then, this is the position I'm much more accustomed to being in. It's been too long." A wicked grin crossed his face.

James drew his sword, doubling the threat to her.

"No!" I shouted, pushing my way through the men in front of me. They were much bigger than me, even James, and it felt like pushing against solid rocks, but I had determination. I pushed Marina aside and shielded her from what was now my father's gun.

Marina turned to run behind me. James cut her off and ensured she wouldn't be able to follow the rest of her squad.

"Zaira, she's working with the Wyranth. This is some sort of trick," my father said.

"No, it's not. I got through to her. Trust me," I said to him. I pushed the wind-blown hair out of my face once more and touched his arm.

My father frowned. "Are you sure about this?"

I nodded. My heart fluttered. It was the second time I'd made a decision and my father deferred to me. Was I getting the hang of this?

Marina breathed a sigh of relief. "Zaira, thank—"

Before she could finish, I grabbed her by the shirt and jerked her toward me. She grunted as I brought her face close to mine. "Listen. I'm giving you the benefit of the doubt because there's some weird creature in that mountain, and we don't know what it's doing to our minds. You'd better not make me sorry, you hear?"

"I hear," Marina said, her voice much more subdued, submissive. "Thank you," she whispered.

"Okay then. Ship should be here, yes?" I asked, looking up to the sky.

Sure enough, I saw the bottom of the *Liliana's* hull, part of her massiveness covering the moon, but not completely blocking out its light. It wasn't that high above us.

Marina spun, tensing as if she heard something. "I think my soldiers realized I lied. They're back!"

James had drawn his gun in his non-sword hand and fired. Cid unleashed his own rounds. Howls of pain came from the trees shrouded in darkness behind us. The fire flickered, which gave away our position and left us sitting ducks while the Wyranth soldiers loomed in darkness.

"Put the fire out!" I yelled. James understood and nodded to me, rushing toward the flame. "Sorry," he said to Talyen who still lay there slumbering. He grabbed the jacket-turned-blanket off Talyen and draped it over the fire.

Before he could get the flames out, several shots fired in our direction. Marina hit the ground in front of me and tugged at my ankle to force me down with her. Surprised, I landed on my backside with a *thud* that sent my tailbone shaking. It would hurt to sit for days. "What was that for?" I asked angrily, trying to catch my breath.

"I'm saving your life," she said.

Now the odds were even. I flipped myself over prone beside Marina. The soldiers could see us as well as we could see them, which was to say not at all. I leveled my pistol toward the darkness, waiting for some sign of movement or sound of footfall.

My father, James, and Cid all crouched. I could see them making hand motions in the darkness. Then James and Cid headed for a different tree to provide cover. My father stayed beside Talyen.

"We should find a good place to hide as well," Marina whispered.

I crawled toward a tree, but my palm landed on a twig. It wasn't much of a *crack*, but with how quiet everyone was being, it was deafening to me. The Wyranth probably couldn't have heard it above the whir of the airship above, right? I held my breath, unmoving for a long moment.

Shots fired in our direction once more, and toward me! The Wyranth had heard.

I rolled away from where I'd been. Bullets sped past me, pelting the ground where I'd been a moment before. My friends returned fire almost instantly. More curses came from the Wyranth soldiers. We did a better job picking them off than they had us, for now.

This couldn't keep up forever, though. There were too many of them, even if we'd managed to get lucky at first. If the soldiers were smart, they would call for reinforcements, and this close to the capital, they could easily arrive before we could escape. Then they would completely overwhelm us. The longer the Wyranth delayed, the greater advantage they had.

I remembered days before, when Talyen projected her voice so loudly that it spurred the *Liliana*'s crew on. If we could get the crew down here, we could turn the tides in our favor. I looked up. Was it even possible for them to hear me from this distance?

The airship hovered, then moved again, back the direction they had come. Panic struck me. What if they thought the flare was a false signal, and they couldn't find us? We would be trapped.

I took a deep breath, summoning all the sheer command and strength my voice could produce. "*Liliana* crew!" I shouted louder than I ever had in my life. My throat burned, but I continued. "We need you here! For steam and country!"

The *Liliana* continued in the same direction, and I thought my efforts were for naught. Hope disappeared as sure as the ship moved away. I instinctively reached a hand toward the sky as if that would do anything to bring the *Liliana* back.

The moon came back into view, shining its light down on the forest. Though everything had a bluish tint, at least I could get my bearings better. I wasn't alone in that thought. My party and Wyranth soldiers alike weaved through different trees, seeking new, better covered positions.

Then the ship stopped, hovering in midair. Someone up there must have heard me. I waved frantically, though I stopped soon after. It was still dark out, the odds of them seeing me were low, but that kind of movement would draw Wyranth attention. I'd been lucky it hadn't already. The *Liliana's* crew either knew where I was or didn't, and nothing would change that.

I peeled my eyes from the ship to look back down at my surroundings. My shout had done as I'd feared. I spotted too many Wyranth soldiers with guns trained on me. They advanced.

Before I could raise my gun to fire, shots rang out in the distance. Several bullets came in my direction. I recoiled, blocking my face with my arm.

The bullets grazed my skin on my sides and my arm. Though none lodged in me, the pain was beyond anything I'd ever experienced. I couldn't hold myself upright and tumbled into some foliage below me. I hit my head on a rock.

"Zaira!" my father yelled, firing off several shots at Wyranth soldiers as he dove toward me.

The world spun around me. Several figures of my father appeared to float about. Just as many or more Wyranth soldiers dropped from gunfire. My father moved in a fury like I'd never seen, and his marksmanship made Talyen's look like child's play. I was so woozy, I couldn't tell if any of it was real.

The end of a long rope hit the ground beside me, then another in front of me. I managed to twist my head upward and saw commandos sliding down on them. Above loomed the familiar darkness from before. It was so cozy, making me want to fall asleep.

I heard shouting, some more gunfire, and then feet upon the ground. The crew who descended the *Liliana's* ropes hovered around me. Though they tried to keep their expressions flat, I could see grave concern on their faces.

Toby, wherever he'd scurried off to during the whole incursion, appeared by my side. He licked my face.

I faded in and out of consciousness, and the next I saw, my father's face was in front of me. "Zaira. Zaira! How badly are you hurt?" he asked. I'd never heard him in such fervor. His voice was so loud, booming. It hurt my head. I wanted to sleep. I was so tired. It was from the hit on my head more than the gunfire, though those grazes stung like none other. I wanted to tell him that, but I couldn't manage to speak. Even keeping my eyes open made my head spin, made me sick.

I succumbed to a darkness much blacker than the forest had been moments before.

CHAPTER 25

It's been a long time. I stopped writing in this journal months ago. It was Theo's idea to keep one to begin with, and I saw it as a way to hold onto him. I don't know what brought me back today. Perhaps it's because it is the anniversary of the day I met him. I miss him more than anything.

An excerpt from Captain von Cravat's log
Day 15 of the Month of Queens
18th Year of Malaky XVI's Reign

I AWOKE IN my father's cabin, tucked into the lavish sheets. Light peered through the shutters, flickering across my face and causing me to turn away. I groaned. Nothing had ever ached so badly in my life. The first thing I saw was my father, slumped against a corner on a stool. He'd been waiting for me to return to consciousness. "Father," I said.

My father shook his face to alertness. His hair was frazzled, face gaunt with age lines showing a profound weariness. "Zaira, you're awake." He placed a hand over his heart as if it ached. "I'm so relieved. You have no idea."

"What happened?" I asked, trying to sit up. That attempt proved overly optimistic. My body refused to comply, and I fell back down onto the bed. It was all I could do to prop my head on my pillow and find a more comfortable position.

"Three bullets grazed you out there and you suffered a head wound. I'm so sorry I got you into this. I truly am. Can you forgive me?" My father leaned over my bed, took my hand, and squeezed it. A protective parent, even two years out.

Before I'd lost him, I would have found that protectiveness annoying, but now it filled my heart with warmth. I had him back. My father lived, and he sat in a chair across from me. "Nothing to forgive. I made my own choices."

He considered for a long moment, brow wrinkling, then gave a half nod. "That you did. That you did. I'm quite proud of you."

A thought occurred to me. "Where's Toby? He's usually the one to wake me up."

"Who? Ah, the ferret. I'll have to ask you how you got that boisterous little thing another time. I sent him to James's quarters so you could rest uninterrupted."

"Oh," I said.

A knock came on the door, and Harkerpal peeked his head inside. "Hope I'm not interrupting. I wanted to see how Zaira was doing."

"Not at all," my father said, inclining his head toward the engineer.

I could barely move to acknowledge the engineer. "Hi, Harkerpal." I said. Then to my father, "How long did I sleep?"

"A little over a day. We took the *Liliana* back out over the sea to recuperate and discuss plans. The elixir the medic gave you seems to be doing wonders. Thank Malaky she was assigned to the *Liliana* all those years ago, and that she hasn't wanted to be anywhere else," my father said. "I've had one or two life-threatening scrapes myself."

"Indeed, I could tell the story of the first time we had a crisis aboard the *Liliana*. Remember, Baron, when you came back with a treasure chest found buried in the Sands of Zarma, and the crew started to get those strange boils? Well, the medic figured that—"

"Perhaps later, Harkerpal," my father said with a knowing smile. "Zaira still needs to relax. She took a head injury."

259

It seemed everyone had the right of how to deal with Harkerpal's exhaustive speaking habits. It didn't annoy me, lying there—I found it comforting. Harkerpal gave me a sense of home as much as anyone else aboard.

"Very well, Baron," Harkerpal said. He raised a finger, then bobbed his head several times. "Ah, I meant to speak with you. The explosive device has been secured and is ready to be delivered dirtside. My team and I have rigged it with wheels and a steam powered gear crank that should be able to traverse a dirt and foliage terrain. We weren't, however, able to secure a steering mechanism. It will require several members of the crew pushing to keep it on course."

"Excellent, Harkerpal. We are blessed that Talyen could coordinate this effort after her injuries," my father said. He shifted his eyes to me and smiled.

"We have a good crew. The *Liliana* can almost run herself," Harkerpal said.

"Almost," my father and I said simultaneously. All three of us laughed, the men more than me, since each instance of laughter jolted my wounds and brought about poignant reminders of my pain.

The creature within the mountain. They were going to strike soon, while I was stuck in bed. "Wait, I want to be a part of that team," I said.

My father patted my hand sympathetically. "Zaira, there's no way. We need to complete this mission *now*. The longer we wait, the more time the Wyranth will have to reinforce Devil's Mountain. Now that they know we've been in there, it'll be dangerous enough as it is."

"I'll leave you two to talk," Harkerpal said, giving me a small wave. "Good to see you feeling better, Zaira." He shut the door behind him.

"This is my mission as much as it is yours," I said.

My father's countenance turned somber. "You're injured, and you don't have the proper training."

"I rescued you, didn't I?" Technically, it had been James and the knights who saved him from my failed rescue attempt, but I didn't need to bring it up. "I'm not just some little farm girl anymore. I took care of myself when I was gone, and I've helped with missions. I'm a part of this crew as much as anyone."

"Zaira, you need to be resting," my father said. "Besides, this is more of a mission for the crew. I'm sure you have all sorts of stories about my swashbuckling this or raiding that, but the truth is, most of the time, I stayed with the ship. The 'Great Baron Von Monocle,' while flattering as a term, makes me a symbol. More than that, I'm in charge of this ship and need to be here in case feces hits the turbines. We're in enemy territory."

"Then you should stay on the ship," I said stubbornly.

"Zaira," my father warned.

"You're trying to protect me, and I don't need protection. I've been living for two years on my own. Danger doesn't frighten me anymore. I've seen it. I've stared the Iron Emperor in the face."

I tried to cross my arms, but I found that impossible due to one of the bullet wounds. Even the slightest twitch set off incredible pain. I winced, but tried not to let it show beyond that. Deep down, he was right about my condition, but a little of the medic's powerful elixir and I'd be fine.

"Of course I'm trying to protect you," my father said, eyes widening. He stood, pacing beside the bed, moving over to his dresser with the photographs of our family on top. He picked one up. "First, because you're my little girl. And I know you're grown up and your own woman now, you don't have to remind me." He blinked. "The Iron Emperor?"

"Long story." I found myself blushing.

"But your name makes you a symbol, as well. And not just because of me now. Did you know that Marina's Baronette title has started to catch on among the crew? They think of you as a leader now, Zaira. It means we shouldn't go out on missions at the same time. If something should happen to me—"

"It won't."

"Last time I ended up in a dungeon for two years," my father said, eyes piercing into me.

Something about the conversation struck me then. "Wait, you mentioned Marina. Before, you said she found something about the creature and the goo?"

"Ah yes, this is where it gets interesting. You see, the von Monocle luck stayed with you when those bullets grazed you. But when you fell, I'm afraid your head wound was far worse than you realized. That's where Marina comes in. You were right. I believe something manipulated her into her betrayal. When she found I had a canteen filled with the blue goo from that monster in the mountain, we could barely hold her back from it. At the time, we had her under guard and bound. She rambled like a madwoman, or so we thought. I posted a sentry to listen to her anyway. It turns out she was actually trying to save you."

He turned back, eyes locking on me with dead seriousness. "Whatever you said to her, it overpowered whatever this blue goo did to her. That's another reason why we need you safe. My diplomacy is better with the sword, you have a way with words. Perhaps it comes from your mother's side."

"I speak from the heart," I said.

My father smiled. "That's my girl. When she calmed down, we found that the goo, which the Wyranth call the vitality ether, has restorative properties, even beyond our medic's regular elixirs. There are side effects, which our scientists will study later, but you had lost so much blood, we took a risk."

I bit my lip. I was restored by this giant goo—vitality ether? It meant I'd drunk some bodily fluid from that disgusting creature inside Devil's Mountain. And what was it doing to me? "Do you know what the side effects are?"

"So far all we've seen is increased aggressiveness in limited quantities. Which I've definitely seen in you thus far in how argumentative you are. Moreover, you were thrashing in your sleep. I almost had the medic restrain you but he didn't want to risk waking you." My father laughed. "I'm very interested in finding out more. This could be a large reason why the Wyranth soldiers are so relentless, if they're being fed a steady stream of the stuff."

My father smiled at me. "I should check on Talyen and let you rest."

"What about her? Did she have to take the vitality ether?"

My father shook his head. "She was able to recover by normal means. Normal by our medic's standards but normal nonetheless. Get some sleep, Zaira."

Did he just dismiss me? I wasn't a simple member of the crew that he could do that to. I opened my mouth to argue, but soon realized it would do no good. He had his mind made up as sure as I did. I would just have to find some other way onto the mission. It felt rather deceptive, but I hadn't promised my father I'd stay put in his quarters.

He waited, watching me, and then slipped out the door.

I stayed still for a few more moments to make sure the coast was clear. I felt like I was a child again, pretending to go to bed while I watched my parents through a crack in the door as they set out presents for the Grand Harvest Festival. My heart yearned for those days again.

I stretched my legs out, tight from having been in the same position for more than a day. Then I pulled the covers off me and dangled my feet over the side of the bed. My new position allowed me to slide to my feet. My toes froze as they hit the cold deck floor. I stayed leaned against the bed, not ready to try my full weight yet. My body ached and protested, and my head spun. So much for a vitality ether. Perhaps they hadn't given me enough of the stuff.

I had to get outside if I wanted to join the mission team. If I couldn't stand, there was no way I'd be able to prove myself ready. Barring being able to do that, I would need the strength to make the rope descent on my own and evade my own people.

I bit down hard on my bottom lip and forced my weight onto my feet. With a stumbling step, I was upright. I held my arms out to keep my balance, then concentrated on the door.

It took me several more minutes to get out of the quarters, but I managed it and, soon enough, I made my way through the mess hall.

Several of the crew sat along the benches, eating and socializing. The ship was moving back toward Devil's Mountain, giving a sensation of a gentle tug forward. I snuck over to the kitchen area to grab myself a snack.

James leaned over one of the tables, chatting with the crew. His eyes lit up as he saw me, and he enthusiastically waved me over. "Zair-bear, you're awake! Come join us!"

I shook my head. "Can't," I said, quickly stuffing a piece of fruit into my mouth. "Need to... uh..." I tried to think of an excuse, looking toward the door in front of me. "...be out on the deck. Later?"

"Baron's orders, hmm? Heard a lot of that since I've been back. Well, glad to see you're up and at it." James made a friendly gesture and went back to conversation with the others at his table.

Step by step, I forced my way to the door. I stayed focused, knowing that with a single stumble, every member of this crew would try to stop me over concern for my injuries. It felt like hours, though I knew it was only a matter of seconds before I made it to the door. A great triumph in my own mind, if nowhere else.

My excuse to James was a good one. I had to go out to the deck anyway. No, I had to find a place to stow myself and hide so I could make the drop when we arrived. I had one problem as I recalled the layout of the deck—the exterior of the ship was too open. It had the turbines, the rope holders, the deck—but all those places could be seen from the main bridge. The pilot would be looking right down on me if I didn't find somewhere to hide.

I twisted the door handle and stepped onto the deck anyway. Looking around, I saw that I was right, but there was some netting up against the bridge I could use as cover. At least I could look inconspicuous there. But walking on the outside of the airship when it was moving at such speeds was a whole different proposition than my already strained maneuvering on the inside.

Within moments of my reaching deck, I'd stumbled over to the port rail. I pressed my stomach against the rail and wrapped my fingers around it to stay secure. My eyes went wide as I stared down at the clouds below and at patches of farms and landscapes as we zoomed overhead. I recalled what my father had said, that the *Liliana* had gone back out toward the sea, and now we had to return to the mountain to complete this new mission. In the daylight, I could see the shadow the *Liliana* cast upon the Wyranth countryside.

Something moved on the ground, which surprised me. From this height, it should have been impossible to make out individual people. I righted myself so I could still see but not be in any danger of falling. Those spots on the ground grew, as if they were moving toward us. Those weren't people at all.

We'd come across the Wyranth anti-airship artillery. A cannonball flew right past my face.

CHAPTER 26

In an odd turn of events, Harkerpal says he's repaired the ship. The Liliana will fly again. I spoke with the attorney, Mathias du Gearsmith, in the capital. He had nearly forgotten Theo's will, but talk of the airship reminded him. Apparently, we are close to a time when Theo, as missing in action, will be declared legally dead. In his will, he bequeathed the Liliana to his daughter, Zaira. I can't believe he'd give a weapon of war to a little girl. Sometimes, that man infuriates me.

An excerpt from Captain von Cravat's log
Day 24 of the Month of Dukes
19th Year of Malaky XVI's Reign

"GET MY FATHER... I mean the Baron! Someone alert the Baron! And the pilot!" I screamed back to the deck crew as I took a couple of steps away from the railing and toward the turbine.

Crewmen took note, first of the shots fired into the air, and then of me. They hesitated briefly.

"Move!" I commanded and glanced back over the side. I wouldn't be able to run and alert someone in my condition.

More projectiles whizzed through the air at ridiculous speeds. One, two, then a third flew right past the ship, arcing overhead and dropping back to the ground below. Scanning the flatland, I could see where the three shots had come from. If we could increase our speed, we could be past this anti-airship barrage in a few minutes at the most.

To my surprise, it wasn't my father, but Talyen who rushed out onto the deck. "What is going on?" she asked. Another cannonball flew by. She whipped her head back toward the bridge. "Helm! Top speed!"

Back on the bridge, the pilot gave her a thumbs up.

Talyen made her way across to me in the time I'd looked away from her. "What do you think you're doing out of bed?" she asked.

I nearly jumped at seeing her so close. "I, uh..." Any excuse I could come up with seemed so inadequate. But why did I need to lie to Talyen? She was up as well, and had injuries worse than mine. She was also the one who had planned to steal the ship when King Malaky said no to the mission. She understood how crucial this mission and these duties were. "I was trying to position myself to go with the landing party when we arrived at Devil's Mountain What're *you* doing out of bed?"

Talyen lifted my chin with a finger to meet her eyes. Where I thought I'd find another argument, her face radiated compassion. "You're very brave. And thank you for alerting the crew to the anti-airship ballistics. I'm out of bed because someone needs to run this ship, which means I have to get to the main bridge, but we'll talk about this later. Okay?"

"Okay."

Talyen lunged toward the bridge, bursting into a full run. She cared so much for me, it made me feel important. She was going to listen, which meant I had a chance to go help the crew to put an end to this ridiculous war.

A cannonball connected with the ship.

The *Liliana* jerked, then swayed. I heard a *crack* in the wood, louder than even Talyen's loudest shouts. A projectile burst through the deck, boards splintering. Wood planks flew in a whirlwind. The area where I'd stood creaked and collapsed inward.

I lunged for the railing, then hung from it for dear life, watching a hole fall into an empty hold below me. Before I could right myself, another *crack* resounded, this time behind me.

A ball burst through the starboard-aft roof of the bridge. It bounced on the deck again, but its weight was enough that the deck collapsed under it. The *Liliana*, with a hole blowing heavy wind through its midsection, rolled to the side. The movement swung me, and one of my hands slipped, leaving me dangling from one arm. It hurt so badly, but I had to hang on for dear life. On the opposite side of the deck, one of the crewmen wasn't so lucky. He flailed his arms helplessly and flew over the side, off into oblivion.

The turbines stuttered. And then they cut out entirely.

I couldn't breathe. The wind blew in my face, my hair frazzled everywhere. My arm felt like it would snap like a twig at any moment. I swung myself like a pendulum until I could reach and grab ahold of the rail with my other hand, fingers clasping. If I could move hand over hand, I could get to a place where the deck still held, back to safety.

Relative safety, with the ship still descending at faster speeds than I could have imagined. The ship fell backward, aft first, with so much weight behind it. Our momentum shifted abruptly from the prior forward movement. I almost lost the meager contents of my stomach.

The engines below made a couple of *clicks*, and then whirred loudly. They'd fired! Harkerpal could work miracles. It was the sweetest noise I could have heard.

The turbines above me spun, slowly at first, and then reached their full speed. We still hadn't recovered from the fact that we were falling from the sky at an alarming rate. We passed through the clouds. Through the hole in the deck, I could see the trees growing larger in the distance below. Those treetops came far too close before we reached sufficient thrust to pull out of the dive. My stomach lurched again as we jolted forward.

I let out a gasp in relief, and then focused on keeping myself alive. I swung myself, using my full body weight, back and forth.

One hand, then another. I was close to the deck, but not quite over it. I had to make a leap of faith. While I did so, the *Liliana* righted itself. We rose into the air and continued forward, though at a slower pace than before. The turbines moaned in their efforts, but we were safe again and on our way.

I shifted my weight once more and forced one final swing to get myself to the deck. On that swing, I lost my grip and pawed at the deck, my body half on it, and half dangling into the hole. I slipped back toward the hole, screaming. This would be my doom.

One of the crewmen saw me as he moved to secure a nearby rope. He dove and grabbed me by the wrist. That stabilized me. A couple of other crewmen rushed over and helped pull me to safety.

"There, there, Baronette," the crewman said, offering a sturdy arm so I could pull myself to my feet. "Nothing we haven't dealt with before on the *Liliana.*"

I laughed. "A new adventure every day." I gave him a thankful nod, then turned to look at the damage to the main bridge.

A good half of the room had collapsed from the hit to its main structural components. The roof sagged toward the floor. It had completely caved in on itself, though the pilot's side still stood.

Which meant the area that had collapsed was Talyen's command post.

I ran hard at a speed I didn't know I could muster and rushed through bridge door. My breaths were heavy, already exacerbated from hanging by my arms for so long.

I pulled the door open, afraid of what I might find inside, ready to call for the medic.

Talyen was inside, leaning against the wreckage, carefully monitoring the pilot's course. They both looked at me like I was crazy.

"I thought..."

Talyen knocked on the wood that had been the roof moments before, now a slanted wall to a much smaller main bridge. "I didn't make it to the chair yet. Two feet to the right of disaster."

The pilot laughed.

One of the other deck crew entered the cabin, saluting Talyen. "Commander, we're clear of the anti-airship artillery."

"Very good, crewman. Please coordinate the cleanup and repairs with the others. Report back casualties when you know them," Talyen said.

"Aye, aye." The crewman turned and left.

Talyen rubbed her forehead. "I have a splitting headache," she said.

"At least you don't have a split head," I said.

Talyen glanced out toward our heading, seemingly in thought. She paced to the window, then looked back. "Pilot, how long until we reach Devil's Mountain?"

"A little over an hour."

She walked over to me, and linked her arm with mine. "Very well, then. Zaira, I promised you we'd be able to talk about this mission, and it looks like, barring any other unforeseen attacks, that we'll be able to do just that for the next hour. To the mess hall, then?"

So soon after such trauma, I could hardly consider myself ready. But what was this but another day aboard the *Liliana*?

"Sounds good," I said to Talyen, trying to formulate a good argument in my head as to why I should be allowed to go on the mission. We walked over to the mess hall together.

CHAPTER 27

We're traveling by horseless carriage to meet with Zaira von Monocle. I hope this isn't a mistake.

An excerpt from Captain von Cravat's log
Day 24 of the Month of Dukes
19th Year of Malaky XVI's Reign

"I TALKED TO Theo before the attack," Talyen said, squeezing a mug of coffee between her hands and bringing it to her lips. She held it there, basking in the steam. "After coming so close to dying myself, it makes me grateful for the little things. To be able to enjoy a cup again."

"I think it's too bitter," I said.

"To each their own." Talyen shrugged. "I know we've disagreed about almost everything in the past regarding your involvement with this ship, how far this should go, but I'm going to remind you of something. Back in the cave, you warned us we were ill-equipped, and we needed to get out of there immediately. You were right, though with Theo, he doesn't always listen. You both have good intuition on things at times."

I tilted my head to her, not sure what she meant.

"So do I, however. I kept this crew together for more than two years after your father disappeared and before you could even dream of the sky. This time, my intuition and your father's lines up. We both believe you're ill-prepared and too injured to come on this mission. You'll slow the crew down with how you can barely walk, and don't think I haven't noticed how you hobble. We can't risk that."

She was right. My father was right. But, by Malaky, I needed to help them. Perhaps I still felt I needed to prove myself after this whole ordeal, but that was silly. I'd taken out two Wyranth soldiers by myself. I convinced Marina to delay her trap, which might have saved us all. I'd been useful, and I'd learned more than I could ever imagine.

"I wanted to inform you of the mission, figure you've earned at least that much. I've assembled the team. We'll be taking the knights with us, two of the ship's scouts, and six of the strongest men I could get in order to help push the device."

It felt strange for me to hear James referred to as one of the knights, but it brought me great pride for my friend. I said nothing, however, still thinking about my role and what would be best.

Though I'd argued a lot with her, as she had said, this didn't feel like the time to protest. It hurt me so much to be left out, but I understood. "Okay," I said, looking Talyen directly in the eye. "I'll listen to you and Father."

She relaxed her shoulders. A tension I hadn't noticed in her before disappeared. "Good. Thank you, Zaira. This is a big decision by you, I know. It proves you're an adult."

An image flashed in my mind. The creature. The mountain. It breathed—or more accurately pulsed—and through that pulsing I could see. Wyranth soldiers surrounded it, a lot more than I'd seen before. I closed my eyes and opened them a few times, until I regained focus on the conversation.

Talyen remained seated back in front of me, tilting her head with concern. "Are you okay?"

"Yeah." I blinked a couple of times to regain my focus. "I'm just seeing something strange."

"Strange?"

"I don't know." More images flashed in front of me. The creature in the mountain pulsed, sending anger, rage at the Wyranth soldiers. They would be ready to kill on sight.

Talyen watched me with concern. "Zaira, you're turning pale. I should call the medic."

I waved her off. "It's not that. It's the creature. It's projecting thoughts to me somehow. I think this mission may be a bad idea. They're ready for us. There has to be another way."

"Like what?" Talyen asked.

I thought hard on it. If I were connected to this creature, it wouldn't help me willingly. It shifted in its chamber, causing another quake down below. Something excreted from out its backside. Gross! I could feel its bowel movements. Like its blood, its waste was different. It ate through the ground below.

As much as that made my stomach upset, it gave me an idea. "Don't go straight for the tunnel's exit," I said. "Go into the forest. There'll be a spot close to where we were before. A big rock and a tall white flower will be there, under a tree. Have your team dig from there. I know it sounds weird, but they won't have to dig far. There's a huge hollow hole under the creature's rear that reaches out to that distance. It was worried about us being there before, when it sensed Marina and me. It's been sitting in its own feces." I couldn't believe I was visualizing this. "You'll be able to—"

Something strange tingled up my spine. I cringed. It made Talyen look at me like I was crazy. Intense pain shot all the way from the small of my back to my skull. My head felt like it was about to burst open. "What's going on?" I asked.

"The creature?" Talyen asked.

Pure rage boiled inside me, so much so that I couldn't see straight. My breathing was quick, shallow, like I couldn't get enough air. "The explosive. Must set off the explosive."

As much as I wanted to control my body, I couldn't. The creature had taken over my faculties. No matter how hard I struggled against it, I couldn't control myself. It was like being stuck in a cell, watching through my own eyes. I bolted toward the mess hall door.

Someone grabbed me from behind. I clawed at the person's arms. The person cursed, but had me fully restrained with the help of a couple other members of the *Liliana* crew. I didn't want to do this at all. Why couldn't I even move my lips to tell them?

The crewmen lifted me from the floor and carried me to my father's quarters. I'd lost complete control, struggling against them the whole way. I squirmed, kicked, and screamed, to no avail. It felt as though a balloon expanded in my skull, pushing outward. At any moment, it would pop.

I thrashed around and scratched at the door. Then I pulled on the handle and screamed at the top of my lungs. I shouted something in a language I couldn't understand. Was that the creature speaking?

Visions clouded my head. A far away land that had a rocky terrain, large boulders the size of the *Liliana*. The sky grew dark, cold—snow hit the ground like a rushing river. The people there had a blue tint to their skin. They panicked. Riots erupted, men with clubs smashed in the faces of other people. The violence was unbearable.

I ran through the forest, down a slope as far as I could go. I ran for so long the skin wore off my feet. My limbs became exposed bone and muscle with blood trailing behind me. I ran across continents, across oceans. It took a millennium, more. All the time, my movements became slower. My legs lost their shape, grinding down into bulbs. The people of this land stood and stared in awe, mocking me for how slowly I moved. I froze, and that's when the real change came. My skin expanded, draping over everything, encapsulating me. It pulsed, and I became afraid I'd drown in it.

The skin kept expanding, changing. It had a rubbery texture, and it throbbed. It was more sensitive to everything—light, touch, the temperature of the air around me. Unable to move, all I could do was watch when it folded over my face. I couldn't see, that skin substance becoming all I had to sense the world around me. Though I should have been smothered from my nose and mouth being constrained, I found that the throbbing and pulsing supplied my lungs with air.

I pushed out with my mind, seeking as hard as I could to connect with anyone, anything. And I was hungry, so hungry. All that running and growth required sustenance. My mind found the small men, could reach them in their puny skulls. Whatever had changed me had given me the tools to survive. Yes, they would do well for me. So many of them gathered around me now. They could find the others, the ones from far away. It would be a bloodbath. The best part was that the humans were on their way to me. I could sense them in the forest. So much pain would sustain me for a long time.

My eyes popped open, and my natural surroundings returned. The *Liliana*. I was inside my father's cabin. The pain lingered, strong and getting worse.

CHAPTER 28

After meeting Zaira von Monocle, I'm torn as to how I feel. Some of the crew has already taken to her. I have to admit, she does have a lot of her father's energy in her.

An excerpt from Captain von Cravat's log
Day 29 of the Month of Dukes
19th Year of Malaky XVI's Reign

IT TOOK ALMOST everything I had to push that creature from my mind, but I finally regained control over myself. My sheer willpower had been enough to overcome that ancient force. I was a von Monocle.

Red skies filled the room with a soft light, one darker than the room I had been thrown into hours before. Despite my still groggy head, I hurried to the door and turned the knob. The creature knew that Talyen and the others were coming. They would be ambushed by Wyranth soldiers if I didn't act.

I was immediately greeted by a crewman who stood guard. "I'm sorry, Baronette. Orders are to keep you confined to quarters."

"I need to talk to Captain von Cravat, now!"

Toby squeaked from behind me, but I ignored him.

"The captain's already left with the commando team," the crewman said.

I frowned. Even with my plan of digging through to the creature's rear, there would be far too many Wyranth soldiers for our team to deal with. They'd find Talyen and the others and slaughter them.

Unless I could provide a distraction. "Then let me go to the bridge. This is my ship, it's my place."

"Orders," the crewman repeated.

"Crewman, what's your name?" I asked, putting on the sweetest tone of voice I could muster. I tilted my head at him and smiled.

The young man in front of me struggled to keep his composure, adjusting his neck collar. "Ah, Glenn."

"Glenn. You called me Baronette. You know who I am. It's my ship. Do you know why they put me in here?"

"Ah, said it was for your health," Glenn said.

"Right. And the medic did a great job. I'm fine now. But the people down below, they won't be unless we do something to help them out. You want to save Captain von Cravat and my father, right?" It may have been laying it on too thick, but I batted my eyelashes at him.

"Well, yeah, but—"

"No buts! That's not the von Monocle way." I inserted my foot in the crack between the door and the wall and pushed it open.

He stepped back, allowing the action.

"Now, be so kind and escort me to the bridge?" I shut the door behind me to make sure Toby wouldn't escape.

Glenn looked unsure, but then nodded and led me down the hall to the main mess cabin, out the door, and around the corner to the bridge. So much of the top deck still lay in wreckage, though the crew had cleared out much of the debris from the earlier anti-artillery attack. With any luck, the Wyranth wouldn't have time to move those blasted contraptions to the base of Devil's Mountain.

The front cockpit still held true, and a couple of crew I didn't recognize stood there. One manned the pilot station, and the other looked ahead through binoculars. "Ensign Matthews?" the latter man questioned my escort.

Glenn saluted. "Sir. The Baronette requested to come to the bridge. Said it was a matter of urgency."

"Baronette?" the man with the binoculars set them down on the wooden dashboard in front of him. He saluted me. "Oh. Welcome to the bridge. How may I help you? I'm Lieutenant Colwell, and this is the pilot, Major Edwin Ral."

I returned the gesture. They stared at me. Was I supposed to do something else? I jerked my thumb toward the window in front of them. "I'm here to take command."

"You are?" Lieutenant Colwell blinked.

"That's right." I tried to sound confident, like my father would be in this situation. I'd seen how he'd handled that Wyranth guard back in the cave. I could talk my way through situations like that. And this was easier because I could be honest. "The Wyranth soldiers down there are ready for our team. They're fanning out through the forest now to try to find and stop them."

"How do you know that?" my all too astute escort asked.

"I have my ways," I said, not wanting to scare him by mentioning the cave giant taking over my head for several hours. "But we need to get everyone ready for a direct assault on the aperture right at the base of the mountain. We can make them think that's where our team is going to attack, and concentrate their forces there."

"A diversion," Lieutenant Colwell said.

"Exactly." I nodded.

"Okay," Lieutenant Colwell glanced past me, out the window to the forest and mountain beyond. "Major, set a course. South by southwest approximately..." He held up his binoculars again, "thirteen degrees."

"Aye," Major Ral said. I watched him move the ship controls. The turbines activated beyond their standard hovering. I heard the pounding of the large gears below their shafts. He operated the controls so smoothly, so precisely. What I had done in controlling the ship on my first flight had been a mockery of his work.

I watched him with deep concentration. Perhaps I would never fly the ship again, but if I ever got to, I wanted to be sure I wouldn't make any mistakes.

The *Liliana* turned and moved forward.

"We need to make sure the cannoneers are ready to fire," I said.

"And the crank turret at the fore of the ship," Lieutenant Colwell said. He motioned to Glenn. "That's your post."

Glenn eyed me as if asking for permission.

"Go. We'll need all the firepower we can muster." I shooed him off.

He left the bridge, which, with the back of the room having collapsed, gave the three of us much more room to stand than we had before. I turned to watch the crew readying the deck and Glenn hustling to his station. "Now what?" I asked.

"You'll have to call them to battle," Lieutenant Colwell said. He motioned to a funnel shape on the dashboard in front of him. "If you call into here, it'll bring your commands to different listening posts in the ship. The cannoneers and deck minders should hear you."

"How come I didn't hear that before?" I asked.

Colwell shrugged. "If you were in the Baron's quarters—he had it outfitted for peace and quiet. I'll let the deck know." He moved and poked his head out the door, shouting to the crew. "Battle stations! For steam and country!"

I repeated his call into the strange cone.

"Cannoneers ready!" came a cry back.

The ship approached the mountain and, as I anticipated, hundreds of Wyranth soldiers stood at the base, ready for any sort of attack. They had a few of those whirring contraptions that had attacked the Gentrys' farm what felt like an eternity ago. I couldn't wait to destroy a few of those. They wouldn't be destroying any more helpless villages with the *Liliana* here to defend them.

"Fire at will!" I shouted.

All at once, the cannons roared. The giant balls streaked from the sides of our ship, down toward the Wyranth below. Each one pelted several of the soldiers, blasting the surface below. The mountainside erupted with plumes of smoke. The Wyranth battle commanders shouted, and their men fired shots at the ship.

Glenn opened up fire with the forward crank turret, which struck several soldiers in a line.

The Wyranth war machine contraptions came to life and tossed their own cannon balls into the air. These weren't as effective as the straight-shooting anti-airship artillery that we'd seen before, but they still provided enough danger that Major Ral thought it best to ensure the ship stayed straight in facing them, to provide a narrower target from the ground. He lifted our altitude considerably.

Our next volley was less accurate as a consequence. It still caused chaos in the army, but not nearly as effectively as that first surprise round. The Wyranth returned fire with another volley of cannon shots from their war machines. I watched the projectiles arc toward us and come dangerously close. The pilot kept the ship mobile, making it harder for them to track us.

Our gambit paid off. I spotted several dozen Wyranth soldiers trickling out from the forest. It meant that they wouldn't be searching for my father or Talyen. The more time we bought to allow them to dig and plant the device, the better. I wished I'd been down there with them to help direct them to the place that I'd seen in my mind's eye.

That was a silly thought. The exhilaration of being up on the bridge, commanding the *Liliana's* crew, leading them in a real battle—it couldn't be matched. Even when I had been naïve, and took control of this ship on my own on that fateful day, I hadn't had this much energy running through me. I hoped that energy wasn't the giant trying to regain control of my body.

KILL! KILL!

Those were the first words in my mind that I'd heard from it since those flashes of its life. Just like before. It wanted more of that energy that the death and destruction brought, unconcerned with the specifics of the situation. Our goals were aligned for now, even if it didn't realize the end result.

We played a game of chicken, moving the ship back and forth, sending in volleys and retreating, even after the sun had set. The glow from inside the mountain lit the Wyranth down below just enough for us to continue our assault, and the *Liliana* was easy for them to pinpoint in the air. The shots from the soldiers' guns did little at this range.

But then a cannonball struck.

It cracked the fore bow, just where Glenn had been standing with the turret. I watched as it ripped through the deck, knocking the gun aside, plowing into the compartment where Glenn had stood. I rushed forward to the door of the bridge.

Lieutenant Colwell stopped me with a hand to the shoulder. "Baronette, there's nothing you can do."

ANGER. PAIN. MORE.

With a single thought, the monster overwhelmed me with emotion. The boy had been so nice, and I had liked the fact that someone took notice of me and found me worth betraying his orders. It meant he had loyalty to me. My heart sank. Lieutenant Colwell was right, however. There was nothing I could do, but that didn't bring me comfort. Quite the opposite.

Talyen and my father had to deal with this kind of thing on a regular basis. Even killing the Wyranth soldiers felt uncomfortable to me, but watching a crewman die, one whose name I knew, it hurt. I bit down on my bottom lip hard. I had to show confidence. Lieutenant Cowell and Major Ral were watching, and what they saw would trickle down to the rest of the crew. I had to lead. My hands shook with rage.

"Keep firing," I said. "Let's take down one of those war machines. For Glenn." I pointed to one. "Focus fire on this one."

YES! KILL THEM ALL!

Lieutenant Colwell stared into his binoculars, then called out some coordinates into the cone for the cannoneers. I held still, staring at that contraption, willing its destruction.

The cannonballs fired. They struck true. All of our ship's batteries in one location. The thing blew into a thousand or more pieces. I clenched my fist.

And then I heard a much larger explosion.

This one came from inside the forest. With all the excitement, I'd forgotten about the team. The mountain itself seemed to shake in front of us. The Wyranth soldiers stopped firing in our direction. Rocks fell from the mountainside, the aperture caved in. It left us in the darkness of night until a massive column of dirt and debris shot into the air. Fire broke out below. Dust filled the sky.

Everything pulsed in a brilliant, baby-blue light. My ears rang. I couldn't see anything in front of me and had to shield my eyes. Lieutenant Colwell and Major Ral did the same.

An ear-piercing, high-pitched noise blasted directly into my head, followed by sudden wave of excruciating pain. It was as if dozens of knives sliced at my head and body all at once, giving no time for recovery before the next wounds stabbed me. Lights flashed like I'd never seen.

"Go pick up the crew," I said, tugging at Lieutenant Colwell's sleeve before I collapsed to the bridge floor. I heard the *thud* my body made, and then darkness came for me.

CHAPTER 29

I have returned triumphant! How blessed I am to have such crew, friends and family. It warms my heart to be able to write in this log again. When you read this in the future, know that I love you and I'm proud of you.

An excerpt from Baron von Monocle's log
Day 13 of the Month of Queens
19th Year of Malaky XVI's Reign

EVER SINCE I'D discovered the *Liliana*, I'd become accustomed to waking up in strange places, having no memory of how I'd arrived there. This time, I awoke in a bed that was both familiar and unfamiliar. The sheets were fine and soft, the pillow under my head was plush, and I'd been tucked into a warm blanket. The scenery didn't match my father's cabin, and it couldn't be construed as anywhere near my accommodations in the Wyranth prison.

I had the kind of fuzzy-headedness I recognized from sleeping too long after I'd been sick in the past. Had I been sick? What happened?

Bad dreams. That was an understatement. I touched my face to make sure I still had one. For a long time after that, I lay still, staring at the ceiling. The shadows formed a comforting pattern there. It was daytime, with natural light trickling through the shutters of the window beside me.

After several minutes of that, aches and cramps signaled to me that my body was tired of residing in the same place for so long. I sat up and let my legs dangle over the side of the bed. Something was missing, but what?

I thought about it for a long while, staring at my toes, wiggling them from time to time. Any movement felt good.

A wet nose pressed against my wrist, followed by a playful lick. Toby. Him I remembered. I scratched under his chin and gave him a pet. Then I ventured to my feet.

I wobbled. That was familiar. I'd been hurt, very hurt. The memories came flooding back to me. Wyranth soldiers had shot me, and I'd hit my head hard. That had left me under recovery aboard the *Liliana*. Talyen had sent a landing party to plant the explosive and destroy the creature inside Devil's Mountain. After I thought my injuries had been healed, I'd commanded the ship, providing a distraction so they could do their job and save Rislandia from a prolonged war.

Just as I pieced things together, someone poked their head through the doorway. It was James. At first, he looked concerned, but then elated. "You're awake!"

"James," I said weakly. "Where are we?"

"King Malaky's palace," James said. He stepped through the door. He wore the dark sleeves of a Knight of the Spire with a tabard bearing the spire symbol in the crimson colors of the Rislandia Kingdom. A sword rested at his side.

"You look so—"

"Knight-ish?" He smirked.

"Yeah, that's exactly it." With a deep breath, I took a couple of steps toward him.

James grabbed onto me, supporting my arm to help me. "They promoted me to a full knight when we returned. Apparently, I performed very well on the mission. This is everything I ever wanted." He sounded so happy, and I was happy for him even though I still needed to get my bearings before I could give a believable smile.

"What happened back there?" I asked.

"I'd better let Captain von Cravat and the Baron talk to you about that," James said.

He left me then so I could dress, which took a considerable amount of time given that I was still weak. Quick movements made me dizzy. I found my way out of the room eventually, wearing the same poof-filled formal garments I had been given the last time I visited the palace.

Though the clothes were scratchy, it was nice to have something familiar. It grounded me in reality, and I hoped that would prove a sign that I might come out of the funk I'd been feeling since regaining consciousness.

In the hall, I found more familiarity. The same servant from my last visit greeted me. He had kind words and well wishes. That was a good sign. I half-expected to be tried for treason for stealing the airship and pulling it from the assigned mission. He told me I was expected in the king's banquet room and led me there.

When I entered, I saw King Malaky, Mr. du Gearsmith, my father, Talyen, the princess, and James already seated. Smiles abounded and everyone rose to greet me and ask how I felt. After several hellos and hugs, and my many reassurances that I was doing fine, thank you, I sat by my father, and we enjoyed the breakfast meal. I'd forgotten how wonderful the king's breakfasts had been. After eating mush in the Wyranth prison, I couldn't be more grateful for the eggs and sausage.

James and the princess shared whispers, resulting in giggles on her part. I raised a curious brow but said nothing as we ate.

King Malaky had spent the time observing the conversations, picking at his own food, and seldom commenting. Over the course of the meal, the topic shifted to the Devil's Mountain mission. I noted that King Malaky learned toward the table when the conversation turned.

"Are you sure you want to talk about this now?" Talyen asked. "The *Liliana's* medic advised us to keep conversation light until you'd regained some of your fortitude."

"I'm sure, I'm fine," I said in between stuffing my face with bites of egg.

My father set down his fork. "We learned that the ingestion of the vitality ether did indeed provide a link to the evolved giant inside the mountain. I'm sure you're aware of that already. Commander Willett fainted from the stress of it the giant's destruction."

I nodded.

"Well," he continued, "because of that, the creature was able to alert a good number of Wyranth soldiers stationed near the capital. It was a good thing you and Talyen revised our original plan to find an alternate route and dig our own tunnel. We brought as many strong men as we could to work the operation, and sure enough, the location you told us was hollow after only a few feet. We were able to get inside a tunnel—which was disgusting, by the way—and make our way to the creature via underground passage."

"We're very fortunate that you decided to take charge, Zaira," Talyen said. "I told you to stay in your cabin, but the crew told us how many Wyranth soldiers they saw coming from the forest, no doubt in search of us. I'm not sure we would have survived without your distraction." She ate in small bites, dainty and proper in every regard. She made the perfect noblewoman as well as military officer.

"Not to say we didn't have our own firefight. We lost a lot of good men and women," my father said, a frown creeping across his face.

King Malaky wiped his lips with a napkin. "And their sacrifice will be remembered. Their names will be proclaimed with honor."

Everyone nodded to that.

"Lieutenant Colwell told me the moment our explosive detonated, you collapsed to the floor. He rushed you back into the medical bay, and you were out until we returned to Rislandia City."

"What about Marina, is she—?"

My father cut me off with the wave of his hand. He wiped his face with his napkin. "We don't need to bore King Malaky with the details of all that went on with individual crew members. Suffice to say, she is on the *Liliana* under the care of the medic."

I peered into my father's eyes. He meant to say he hadn't told the king she'd betrayed us. That meant he protected her. For my sake, or because she had proved a useful member of the crew? I had much to learn of my father's sense of loyalty.

"You were very brave," Talyen said with a reassuring smile.

King Malaky cleared his throat then, garnering our attentions. "Brave indeed. I'm told by our spies that the Wyranth Empire is in disarray over this. Apparently, that creature had an incredible amount of control over their forces. After the explosion, many of their soldiers refused to fight anymore. It's a curious situation that our alchemists will study now that we have a good sample of this vitality ether. You did good work. I believe this will be a turning point in the war," King Malaky said. "That brings us to a discussion on what transpired to take the *Liliana* there to begin with."

"I took full responsibility for that, Your Majesty," Talyen said, bowing her head slightly.

King Malaky huffed. "Everyone on that ship was complicit in violating my explicit orders. Under normal circumstances, that would be defined as high treason. You had a clear mission given by myself and General Carwell to assist the Grand Rislandian Army near Plainsroad Village. You could have left them stranded at the mercy of the Wyranth. That's very dangerous."

"Have mercy on my crew," Talyen whispered.

"Your Majesty," I said, despite Mr. du Gearsmith's prior warnings not to speak until spoken to. I had to do something or Talyen might be executed for saving my father. "I believe I gave Captain von Cravat the idea. I'm the one to blame."

The king considered for a long moment. He looked to Mr. du Gearsmith, who had watched the entire time without any comment, then back to me. "I did say that these were extenuating circumstances. You technically achieved your objective in assisting the Grand Rislandian Army, even if you didn't do so in the way you were told. Since the Wyranth have, for the most part, stopped their fighting and turned back, your work, albeit a couple of days late, cannot be discounted in that. Returning one of my best advisors to my side can't be scoffed at either."

I held my breath. Talyen didn't appear to worry, however. In fact, no one else around the table looked as worried as they should be. What was wrong with them?

My father grinned at the king. "What happens next?"

King Malaky noted my father's smile with a small chuckle. "You have such a profound influence on everyone you meet, Theodore. I see your young daughter proves to be no different than you."

My father and the king laughed together.

I wrinkled my nose. What was that supposed to mean?

King Malaky let out a sigh. "I can't in good conscience follow the letter of the law in this example. It's my job to adjudicate responsibility and make exceptions where they are warranted. But!"

I held my breath.

This time, King Malaky set his gaze directly on me. "If I find in the future that you manipulate any of my officers to treason for some harebrained scheme, your status of the daughter of my friend won't protect you. Do you understand?"

I exhaled and nodded.

"Excellent. Then let us rejoice in our victories and the return of the great Baron von Monocle. We'll have a parade and three days of rest before we return to our respective duties." King Malaky smiled the biggest smile I'd ever seen.

The princess clapped for that, and James followed her lead.

"Excuse me," Mr. du Gearsmith said. "Legally, an error was made. The *Liliana* will need to be transferred to its rightful owner, the Baron proper, due to the false pronouncement of his death. I'm sure you wouldn't mind signing the forms of consent, Miss von Monocle?"

"Of course," I said. Though I'd been filled with relief a moment prior, my heart sank. I had enjoyed owning the airship, being the "Baronette" for the short time I'd had the privilege. I'd had little time on my own to explore what that meant. The taste of adventure had been wonderful for me, and this meant that my father would be returning to his post. I would be set up in some civilian life somewhere in an effort to protect me from all of this. I frowned.

My father held a finger up in the air. "Hold on a moment, if you would."

"Yes?" Mr. du Gearsmith asked.

My father stepped around the table and took my hand. "Zaira, if there's anything I've noticed in my time apart from you, it's how much you've grown. You're a woman now, and a beautiful one at that. I know the initial attempt at rescuing me wasn't altogether successful, but look what we accomplished because of the way events unfolded. Wouldn't anyone say that was a job well done?"

"Thanks," I said with some skepticism.

"Before you woke, I'd discussed much of this with King Malaky. I've accepted a position with him as his chief of foreign relations. It'll be, in large part, hobnobbing and paperwork. All sorts of things I'm sure you'd find boring. For a man of my age though, it's a welcome post."

I looked to Mr. du Gearsmith, then back to my father. "Does this mean you want me to sign over the *Liliana* to Captain von Cravat?"

"Not exactly," my father said, beaming a wide smile.

That brought Talyen's attention to me. She smiled, but not with her usual confidence. Something was amiss. "With your permission, your father and I would like to get married," she said.

I blinked. In a lot of ways, I couldn't say I didn't see it coming, but I didn't expect to be consulted on the matter. "Of course. It's your choice—"

"Talyen's much younger than I, and she's looking forward to a ground-bound post as well. We're hoping to have more children, Zaira."

"And so I've promoted Captain Talyen von Cravat to Commodore of the Grand Rislandian Air Force," King Malaky said with a nod. "She's too valuable, and I believe her best place would be in my strategy room."

"Air Force? That means there'll be more airships than just the *Liliana?*"

"We plan to oversee the construction of a new fleet. Airships are so effective, I believe returning to our original scope of five of them would be a good long-term strategy," Talyen said.

"I agree with her recommendation," King Malaky said.

"What of the *Liliana* then?" I asked.

"If you don't sign it back over, you would be legally contesting that your father has a right to its ownership," Mr. du Gearsmith said. He stroked his chin.

"Mr. du Gearsmith, I plead no contest. Miss von Monocle certainly has earned the ship in her own right," my father said, his tone one of wry amusement.

"Very well then," Mr. du Gearsmith said.

King Malaky rapped his fingers on the table. "We can't let the airship fall into a civilian's hands, however. Zaira has no lands, no title."

"The crew calls her the Baronette," James said.

"That's not a real word, Knight." King Malaky gave James a placating smile, and then pondered with narrowed eyes. "Ah, I know the solution. Miss von Monocle?"

"Yes, Your Majesty?" I couldn't help but be lifted by everyone else's jovial attitudes. They'd had one over on me, and the amusement was clear on all their faces. Even with that, all of this held far too good to be true. I could hardly believe it.

"I, King Malaky the Sixteenth, of the Rislandian Kingdom, hereby bestow upon you the rank of Baroness, true owner of the airship *Liliana* with all the duties and privileges thereby."

My heart nearly leapt from its chest. I couldn't believe it. I was going to be able to keep the airship! Then I frowned as I thought about the logistics.

"What's wrong? Did you not want this?" my father asked.

"No, it's not that. It's just...with Talyen being promoted to Commodore, who's going to help with the operations of the ship?"

"Well that would be up to you," my father said. "You're the Baroness."

"I think I'm going to go with Baron. Baroness sounds funny, and that way people might think they're still dealing with you."

"Wise," King Malaky said. "An intimidation factor."

I sat there stunned for a long moment. My face was as hot as it ever had been, and I felt as if I could float on air without the *Liliana's* help. "Thank you all. I don't know what to say."

My father raised his glass in toast to me, and everyone else followed. "Don't worry about it, Baron von Monocle. There'll be plenty of time to figure it out."

Next in the Series...

Thank you for reading *For Steam And Country*. If you enjoyed the novel, please review the book on Amazon and be sure to read Book Two of The Adventures of Baron Von Monocle, *The Blood Of Giants!*

Danger looms on a foreign continent...

Zaira von Monocle is getting the hang of commanding her airship, when crisis hits her homeland, Rislandia. Caught in a terrible cycle of withdrawal from their power-serum, Wyranth soldiers are ravaging the countryside in a berserk rage. The Grand Rislandian Army has been unable to slow their bloodthirsty advance.

The Wyranth's serum has its origin in legend, a children's tale about giants roaming the land of Zenwey, far across the ocean. Zaira must take the Liliana and her crew to this faraway land, in hopes that she might find a cure before the Wyranth take even more lives.

When Zaira arrives on Zenwey, she finds the continent to be a mysterious and hostile environment. She must navigate her way past savage jungle warriors, fantastic creatures and terrors, and evil forces that have flying machines of their own. Before she can try to save Rislandia, she has to survive!

The Steam Knight Series...

Want more of James Gentry? He has his own series of novellas in The Steam Knight. Read Book One, Knight Training.

The Special Forces of Steampunk!

Airships, Guns, and Gadgets! The Knights of the Crystal Spire are more than ordinary fantasy knights.

Life as an apprentice knight hasn't been easy on James Gentry. As a commoner and an outsider, he's been ridiculed, picked on, and shunned by the other boys. But he's determined to become one of the finest knights Rislandia has ever seen.

During his training, James stumbles upon a master knight selling information on Rislandian troop movements to a Wyranth spy. To keep Rislandia safe, he must root out the traitor and put a stop to the enemy's schemes. Does he have what it takes?

Read this action-packed steampunk novella and #1 Amazon bestseller today!

Rislandian Timeline

23rd Year of King Malaky XV Reign – *20 years before the events of For Steam And Country, Baron Theodore von Monocle flies his ship on its first mission to Tyndree on the east coast of Rislandia between Wyranth at High Mesa Castle. He rescued duchess named Liliana, fell in love, and named his airship for her.*

24nd Year of King Malaky XV's Reign – *The Liliana travels to the One-Eyed King's domain on the Ebony Sands Coast. Theodore convinced the king he'd work for him as a mercenary, was imprisoned in the ruse, and escaped with the help of his crew. Theodore returns to Rislandia and marries Liliana.*

25th year of King Malaky XV's Reign – *King Malaky XV is assassinated by Wyranth. A new airship is commissioned. A big battle occurs, and an uneasy peace is achieved.*

1st Year of King Malaky XVI's Reign – *Von Monocle takes the Liliana on an exploratory world tour. The new king wants trade relations and peace, a new positive outlook for the world.*

2nd Year King Malaky XVI's Reign – *On a 2nd exploratory tour, the Liliana travels to the Sands of Zarma, where they find a treasure chest and the crew had a strange disease. The Tyndree Kingdom folds into the Wyranth Empire.*

3rd Year of King Malaky XVI's Reign – *Zaira is born. The Atreblan Kingdom sends an expedition around the world to find treasure, and comes back with a supply of aether-fuel ("Black Gold"). The Rislandians desperately need the fuel for their airship fleet, and seek trade. Theodore von*

Monocle agrees to go to the Island of the Fae to help an Atreblan noble in exchange for fuel ("Baron von Monocle and the Island of the Fae").

5th Year King Malaky XVI's Reign (Zaira is 2) – 3rd expedition across the world. Trade negotiations with the Tribes of Zenway. Theodore comes across a book given by a shaman attached to chief, she told that the Areth continent didn't have a grasp of true history, the settlers a thousand years ago had forgotten much. The book had legends about giants who roamed the land in ancient times.

6th Year of King Malaky XVI's Reign (Zaira is 3) – Small skirmishes occur with the Wyranth at the border, frightening the Rislandian people. The Airship takes a number of casualties, grating on the crew. Baron von Monocle turns to a young chef's assistant, Talyen von Cravat, to come up with an idea to help the crew's morale ("The Battlecry Of The Liliana")

7th Year King Malaky XVI's Reign (Zaira is 4) – Twin Tops Mountains rescue mission in winter (during the month of fools) to save starving dying people.

8th Year of King Malaky XVI'S Reign (Zaira is 5) – Baron von Monocle travels to the Dragonmist Isles to retrieve a rare flower for his anniversary with his wife.

15th Year of King Malaky XVI's Reign (Zaira is 12) – Wyranth are getting aggressive again after a period of relative peace. Portsgate floods after a recent hurricane. Zaira's mother Liliana dies while Theo's away fighting. 1st battle at Border River.

16th Year of King Malaky XVI's Reign (Zaira is 13) – The 2nd Wyranth War begins.

17th Year of King Malaky XVI's Reign (Zaira is 14) – The 2nd Battle of the Border River. Baron Theodore von Monocle goes missing. Commander Von Cravat leads a counter assault 9 days later. Afterward, von Cravat can't handle the loss of the Baron and grounds the ship in Loveridge ("Tangled Web").

18th Year of King Malaky XVI's Reign (Zaira is 15) – Captain Von Cravat tries to get the crew back together and fails.

19th Year of King Malaky XVI's Reign (Zaira is 16) – Zaira von Monocle inherits her father's airship and mounts a mission to rescue her father based on rumors he may still be alive (For Steam And Country). James Gentry is trained as a Knight and uncovers a Wyranth plot ("Knight Training"). Zaira takes the airship to the Zenwey Continent in hopes of finding more giant's blood to help cure the Wyranth soldiers of their addictions (The Blood Of Giants). When she returns, she finds the Wyranth have invaded and she must save her kingdom (The Fight For Rislandia). James Gentry is sent to guard King Malaky and Princess Reina at their retreat ("Guard Training").

20th Year of King Malaky XVI's Reign (Zaira is 17) – The knights play a prank on James Gentry ("Hazing").

ALSO BY JON DEL ARROZ

The Adventures Of Baron Von Monocle:
For Steam And Country
The Blood Of Giants
The Fight For Rislandia

The Steam Knight Series
Knight Training
Guard Training

Other Books
The Stars Entwined
Make Science Fiction Fun Again
Alt-Hero: Covert
Star Realms: Rescue Run

Short Stories
Gravity Of The Game

Graphic Novels And Comics
Flying Sparks Volume 1
Flying Sparks: Meta-Man Special
The Ember War

ABOUT THE AUTHOR

Jon Del Arroz is a #1 Amazon Bestselling Steampunk author, "the leading Hispanic voice in science fiction" according to PJMedia. com, and winner of the 2018 CLFA Book of the Year Award for his novel, *For Steam And Country*. As a contributor to The Federalist, he is also recognized as a popular journalist and cultural commentator. Del Arroz writes science fiction, and comic books, and can be found most summer weekends in section 127 of the Oakland Coliseum cheering on the A's.

Twitter: @jondelarroz
Instagram: @jdelarroz
email: jdaguestposts (at) gmail (dot) com

ACKNOWLEDGMENTS

I want to thank everyone involved in making *For Steam And Country* happen. Editor Tim Marquitz did a killer job, as did Ben Zywycky and Avily Jerome with copy edits. Shawn King made the most beautiful cover possible. Thank you to all at Superversive Press for believing in the book.

The kind folk who helped me along on early reads: Stephanie Caporusso, Katie Cord, Setsu Uzume, Karen Junker, Stephanie Bissette-Roark, Fred Wan, Herma Lichtenstein, Tim W. Long, Todd McCaffrey, and Dario Ciriello.

Big thanks to The Grand Rislandian Army, the friends via my email list and Facebook group who helped out with the promotion: Declan Finn, Marina Fontaine, Corey McCleerey, Genie Garcia, Morgan Tysor, Stephanie Sounders, Paul Clithero, Joshua Kanapkey, Julian Thompson – couldn't have done it without you.

More thanks and love to Peter Grant, Vox Day, L. Jagi Lamplighter-Wright, Laurie Forest, Nick Cole, everyone in the CLFA, the #PulpRev, and at the Castalia House blog. Your faith in me has kept me going and it means more to me than you know!

If I missed you – I'll get you in the next book. But know I love you all the same!

Finally, thanks to my wife and kids for being patient while I spend late nights immersed in the world of Rislandia!

Made in United States
North Haven, CT
11 October 2024

58745945R00182